THE BOOK OF STONES

MÓRDHA STONE CHRONICLES - BOOK 9

KIM ALLRED

STORM COAST PUBLISHING, LLC

The Book of Stones
Mórdha Stone Chronicles, Book 9
KIM ALLRED

Published by Storm Coast Publishing, LLC

Cover Design by Amanda Kelsey of Razzle Dazzle Design
Print Edition August 2023 978-1-953832-26-9
Large Print Edition August 2023 978-1-953832-27-6

To all my readers who've taken this journey with me. Thank you.
These characters wouldn't live without you.

You will never be completely at home again, because part of your heart always will be elsewhere. That is the price you pay for the richness of loving and knowing people in more than one place.

Miriam Adeney

1

England - 1805

The ride from Ipswich to London was painful, numbing, and unforgettable. Stella Caldway, a woman out of time, seemed more isolated than she'd ever been. Her horse followed the one in front of her, keeping pace without having to do much thinking other than not falling off the animal. Not nearly stimulating enough to stop the images from bombarding her—kneeling in front of Gemini, Beckworth giving himself up for her, the two-by-four as it came down on his back, then again on his head, him falling before being dragged off... It was a manic reel that played over and over, her own personal nightmare.

For the first several miles, she followed Morton and Lewelyn, who, from what she'd gathered, had returned to the warehouse and then the docks when she and Beckworth never arrived at the meeting place. They said nothing. What was there to say?

Her gaze kept falling on Beckworth's riderless horse that trailed behind Lewelyn's horse. The sight was a constant reminder of her failure. If she'd paid more attention when running for the meeting spot. If she'd been able to get out of the man's grasp before the second one arrived. If. If. If. Unable to stand it anymore, she kicked her horse faster until she rode next to them and asked if they couldn't ride ahead and let Hensley know they were coming.

"Finn already sent Fitz ahead." Then Morton noticed her staring at Beckworth's horse, and she caught Lewelyn's nod. Morton squeezed her hand. "Of course. We'll be waiting for you." And without so much as a nod in Finn's direction, they took off.

If Finn wondered about the exchange, he never said a word. AJ rode alongside her for a while, but Stella couldn't look at her. She finally understood the wordless days AJ had spent on the back deck of the inn, staring out to sea, wondering why Finn hadn't followed them home. Had she spent those days kicking herself for leaving or not doing more?

When the sight of London appeared, the city still several miles away, she didn't see it with the same excitement as that first time on the knoll. Her chest ached, remembering how Beckworth had waited patiently, watching her emotions as she'd taken it all in. He'd wanted to hear her first impressions.

The city didn't look the same. Instead of the bustling metropolis she'd originally seen, now she only saw a monstrosity harboring the poor and sick while the rich went to their parties. It was wrong to be looking at it now without him. She closed her eyes. He couldn't be dead. Gemini had plans for him. If there was only one thing she was grateful for, it was the spiteful woman's personal interest in him. That alone would keep him alive—for now.

When they reached Hensley's manor, Finn helped her off the horse, and AJ wrapped an arm around her as they trudged up the steps. There wasn't a happy greeting with Mary running down the steps, though a couple of footmen arrived to collect bags, and stable boys took the horses.

Mary waited just inside the door and took Stella from AJ, clucking at her friend. "You've had your own harrowing journey. You have to take care of yourself before you can take care of others."

Then Finn pulled AJ away as Mary guided Stella to her room, where Sarah waited with a bath.

"I'll have food brought up. Sarah has strict orders to make sure you eat something. What would Teddy think if you're nothing but a mere shadow of yourself when he returns?"

Though she didn't respond to Mary's words, they nestled in the back of her mind, and she knew Mary was right. But as Stella had always told AJ, everyone deserved a pity party, and she sure as hell had earned this one. And if it lasted more than a day, they'd all just have to deal with it.

Sarah was an angel who pampered her to a point. She took Mary's orders quite seriously and sat on the bed as she coaxed Stella to finish the light meal. Fortunately, neither she nor Mary forgot Stella's penchant for coffee. There was always a fresh carafe provided until shortly after lunch, when Sarah replaced it with a bottle of wine. These women were too good to her and more than she deserved.

AJ watched Stella stumble up the stairs. In all the time she'd known her, she was typically upbeat. She had her moods, mostly an overload from her clients, and she'd disappear into her garden. It would be a day, sometimes two, before Stella rejoined the world. But AJ could count on one hand and, quite frankly, a couple of fingers when Stella had been so distressed over a man. It was always Stella that walked away—all for solid reasons—but she took each of them to heart.

All the time she'd worried about Beckworth watching out for

Stella, she'd never imagined them becoming that close. She tilted her head as Stella disappeared down the second-floor hall. It was obvious she had strong feelings for him. They'd been on the run for a long time, which might have put them in intimate settings. The question was how long their relationship—or whatever it was—had been going on.

Beckworth would never take advantage of Stella. Not without the knowledge that either she or Finn would kick his ass. But this wasn't the time to ask. Stella had disengaged from the world, and something told AJ it was going to take more than a day's worth of pity party to come out of this one.

Finn put an arm around her shoulder. "Let's go to the study. Hensley will want to debrief. You know there's nothing you can do for her now."

"I know. It just wasn't the homecoming I was expecting."

He kissed the top of her head. "I know. We'll work it out."

Hensley was already behind his desk while Sebastian sat by the hearth, staring into the fire. Morton and Lewelyn stood against the wall near Lando, and Fitz sat on the floor in a corner. Thomas pulled two chairs over for them.

Hensley wasted no time. "What happened?" He looked at his two men to start the replay. Morton gave a detailed report from when they left London to their role in setting the diversions to give Beckworth time to sneak into the warehouse. After setting their charges, they went to the livery, which was their second meeting point. They were to arrange for a wagon in case the smithy needed to be transported to London for his injuries. Lewelyn had a bad feeling, so they'd run to the church where Stella and Beckworth were to take the smithy if his injuries could be treated locally. When no one was there, they followed the most likely route to the docks in time to see Beckworth fall.

Finn took over and gave their account of going to the blacksmith's shop. The smithy hadn't been there for a couple of days, and they found his body in the warehouse after the *Phoenix* had set sail. "We didn't want to leave him there, so we contacted the local constable."

"We told him we'd been looking at warehouses available to store cargo." Thomas looked exhausted. He'd been racing from one city to another since leaving Bransford and dealt with a harrowing ambush that took one of his men. Two others were in upstairs guest rooms, healing from their injuries. "The constable had been concerned when he heard of the smithy's strange disappearance and was genuinely upset to discover he'd been tortured so close to home."

"He'll never get the answers he wants," Finn said. AJ stroked his arm, remembering her inability to look at the man's body, and knew Finn had found it difficult. They all had. "The man was a loner, and though he'd been a devout man, the constable knows we all have a history. And this time, his past caught up with him."

"He was a good man," Sebastian said from his seat by the fire, never turning away from the flames. "Your story wasn't far from the truth. He had a troubled childhood and ran with the wrong crowd until a few years before I met him in London. He was visiting his mother, who'd been sick and didn't recover. He'd turned to the church for salvation. I never thought he'd give his life for the chronicle."

"I'm not sure it would have mattered if he'd given them the chronicle the minute they stepped into the smithy," Lando said. "They somehow discovered he had the book. Gemini had been in Ipswich a long time, and she had plenty of men to scour the area. She knew we'd be coming for it and used the smithy to lure us in. And it worked."

"The smithy was most likely past saving when we first saw him in the warehouse, but he was heavily guarded." Morton's remorse was plain to see, as was Lewelyn's, but they were most likely blaming themselves for the loss of Beckworth. "Our plan was solid. Only Stella can tell us what happened once the diversion started."

"And I expect that will take some time to get from her." Hensley tapped his desk as he stared down at it.

"Once we made it to the docks, Stella was on her knees in front of Gemini and Gaines." Finn continued with his report. "I can see why men fall for Gemini's guise. She's a beautiful woman but hard as nails from what little I heard. There were too many men for us to do anything, and it was sheer luck we got as close as we did. We were all surprised when Beckworth walked out of the shadows with the chronicle, ready to trade it for Stella."

"Do you think he knew I had a man on the roof?" Thomas asked.

Finn shrugged. "I think he was bluffing, though he'd seen Lando and must have known we had more men. He probably guessed we didn't have as many as we needed to make a difference. Thomas's man had orders to take out either Gemini or Gaines or whoever threatened Stella. But it would have been a bloody scene if fighting had started."

Hensley nodded. "Which is why Beckworth suggested the trade. He must have known Gemini could have easily walked away with both him and Stella."

"He blew her cover." Finn tapped his finger on the armrest, his brows furrowed. "He wanted to remove Gemini's need for her since she would no longer be a valuable trade for the Heart Stone. But in doing that, Stella became collateral damage. He traded himself for her safety."

AJ had been holding it together up to that point. All the time they'd been chasing Stella and Beckworth, she'd been worried that no one would look out for her when it truly mattered. To put their own life on the line for her. Beckworth was a good friend, a trusted friend. Yet, when he gave himself up for Stella, she'd known then he was a better man than she ever gave him credit. She would never have guessed something deeper might have developed between them.

Was their unique relationship the simple fact of him rescuing her in the first place? Perhaps some reverse form of Stockholm syndrome. She'd have to wait until Stella was in a place to discuss it. One thing was for certain, something serious happened if Stella refused to go home.

AJ vaguely listened to the plan, which was nothing more than sending men to watch the coast to see if they could find the *Phoenix*. All bets were on Southampton or back to France and the monastery.

Until they knew more, her focus would be set squarely on Stella. Then another thought came to mind. Stella and Beckworth had been in London for several days before leaving for Ipswich. If anyone knew what went on in this house, it would be Mary.

2

Baywood, Oregon - current day

Maire desperately wanted to grab her stomach, but she clutched the chronicle to her chest with one arm and held tightly to Ethan with the other. The duffel over her shoulder weighed heavy and threatened to topple her over.

She kept her eyes shut tight in an attempt to ward off the blinding light and grimaced against her need to vomit. Her last thought before she was pitched aside was whether the books held any advice to make the time jumps smoother.

She hit something so hard her teeth rattled and vaguely remembered the duffel. Ethan let go of her hand, and she immediately clasped her stomach and rolled over, the strap of the duffel slipping off her shoulder. All she did was gag, her stomach still twisted in knots. She hadn't eaten anything since early that morning in Stokenchurch, and it had only been cheese and bread. There wasn't anything left to throw up.

Then she remembered the ambush and their need to jump. She rested her forehead on the wooden dock, hoping their gamble had been worth it and that Fitz, Thomas, and the men found safety. In a frantic movement, she searched for the chronicle and thanked the heavens when her hand touched it. It took a minute while her eyes adjusted to the natural light of the sun rather than the intense whiteness of the jump.

She reached out for Ethan, who lay on the dock motionless. That wasn't right. She crawled to him. "Ethan? Ethan? What's wrong?"

He was on his side, the duffel still against his back, acting as a prop to keep him upright. She pulled the duffel from him, and he fell onto his back. That's when she saw the blood.

"Oh my god, Ethan. Can you hear me?"

She checked his pulse at the wrist. It was weak, but it was there. He groaned, and while the sound didn't ease her panic, it settled her enough to think. The blood was heaviest near his stomach. He must have been shot before the fog took them.

"Ethan. You need to wake up."

The sound of footsteps startled her, and then the dock shook. She glanced up, terrified of Gemini's men somehow finding them.

"Maire. Are you alright? What the..." The man looked familiar. "Is that Ethan? He's been injured."

The man pulled something out of his pocket. Her fuzzy brain cleared enough to recognize Isaiah. Oh, god, no. She turned around, scanning the area. The wooden dock was the one in Baywood, not somewhere in London. That would explain the cleaner-smelling air. But this wasn't what they'd expected. Not with both Heart Stones in London.

Her focus turned back to Ethan. At least he had a better chance of survival in this time period.

"Adam. Code red." Isaiah glanced at Maire and then at Ethan. "Maire and Ethan are back, but Ethan's been injured."

Silence as he listened. "There's a lot of blood, but I haven't had a chance to look. I wanted you to know first. Bring everyone." He stuck the phone in his back pocket, then looked at Maire.

"Are you okay? Any injuries."

She took a moment to consider his question, but other than sore muscles and a stomach cramp, she felt alright. She nodded. "I think Ethan's been shot."

"Alright. Let me check. Adam is on his way, and he's bringing help." Isaiah felt for a pulse as she had, but rather than check at his wrist, he laid two fingers on Ethan's neck. "He has a pulse. I've felt stronger, but it's there and seems regular." He opened an eyelid. "Ethan, buddy, are you awake? Can you hear me?" He turned to Maire. "Come over here and hold his hand. Let me know if he squeezes it or if you feel anything."

She did as she was told, her nerves settling with Isaiah's calm tone.

"Ethan, it's Isaiah. If you can hear me, try to squeeze Maire's hand. She's right here with you, and she's fine. You both made it back." He glanced up at her, but she shook her head. "That's alright. From what I remember AJ saying, the jump takes quite a bit out of you. He's obviously lost blood and is just unconscious. Let's not read too much into that." When she nodded this time, Isaiah began pulling Ethan's shirt up.

The shirt, sticky with blood, was pulled away slowly, Isaiah pressing lightly on Ethan's skin as more and more was exposed. "You wouldn't happen to have a towel or something we can use to wipe away some of this blood in one of those duffels?"

The question caught her off guard, then the healer in her finally kicked in. "No towels but plenty of shirts." She opened Ethan's duffel since it was closer and rummaged past the weapons until her fingers found the edges of fabric. She tugged and pulled out a shirt, tossing it to him before digging out another.

Isaiah blotted away the blood, but from where she sat, she couldn't tell how much was still seeping from whatever wound Ethan had sustained.

He nodded. "I think we're okay. It looks like a flesh wound, though it's decent-sized. Help me roll him over so I can see what his back looks like. I'm going to roll him toward you."

She moved back a couple of inches and pulled Ethan to her while Isaiah prodded the wound and Ethan's back.

"I think we're out of the woods. There's no hole, markings, or bruising on his back. What I don't know is why there's so much blood. The wound isn't near any vital organs, though it might have nicked a rib."

"The jump presses in on you. It feels like a large hand grabbing your stomach and twisting as it tries to rip it out."

"Something like squeezing a sponge?"

She shrugged. "Close enough."

"Maybe the pressure created by the jump forced more blood to his extremities, and when it found a hole, it just pushed more out."

She laughed and shook her head. His explanation, while making eerie sense, sounded completely crazy. "Like making orange juice."

Isaiah chortled. "More like tomato, but it's the best guess I have. Unless we find something else when we get him to the inn and get the wound cleaned, I think we're dealing with blood loss more than anything else."

"Where did you learn to be so calm with so much blood?"

"I spent a summer on a fishing trawler out by the Aleutians. They're a string of islands off the Alaskan coast, and we were far from any medical facilities. You'd be amazed at the type of injuries one can get on a fishing boat, especially with all the hooks and spearguns."

They spoke of his fishing days while they waited. He

appeared to intuitively understand she wasn't ready to discuss why they were back without the others. It was another fifteen minutes before Adam was running down the hill toward the dock, Madelyn a few steps behind him.

Adam slid to a stop and dropped to his knees. "What happened? How bad is it?"

Isaiah gave him the rundown of what he'd found. "The wound is still bleeding, but it's more of a trickle now. We need to get him stable and determine if he needs blood."

"I'll get the couch ready for him." Madelyn hefted a duffel. "Bring him straight to the living room." She began the trek back up the hill but turned after a few steps. "Maire, I could use your help with preparing hot water and then grabbing sheets, towels, and everything you can find in the medicine cabinet."

Maire nodded and stood, her gaze locked on Ethan. She wanted to watch over him.

"The men will get Ethan to the house. We need to have everything prepared." Madelyn prodded with the best of intentions.

If Maire focused on the injury rather than the man, she'd know what she needed to do. She set aside the fact it was Ethan bleeding and picked up one of the bloody shirts. The other had been tied around Ethan's waist to staunch the bleeding and would have to do until they got him moved. She strung the other duffel over her shoulder.

"Where are the others?" Adam asked as she walked away.

"I don't know."

Maire knelt on the floor next to Ethan, who lay asleep on the couch. Once they'd been able to clean the wound, it was easy to see Isaiah had been right, a flesh wound from a flintlock. She'd stitched it and applied a salve. Ethan woke long enough to drink a few drops of her herbal remedy mixed with a drug Doc had given her.

All she wanted to do was curl up next to him and sleep, but Adam and Helen, who'd arrived with Emory shortly after Adam, had dozens of questions, most she couldn't answer. She went over the main highlights of their trip since first jumping back when Stella had been taken, which in this time period was about three days, but had been several weeks for her and Ethan.

"Let me make sure I understand." Adam had pulled out a pad of paper and pen as he usually did, writing down what she presumed were the salient points. "You were ambushed, fully surrounded, and Ethan decided to jump. This was what you did that time at Waverly, right? When Finn got left behind."

She nodded. "The problem was, Ethan knew both Heart Stones were in the past with us. We thought the incantation would take us to Parliament or to AJ, who we assumed would be in London by then."

"That confirms one thing," Isaiah said. When everyone glanced at him, he shrugged. "Didn't we wonder if the incantations would take you to a Heart Stone if they were in the same time period? This confirms they don't."

"So it would seem," Maire replied. "Or maybe we just needed a different incantation."

"All that time and you and AJ never caught up with Stella?" Madelyn asked.

"No. We were so close when we docked in Saint-Malo, but she'd been abducted again. AJ's been beside herself with worry."

"But it sounds like she's safe now." Adam glanced at his wife.

Maire wished she had something more to offer them. "We know Beckworth has been traveling with her, keeping her safe as he can, and now Sebastian is with them."

"AJ trusted Beckworth, right?" Isaiah asked. "I mean, I know he was the enemy when he was here in Baywood, but he's part of the team now. Did Finn seem worried?"

They were fair questions. She took a moment to consider whether she believed Stella and Sebastian to be in good hands with Beckworth.

"My relationship with Beckworth is colored with bad days and better days where he's concerned. But if I think about his behavior since the time we returned to find Finn, there's no question he's been trustworthy. For AJ to have trust in him gave me a different perspective on the man. At the monastery, after Stella had been kidnapped again, he'd beared full responsibility, though it hadn't been his fault. He'd done everything he could to get them as far as he did, considering the number of men Gemini sent after them.

"The fact he was willing to board the kidnapper's ship so he could watch over Stella and Sebastian told me everything I needed to know. That and the fact I'd seen how miserable he was before then. If anyone can keep them safe, he can. Besides, the earl received a message from Barrington just before we arrived in Hereford, letting him know they were safe and heading to London. Hensley will protect them."

"And AJ?" Helen asked. Her eyes were teary bright, but she held her head up, ready to hear any tidbit regarding her daughter's whereabouts.

"They had a long journey to Bréval, which is close to Paris. I know times are dangerous to be in France during the war, but she's as safe as can be with Finn and Lando. It will just take them longer to reach a port and find a ship to England, which shouldn't be a problem since Finn knows many captains."

Helen nodded, but there was little she could do to prevent a mother from worrying over her child.

"I'm sure Ethan can tell you more once he wakes. The problem is, we need to return, but I'm not sure how to get us back to the right moment in time."

3

England - 1805

After Hensley excused them, AJ followed Finn to their room. She shooed Willa, Mary's newest lady's maid, away since all she had to peel off were her pants and shirt. A tray had been left filled with an array of meats, cheeses, and treats, along with a bottle of wine and an urn of coffee. AJ poured a cup and nibbled a strawberry tart.

"Dessert before the main meal." Finn stepped behind her and wrapped his arms around her. "You Americans are heathens."

She made an exerted effort to lick her fingers clean. "And I'm proud to be the shining example." Then she took another bite.

He laughed as he took off his shirt and pants.

She glanced around. "I see water simmering by the fire. Were you expecting a bath?"

He swung her around and kissed her soundly. "It was more to attend to my wife." His gaze softened. "I know you're hurting, too."

She hugged him tight. “I don’t know what to say to her. I suppose I’m lucky she’s not ready to talk.”

“Let’s get you into something more comfortable, and I’ll make a plate. We can eat in bed. How does that sound?”

“A picnic?”

“Absolutely. Wine or coffee?”

“I’ll stick with the coffee. But I’ll have a glass after a nap.”

They settled into bed, each sitting cross-legged while moving the food onto napkins.

“Did she tell you anything about Beckworth?” Finn placed two pieces of cheese on her napkin and then on his.

“No. I was totally blindsided. Whatever happened, it seems pretty serious if she won’t go home.”

“Do you think Beckworth has the same feelings for her?”

The question startled her. “He saved her.”

Finn shrugged. “I wouldn’t expect anything less of him. Whether it was for his own honor, for you, or for Stella, we might never know if we don’t find him. Maybe he did it for all those things.” He finished his meal and placed the remains on the tray. “Until we locate the *Phoenix*, all we can do is wait. To be honest, I’d prefer not doing anything other than search for him until Ethan and Maire return.”

“Since it’s been a few days since they jumped, and they haven’t shown up yet, we should assume they went to Baywood. If that’s true, and she uses the same incantation, it could still be a couple more days.”

“Fitz says she took the chronicle with her. Maybe she’ll find something in it to improve the timing.”

She grimaced. “Or she’ll monkey with it and end up years off.”

“There’s my optimistic lass.”

“What location do you think they’ll try for? Hereford seems plausible since that worked before. I wonder what would happen if they arrive at a time before they jumped back." All the different scenarios she'd seen on science fiction shows flitted through her brain. None sounded promising.

"There you go, getting ahead of yourself. Let's deal with what's in front of us. We need Stella to share her story. I'd also like some time with Sebastian." His gaze took on a faraway look, and when she tapped his knee, his grin instantly appeared, but his eyes were still shaded.

"You're worried about Jamie."

"Aye."

"When would you have expected him to arrive?" She scooted off the bed and picked up the tray. "It should have been safe travels if he stuck close to the coast."

"I wouldn't have expected him to arrive before Beckworth and Stella, even with their stop at Waverly. But he should have arrived before us."

"What about weather?"

"It's possible. He might have stopped at Bristol on his way south. He wouldn't have wasted an opportunity to haul cargo."

"As he was trained to do." She climbed into bed and knelt behind him, moving her hands over his shoulders and gently kneading them.

Finn leaned into her, and his soft groan encouraged her to deepen the massage. Before long, and an hour later, they were both lying in each other's arms, staring at the ceiling.

"After our nap, I'm going to ask Mary to join me for tea."

"You think she has gossip?"

She snorted. "I can't believe you're asking that question. I heard one of the maids grumbling about Lady Agatha. It sounded like they'd recently been here."

"While Stella was here? That couldn't have gone well."

"That's what I'm hoping to find out. And maybe she'll know what was up between Stella and Beckworth."

"Not only a heathen but a strategist. I'm impressed, Mrs. Murphy."

"As you should be, Mr. Murphy."

AJ stood in front of the mirror and turned to check the back. Her hair had grown long enough for Willa to add a few curls. And the jade-green day dress was a good color for her complexion and hair. She was starting to enjoy dressing up for social events.

Mary had decided to go all out for the engagement. AJ would be treated to a full tea service for two in the solarium. She placed a hand over her stomach, hoping there was room for the food Mary was sure to provide.

She'd been lining up her questions since rising from her nap while Finn dressed for an afternoon with Sebastian. The monk had expressed an interest in visiting Westminster Abbey, wishing to pay his respects. To whom, Finn had no idea and decided it wasn't his business, but she suspected his curiosity was piqued nonetheless.

He'd given her a swift kiss before leaving. "Don't overthink it. Let her drive the conversation. You only need a word or two to steer her in the right direction."

"It sounds like manipulation."

He'd laughed. "Says the reporter."

"Fair enough."

Her hand shook when she tugged at her bodice and the pinch of material at her waist. She wasn't nervous to spend time with Mary. It was more that she might not be ready to hear whatever Mary was willing to share. She should wait for Stella, but she had to know if something truly connected the two or if Stella was dealing with a one-way attraction. That answer would guide her on the best way to respond. If it was a one-way thing, that was something they'd both dealt with in past relationships. But if there was any indication Beckworth felt the same way, what would happen when it was time to go home? She wasn't sure she wanted to know the answer.

"You look perfect, my lady."

AJ slapped the maid's arm with her folded fan. "Enough of that, Willa. I know it's the proper way, but I prefer Lady AJ if you have to use the title at all."

Instead of looking admonished, the maid gave her a wink. "If you stay with us much longer, you'll be here for Lady Agatha's next visit."

"Well, now, that's just mean."

They both chortled as Willa followed AJ out the door.

Mary was already in the solarium, which was smaller than the one at their estate in Bristol but had a perfect view of the garden. She set down her embroidery when AJ entered and moved to the table for two by the windows. The sun was out, but a nearby tree shaded them from the glare.

"Oh, my dear, you look wonderful. I'm not sure why we haven't done this before." Mary sat, and once AJ was settled, a footman poured their first cup of tea.

"So much is usually going on with our arrivals, it's lucky we ever found time to relax. This is the first time I can remember having so much free time."

"This isn't the best of times with Teddy missing, but he would want us to carry on while we have people searching for him."

"The two of you have grown quite close." AJ smiled. Finn had been right, but she should have remembered Mary's love of conversation.

"It's like we've known him for years. Hensley was guarded at first, but actions speak louder than words, and Teddy has been nothing but loyal and honest. He does so much for Hensley, and not just with their business dealings."

"And now this thing with Gemini. We're still trying to figure out her end game. She's not very predictable."

Mary giggled. "What woman is?"

AJ laughed with her. "Truer words."

Footmen arrived carrying trays of food, and as expected, AJ could already feel her stomach swelling before she ate the first bite. She bit into a cream-filled biscuit and inwardly sighed. "I hear we just missed Elizabeth."

"And what a lovely visit it was. Agatha came along, of course, and I hosted a few other guests that night." Mary nibbled a thin sandwich with some type of chopped meat filling. "You should have seen Stella. When Beckworth first introduced her, I knew I'd like her straightaway. That evening she was dressed as if she'd lived here all her life."

"Really? I wish I could have seen it."

"She still has the dresses. The blue one was luscious, but nothing compared to the periwinkle masterpiece." She sipped her tea and gave her a wicked smile. "You should have seen the men gawk when she walked into the room for dinner." She chuckled. "I suppose the women as well, for that matter. Of course, Teddy kept her by his side the entire evening until Elizabeth stole her away at dinner."

AJ considered that. There could be several reasons why Beckworth kept Stella by his side. The first one that came to mind was ensuring she didn't talk her way into trouble. But was it more than that? AJ finished a tart and selected a slice of spiced bread. "I can't say I've ever seen Beckworth with a woman at a party." Not that she'd seen him at any social gathering other than her first stay at Waverly, and she didn't count that.

"We hadn't, either, but even Hensley commented on Stella's hold on the man. You know he paid for both her dresses, including the fittings. And if that wasn't enough, Agatha was speechless when she noticed the opal necklace and bracelet Teddy had given her."

AJ's cup rattled in its saucer, and she almost knocked over her plate. He'd bought jewelry for her? The dresses were one thing, but jewelry?

"I think those two have a very special relationship. He took her all over London. From what I hear, Eleanor adores her as well."

AJ sipped her tea before she choked on spiced bread. Sebastian hadn't mentioned they'd stopped at Eleanor's. But that would make sense if Waverly was being watched by Gemini's men.

"She must truly be heartbroken without Teddy."

The statement startled AJ out of her musings. "I think she feels responsible."

"That's only natural in these circumstances." Mary refilled their teacups and glanced out the window. "I think the lilacs will be glorious this year. Teddy took Stella to Whitechapel to visit the flower vendors."

"Whitechapel? Isn't that a dangerous area?"

Mary shrugged. "It can be, but Hensley says that's where Teddy's old friends live, so I imagine he felt it safe enough for Stella."

AJ pulled out her fan and waved it fast enough to lift the edges of her napkin. Had Beckworth taken her to meet his old crew? Boardinghouses and the East End. What the hell had he been thinking? Someone had some explaining to do.

4

Baywood, Oregon - current day

Ethan listened to the voices, unsure of where he was, and groaned when he tried to lift an arm. A painful twitch on his side reminded him of a glade and a run-in with a sword. He opened his eyes to the most beautiful sight in the world.

Worried green eyes stared down at him, lines forming between her brows. He smiled when she ran a hand over his cheek.

"Hello, beautiful." His throat was scratchy.

"You worried me to death."

He blinked, then memories slammed into him, and he turned his head, the motion forcing another groan. The voices had stopped, and his eyes darted around, taking in as much information as he could since he seemed incapable of moving for the moment.

The ceiling should have given it away, but he didn't have to look farther than Maire's crisp flowered blouse covered with a light sweater to know they weren't in 1805 anymore. He sighed, not really surprised they'd returned to Baywood.

"Ethan. How do you feel?" Adam's voice came from somewhere over Maire's right shoulder, and soon his face came into view. "You had us all scared when we found you on the dock covered in blood."

He tried to rise, but his side burned.

"Here, drink this." Maire shoved a glass in front of his lips.

Without thinking, he did as she commanded and then almost spit it out. "Good Christ, that's horrible. Now I know why Finn and AJ grumbled so much."

Maire tsked. "It will help you heal."

"There must be something in this time period that tastes better than that and provides the same effect." He ran a tongue around his mouth, trying to ease the horrid aftertaste. "How long have we been here?" His voice sounded more like his own, and he tried to sit again.

Strong arms lifted him as pillows were stuffed behind him. He stifled another groan, but at least he could see the room without straining his neck. Then Isaiah moved into his peripheral vision.

"A couple of hours. You have a flesh wound from what Maire believes to have been a flintlock rifle." Isaiah offered him a glass of water, and Maire held it to his lips. The water was cool and revitalized him while washing away the rest of the bitter medicine. He didn't taste any additives in the water, but he refused to ask for fear Maire might force him to drink more of her vile herbal remedies.

"I remember feeling pain just as the fog took us. I thought it might be worse than it was."

"Thank heavens it wasn't. I'm not sure how I would have explained it to the paramedics if we had to call them." Adam pulled his chair closer.

He scanned the room to find Madelyn, Helen, and Emory hovering close. "Did Maire tell you what happened?" He hoped so because he wasn't sure he had the energy to go over it all.

"The highlights from when you left Baywood to the ambush outside Stokenchurch." Adam glanced down at a pad of paper in his lap. "I checked a map. It's hard to tell two hundred years later, but it appears to have been a fairly wooded area at one time. It would have been an excellent spot for a trap."

"Maire also told us how everyone split up to look for the chronicles." Helen's eyes appeared watery. "She thinks AJ is alright, but she was still in France the last time you'd seen her."

He nodded, and when he shifted on the couch, it didn't hurt quite as badly when he pushed himself up to a better-seated position. "She was with Finn and Lando. I know it seems a dangerous time to travel through France, but Finn speaks the language, so it will help. The role of the Irish in the war is complex as they fight on both sides. I wouldn't worry too much about them getting to London. The question is whether they were able to retrieve the chronicle."

Then he gripped Maire's arm, but she was already nodding. "We have the second chronicle. It's safe."

He relaxed, not realizing how tense he'd been until he heard they'd completed part of their mission. "I suppose it was too much to hope for a jump to London."

"You're lucky you didn't end up back at the monastery." Emory held Helen's hand, and it appeared she was squeezing it tight. "The incantation might have taken you to the torc rather than the earrings. It's amazing for their small size that they still hold the power of the Heart Stone."

Maire gave Emory a quick glance. Her brows rose as she considered his words. "I hadn't thought of that, but you're right. It was a possibility."

"We didn't have a choice," Ethan insisted, suddenly questioning their decision.

"Of course not." Adam's words weren't said to make him feel better. There was honesty behind them. "It worked before, bringing the fog. From what Maire says of the situation you were in, it was your best recourse to save the others. We can only hope it worked."

Maire turned to Isaiah. "Why were you so close at hand to find us on the dock?"

"We weren't sure how long you'd be gone, but we thought it best to have someone at the inn in case there were any more surprises from the past. My schedule is more flexible since I can do most of my schoolwork remotely. Adam and Helen fill in to give me a break, and you've only been gone for three days."

"We need to go back." Ethan caught Maire's grimace. "You got us back there before, you can do it again."

She shook her head. "The timing was off by several days."

"It was off by two days, and now that you know that, you can work on improving it. I'll need a day, maybe two, before I'm ready to travel."

"I'll be the judge of when you're ready." Maire used a damp towel to wipe his forehead. "We need to make sure there's no infection, and you'll need your full strength back."

He recognized her hunched shoulders and wrinkled brow. "Have you had a chance to review the chronicle?"

She shook her head.

"She wanted to read it, but we made her take a shower and then had to force her to eat something." Helen laid a quilt over him. "I think it's best you get some more rest before we move you upstairs to the guest room. Adam can help Maire get you into a bath when you feel up to it. Once you're both rested and fed, we'll give her the chronicle."

He chuckled. "I assume you've hidden it from her."

"It's not funny." Maire's lips twisted anyway, and it made him feel better that she understood the group's concern for her.

"I might be a bit rusty with my Celtic, but I had a few moments to review some of the pages." Emory appeared to be the cheeriest of the group. "I'm also fairly good with encryption. I might be of some assistance to Maire, if only as an observer, but perhaps I can also be a second pair of eyes."

Ethan remembered that Emory had been a professor of ancient studies at the university in Eugene. His specialty had been in Celtic and Irish studies, which was how Adam and Stella met him.

"It couldn't hurt," Maire agreed as she stood. "Let me get you a bit of soup, and then you can rest."

He knew she would hide a sleep potion in the soup, but he nodded and squeezed her hand. As much as he wanted to jump back immediately, they had to be smart about their return. There was an advantage in coming back to Baywood. Maire would have the proper time to study the chronicle to see if there was anything useful in fine-tuning the incantation. Even if it took a month and they had to use their last incantation, being a couple of days earlier or later than when they left would be better than nothing.

He could only hope that whatever the outcome, it wouldn't be too late.

5

England - 1805

Stella was true to her word, remaining in her room for two days to participate in her solo pity party. AJ visited twice to make sure she was still breathing and to share what Hensley and Finn were doing to find Beckworth. Her wine-clouded brain picked up various words—men watching the coast, a message to the monastery, a dispatch sent to Waverly. It didn't matter. Nothing would come of it. Something tickled at her, nudging her with a forgotten memory. She was self-aware enough to know focusing on the problem wouldn't force the answer. Her best option was to do what came naturally—let her subconscious do the heavy lifting. The answer would come. She just needed to wait.

On the third day, Sarah pestered her about getting air, and a walk through the garden would do her good. It's where she'd be if she were home, so she relented. She found AJ sitting on a bench near a willow tree. It was the same bench she'd shared with Beckworth on their last day in London.

"I hope you don't mind." AJ patted the seat next to her and

nodded to Sarah in a way that said she'd take over babysitting duty.

Stella patted Sarah's hand. "It's alright. Come find me in an hour."

When she sat, AJ took her hand. "You don't have to talk. We can just sit here. I know what you're going through. You know that. So, I'll be here when you're ready."

And they sat without speaking for the entire hour. They leaned against the back of the bench and watched the birds flit about in the beautiful sunshine. Though she tried to focus on the flowers and trees around her, the same questions played over and over. Was he being held in the dark hold of the ship? Were his wounds being cared for? Was he resting comfortably in Gemini's cabin? She almost cried with relief when Sarah came for her.

The next day, when she met AJ in the garden, she felt a bit more like her old self. But that nagging feeling they were looking for Beckworth in all the wrong places still plagued her. Instead of worrying over it, she glanced around and noticed the world around her for the first time since returning from Ipswich.

"Where's Maire? I would have expected her to join us."

When AJ didn't say anything, her worry for Beckworth slid aside. "What aren't you telling me?"

AJ pushed her hair back and sighed. "They retrieved the chronicle without a problem. On their way back, the team was ambushed before they made it to London."

She stared at her. Something didn't compute. "Wait. Fitz and Thomas had been with them, but they were at Ipswich."

AJ nodded. "They were surrounded. Gemini's men planned on taking Maire and the chronicle, then killing everyone else. They had no way out."

She let the words sink in, then she understood. "She jumped with Ethan."

"And it worked as well as it did at Waverly. Fitz, Thomas, and the rest of the men were able to get away under the cover of fog. Since Maire and Ethan haven't shown up, we assume the jump took them back to Baywood."

Beckworth had mentioned Maire modifying the incantation when they followed her to the past. "So, they might already be back and on the way here."

"If the incantation works like it did the first time. There's no way to be sure until they show up."

That was the problem. There was nothing to do but wait. "That's as much information I can take for one day. If you don't mind, I'd like to go back to my room now."

"Of course." AJ stood and took Stella's arm as they strolled back to the manor. "Do you think you'll feel up to eating with us tonight?"

She patted AJ's hand and stepped back. "We'll see." She turned for the foyer, leaving AJ to watch her walk away.

Stella woke with a start. Her short time in the garden had zapped her strength, and she'd fallen on top of the bedcovers, drifting instantly to sleep. Sarah's footsteps brought her to partial consciousness, but not enough to fully engage before she was out for the count.

At some point during her deep sleep, her subconscious musings paid off. With a certainty she couldn't explain, there wasn't a doubt in her mind the team was searching for Beckworth in all the wrong places. She scoured her room for Beckworth's saddlebag, which she insisted on keeping for him, and found it stuffed in the back of a wardrobe closet.

She dragged it to the bed and picked through it, removing the contents item by item. It made sense to give everything a thorough review in case there was something Hensley might find important. She set the coffee pot, utensils, and other supplies to the side. After taking a long sniff of his two shirts that still held his scent, she set them in a separate pile. There was a pouch the size of a cell phone that she expected to hold coins, and it did hold a few, but there were other items stashed inside. One was the map she'd been looking for, and the other was a dozen of her origami swans. She could understand one, they'd become a bit of a joke between them, but twelve seemed odd. She put them back in the pouch and opened the map.

It was the one they'd taken off the dead guy at Eleanor's. It showed the three locations of the chronicles—Bréval, Worcester, and Ipswich. The fourth and final mark was London.

When she'd discussed it with Beckworth and Sebastian, they'd assumed Gemini expected their team to join Hensley at his London house, where he would be in residence for the season. But maybe London was selected for another reason. Gemini had proven to be clairvoyant before in guessing Beckworth's strategy when they'd run for Southampton. Though it made sense their team might meet in London, they could have easily decided on Bristol or a southern port before sailing for the monastery.

She tapped her finger on the X. If she'd learned anything after spending time with Gemini, the woman was crafty. Dollars to donuts, the woman was up to something. Something no one would see coming.

"Sarah!"

When the maid didn't respond, Stella raced to the door and swung it open. She yelled down the hallway, "Sarah!"

It didn't take long to hear stomping feet as Sarah burst from the servant's stairs. "Lady Stella. What's wrong?"

"Have they been seated for dinner yet?"

Sarah shook her head. "Another half hour."

"Then let's get busy. I'm going to dinner."

Sarah smiled, happy she'd finally relented. If the poor thing only knew there was a storm brewing.

Stella breezed into the dining room with two minutes to spare. All conversation stopped when everyone stared at her stunning cobalt-blue dress that Beckworth had bought when they'd first arrived in London. Her hair was pinned up in a simple style, with her leaf hairpin placed in a prominent spot. Her opal necklace settled just above her bodice, and the matching bracelet was warm on her skin.

Stella was back, and she had a mission. With any luck, they'd see the answer as clearly as she did.

Finn was the first to greet her, and he bent in a deep bow, making her laugh. Hensley and Lando followed suit before they introduced her to Thomas. She wondered why Lando and Thomas weren't part of the search for Beckworth, but it wasn't her place to ask, as much as she wanted to. But with Ethan and Maire missing and Jamie and the *Daphne* still unaccounted for, they might be waiting should their friends need them. That was something she understood.

When the butler called them to dinner, Finn held out his arm to escort her. Lando offered his arm to AJ, who took it with a pleasant smile, but her eyes squinted when she glanced at Stella. She responded with her most innocent smile, though it was impossible to hide anything from her. AJ was quite aware she was up to something, but if she'd told AJ her plans, she would have to tell Finn. And Stella wanted to share her idea in her own way and not have it diluted through Finn's eyes.

The conversation was lively throughout most of the meal, with Hensley and Mary dazzling them with stories of their trips taken abroad years before. It all worked into Stella's plan for the group to be at ease as she waited for dessert to be served before making her first move.

"How's the search for Beckworth going?"

The room quieted with forks raised over their spiced rum cake with gingerbread frosting, eyes darting from one person to another.

Finn took the bullet for them. "We have men searching up and down the coast for the ship."

"I know it's only been a handful of days, but how long do you think it will take to scour the coastline?"

"There's a great deal of land to cover with plenty of coves where the ship could have docked."

She nodded. "So, we're talking weeks rather than days."

He glanced at AJ before answering. "Very likely."

"I think we're looking in the wrong place."

Heads that had previously been lowered as if the dessert was the grandest they'd ever eaten suddenly rose. Stella held back her smile. Now they were getting somewhere.

"What do you mean?" Hensley asked.

She glanced around the room, her gaze touching on AJ, who was shaking her head. It wasn't that she didn't understand what Stella was doing. She understood quite well and was begging her to stop talking and not get in the middle of it. AJ had to have known that was a fifty-fifty shot at best.

She opened a small coin pouch she'd tied to a button sewn at her waist and pulled out the map, handing it to Finn. "I think Beckworth showed this map to Hensley. It was the one we took off Gemini's man at Eleanor's. Pass it around, and you'll see that London was important to Gemini."

Hensley waited until he looked at the map, most likely ensuring it was the same one he'd seen before. "I did speak with Beckworth about this. We both agreed that it was highly likely she planned on returning to London if she thought it was the best way to barter for the other chronicles, or perhaps steal them back. But capturing Beckworth with the third chronicle would have changed that. She would be mad to sail up the Thames with all of us actively searching for him."

"Well, that's the point. We're not actively looking in London." Stella spread her arms wide, encompassing everyone at the table. "Besides, I think we can all agree she's unpredictable."

"It wouldn't be strategically prudent to sail into London," Finn replied.

Stella glanced at Sebastian, who she hadn't seen since her return. He didn't look at her with the same pity as the others. He wore that silly grin that made you wonder if he understood the magnitude of the situation or was mentally drifting in another dimension. His gaze sparkled with humor, and he gave a slight nod.

He believed her. He understood the unconventional thinking that appeared to run in the Belato family.

Stella held her ground, unwilling to give in. "You haven't met her. You heard her at the Ipswich dock. Her plan went awry, and while others might take a step back and reconsider their position, she doubled down. We can easily look at her and say she's mad as a hatter, or you can see someone who's been making plans for years and always has another option in her back pocket."

She caught Finn's glance at Lando, and she knew she'd hit a chord, but it wasn't enough to come to her aid. She added her last assurance in her most convincing broker voice.

"She's coming to London, if she's not already here."

If for no other reason than to get back to dessert, Hensley made an offer. "I can send a couple of men to monitor the docks on the off chance the ship sailed under cover of darkness."

The others nodded, and though she knew Hensley would be

true to his word, two or three men weren't sufficient. The Thames was a long river with just as many places to dock as the coast.

The men continued the discussion with how committed they were to the search while providing sound reasons why London would be a terrible risk. She listened, letting the matter rest as she took a bite of cake.

The men's response wasn't a surprise. She'd expected it, which was why she would retire early and spend the rest of the evening preparing for phase two. She had no choice. This group wouldn't discuss it with her because Finn and AJ could only see the real estate broker. They hadn't seen what she was capable of. They couldn't understand, but they would soon enough.

6

Baywood, Oregon - current day

Ethan carried a tray to the back deck where Helen had prepared the patio table for lunch. Adam manned the grill, cooking hamburgers while Madelyn fed the kids at a smaller table, helping them add fixings to their hotdogs. They'd been back a week, and he'd become stir-crazy trying to stay busy.

Jackson welcomed his assistance on the new deck being added to the inn's master bedroom while he split part of his time at the McDowell house puttering with minor repairs. The work gave him time to consider their next steps once Maire developed an improved incantation.

He glanced around, noting the only two missing from the scene were Emory and Maire, who both spent long days locked in Finn's study. Maire translated the second chronicle while Emory reviewed the piles of notes and journals she'd collected from the druid's grimoire and the first chronicle which were safely hidden at the monastery.

"Lunch is about ready." Helen filled glasses with iced tea. "Do you want to get them, or should I?"

Ethan glanced at the table with dishes of potato salad, green salad, fruit salad, baked beans, potato chips, and all the toppings one could want for a hamburger. He had to admit, he missed this century's food. His preferred tastes might have been altered by the limited choices when moving from one inn to another, or it might have been the improvements in modern-day convection ovens and proper refrigeration. Of course, Maire found solace each evening with her ice cream maker. He rubbed his stomach. A five-mile run would be in order to fend off the effects of the sweet dessert.

He placed a hand on Helen's shoulder. "I think it's my turn to fetch them and hear their wrath about leaving at a critical moment."

She laughed. "If we didn't force them out of that room every few hours, I'm afraid we'd find them passed out over piles of paper, dehydrated and half-starved."

He was still chuckling as he strode toward the library and was surprised when Maire and Emory met him at the stairs. The first thing he noticed was their huge grins.

Maire nodded. "We think we have what we need for a new incantation."

"It required bits from her excellent notes from the grimoire, what she'd put together from Sebastian's last journal entries, and pieces of a new incantation from the second chronicle." Emory seemed to have grown younger after a week locked in a study. But Ethan imagined it was more the professor's enthusiasm to continue his life's work.

The two of them continued to chatter on their way to the deck. He didn't understand most of it, but he found humor in their ability to complete each other's sentences as if they were an old married couple.

Helen laughed and blushed when Emory took her by the waist and twirled her around in a short dance.

"I didn't think I'd be so happy in helping to send Ethan and Maire back to their time." Emory released Helen, the kids laughing at their grandmother, and looked over Adam's shoulder as he took the last of the burgers off the grill. "Those look wonderful." He rubbed his hands together. "I have to admit, reading those old texts has made me hungry."

"I can't believe how famished I am," Maire said as she dropped a large helping of potato salad on her plate.

Adam laid the platter on the table, followed by a stack of gently grilled buns, then sat down next to Madelyn. "So, the second chronicle proved helpful?"

Maire nodded. "At first, I wasn't sure, then Emory reviewed portions of text from the chronicles and the grimoire. He was the one who saw the pattern."

Emory nodded. "It was my experience working with encryption in the military."

Adam glanced at Madelyn, who shrugged. "When was this?"

"It was right after the end of the war in Vietnam. I was attending college at the time, considering topics for my doctorate when the military came calling. While my passion was history, I had a way with math and various languages. I put my studies on hold for a couple of years with the army before deciding my direction lay with ancient studies. It's all about the patterns."

"Emory was right." Maire licked ketchup off her fingers after taking a bite of her burger, then washed it down with tea. "Without realizing it, Sebastian and I had discovered part of the pattern when we found the various bits of the incantations. After Emory pointed it out this morning, everything fell together like coming to the end of one of those jigsaw puzzles Helen loves." She gave Helen a wink before swallowing potato salad. Ethan couldn't remember the last time he saw her so animated. "We're obviously missing a large piece of the overall puzzle where the torc is concerned, but I believe we have enough to take us to a general location with a date that will put us a day at most from when we jumped."

"You're sure?" Ethan asked. The new incantation alone made jumping to Baywood worth it. He'd already been contemplating the best location to jump if they had a choice. Now it was just confirming the date.

Maire gave Emory a quick glance before confirming. "We should be able to finalize the incantation this afternoon. And if all goes well, we can leave in the morning."

Her words gave Ethan's heart a solid thump. He was anxious to get back in the fray. He'd been worried about Thomas, Fitz, and the men they'd left behind, as he knew Maire was. Thankfully, the chronicle had taken her mind off them and the fate of the other teams.

"The question is, where do you want to go?" Emory asked.

"You definitely don't want to end up at the monastery." Adam finished the last of his hamburger and sat back, picking at the potato chips. "But dropping into London could be problematic."

Maire squeezed Ethan's hand. "We could go to Hereford. You can see the earl again."

It was an excellent suggestion, but as much as he wanted to see the earl, it put them too far away from London. If their timing was right, and they would only lose a day, Gemini's men could still be around.

He reluctantly shook his head. "We need to get to Hensley's as quickly as possible, and I agree with Adam, trying for London would create more problems."

"I don't think London is a possibility at this point." Maire glanced at Emory, who nodded and supplied the rest of her thoughts.

"While we can produce an incantation for the right date, we believe the Heart Stone is required for directing the incantation to a specific location it hadn't been before. The smaller stones don't have enough power, so we believe they can only travel to a location from one of its previous jumps."

"But the Heart Stone is in London," Adam said. "Couldn't an incantation to find the Heart Stone get you there?"

Maire shrugged. "Yes, we have the original incantation Finn and Ethan used during their travels, and we can attempt to modify that one, but since the Heart Stone is in the same time period as the torc..." She shrugged and ate a potato chip. "It's possible we could be pulled to the monastery."

"That doesn't sound like a wise choice." Madelyn joined them at the table after sending the kids to the family room to do their homework.

"We need to go to Waverly." Ethan had gone over multiple scenarios, and each time, he came to the same conclusion. "Gemini probably has men watching the estate, but Barrington will be in contact with Beckworth and Hensley. He'll also be able to provide us transportation."

"Then two days to London." Maire tilted her head and stared out to sea. "The stone has traveled there before, so the incantation will be easier to finish."

When Ethan glanced around the table, everyone nodded. "Then, not to be a taskmaster, but if you're done with lunch, I suggest you get back to work."

"And we'll prepare a feast for this evening," Helen added. "After a good night's sleep, we'll send you back in the morning. But no breakfast. From what I understand of the effects from a jump, you'll just throw it all up when you arrive."

The following morning, Maire finished packing her duffel and left it by the bedroom door. Ethan would retrieve it after his meeting with Adam to discuss the McDowell house should they not return after a specified amount of time. Pinpricks ran over her body with the thought.

The first time she'd been forced to the future, she'd expected to hate every moment of it. And it disturbed her to discover she'd been terribly wrong. If she'd been on her own, it might have been a different story, and the thought reminded her of Beckworth and when he'd been stuck in this time with little hope of returning home.

She hadn't considered it at the time, and who could blame her, but now as she looked back, some of his actions at the time made sense. He was a different man now, or maybe he always had been, and his guise as viscount and the duke's henchman was a mask for the benefit of his father. Such displaced loyalties, but she still understood.

Her problem was that she'd made friends here, and Ethan had made a comfortable life for them. She never thought someone like him, and an Englishman at that, would make such a difference in her life. He warmed her blood and calmed her. In this modern era, the better phrase was that he centered her. She couldn't predict their future—whether they'd stay in the past or return to this time. She'd be happy in any era as long as Ethan was with her.

She'd come to that conclusion some time ago. At the same time, it was easy to sense his own questions about the future, yet neither of them brought it up. He was most likely waiting for this business with the stones to be done, but what if it took years? Wasn't it worth living each day and not worrying about what tomorrow brought?

Her life might belong in the past, but she'd learned a thing or two in this time period. And it gave her the perfect answer. When the time was right, she'd see it done.

She glanced around the room, then picked up the backpack Helen had given her and rushed down the stairs. Ethan and Adam were meeting in Finn's study, so she'd asked Emory to meet her in the library. He was already there, slowly working his way through the shelves, when he stopped and selected a book. She watched him, curious at his reverence for the delicate binding as he read the first page while his finger rubbed the edge of the cover—a purely subconscious act. He flipped through the next few pages and then turned, realizing someone was watching him.

She smiled. "I didn't want to disturb you. Is it what you expected?"

He returned the grin. "Oh, yes. It's a Dicken's book. I've read them all several times. He has the most marvelous way of starting a story."

"I don't recognize the name."

He chuckled. "You're right. From your perspective, Charles Dickens will be born a few years after you jump back. If you return to us, I'll personally buy you his complete works. I'd love to have someone to discuss them with. They're not everyone's preferred reading."

"Well, that's a true shame. And it's a deal." She walked to the antique desk, opened the backpack, and pulled out the chronicle along with a stack of bound pages.

"What's all this?" He stepped next to her, and his hand automatically reached for the chronicle. His fingers once again caressed the book, this time on its spine.

That action alone told her she was making the right decision.

"This, as you know, is the second chronicle. I've taken notes of the more critical portions." She pulled the stack of pages over and tapped them. "These are my more salient notes on the druid's grimoire. You've already read most of them." She turned to face him. "I'm leaving these in your care."

He stared at her, his gaze unfocused and completely blank. It was another moment before he blinked. His expression turned hopeful. "Why would you leave them in this time period, and why with me?"

"I think the answer as to why you would be obvious. You're tied to this family now, you're a historian, and you can actually read the material. You also know their importance as well as their dangers. We haven't known each other very long, but I trust you to keep them safe. And should you never hear from me again, I know you'll find a permanent resting place for them."

His eyes misted. "Well, I hope that day never comes. But I'd be honored to be entrusted with them. But you know I won't be able to keep them close without spending time with them."

"I wouldn't expect anything less." She slipped everything back into the backpack and pushed it toward him.

He eyed it, drumming his fingers on the back of the Dickens book he still held. Then he looked past her to the far wall. She turned to see what caught his attention and saw the door to the armory and the security keypad next to it.

She touched his arm. "It's a perfect spot for now."

Ethan walked the path to the dock with Adam, Isaiah, and Jackson. The four of them had drunk coffee while discussing what he and Maire might be jumping into and how difficult it would be to challenge both Gemini and Belato. Then they asked what he'd miss if he never returned. Whether they'd meant it to or not, their question had thrown him, and when he considered his answer, there were too many things to name. But not returning was a real possibility, and the one thing that kept repeating was the word "family." He pushed aside the strong pull to this place and enjoyed their game and the outlandish items Isaiah continued to suggest.

Before they reached the dock, he changed the subject. "How much longer will the renovations take?"

Jackson rubbed his jaw. "With AJ and Finn? Most likely a lifetime." When everyone laughed, he shook his head. "Do you know they made a five-year renovation plan? After a year working for them, I can tell you those five years will stretch to ten."

"All the more reason for you to stick around, old man." Isaiah put an arm around his grandfather's shoulder, who immediately shoved it away, grinning the entire time.

Jackson pulled his sweater tighter and rubbed the back of his neck. "I'd say it was all AJ's doing, but Finn told me about his plans for making furniture. I wouldn't be surprised if there isn't a shop built at the end of the parking lot in the next couple of years. There's plenty of room for it since the house won't become the bread and breakfast it used to be."

"He's talked to me about that as well," Adam said. "He's worked through several different floor plans, but for now, his focus is on the second floor."

"It will be another several months before that work is completed." Jackson glanced past the others to Ethan. "If you come back and decide to stay, we need to talk about the McDowell house. I suggest you buy it, then we can discuss the changes you should make."

Isaiah threw his head back and laughed. "I knew you wouldn't let him jump without getting that said."

"He already knows it, even if he don't know he knows it."

Ethan was shocked by the emotions that crept over him. They were similar to those he'd felt the last time he looked down at the Brun Manor. Without realizing it, he'd created a family here. And the fact these people accepted him as one of their own meant the world to him. It left him with a difficult decision of where his future lay. Of course, it wasn't his alone to make, and he glanced at Maire as they reached the dock where she waited for him, a smile on her soft pink lips.

Helen stepped away from Emory to hug him tightly. "I just want you to know that if you don't come back, I'm going to be extremely unhappy with you. You have to make your own decision, but that doesn't mean it won't take some time to forgive you if you don't return."

He leaned in and kissed her cheek. "I'll understand as long as you eventually do forgive me."

He hugged Madelyn, then shook Patrick and Robby's hands before rubbing Charlotte's mess of blonde curls. Maire took his arm, and they walked to the middle of the dock and turned around.

Ethan gripped her hand, and she squeezed back as they took a moment to watch this group of strangers who'd become their family.

"We can't promise if we'll be back. The wind continues to blow us around as it sees fit. What I will promise is that AJ, Finn, and Stella will be returned to you. That is my personal guarantee."

Adam wrapped an arm around his mother as she dabbed at her eyes with a tissue. "I'm not good with Irish sayings, or any sayings really, but I'll give you the only one I know. May the road rise up to meet you."

"Sláinte, to your health," Maire responded. She took out a piece of paper and Ethan's stone, then read the new incantation.

Soon the white tendrils surrounded them, grabbing them gently at first, then sucking them into a whirlwind of light.

Ethan dry heaved and was thankful the coffee didn't come up. Then he heard the tell-tale sound of a flint-lock being cocked. He froze, his eyes darting around for Maire. She was to his left and an arm's length away. Her face was sickly pale, probably from her own retching.

She gave him a side glance, then turned her gaze upward as Ethan did.

Two men stood in front of them, muskets pointed at their heads.

Ethan wasn't sure where or when they'd landed, but if these were Gemini's men, the fates weren't kind.

7

England - 1805

Stella woke before dawn and drew on her pants, shirt, and boots. She tied her hair back with a black ribbon, then glanced around with the feeling she was forgetting something. Before she made it to the door, she snapped her fingers and backtracked, pulling her old raincoat out of the dresser. It was unrecognizable from how it looked the day she bought it, but other than missing buttons and tears from the bushes she kept jumping into, it had held up well. She'd have to buy another one when she got home.

The thought hit her like a baseball bat to the head. It had been weeks since she'd thought of home. AJ's suggestion to jump back as soon as they returned to London had appalled her. With Beckworth taken, now was the worst time to think about leaving. Or, more to the point, to consider why she wasn't stomping her foot in frustration as to why they couldn't leave that very minute.

She slid on the coat and gently opened the door, closing it with the same care. Rather than using the main staircase, she took the servant stairs to the main floor. The kitchen staff was already busy baking bread and preparing ingredients for breakfast. She nodded to them as she passed through, and while she received a few odd stares, they returned to their previous conversations.

The stable was quiet in the predawn hour, and she ducked in before anyone rising early might see her. She found a young stable boy seated on a stool in front of a stall, his chin resting on his chest.

"Wake up, young one." She smiled when the boy, who must have been eleven or twelve, fell off the stool.

He jumped up. "Sorry, my lady."

"I'm really sorry to bother you, but I need a horse saddled as quickly as you can."

The boy stared at her, finally taking in her pants and shirt.

"Well, what's the problem?"

"Did Lord Hensley say it was alright to take a horse?"

The kid was smarter than she expected. Just her luck. She gave him her sugar-sweet smile. "The horse doesn't belong to Hensley. It belongs to me. You must not have been working the day we returned from Ipswich."

"You were there?" The boy's misgivings about her vanished, and his eyes grew large.

She nodded.

"Someday, I'll be able to go on missions with Morton and Lewelyn."

His devotion to the pair could be seen more in his starstruck gaze than in the intensity of his tone. The boy was definitely smitten with adoration.

"They are honorable and brave men. You've chosen well."

He stood straighter, his thin chest puffed out. "Which horse is yours?"

She glanced around as if she was concerned someone might overhear her. "He's the horrible colored gelding called Smudge."

He screwed up his nose. "Well, at least he's well-behaved."

She watched him run down the aisle, grabbing a bridle as he went. He turned down another aisle and disappeared from sight. She fidgeted, positive that either Hensley or Finn would storm in and stop her.

She mounted the horse with more ease than expected and glanced down at the boy. "Thank you for your help." She leaned over and handed him a coin.

His eyes grew wide, and then his grin showed a missing tooth, which, at his age, would stick with him the rest of his life. He gave her horse a long look. "He is something awful. I can see why you prefer to ride at dawn." Then he laughed and ran off.

The little stinker.

Dawn was just breaking over the tops of buildings. She was fairly certain she remembered the way and remained alert to everything around her, occasionally touching the pistol resting in her coat pocket. The streets were mostly empty until she grew closer to the East End. Every block or so, a man would step out of the shadows and nod before stepping back. She wasn't sure what the behavior meant and decided they didn't believe her to be a worthy target and were giving her a pass. No one else approached her, but she was relieved when the two-story house came into view.

Smoke curled upward from the chimney, and she hoped she wasn't too late. She wasn't sure when he left for the day, though he might conduct business at home. The topic never came up.

She tied the horse to a post and knocked on the door.

A minute passed before she heard heavy boots, and the door swung open.

Chester gave her an appraising look before glancing past her to the horse.

He smiled. "I've been expecting you."

AJ stared at Stella's bedroom door, unsure of the best way to approach her friend. She couldn't remember being in a position where she'd been scared of how Stella would greet her. They'd had disagreements, but they were rare. And one of them would always send chocolate, coffee, or wine to patch things up.

She looked down at the bottle of wine and two glasses in her hands. Some things never changed. Yet, her best friend, someone she'd known for years, who'd never been near a horse, had taken one from the stables and ridden off at dawn. And she refused to say where she went, other than she went for a ride. A ride. Who was this woman, and who took Stella?

At first, Hensley was upset she'd taken a horse without asking, but Stella pointed out the horse belonged to her. Beckworth had bought it for her. AJ shook her head at the fact he'd purchased a horse and opal jewelry for her.

Hensley's other concern was that she'd gone out unprotected. Gemini's men could have grabbed her at any time. Stella countered the argument that since her cover had been blown in Ipswich, there wasn't any reason for Gemini to seek her out.

No one had even been aware she'd left the manner until later that afternoon. The information worked its way from the stables, to the kitchen, to a footman, and finally, the housekeeper, who mentioned it to Mary after she'd taken Stella and AJ to lunch with friends.

Finn and Hensley both wanted to restrict her from the stables for her own protection, but AJ asked them to back off. She might not understand how Stella arrived at her current thinking, but she knew a great deal about guilt and loss. When she was forced to jump home after a botched mission at

Waverly, she blamed herself for leaving Finn behind. And she suffered for weeks, not knowing if he was alive or dead.

Stella was going through the same thing with Beckworth, and it didn't matter if AJ approved or understood. She forced the last couple of days away and knocked on the door.

"Come in." Stella sounded like she was in a good mood.

She shifted the wine bottle under her arm, then opened the door and peered in. "It's just me. I come with a peace offering." She held the bottle out.

Stella chuckled. "You know me, never one to say no to wine." She was sitting cross-legged on the bed with a flock of swans around her. AJ couldn't imagine what she did with them all, but she stopped when AJ entered. "I see the bottle is already open. You didn't get a head start did you?"

She laughed. "And test fate? Hardly." She climbed on the bed and poured two glasses, stuffing the bottle between pillows to keep it upright.

Stella finished the swan she'd been working on and set it with the others before she moved to lean against the headboard, her legs stretched out before her. "Are we celebrating something, or is it time for girl talk?"

AJ took a long swallow of wine and let it spill. "I hadn't seen you for weeks. Not since before our sail down the Oregon coast. Once we jumped back, it seemed like we were always chasing you, always a day behind. When we came across people who'd seen you, they said you were doing fine." She wiped an eye. "But I wasn't able to see it for myself." She stopped to take a drink in some vain attempt to keep the tears in check.

Stella patted her leg and stared up at the ceiling. "I never considered it from your point of view. Not really. I thought about you all the time and how you'd worry, but I'd just assumed you'd know I was alright. Though, looking back, I can see that was a mistake.

"Those first couple of days, I was so terrified but also pissed off. You know how it is; you fall into survival mode. Gemini had a lot of men—mean men. I didn't know how long it might take for you to find me, and then all of a sudden, Beckworth was there. I hesitated to leave with him because I wasn't sure if I could trust him, but you trusted him, and in the end, that was all I needed to know." She swallowed a gulp of wine and pushed her hair back. "Sometimes he was so insufferable, but he took care of me, watched out for me. He killed two men trying to keep me safe. My entire purpose was to find you and Finn, but as the days went by, I learned new skills. I learned to adapt and gain some control over my life." She chuckled and gave AJ one of her quirky smiles. "I'm the same Stella but with upgrades."

AJ nodded in understanding. She'd developed her own skills during her time in this era. It would be foolish to think Stella hadn't. They were both survivors—strong and capable. She picked up a swan, holding it gently in the palm of her hand. "When did this thing with Beckworth start?"

Stella's expression took on an ethereal glow. "Somewhere on our way to Southampton, we became friends. I suppose riding the same horse for days brought a certain intimacy. There were hours we never spoke, but it wasn't awkward. Then we'd talk nonstop." She laughed. "Maybe it was just me talking."

AJ snorted. "That sounds about right."

"In the end, maybe it came down to him putting up with my moods like he understood what I was going through. Even on the ship to France and surviving the storm. My god, AJ, you should have seen us. Nothing more than a couple of drowned cats."

"The second kidnapping must have been horrible."

"I was raging mad. We'd been so close to the monastery. I didn't know if they'd killed Beckworth when they took me. Then I woke up and discovered Sebastian in the cell next to me. It helped. But when I found Beckworth and Lando on the dock in Saint-Malo, I'd never been so happy to see someone."

"And now you have some pretty strong feelings for him."

"Well, enough for us to hit the sheets."

She'd taken an inopportune moment to finish her glass of wine and began choking. Stella was up on her knees, slapping her back until she pushed her away.

"My god, Stella. Give a woman some notice when you blurt something like that out."

Stella gave her an impish grin. "It only recently happened. When we arrived in London. I think it was wearing those fine dresses, especially after living in filthy pants and shirts for weeks. And you have to admit, he cleans up rather nicely."

AJ thought back to the first time she'd met him as the Viscount of Waverly. She'd noted his beauty at the time. And he had a sharp wit that could keep up with Stella, which was most likely one of the reasons she was so enamored by him.

"Why are you so sure he's in London?"

Stella considered the question while she refilled their glasses. "I'm not sure I have a simple answer, and I know the map doesn't seem like enough reason to spend the resources searching the Thames. But Beckworth and I are the only ones that have met her, have spoken with her, and have seen how she interacts with her men, especially Gaines.

"People say she's mad for the things she's done, although you know as well as I they wouldn't be saying that if it was a man making the same decisions. But if she is off her rocker, it's not a lock her up in a sanitarium situation. This is more of a Cruella De Vil take-over-the-world persona. I don't know what her story is or her relationship with her uncle and brother. She never mentioned either one while I was her prisoner, but she's been on this quest for a long time. I'm not sure she's playing the same game anymore. Maybe it was Dugan's death or that she'd been following someone else's plan for too long.

"I guess the point I'm trying to make is that I have a bit more insight into her than Hensley or Finn. And I'd like for them to give me a little credit in that column. But when I think about it from their perspective, maybe they need some proof that I'm not a fragile flower who can't accept where I am or how things work. If anything, I've been counseled by the best. Or at least, insights as good as Beckworth can provide."

AJ took a long sip of wine, then gave Stella a long look. Past all the trappings of their current time period, she saw her friend. The same Baywood broker who knew her own mind. She hadn't broken under the conditions she'd been put through, a journey not of her own making. No more than AJ had when she was transported to the past without her consent. They'd both had rocky starts in this time period, but Stella understood the game.

"You're right. If I think back to those earlier days, it took Hensley some time to accept my opinions." She played with the swan she'd picked up, bending its wings back and forth. "Finn knows you and trusts your judgment, but when he travels back to this century, he falls into his old habits of how to protect everyone." She glanced around the room, anywhere but on Stella. Then she had no choice but to pull up her big-girl panties.

"I might have added to Finn's perceptions. I've been a mess since you were taken, and I didn't give you enough credit that you could land on your feet. Maybe I had cause for concern because you were with the bad guys, you know? But once I heard you were with Beckworth, I should have thought better of you. Of your ability to adapt. And that's on me, but it might have colored Finn's view as well."

Stella turned the wineglass in a slow circle and watched AJ pick at the swan. Then she patted the spot next to her, and AJ complied. "I think we both have good reasons to be a bit off-kilter with our current circumstances. But we're in this together—as always."

She lifted her glass, and AJ clinked hers against it. The weight of the last few weeks fell away like petals in the wind.

"As always."

8

Ethan stared at the musket pointed at him and then at the surrounding landscape. The trees had sprouted new leaves for spring. The season appeared to be correct, and when he tilted his head to peer around the man in front of him, he could make out the edge of a garden.

"Are we at Waverly?" he asked and glanced at Maire.

She stared up at the man who held a musket at her head as if daring him to shoot a woman. Sometimes she was too foolhardy for her own good, but when he considered her taunt, he would have a hard time firing on a defenseless woman. And if these were Gemini's men, who ended up shooting the scribe, they'd be marking their own deaths.

"You sneak onto private land, and you're not sure where you are?" The man was wiry and of average height. Ethan would be a fool to think he wasn't an expert with the flintlock and equally scrappy in a fight.

"Is Beckworth at home by any chance?" Even without knowing the date, Ethan assumed Beckworth would be in London, but it couldn't hurt to ask.

"Keep your head down."

He complied, unsure how long he was supposed to stay on his knees. When he heard the crunch of boots, it wouldn't be long now.

"Most guests of Beckworth's come up the drive, but it is wonderful to see you again."

Ethan recognized that voice and dared a glance up. Barrington. Relief flooded over him, and when he turned to Maire, the man holding the musket had lowered the barrel and was helping her stand.

He stood and brushed the dirt from his pants. "Sorry for the unexpected visit. We had every intention of knocking on the door."

Barrington smiled, and the two shook hands.

"We thought the fog would keep everyone away."

"Beckworth doesn't like surprises, so he shared the secrets of the fog with his most trusted men." He led them toward the manor, the two guards taking their duffels and following behind. "After hearing that one of Gemini's men had traveled to the future to kidnap AJ but brought Stella back instead, we decided that any strange fog should be met with force, just in case."

"You've seen Stella?" Maire asked.

"Yes, and Sebastian. The three of them stayed with Eleanor for a few days before moving on to London. Gemini has three men watching the manor. There was a fourth, but he became too nosy."

When they reached the back of the manor, they entered through the solarium doors. "You've arrived just in time." Three people stood by the windows and might have seen the strange fog for themselves.

"Eleanor!" Maire called out, and the two women hugged. Then she noticed Doc and Lincoln and greeted them with a hug that Doc tried to brush off, though he couldn't quite hide his smile. Lincoln's response was to simply blush to his roots.

Ethan shook their hands and gave Eleanor a kiss on her cheek. "I suppose this gathering isn't a social call."

"No. Have you eaten? I'm afraid your travels are only beginning." Barrington pointed to the sofa, and everyone found a seat around the hearth.

"The effects of the fog have a negative effect on one's constitution. We thought it would be best to travel before eating."

Barrington nodded to a footman, who disappeared through the door. "Why don't you tell us of your long journey, then I can update you with current events."

"Before we do that, can you tell me the date?" Maire asked.

"It's the twenty-seventh of March, and the year is 1805."

She grinned and looked at him. "It worked."

Ethan nodded, then launched into their story from the time they arrived at the monastery, their trip to Southampton to discover Beckworth and his charges had escaped Gemini, and their journey on to Heresford and Bransford to locate the second chronicle. He finished with their race to London and the ambush.

"So, you traveled back to the future in order to save the rest of the team, like you did when escaping Dugan's men when Reginald held Waverly." Barrington stopped when three footmen arrived carrying trays and coffee service.

Once plates of food and cups of coffee had been passed around and Barrington dismissed the footmen, Ethan asked, "You knew the reason for the fog back then?"

Barrington shook his head. "Not at the time, but Beckworth filled me in later. That's why I didn't say anything to the handful of men Dugan had left behind when the fog returned a few months later."

"You saw the fog when we returned?" Maire asked.

"Quite by accident. The only time I could move about the manor without one of Dugan's men following me was once everyone had turned in for the evening. After Dugan left with Reginald on one of his crazed searches for sacred druid locations, the men left behind became lazy. I happened to be in the solarium when I saw a bolt of light and noted the heavy fog. I stepped outside and realized it wasn't a normal fog, and something told me someone had returned, though it was much later before I knew it was the two of you and AJ coming for Murphy."

Ethan shook his head. "It was fortunate we had friends at Waverly."

"Indeed."

"So, what have we missed? I assume we're leaving straightaway for London?" Ethan finished his plate of food while Barrington brought them up to speed on what Beckworth had shared of their travels.

"I received a missive from Hensley a day ago. The mission to Ipswich was a trap. Beckworth and Stella, along with two of Hensley's men, had retrieved the chronicle, but Stella was captured. Beckworth traded himself and the chronicle for Stella's life."

"Oh, god. What of Sebastian?" Maire had set down her plate.

"As far as I know, Sebastian is safe at Hensley's."

"Have you been able to locate where Gemini's ship went?" Ethan couldn't imagine that would be an easy task.

"Not yet. But we know Beckworth was injured before being taken aboard."

Maire nodded at Doc. "Which is why you and Lincoln are here."

"I wouldn't think of going back to London for any other reason. I brought what supplies I had on hand. The one good thing about being back in that hell hole of a town is the ability to gather whatever else we might need, depending on Beckworth's condition when they find him."

The sound of that didn't bode well, and he looked at Eleanor. "And you're coming as well?"

Eleanor's demeanor had turned inward, and it took her a moment to understand the question was directed at her. "My skills might be needed, and he would do the same for me."

"Of course. I'd presumed as much." Ethan drained the cup of coffee. "Anything else we should know before we head out?"

"Only that Gemini knows Stella isn't AJ. It seems Beckworth felt that was the only way to ensure Stella's safety. And we have confirmation that Belato—and however many men he brought with him—is now in England."

Ethan trailed behind the carriage, relieved he'd taken Barrington's offer of a horse. Once they'd entered London, he rode near the back window so he could gaze at Maire. Then Doc began complaining about the filth of the city, his disappointment in the king for his disregard for the poor, the lazy aristocrats, and so it went until Ethan put enough distance between him and the coach to be out of earshot.

He remembered the manor as soon as the carriage stopped in front of it. It belonged to a friend of Beckworth's, who spent most of his time away. He offered it to Beckworth whenever he was in need, and no one else was in residence.

Lincoln jumped off the coach to help the women down, then Barrington stepped up to assist Doc.

"I'm more than capable of getting out of a carriage on my own," the old man growled.

Ethan was certain he'd end up on his face if Barrington and Lincoln weren't there to keep him upright. They let him totter up the steps on his own but remained close as he weaved his way to the door.

Maire and Eleanor watched as they held their chuckles behind huge grins.

"Thank heavens we're here." Eleanor picked at her skirts and glanced both ways down the street. "He didn't stop complaining for the last hour."

"At least he slept most of the way here," Maire said as they followed the men at a safe distance.

"Was he really that bad?" Ethan stepped up after tying his horse to the coach, working hard not to laugh.

"I see you didn't waste any time accepting Barrington's suggestion of a horse." Maire poked him in the ribs with her elbow. "I also noticed you disappeared from my view the farther into London we got and the louder Bart complained."

"It was purely for security reasons." He followed Eleanor's visual sweep of the street as proof of his concern before ushering the women through the door. He waited several more moments before closing it. If Gemini's men had somehow followed them, he didn't see anyone. The men who'd been watching Waverly had stayed well out of sight. Their first night on the road, one of Beckworth's guards had caught up with them to report her men still watched Waverly. It made sense. No reason to have her men follow them when she knew their team would meet with Hensley.

Everyone adjourned to rooms to rest while the staff prepared a midday lunch. Barrington sent a note to Hensley to let him know they'd arrived and would join them in the afternoon.

An hour later, Ethan stared at the ceiling of their room, Maire asleep beside him. It seemed to be the first fitful sleep she'd had since arriving at Waverly. Her relief that the incantation had worked so well was soon replaced with fear for their safety. Now that she was in the middle of London, she was able to let down her guard.

Ethan slid from the bed and slipped into his clothes before

strolling through the manor on his way to find Barrington. Something told him the butler wouldn't be resting and was most likely sending messages to Beckworth's friends.

A quick peek through a door confirmed the dining room was set for lunch, and he continued wandering the halls when Barrington strode out of a room with another man beside him. Their heads were down as they conversed, and they were almost upon him before the butler lifted his head. There was a flash of surprise and a glint of something else in his eyes. Were the two of them cooking something up?

"Ah, Sir Hughes, I should have known you wouldn't rest long."

The man next to him wore a bland expression with the ease of someone who'd done it for years. Ethan recognized a street hustler and had no doubt he was a friend of Beckworth's.

Barrington seemed to note Ethan's curiosity. "This is Chester, a friend of Beckworth's. I was just updating him about the events at Ipswich."

Ethan nodded at the man. "Why am I having a hard time believing that's all it is?"

Barrington glanced at Chester, who shrugged. "Very well, but I'd rather discuss this in the study." He turned, and Chester, giving Ethan a lazy grin, followed.

Ethan wasn't sure what the two were up to. Beckworth could be anywhere. Until they found the ship he'd been taken aboard, and he assumed Finn and Hensley had men searching the coast, there wasn't much they could do. Not unless Gemini made an obvious move.

The two men stood by the hearth and didn't show any signs of sitting.

"So, tell me what's going on." Ethan stopped by the corner of the desk.

Barrington scratched his head, and Ethan figured it was a

fifty-fifty chance the man would change his mind about giving up any information. "This is rather sensitive and something I'd like to keep from Hensley and Murphy for now."

"Do you know where Beckworth is?" Ethan asked. Why would they want to keep that a secret? Hensley had men who could help.

"Not yet. Chester leads one of the largest crews in the city and has connections with several others. He has the ability to engage all the crews to assist in a search."

"Alright. I can see how that could help if we thought Gemini was in the city, but she'd be foolish to sail into London now."

"Yet, we believe that's exactly what she's done."

"Why would you think that?"

Chester crossed his arms and leaned a hip against a chair. "I had a visit from a mutual friend, who has information that supports the theory."

"I need more information than that." When neither man appeared willing to budge, he blew out a breath. "I don't like keeping secrets, but if you give me a good enough reason, I'm willing to hold my tongue for a short while." He gave both men a long glare. "And I do mean a short while. This isn't something we can keep from Hensley."

Something passed between the two men before Barrington nodded, and Chester said, "Stella came to me with information reliable enough to act on."

"Stella? How did she know to come to you?" a woman's voice demanded.

Ethan squeezed his eyes shut before turning to face the woman he'd been certain was fast asleep when he'd left their room.

Maire stood at the doorway, hands on hips and an Irish storm in her gaze. Then Eleanor was behind her, pushing her into the room before closing the door.

"This could have all been handled better." Eleanor walked to a side table, looked at the bottles of alcohol, and pulled one out. She set out five glasses and quickly poured what looked like expensive scotch into them. "Everyone sit, and let's get this done. Lunch is ready, and Hensley will be expecting us. I'm surprised AJ hasn't already stolen a horse to race over here."

"It's only because she doesn't know the way here." Maire huffed but swallowed a healthy amount before sitting.

Ethan held his glass, his focus on Chester. "Tell us from the beginning. How does Stella know you?" For being here such a short time, she seemed to have fallen deeply into the curse of the stones.

Chester sat in the chair he'd been leaning against and explained the visit he received from Beckworth and Stella when they'd first arrived in London. It seemed Stella wanted to meet Beckworth's friends, and she didn't seem to care what station in life they came from. He chuckled when he spoke of Stella pitching in to help with dinner and the cleanup afterward. It was obvious the man had been smitten with her bold personality. Although, why she wanted to meet street gangs and why Beckworth would allow it escaped him for the moment. When he glanced at Maire, she seemed curious as well.

"It didn't take the crew long to hear whispers when Stella returned from Ipswich with Murphy but without Beckworth." Chester finished his scotch and set the glass down. He scratched his chest and smiled. "I know what you're thinking, but Beckworth asked us to keep an eye on Hensley's place. We knew Gemini had men watching, and we watched the watchers. When Beckworth's horse returned without him, we knew the mission had failed. It was a few days before Stella knocked on my door. I'd been expecting her but wasn't sure how she'd get out of the manor without a coach or Murphy by her side."

"She came to you on her own?" Maire's question should have

been one of shock rather than her increasing curiosity and, if he read her expression correctly, admiration.

He doubted AJ would have attempted a stunt like that for anyone other than Finn. But the more he considered Stella, maybe he hadn't known her as well as he'd thought.

Chester grinned. "Rode over on a horse wearing pants and a shirt while dawn was just breaking."

Eleanor snorted. "I knew I liked her. The woman has gumption."

"But why did she feel the need to come to you on her own?" Maire persisted in her need to understand.

"She had a hand-drawn map of England and the north of France," Chester answered. "A rather poor one at that. Four cities had been marked. One in France and three in England, of which Ipswich and London caught my eye."

Chester didn't have to mention the other two cities to know what they indicated.

"Where did she get the map?" Ethan asked.

"From one of Gemini's men who Beckworth killed when he came snooping around my place." Eleanor set her glass down and folded her arms across her chest, a sneer on her lips. "The man had been sneaking around the woods and found Stella, who'd gone for a walk. Beckworth didn't have a choice. The map had been hidden in the man's hat."

Now it made sense. Gemini knew the locations of the cities and had shared them with her men.

"But why London?" Ethan spoke out loud, though the question was more for his own understanding. "She's predicted our movements in the past, but London was a reasonable guess. She'd expect Hensley to be here, especially since she's had eyes on his estate in Bristol. But after Ipswich, she'd be crazy to sail here."

"And that's exactly what Hensley and Murphy told Stella."

Chester leaned back in his chair and crossed a leg over his knee. His posture appeared relaxed, but Ethan suspected the man held everything inside. If he ran one of the largest gangs, it would make sense he didn't rattle easily. "Stella suspected London meant more to Gemini than just Hensley. She couldn't explain why, but from what Beckworth shared, Stella spent more time with Gemini than anyone else. And being a woman, we assumed she probably had more insight into what Gemini might be thinking, even if she couldn't provide any more information than that."

Maire and Eleanor nodded, which, for Ethan, added more weight to the possibility.

"And when Hensley and Murphy placated her with their plans, which probably wasn't sufficient for her, she decided to take matters into her own hands." Maire grinned. "It seems Stella has adapted well during her time here."

"But why keep this from Hensley?" Ethan couldn't fathom how adding more people to the search could be a hindrance.

"The crews have a code," Eleanor answered, "especially when one of their own is in trouble. Sometimes they can help, and sometimes they can't. Most of the crews have known Beckworth for a long time, some since their youth. He continues to give them jobs and help them out of tough situations when he can. It goes without saying they would do the same for him."

"The crews can be invisible to almost everyone when they need to be," Chester added.

Now, Ethan understood. He'd seen the crews in action when the local constable sent watchmen to capture Reginald. When he escaped the trap, their team pursued him through London, making for the *Daphne Marie* while dodging Dugan's men. Beckworth had put the crews to work, steering them through the safest route to the docks. They had stepped out of the shadows like wraiths and then disappeared just as quickly.

"And Hensley's men aren't as silent." Ethan gave Chester a long look, then grinned. "They'd get in your way."

Chester returned the smile and nodded. "We work best on our own."

"Have you found the ship?" Maire asked.

Barrington and Chester glanced at each other before Chester answered, "Not yet."

Ethan wasn't sure he believed him, but based on their expressions, neither would commit to anything more. "Then I suggest we eat, then see what Hensley and Finn have come up with. For now, we'll keep your secret."

9

Stella heard the news straight from Mary. Barrington had arrived in London with Maire, Ethan, Eleanor, and others she'd never met. They were staying at some manor Beckworth used on occasion, resting from their travels, and would join them later that afternoon.

She hadn't seen Maire and Ethan since she'd been taken from Baywood. It would be wonderful to catch up, but it was Barrington's arrival that excited her the most. The question was how to arrange time alone with him. To everyone else, he was Beckworth's butler, but he was so much more than that. And if he played his role, he probably wouldn't stay long after depositing Maire and Ethan at Hensley's front door.

If he'd traveled to London and brought Eleanor, he must know about Beckworth. She had to find a way to at least get a message to him about Chester, to let him know they were running their own search.

The day before, she'd told AJ they were in this together, and as much as she trusted Finn, nothing changed in her decision to keep Chester and the crews a secret. She wanted to be honest with AJ, but after their little caper during their vacation to

France in search of Sebastian's journals, AJ had promised Finn not to hide anything from him, and that was as it should be. The pact they'd made yesterday over a bottle of wine didn't change that.

She left her room and joined the others in the library. Hensley preferred his study, but it wasn't large enough for the number of people he was assembling, and he chose the library over the sitting room to accommodate Sebastian. When the monk wasn't writing in his journal, he spent his time in the library, where he could be found by the hearth reading a book. AJ had to retrieve him for meals, or the man might never eat.

She played a game of chess with Hensley while they waited for Maire and Ethan. She never beat him, but she'd gotten close. He was an excellent strategist, and it showed in his moves. She respected him for playing his best against her, and from what Finn said, their games lasted longer than most others. She recalled AJ's comment about Hensley requiring time to assess and trust others' opinions. With any luck, their games of chess would help toward that very point.

They were beginning their second game when the foyer erupted with voices. Even though the library was a few rooms down, it was easy to hear Mary's bubbly laughter. Within seconds, AJ almost tripped over her dress in her rush out of the library. Finn grabbed her elbow to keep her upright.

She glanced at Hensley. "Are you going to race out of here, too?"

His focus was on the chessboard, and he never looked up. "They'll find their way here soon enough. I'll wager Maire will want to see Sebastian straightaway."

With the mention of his name, they both turned their heads toward the hearth. Sebastian had his nose in a book, and she doubted he'd heard any of the ruckus.

Hensley winked at her, and they chuckled as they turned

their attention to the board. He moved a rook just as Maire raced into the room.

"Sebastian?" Maire called. Her gaze touched on Hensley and Stella, then around the room until they lit on the monk. He was just turning around when Maire dropped to her knees in front of his chair and took his hands. "I've been so worried."

"Apparently, I'm chopped liver," Stella said and smiled. "I suppose the game will have to wait."

"Maire. I knew you'd find a way back to us." Sebastian gripped her hands tightly. "I've been well cared for. I met the most marvelous woman in my cell." He glanced at Stella, his eyes twinkling as they did when he was happy and perhaps a bit mischievous. "And then Beckworth came and helped us escape. It was all quite exciting."

Maire's laugh was almost lyrical. "Of course, it was." Once she confirmed Sebastian was well, she stood and strode to Stella, giving her a huge hug. "And the woman at the heart of it all."

"You don't think I'd have it any other way, do you?" She laughed and glanced up to see Ethan smiling down at her.

"Your ordeal gave us quite a start, but it's good to see you alive and in one piece." Then a thin frown marred his expression. "I'm sorry it wasn't under better circumstances. We were very sorry to hear Gemini took Beckworth. I'm sure with enough people searching, it won't take long to find where he's being held."

There was something about his gaze that made it seem there was more he wanted to say, but he squeezed her hands and turned toward the door. Barrington had entered and was shaking Hensley's hand. Was she reading too much into Ethan's gesture? Something he didn't want to share with the rest of the room. Maybe Barrington would stay longer than she'd previously thought. With the search still underway, everyone spent a great deal of time not doing much of anything. Perhaps it wouldn't be too unseemly if she asked him to take her for a stroll around the garden.

He glanced her way several times as Maire and Ethan shared their travels after leaving Bransford. Ethan weaved almost as good a story as Fitz regarding the ambush. She was tempted to make her way to Barrington, but at the same time, she was nervous about his condemnation. It was her fault Beckworth wasn't here. If she hadn't gotten caught, they'd be planning their next steps to take Gemini down rather than sitting around waiting for word.

The group settled into sofas and chairs while footmen served light refreshments. Hensley wanted to review the details of the various missions that finally brought them all together. Her heart sank at having to repeat her involvement at Ipswich, and she was inching her way toward a chair close to the door in case she needed to make a quick exit when someone touched her elbow.

Barrington gazed down at her with a soft smile. "I was wondering, Lady Caldway, if I could spare a minute of your time."

"Sure." She wanted to say how good it was to see him, but her nerves chickened out. He was still smiling, and she was positive it was for appearances. It was more likely he wanted to take her to a broom closet for an ear-splitting, raging lecture.

She followed him, but he didn't leave the room, stopping just shy of the door. When she gave the room a quick scan, she noted several sets of eyes on her, specifically AJ and Maire, though Finn and Ethan glanced her way.

Hensley stepped to the other side of her. "Is everything alright, Barrington?"

She was somewhat surprised by Hensley's question and wondered if he asked because it was his way of keeping tabs on everything. The man was devious, so anything was possible.

"It's Eleanor," Barrington started.

"Is she okay?" Stella interrupted, her other concerns vanishing.

He gave one of his prudish facial expressions. "Healthwise, she's fine. I'm more concerned about her mental state." He cleared his throat as his eyes darted around the room. "She's quite worried about Beckworth, as we all are, but other than Bart and Lincoln, she has no one else at the manor in whom to confide."

"Oh my," Stella said, but her forehead wrinkled as she considered his words. Eleanor was strong, lived alone, and went weeks, sometimes months, without seeing Beckworth. This certainly wasn't the first time he'd found himself in trouble. She had to give Barrington credit. He seemed to be as cunning and manipulative as Beckworth. He was up to something, she just wasn't sure what.

"She's more than welcome to stay here," Hensley answered. "We have more than enough room, and she's stayed with us before."

Barrington lowered his head, seemingly at a loss for words, before he glanced up. "I asked her before we left, and she could have come with us, but she refuses to leave the manor. She's not fond of London. I was wondering, and I hate to even ask, if perhaps Lady Caldway might come over, maybe stay for a day or two while we wait for word. She seemed quite eager to see you again." This time his gaze bored into hers, though it was nothing more than a flash.

He was a sly one. There was a great deal more to learn about him, and she'd already pegged him as more than a butler.

"We did get along well. She was an angel when the three of us showed up on her doorstep." She grabbed Hensley's arm. "Would it be too much trouble? Would Mary mind? I hate to leave everyone…" She glanced around the room. Damn, if Maire and AJ weren't watching them like little vultures.

Hensley took her hand and squeezed it. "I think that's quite a generous offer, and Mary would completely understand on one condition. We want all of you, Bart and Lincoln as well, to join us for dinner tomorrow night."

"I think that would be doable, sir." Barrington bowed his head. "If Lady Caldway wouldn't mind. I'd like to leave in the next half hour."

"Can you be ready that quickly?" Hensley asked.

"Ready for what?" AJ stepped up next to them, Maire behind her.

Hensley explained the issue, and AJ gave her a probing look, which she shrugged off as if she was as surprised as the rest of them by Eleanor's request.

"Maybe I should go as well," AJ suggested.

Stella would have kicked AJ as a signal to butt out, but first, it wouldn't be proper in the current setting, and second, she was fairly certain this was all a ruse to get her out of Hensley's manor. And she wasn't sure how to tell AJ no without triggering her reporter instincts.

"Must you go, too?" Maire asked. "I wanted to catch up on your travels to Bréval and your meeting with this Lavigne who works in Napoleon's court."

This probably wasn't the best moment to kiss Maire smack on the lips for her save. She wasn't sure if Maire was in on the ruse or whether she simply missed AJ. It was most likely the latter, but either way, she decided to stay out of the conversation to deter AJ's suspicions.

After a long moment and a quick glance at Barrington and Stella, AJ put an arm around Maire's waist. "You're right. We have many things to catch up on." She gave Stella a pointed stare. "No excuses for not showing up for dinner. And as soon as you cheer Eleanor up, I think we all need a ride through Hyde Park."

At that moment, Mary hustled into the room. "Did I hear something about a carriage ride through the park?"

They all laughed at her incredible timing, and Hensley nodded with an endearing smile. "And a dinner party tomorrow night. You can add five more to the group."

Mary clapped her hands in excitement, and Stella took this moment as her way to extricate herself from the group.

"If you don't mind, I need time to pack a few things." She stepped back and took Mary's arm. "I need Sarah to help. I'll be staying with Eleanor for a couple of days to see if I can't cheer her up."

"Oh, the poor dear. I didn't know she was in town. Wouldn't she prefer to stay here?"

"Nothing to worry about, my dear." Hensley nodded to Barrington. "It appears Eleanor would feel better without a crowded house."

"Oh, quite understandable," Mary said. "Let's find Sarah." She glanced up at Barrington. Tears instantly sprang to her eyes, and she mopped them away with a kerchief. "It's a pleasure to see you again, though I hate that it's under such trying circumstances. I'm so worried about Teddy, but I know we'll find him and bring him home."

"Indeed," Barrington replied.

Then Stella was dragged away as Mary rushed them up the stairs, calling for Sarah. She didn't miss AJ sticking her head into the hallway, squinting after them.

10

Stella viewed her reflection in the standing mirror. The day dress was the same one she'd worn when Beckworth had taken her to the East End. She never wore it at Hensley's, but it was the first dress she'd asked Sarah to pack. In her rush to leave for her short stay at what she referred to as Beckworth's manor, even though it wasn't, she should have considered her clothes more thoroughly. She'd meant to bring her tattered raincoat instead of the dove-colored cloak Beckworth had bought her, but at least she'd remembered her pants, shirt, and boots. Eleanor thought she should have brought more day dresses, but her mind had been on Beckworth, not her wardrobe.

Before she'd left Hensley's earlier that day, and after a brief goodbye to the team, AJ hugged her fiercely.

"I can't believe you're leaving me already." Her gaze was tearier than Stella expected.

"Good grief, I'm going, what, five blocks or so away. I'd hoof it over there if these shoes weren't squeezing my toes." She wiped a tear of her own away, unsure where it had come from. "I'm perfectly safe with Barrington, Eleanor, and whoever the others are. You know that. And I'll be back tomorrow for dinner and then for our day-long excursion in the park. You'll hardly miss me."

AJ ran a hand under her nose. "I always miss you, and it was nice having us all together for five minutes."

She let out a short laugh. "Then you remind that husband of yours to keep his eye on the prize and find Beckworth."

With nothing to add, AJ had stepped back and let Maire have her minute with Stella.

"I haven't had the luxury of spending the last few days with you, so I'll want to hear all about your adventures after dinner tomorrow. So be prepared." She laughed and pulled Stella in for a hug, whispering in her ear, "Be careful tonight." Then she pushed her away and took AJ's arm. "I'll keep you so busy with tales from home you'll barely notice her gone."

"I'll want to hear those as well," Stella called out as she climbed into the carriage.

The two women walked arm in arm up the steps to the manor, but AJ gave Stella one of those squinty-eyed stares before the coach rolled away.

Stella stewed over what to tell AJ when this business with finding Beckworth was over, but she forgot all about her friend when she entered the manor. Beckworth did have friends in all levels of society, but her perusal of the splendid finery of the grand house was interrupted by Barrington's low growl and the sound of yelling coming from farther in, most likely a sitting room or maybe the library.

They discovered the loud voices, which were more of a high-volume argument between an old man and a footman. The footman was young, his face red with a stubborn expression. There was another man, who looked even younger, dressed in very casual clothing for the manor, tugging at the old man's jacket, trying to pull him away.

Eleanor appeared oblivious to it all as she focused on her task of stitching a garment, most likely repairing a tear. This argument must not have been the first one since she paid no attention to it.

Stella glanced at Barrington, who sighed. Whatever part of his persona that was the strict, uptight butler must have been left at Waverly. He showed decorum at Hensley's, but here, he seemed to care less, though he did make an attempt.

"Bart, can you stop your bickering long enough to meet our guest?" He'd raised his voice to be heard over the old man's continued shouting.

Bart, who must be the old man, lowered his voice but apparently had a few more choice words he needed to get out of his system. The younger man stepped back and walked toward her. Eleanor had popped up, dropping her sewing on the chair. She slapped Bart's arm on her way by, which finally got his full attention.

"A visitor? Why didn't you say so sooner." Bart hobbled over faster than one would expect for his age and stooped posture, allowing the footman to make a hasty retreat. He barreled his way past Barrington and, when he reached Stella, gave her a quick once-over. "I'm Bart, but everyone just calls me Doc. That's because I'm a doctor."

She grinned. "Well, hello, Doc. I'm Stella Caldway, and you can call me Stella."

Eleanor hugged her. "We were devastated to hear about Beckworth, but between Barrington and Chester, there's not a doubt he'll be found." She turned around and waved for the young man to come closer. "This is Lincoln. He lives with Doc and watches over him."

"You mean I watch over him." Bart turned and lumbered to a chair near a chessboard. "He's too young to know what's good for him. Someone has to keep him in line."

Stella gave Barrington a skeptical glance. "It appears Eleanor needing womanly company might have been overstated?"

His chin lifted in that stuffy butler manner, apparently not an ounce of regret, and Eleanor answered for him. "We had to find a way to get you over here for a couple of days, but to be honest, the men are driving me crazy. I could use a bit of sanity."

When Eleanor steered Stella to her room, she was advised to take a nap. Dinner would be served late because they were going out afterward, and when Stella asked where to Eleanor had shaken her head.

"You'll know soon enough. Get as much sleep as you can. It will be a long night."

Now, she was rested and ready for whatever came next. She grabbed her coat and strolled down the stairs, finding the group in the dining room. A coffee urn and two pitchers of ale sat in prominent positions on the table.

Barrington sat at one end of the table, Chester at the other as Eleanor refilled cups. Bart was nowhere to be seen and was most likely in bed. Lincoln sat at the table with several other men that Stella didn't know. Scratch that. She'd met one of them on her visits with Beckworth, and she nodded at him. He smiled and returned the nod.

When Chester noticed her, he stood and grinned at her. "Are you sure you're ready for this?"

"I'll let you know as soon as you tell me what you expect me to do."

He scratched his head and glanced at Barrington. "You didn't tell her?"

Barrington shrugged. "I thought it best to make sure you had everything in place."

"And now it is. Shall we get on with this?" Eleanor took a seat in between two men Stella didn't know.

"Always in a hurry, old woman." Chester laughed. "Somethings never change."

Eleanor mumbled something, but her gaze shone with amusement.

"Then let us proceed." Barrington pointed to a chair across the table from Eleanor, and Stella sat. "As you all know, Beckworth was taken by Gemini in Ipswich. Your crews have been searching for the *Phoenix*, which Stella believed would be sailing to London, even though Hensley and others thought otherwise."

Stella glanced at the men she didn't know. "Wait. Did I understand that correctly? Are you all gang leaders in the city?"

"Everyone in this room has been a member of a gang, with the exception of Lincoln and you." Barrington gave her a wicked smile. "And yes, me too."

"Well, I'll be damned."

The men chuckled, and Eleanor clucked her tongue.

"After tonight, you'll also be part of our crews," Chester said. Then he added, "Honorary, of course."

Stella laughed. "Of course, a trial run for entry."

"We prefer to call it training." Chester swallowed some ale. "An assessment of one's skills and loyalties before determining where they best fit."

"That's smart. So, what's the task this evening? I assume we'll be searching some part of the Thames looking for the ship."

Chester smiled. "That's no longer necessary. We've found the ship."

Stella climbed into the coach and tugged at one of the loose tendrils the lady's maid had created. With her fine, dove-colored coat and updo, any quick glance would say an aristocrat. If they took a closer look at the edges of her day dress, they might think imposter or perhaps a merchant's wife. Someone with just enough money to be a pretender.

Eleanor and Barrington joined her in the carriage while Lincoln, who was already seated on the box, played the role of coachman. Chester was with his crew at the warehouse.

Once they were off, Stella tugged at her gloves. "I think we need to tell Hensley we've found the ship."

"Not until we locate Beckworth." Barrington hovered near the window, his gaze focused on the streets. His ruffled hair took ten years off his age, leaving her to wonder how old the man was. Older than Beckworth, but not more than ten years if she had to guess. It was odd to see him dressed in something other than his butler attire. His pants were worn, not in the way of someone unable to buy new ones, but something more comfortable, like Stella's orange capri pants she refused to toss. They were her go-to summer pants when nothing else would do.

"We can assume he's on the ship," he continued. "But they might have moved him. It would have been risky but not impossible. If we spook them too soon, we'll have no assurances they won't keep moving him." His gaze locked on hers. "I don't mean to be so blunt, but if that happens, it might take months to find him. And perhaps not that long if he loses his value to Gemini."

Eleanor patted her knee, her gaze monitoring the other side of the street. "Barrington's right. These crews have worked together before, but most of the men are Chester's crew. Adding you to the normal routine is one thing, but Hensley would have too many men involved. Even if we could convince him to only send three, that's three more who don't know the signals."

She rubbed her coat, feeling stuck in the middle, but she had to face facts. Hensley's team had been searching the coast for almost a week with no success. Within two days, Chester had found the ship and was narrowing down where Beckworth was being held. If only Hensley would have listened to her, but he and Finn had made the call. Now, they'd have to deal with the consequences of their decisions.

"Alright. But as soon as we confirm where Beckworth is, we tell Hensley."

"Agreed," Barrington said. "Now, are you comfortable with your role?"

It was a simple part, almost not worth the time, but it was meant to be brief. The crew wanted to send a message that an elusive player had joined the game—a riddle they'd be unable to solve. Something to make Gemini nervous and force a mistake.

She nodded. "I walk in, give them my line, then walk out. And try not to trip and look like an idiot while doing it."

Barrington chuckled. "That's the gist of it."

"Just remember the man can't do anything to you." Eleanor turned from the window, her gaze unwavering. "The crew will be there, more of them than you'll be aware of. So don't worry about your safety. Focus on your part and trust the rest will fall into place."

"Easier said than done." Now, Stella understood Barrington's need to keep Hensley out of this part of the plan. It also drove home her appreciation of Beckworth's droning on with continually repeated details until she bristled. Finn and Ethan had worked together for a long time and could anticipate the other's actions. If Chester added others into the mix, it would take time to work out the kinks. Even someone experienced as Finn would have trouble understanding the cues.

"This is why we stick with the crews until we locate Beckworth." Barrington confirmed her thoughts while sharing a tight smile. "That reminds me. We need more of the swans."

She reached into her pocket and handed over a dozen. "Will this do, or do you need more? I'm not sure how paper swans will get back to Gemini, let alone make her nervous."

"The main goal is to make her men nervous. Keep them looking over their shoulder. If her men are spooked, Gemini will have a tougher time controlling them."

"Which will agitate her." Stella forced herself to relive the events at the dock in Ipswich. "When Gemini told her men to release me, they glanced at Gaines first, who nodded. I'm not sure Gemini noticed."

Barrington grunted. "That's valuable information that strengthens our plan. That could put the two of them at odds. You should have told us that sooner."

She dropped her gaze. "I'm sorry. I avoid thinking of how that all went wrong."

Eleanor gave Barrington an admonishing glance. "Of course, you wouldn't want to be reminded of that. It's enough you shared what you thought important." She gave him a final withering glare before turning back to the window.

Barrington released a long sigh. "Apologies. His loss strains all of us." He didn't seem comfortable with that admission, and Stella decided to let him stew. He'd deserved it.

"Gemini had previously been left two swans," he continued. "One was left in your cell onboard the *Phoenix*. Another was left on the dead guy at Eleanor's. We're not sure if anyone questioned them or even passed them on to Gaines or Gemini. And we've picked up six of her men since yesterday morning."

"How do you find them?" Stella asked.

"We have tiny eyes watching the ship who follow the men when they leave."

"Tiny eyes?" Stella questioned.

"The youngest of our crews. Street urchins go unnoticed and make useful watchers. Once the men head back to the ship, we pick them up and take them to the warehouse. We tell them we work for The Swan, and if they'll tell us where Beckworth is, they'll be let go. Otherwise, it's off to Newgate."

"Newgate?"

"The prison," Eleanor said. "For some, once they go in, they don't leave. It's usually enough of a fear, but many of Gemini's men are hardened mercenaries. Even so, some will crack if Newgate is their next destination."

"Once we decide we won't get further information from them, we take one of their personal belongings, add the swan, then our tiny eyes place it somewhere for the ship's crew to find. Each piece is always left in a different spot. We're hoping six swans are enough to start the men talking, but we'll see how this evening goes. If he's not willing to crack, we continue on until someone does."

Eleanor sat back and smiled at Stella. "Don't worry. I have a good feeling about tonight."

11

The cool night air created a fog over the river, at first startling Stella into thinking it was the mist that brought her to this time. But on further reflection, the sound of hoofs on cobblestone and the creak of the carriage told her it was only her imagination and lack of sleep. The coach rolled up to a dark building where two husky men stood on either side of an aged and warped door.

"Wait here until they're ready for you." Barrington studied her, and after several seconds under his stern gaze, she turned to the window, her fingers playing at the edge of her cloak. "We don't blame you."

"What?" Her head snapped around, and when he didn't say anything more, she fidgeted. A powerful wave of claustrophobia seized her, and she reached for the door handle, but he stayed her hand.

"Starting tonight, things will move swiftly." Eleanor left the bench seat to sit next to her, which, for some inexplicable reason, made the coach feel smaller. "You have to put your guilt aside. There's no reason for it, and there's no place for it here."

"What makes you think I feel guilty?"

"Honey, it's written all over your face whenever you look at

Barrington or me. Even Chester. Things happen that aren't within your control no matter how well you prepare."

She gave a nervous laugh, her fingers still moving over her coat before tugging at the wayward tendrils of her hair, wishing she'd brought a small stack of paper with her. "I was almost to the meeting place." Her voice was small, burdened with a heaviness that at times felt as if it would crush her. She thought she'd hidden it well enough. AJ hadn't seemed to notice, or she would have said something.

But these were Beckworth's friends. Many he'd only agreed to introduce her to after a great deal of nagging on her part. And this was how she'd repaid their kindness. She'd gotten him captured—maybe worse.

"I was being careful, watching for Gemini's men, but this huge shadow popped up out of nowhere and grabbed me. I was almost free, then the second guy showed up." She leaned back and stared at the roof of the coach, anywhere other than their penetrating gazes. "I felt so useless. Such a burden. All my self-defense training and I was still trapped." Her eyes blurred when she finally looked at Barrington. "He saved me. It's my turn to save him."

Barrington grabbed her arms and squeezed until tears threatened. If nothing else, her fingers stopped spasming with nervous energy. "Eleanor's correct. Sometimes we make mistakes. Sometimes things just don't go our way. It's the life, and Beckworth knew what he was walking into. He would have done it with or without you. And it could just as easily have been someone else who got nabbed." He raised his hands as he sat back. "Yes, a man would have been in a better position to fight off the first attacker, but with a second one? A fifty-fifty chance, depending on the man's skills. Now that you've come clean, we're not going to toss you into the Thames if for no other reason than not wanting to deal with Beckworth's wrath should he discover we'd abandoned you. Besides, you're our friend, too."

She stared at them. The guilt didn't magically disappear—she'd always retain a portion of it—but a lightness crept over her that she hadn't felt in days. She shook her hands in an attempt to throw off her restlessness, then settled on rubbing them together.

"Alright, let's get this done."

Barrington appeared relieved, and he nodded at her and Eleanor before he exited the coach and entered the building. Eleanor moved back to the other bench as they watched the door together. Ten minutes went by before it opened, and Barrington waved to her.

She sucked in a deep breath and reached for the door, then paused. "You said you use to work in the theater."

"A long time ago."

"Any last words of advice before I go in?"

"Stick to your lines and don't overstay your welcome."

Eleanor's quick wit and wry smile bolstered her spirit.

"Right. Eye on the prize." She nodded and opened the door to find Chester waiting for her. He held out his hand, and she grasped it tightly.

He led her to the door and stopped before entering. "You need to know, the men weren't gentle."

She let the words sink in. "Good. Let's do this."

When he opened the door, she squared her shoulders and lifted her chin, tugging at her cloak.

The warehouse was dark, but several lamps lit a path to the middle of the room, where more lights revealed a man slouched in a simple wooden chair, his arms and legs bound to it. Four men stood around him. She'd never seen them before and assumed they were part of Chester's crew.

Chester was right. The man had been worked over. It was

difficult to tell from where she stood but one eye appeared shut, his lips swollen and bleeding, and he hunched over as if his stomach hurt, probably from several punches. Her first thoughts weren't of Beckworth but of Finn and Ethan. She'd heard the stories of the beatings they'd taken at the hands of Dugan and French soldiers. Then the memory of a two-by-four as it slammed into Beckworth's back and then his head. In her opinion, the man in front of her had it easy.

The man lifted his gaze, and his one good eye squinted. She stood at the edge of the lit area, so he could probably see her form but not much else. Her role was simple—walk in, deliver her spiel, then walk out. When she had the time, which wasn't often, she'd always enjoyed a good suspense novel, and the thought bolstered her.

So, she remained where she was until the crew began to fidget, probably assuming she was flustered by what she was witnessing and had forgotten her lines. But her focus was on the man in the chair. He watched her, and eventually, his leg began to bounce, slowly at first and then faster.

When it reached the perfect tempo, she strode toward him with measured steps, enjoying the sound of her boots on the wood floor. When she was six feet from him, she stopped and stared down. It took a moment before he slowly lifted his head, his one good eye still squinting.

She caught the moment of recognition when he realized she was a woman. His eyes darted to the men, then back to her. His leg still bounced a steady rhythm. She maintained a blank expression that she let stretch for several seconds, then she gave him a sweet smile.

"Hello. You might have heard of me. They call me The Swan."

Stella paced along the stretch of bookcases, stopping to look over Bart's shoulder at the book in his lap. On her tenth—or maybe twentieth—pass, she asked, "How can you read with just the firelight?"

"You get used to it. Just like one gets used to your constant tromping back and forth."

"Are you always so cheery?"

"Yes."

"No."

Stella turned and smiled as Eleanor walked in with a tray. "Believe it or not, this is his better nature."

Bart grunted and glanced around. "Is that fresh coffee?"

"Yes, it's good to know your nose still works." She fussed with the cups, but she grinned.

So did Bart before he returned to his book.

Stella considered the two, curious if there was something cooking between them. Bart had to be ten years older than Eleanor, but it was good to see love blossom at that age. And suddenly, her heart seized, and she eagerly took the cup Eleanor handed her.

It was predawn, and she didn't understand what was taking so long for Barrington to return. Lincoln had driven the coach back, and they'd arrived at the manor around two in the morning.

Her part had ended after she'd told Gemini's man who she was. His eye, the one that wasn't swollen shut, had grown wide. Six of their crew were already missing, so he must have suspected who'd grabbed him. After the crew threatened the man with additional gruesome possibilities, he'd blubbered, but to her, it was mostly incoherent babbling. With a nod from Chester, she'd turned and walked out.

It was all theater, with the intent to scare the man into giving them truthful answers rather than lie to avoid any additional torture. Perhaps it should have bothered her, but she suspected the most the crew would do was perform another round of beatings before carting him off to prison. From what Eleanor told her about Newgate, it should have spurred the prior six men into spilling what they knew. Gemini, or Gaines, had a strong hold over them.

Another thirty minutes passed before Barrington returned. By then, the kitchen staff had prepared a simple breakfast of porridge and sausage, which he dug into. Ten minutes ticked by before he pushed the empty bowl aside and swallowed the entire cup of coffee, wiping his hand over his mouth.

"Are you going to keep us in suspense?" Stella had eaten a portion of the porridge and a single sausage to settle her growling stomach, drinking two cups of coffee to the other's one. "I'm drop-dead tired, but I can't sleep without knowing if we have what we need or whether I have to play The Swan again tonight?"

"It took longer than we anticipated, but instead of Newgate, we proposed another option. He kept asking for one of the crew by name, so we had to wait while we located him and then bring him to the warehouse so Gemini's man would know our offer was sound."

"Which was what?" Eleanor asked as she collected empty plates. Even as a guest in the manor, she couldn't seem to stop her need to clean.

"To leave London. Apparently, Gemini has contacts in Newgate, which could be why the previous men didn't talk. She's probably pulling them out as fast as we hand them over. But this bloke was more terrified of her than of us. His brother's in town from Liverpool on some business, so we took him over to the Wapping house. We'll hold him there until his brother can pick him up."

"That explains why it took so long," Bart grumbled as he held up his bowl, and Eleanor spooned more porridge into it.

Stella fumbled with making a paper crane, which required more effort since she hadn't made one in ages. One of the maids had asked if she could create any other bird because her daughter was fascinated by the flock of swans Stella had given her. She unfolded the crane, which didn't look anything close to one, and made two new folds before blowing out a long sigh, pushing the mangled bird aside.

"Can you just get on with it? Did he provide anything of value or not?"

Barrington grinned. "Beckworth mentioned how impatient you were at times. I was curious how long it would take you to ask."

She mumbled something that would probably make the crew blush.

"Calm yourself. Beckworth is still onboard the *Phoenix*, being held in one of the cargo holds. The man also shared what he knew of the guards patrolling the ship." He gave her a sly grin. "Now, we tell Hensley."

12

Finn slammed a drawer shut and glanced around the room. "Where's my blue cravat? I can't find anything in this room." He stormed to the wardrobe closet and scowled.

Soft hands touched his lower back and slowly moved upwards, kneading and massaging as they went. The tension receded, and he gave a little moan. "If you're trying to seduce me, you'd better be quick about it before my wife comes back."

Warm breath touched his ear and stirred his cock. It was followed by a whispered, throaty voice. "I don't think she'll mind."

He spun around and swept AJ up, realizing she only wore one of his shirts. Instead of tossing her onto the bed as he'd originally planned, he fell into it with her clutching him. They landed sideways, and he slid a hand under the shirt to caress her stomach and then higher to a breast.

"You think it's this easy to calm the savage beast?" he asked.

"If it were only the beast, I'd say yes. But I'm afraid dealing with a man who's worried for his friends is a bit more difficult to navigate." Her kiss was demanding as her leg wrapped around his.

Once she released his lips, he gave her a rueful smile. "Am I that transparent?"

"It's either that, or you've become overly attached to your wardrobe choices. I might expect that of Beckworth, but not you."

He chuckled. "That would be a correct assessment."

She ran a hand over his cheek, then ruffled his hair. "So, you want to get busy?" She stretched her body, her arms rising high enough for the shirt to ride up her legs, revealing the bottom of her backside.

"You are so tempting." He growled and pulled the shirt up to kiss her stomach and both breasts before standing. He stared down at her and shook his head. If he thought he could have a peaceful afternoon with his wife, he wouldn't hesitate. But Hensley was expecting him, and if he was late, the man was sure to send a footman or maid. "I'm afraid we'll have to postpone until this evening. Although..." His wicked grin made her giggle. "We might have time before dinner if Mary doesn't keep you busy."

Her lips formed a perfectly kissable pout, but he resisted.

"Actually, Maire thought a game of cards on the patio would lure Sebastian out of the library and into some fresh air. I'm surprised he hasn't been sleeping on the sofa."

"Maybe Mary could move a dining table in so he could eat there as well."

She laughed. "I think Maire's light touch with Sebastian would be easier, though Mary doesn't seem hindered by moving furniture around."

"Without a doubt." He held out his hand and pulled her into his embrace. "I guess I'll have to do without the blue cravat." He kissed the top of her nose and gave her a soft slap to her backside. He was still grinning as he strode down the hall.

The smile faded to a frown by the time he reached the

bottom of the staircase, and his mood turned completely morose by the time he reached Hensley's office. The door was closed, but multiple voices managed to reach the hall. His mood instantly changed when he recognized them.

He threw the door open and stared at the new arrivals. Jamie, Lando, Fitz, and Thomas leaned back in their chairs, each with a glass of whiskey. Ethan sat by the hearth while Hensley sat behind his desk, chuckling at something Fitz said.

They all turned at his abrupt entrance. Jamie jumped up, setting his whiskey on Hensley's desk as he rushed over and grabbed Finn's hand, pulling him into a quick embrace.

"It's about damn time." Finn couldn't believe his eyes, nor did he understand how all four of them were there at the same time. "And why didn't anyone send for me when you arrived?"

"We were going to send a footman up," Fitz said. "But we didn't want to interrupt any marital duties, seeing as how you've had quite a bit of free time on your hands."

They all chuckled, and Thomas handed him a glass of whiskey. "Find a chair. Jamie only began his tale, but he can start over. I think Fitz was having a hard time keeping up."

Finn grinned. Thomas and Fitz had worked together for a long time now but had never seemed overly chummy. Their experience with the ambush outside Stokenchurch seemed to have created a tighter bond.

He took a seat and a sip of his drink as the heaviness that had been building these past days dissipated. With the full team back together, they could focus solely on finding Beckworth. "Please, continue."

"As I was telling everyone..." Jamie refilled his glass and sat, resting his boots on a footstool. "We left Newport after dropping off Ethan, Maire, and Fitz. Since we had some time, we decided to take a quick run to Dublin to fill our stores and pick up some cargo."

"You mean crates of Jameson," Finn added.

Jamie chuckled. "It's not my fault if demand has increased with the war. Besides, I felt it my duty to support our brave soldiers." He scratched his chin as the others grinned. "I suppose that was my first mistake, but it turned out alright in the end. We had just finished taking on the cargo and were prepared to sail at first light. I decided to follow a few of the men to a local pub for a meal, and that's when I spotted Thaddeus McDuff."

"I thought he ran to France to avoid hanging at Newgate." Finn hadn't heard the name in years. It had been one of his earlier jobs with Hensley and a test of where his loyalties lay when pitted against an Irish rebel. His mission had been to infiltrate McDuff's crew as a smuggler. McDuff claimed to be an Irish sympathizer, but his true roots were Scottish. What most didn't know was that a portion of his finances came from an English lord with a voice in Parliament and a desire to keep a chokehold on Ireland.

"McDuff has been on the run for a long time." Fitz took a puff off his pipe, its spicy scent mingling with the earthy aroma from Hensley's cigar. "I'd heard his loyalties to Ireland were being questioned in some ports."

Jamie shrugged. "I'd heard that as well, but with the war, he's found more opportunities to create turmoil. I was never able to discover what his plans were, but having him on Irish soil wasn't going to be a benefit and would most likely get innocents killed rather than fed. So, I had a dilemma. It wasn't the job I'd been tasked with, but in good conscience, I couldn't ignore what the man might be up to.

"So, there I was, counting how many days it would take Ethan to get to London against how long it would take Finn to cross a good portion of France before finding a ship. I figured we had two or three days and didn't want to miss the opportunity. It might have been a waste, but you have the names of the men and the villages he visited, which pretty much covers a good portion of the southern coast."

"Do you think he was looking for port cities willing to accept French warships?" Lando asked. "It would make sense if Napoleon thought he could get a few past the Royal Navy."

"Maybe. Though from what we gleaned as McDuff moved from one town to the next, he wasn't finding many willing to trade one master for another. France might leave Ireland alone or see it as fodder for their stepping-stone to England. We did all we could before turning for London and would have been here a couple of days ago if we hadn't run into a squall. Then several British Patrols drove us deeper into the Channel. But now we're here, and the men could use a good rest."

A knock on the door made the men turn. Maire stuck her head in, then pushed her way through when she spotted Jamie.

"Well, it's about time you showed. And here you all are, hiding away and telling tall tales." She tapped a foot. "If you're finished with that, Mary has set out food that should see you through to dinner. And you'll not be making plans around Beckworth without the rest of us."

Jamie's brow rose, and his smile faded. "Fitz and Lando filled me in. You haven't found him yet?"

Hensley stood and set the bottle of whiskey on the side table. "No. And I assume since you picked up Fitz, Lando, and Thomas in Southampton, there's been no sighting of the *Phoenix*."

"It was the luck of the Irish that we saw the *Daphne* sail into port." Lando stood and accepted a hug from Maire. "We'd just arrived the day before and decided to stay a day to see if we could get any information at the pubs. There wasn't a scrap of news about the ship anywhere down the coast. But then we found a sailor, way into his cups, who provided one interesting bit. He'd been on watch as their ship passed the estuary to the

Thames. He swore he saw a ship matching the *Phoenix*'s description turned toward the river, but it was too far away to make out the name."

"Did anyone else see it?" Ethan had made his way to the door, an arm around Maire.

"No," Jamie said. "It was just after dawn, and he was the only one on the forward deck at the time. It was one of dozens of ships he'd seen and didn't think much of it, so we can't be sure of his information."

Lando nodded in agreement. "We monitored the docks on the way upriver, but there wasn't any sign of the ship."

Hensley glanced at Finn. "Perhaps we should have given more credence to Stella's insight."

Finn ran a hand through his hair. "We might have been looking at this all wrong in not giving her the benefit of the doubt. She'd been through a great ordeal, and we assumed she'd been struggling with the trauma of Ipswich. We also assumed since we've been at this game longer, our experience held more weight."

"Well, she'll be here in a few hours with Barrington and the others. Now that the entire team is on hand, we should turn our efforts to the Thames."

13

Stella dragged her feet through Hensley's manor with Barrington, Eleanor, Bart, and Lincoln trailing behind. After their breakfast and recap of the night's events, they'd all retired to their rooms. She'd fallen face-first into the bed and didn't move until her lady's maid shook her awake. AJ had told her on more than one occasion that she could sleep like the dead—apparently, she was right.

Everyone had waited in the sitting room for thirty minutes before she stomped down the stairs. She wore the day dress from the previous evening, ignoring the maid's plea to wear something different but agreeing to a quick updo that showed off her leaf hairpin, which made her think of Beckworth.

He was rarely out of her thoughts, and knowing how close he was, she wanted to throw on her pants and beg Barrington to take her to the ship. It was stupid, but she couldn't seem to disconnect from her one-track thoughts.

When they arrived at Hensley's manor, Mary welcomed them with her high spirits and mile-a-minute chatter.

"Hensley wanted to meet in the library, but there are twenty of you now, and more of Thomas's men keep arriving. The poor things are so exhausted when they arrive that I shoo them up to their rooms. I'm afraid most are doubling up. I wasn't expecting a full house."

"Perhaps a few could move to where we're staying," Barrington offered. "There's plenty of room, though we don't ask much of the smaller staff."

"That's a marvelous idea. We'll sort that out after dinner." Mary swept them into the sitting room, where they seemed to be the last of the group to arrive.

She didn't recognize everyone, but Fitz and Thomas were back. AJ smiled at her and shrugged, which Stella assumed had to do with the full sofa where Finn and Maire sat next to her. Ethan stood behind the sofa, his hands resting on Maire's shoulders.

She took a seat on a second sofa with Barrington and Eleanor on either side of her like sentinels while Bart settled into a chair next to them. Lincoln found a spot on the floor in a corner as if purposely staying out of the way. When she scanned the room, it seemed like they'd been partitioned off. Part of the team, but not fully.

"Now that we're all here, let's review where we are." Hensley entwined his fingers over his belly and glanced at the room at large. "I'll start with laying out what I know, and then others can chime in as we go." He went back further than she'd expected—from her original kidnapping in Baywood to Beckworth's capture at Ipswich, ending with scouring the coastline for the *Phoenix.*

The team added bits and pieces they felt relevant, but the only surprise to her was the discovery of a sailor who thought he'd seen the *Phoenix* sailing for the Thames, but where it had gone was a mystery.

"Not a mystery." Barrington seemed to hover between his

butler and crew personas. He didn't flinch when all eyes turned to him.

She barely twitched when AJ's gaze fell on her, and she returned a half-shrug, preferring Barrington to take the hit for what was coming next. It didn't matter to him. He wasn't beholden to anyone in the room except the small group they'd come with and Beckworth.

"What does that mean?" Finn was the first to speak. He kept his tone level, but AJ laid a hand on his arm, so he was probably working up a good steam.

"While your teams explored the coast, we had several crews searching the Thames." His delivery was so droll she almost laughed at the others' wide-eyed stares and grumbles. The only two that weren't surprised were Maire and Ethan.

"We knew Stella went to the East End, but she never said where she went. I assume she met with the crews after we basically ignored her intuition." Finn glanced around and paused on Ethan and Maire, the two of them staring off at some distant point. "Perhaps some of us were more aware of events than others." He frowned at his sister, and when Maire lifted her head, she appeared defiant.

"Yes, Ethan and I knew they had all the crews out searching. They believed Stella and decided it was worth the effort." Maire sat back, her chin lifted in a stubborn tilt as Ethan slowly massaged her shoulders.

"And you found the ship?" Hensley asked. His shock had worn off quickly, and he redirected the conversation back to topic.

"Yes, with Stella's continued support." Barrington elaborated on finding the ship and the intimidation tactics they used, capturing Gemini's men one at a time and leaving an origami swan behind in an attempt to instill confusion and fear.

"Why didn't you tell us?" Finn asked, his irritation growing if she read his rapid tapping on the armrest correctly.

Barrington shrugged as if it was no big deal. "You took one path, we took another. What does it matter as long as we found Beckworth?"

"You think he's on the ship?" Hensley asked, though he was nodding as if answering his own question. "It would make sense. It would be risky to move him."

"We have solid confirmation."

"How old is this information?" Fitz asked.

"Less than twelve hours."

Fitz nodded and glanced at Hensley. "We should strike fast before Gemini becomes worried by the number of missing sailors."

"Aye." Jamie, the new captain of the *Daphne* nodded. AJ had mentioned he was a looker, and she'd been right. His hair was lighter than Finn's, and though it was tied in a queue, Stella caught the slight curls at the tips when he turned his head. His elegant jacket showed off his broad shoulders, and his quick smile must have the women following him in every port. Beckworth seemed fond of Jamie the few times he'd mentioned him, and she hoped the feeling was mutual. "We can't take a risk in them deciding to move him."

"We have multiple eyes on the ship," Barrington replied. "If they move him, we'll follow. But I agree, it's best to take him on the ship. They've found a quiet berth."

"Can we back up a minute?" AJ asked. "You said something about Stella's continuing help. What exactly did you mean by that?"

Barrington scratched his head and glanced down at Stella. She sighed. AJ would get it out of her one way or another, and it might be easier to have it explained in front of everyone. Maybe then they'd see she wasn't dead weight. That she had something to offer.

"Go ahead." Stella reached for her leaf pin. It was becoming her good luck charm. "You might as well tell them the rest."

Barrington explained Beckworth's idea to use Stella's origami swans as some form of message, though neither were sure how they could be used at the time. "A couple of swans had been left behind before he gave himself up to Gemini. Chester and I thought they could be left along with one of the missing men's possessions. We weren't sure if they were noticed or created the fear we wanted, but based on the last man we questioned, the sailors were aware of them."

"It could also make Gemini strengthen her forces," Finn countered.

"That was always a risk, but as each man was taken, the number of men on the ship didn't appear to increase. When we found one of the men more intimidated than the others, we decided to bring Stella in to see if he would break."

"Excuse me?" AJ said. "Bring her in where?"

"Stop coddling me," Stella snapped, then softened her tone. "I went to meet with the man." She held up her hands before anyone exploded. "There were at least twenty of the crew present, and the man was tied up like a Christmas goose. All I did was stride in like I owned the place and told him I was The Swan."

Lincoln laughed from the corner. "The man almost pissed himself."

AJ turned red with anger, but Finn held back a smile as the others chuckled.

"Then I hopped back in the carriage and paced the study until dawn, waiting for Barrington's return to tell us whether it worked or not."

"I can attest to that," Bart said. "She paces like a wild buffalo."

Eleanor tsked. "What would you know about wild buffalos, old man? Besides, you slept through most of it."

Bart grumbled. "Just resting my eyes."

Hensley tried to return everyone's attention back to the discussion, but side conversations started, then Fitz shared a story of something similar he and Jamie had pulled off on one of their cargo runs.

Mary, being the consummate hostess, timed her entrance as if it had been choreographed and nodded to a footman. A minute later, the butler arrived to call them to dinner.

Stella tried to sneak out with Eleanor, but AJ snagged her arm.

"I'll wait until after dinner, but you have some 'splaining to do, Lucy."

14

After dinner, the group split in accordance with local customs of the time, meaning the men went to the library to smoke cigars, and the women gravitated to the drawing room. AJ fell behind when she stopped to give Jamie, Lincoln, and Bart a hug, the latter grumbling through it all while his cheeks turned red.

Before she reached the drawing room, Finn grabbed her elbow and pulled her to a stop. She turned around and grinned at him.

"What's up?"

He placed his arm through hers. "I thought I'd spend a few minutes with the ladies." He led her through the door, where Stella sat on the sofa with a piece of embroidered fabric covering her lap. A needle had been stuck through the piece.

"When did you learn needlework?" AJ dropped next to her and marveled at the intricate work.

Stella snorted. "We haven't been separated that long."

AJ grinned. "It's Mary's, isn't it?"

Stella ran a hand over the design. "I never appreciated the amount of work that went into a piece like this. I mean, I've always found hand-stitched designs to be unique, but I never considered how long it took to create one."

"I wouldn't have the patience."

"Well, if you wouldn't, there's no hope for me." She glanced up and tilted her head when she saw Finn. "Aren't you supposed to be sitting in a smoke-filled room drinking some fine Irish whiskey?"

He gave her his signature grin. "There will be plenty of time for that." He took a seat in the chair next to the sofa.

Stella glanced around. "Where did everyone else go?"

"Mary wanted to show Eleanor and Maire something." AJ fluffed her skirts as she shifted her seat to face Stella. "I didn't catch it all, but they should be here soon."

Stella's brow rose as she appraised Finn, then she sat back, dropping the embroidered work to the sofa and crossing her arms over her chest. "So, you've come to lecture me about last night."

AJ didn't waste a moment. "What possessed you to do something so dangerous? You could have come to us."

"I did. No one was interested in my opinion," Stella snapped.

She leaned back, surprised by Stella's anger. "You mean that night at dinner?"

"Yes. And when no one took me seriously, I went to Chester. He's a friend of Beckworth's, and I knew he'd at least listen."

"That's where you went when you went to the East End?" Finn asked.

Stella nodded. "Beckworth introduced us before we left for Ipswich. I thought he'd listen, and he did."

"So, he put the crews to work." Finn nodded and leaned back, resting a leg on his knee. "Why didn't you tell us?"

"It was Chester's decision." She quirked her lips. "He thought you'd get in the way."

Before Finn could respond, AJ jumped in. "Fine. So you

asked Chester for help. That was bad enough, but then you went with Barrington in the dead of night to interrogate Gemini's men." Her voice had risen, and Finn touched her knee, calming her. She was as angry as Stella and aware enough to know it was fear driving her. Then something occurred to her. "When Barrington asked you to come over so Eleanor wouldn't have to be alone, that was a ruse, wasn't it? He wanted to get you away from us."

Stella rolled her eyes but averted her gaze, suddenly interested in the embroidery again. "That's nonsense." When her hands fisted around the fabric, she sighed as she ran a hand over it, trying to smooth its edges. "Okay. You're right. Barrington had news of the ship." She lifted her head, and her jaw tightened. Stella had her stubborn on. "The crews had a plan to confirm where Beckworth was being held. They wanted me to be involved since I gave them the initial lead."

AJ shook her head. "If Barrington found the ship, he should have said something, not stick you in the middle of it. Why was it so important for you to be involved in the interrogation?"

"Ever since we've caught up with each other, everyone walks around me like I might break. No one gives my opinions any consideration, preferring to patronize me as if that will settle everything." She gave Finn a side glance, and her tone softened. "I've said this before, but I'll say it again for Finn's sake. We haven't spent much time together since I arrived here, but I've changed. I have new skills. I've adapted. And I have friends here, just like you."

"You could have said something before you snuck out of the house a second time." It hurt to think Stella couldn't trust her. How had that happened?

Stella glanced at Finn again. "I wanted to tell you, but then you'd tell Finn, and then he'd stop me."

"That's not true..." AJ looked at Finn and the mixed

emotions crossing his face. She was reminded of their vacation to France when she, Stella, and Maire had sneaked around the monastery in search of Sebastian's secret journal, hiding their actions from Finn and Ethan. She'd promised Finn never to leave him in the dark.

"Oh, honey, I get it." Stella grabbed her hand and squeezed it, giving Finn a smirk. "Husband trumps girlfriend. That's the way it's supposed to be. Well, unless the guy's a total dick, or he's abusive, or he's cheating on you. Then girlfriend trumps asshole."

AJ burst out laughing, and Finn chuckled. But when the laughter died away, she murmured. "It was still dangerous."

"And so was the time you went back to find Finn. If I remember the stories correctly, you went with the men each time they thought they'd found him. You used your skills to save him. I have skills, too."

"That doesn't really explain why you and Barrington didn't come to us the minute you found the ship." Finn's tone was mild yet stern, attempting a balance that wouldn't set Stella off again. "Hensley could have added resources to it. Ethan and I would have helped."

"That was the exact reason Barrington and Chester didn't want you to know until after they confirmed Beckworth's location. If it's any consolation, I said you needed to be informed. But they have crews that have been working together for years. They have their own signals and ways of doing things. You and Hensley are take-charge kind of men. You would have pushed Chester and Barrington aside."

Finn started to say something but seemed to think better of it.

"They weren't going to try to extract Beckworth without bringing you in, but you keep forgetting something. Beckworth is their friend, too. In fact, they have years of history with him.

They have a stake in helping their friend, and they understand the importance of not screwing it up."

Finn sat back, and AJ knew what he was thinking. Neither of them had considered what Stella so eloquently reminded them.

"You're right," Finn conceded. "As much as I would have preferred Barrington bringing the information to us straightaway, if I'd been in his place, I would have done the same thing."

Stella seemed surprised at his admission, but she nodded. "Thank you for that." She knitted her fingers together. "What about Hensley? I don't want him to be cross with me."

Finn chuckled. "I don't think that could happen, or if it did, it wouldn't last long. You intrigue more than irritate. Though I will admit, he was annoyed at not being brought in earlier, but he knows he was wrong in not giving London more consideration. Your actions didn't impact our search, and while Fitz discovered a reason to search the Thames, we would have lost valuable time and could have alerted Gemini to our presence. This time it turned out to be a win for all of us, and hopefully Beckworth as well."

Stella nodded as she considered his words. "If I thought we were doing anything that interfered with your efforts, I would have said something."

AJ leaned over and hugged her. "We know."

Stella heaved a sigh. "So, now what?"

Finn stood. "That's what I need to check on. I imagine the men have been discussing that very fact."

"Of course they are," Stella grumbled.

"And it's just like the men to think they have all the answers," Maire said as she entered the room with Mary and Eleanor behind her.

Mary giggled and waved a hand. "That's why they're in their smoky room. They'll go round and round with their ideas, but my Hensley is just gathering opinions. I have no doubt I'll be setting up tables like before. If we rearrange a few items, the library should fit everyone. Sebastian can participate while looking at the books."

"That will keep Bart occupied as well." Eleanor picked up the embroidery Stella had been mangling and studied the stitchwork. "He and Sebastian are getting along well with their mutual love of books. This is just lovely, Mary."

While the talk turned to more domestic topics, AJ watched Finn slip out the door. He turned at the last moment and winked at her. She glanced at Stella, who sipped wine as the discussion turned to the best herbs to grow in a garden.

She still feared for her but for a different reason. Stella blamed herself for Beckworth's capture, and AJ understood her need to make amends. But there was more to Stella's need to find him, and it was more than making up for what she considered her failing. AJ saw it for what it was because she'd experienced the same thing the first time Finn had taken her through the fog. At some point, they would complete their mission, and it would be time to go home.

Stella would have to make a decision. One that AJ thought would have been simple. But something happened between her and Beckworth, and for that reason, AJ might lose her friend. Or, Stella was setting herself up for major heartbreak, and there wasn't anything she could say or do that would change that outcome.

15

The following morning, Finn left Hensley's study in search of AJ. The conversation the previous evening with Stella had gone better than he'd imagined. They'd been so worried about her since arriving home at the inn and finding her gone, they hadn't taken the time to consider who Stella was—not completely. They only had AJ's experience of finding herself two hundred years in the past to draw from.

But Stella knew everything about their travels. Names, locations, and how their story had played out until this very moment. He stood at the door leading to the garden where he found the women. He'd watched AJ and Stella's interactions at breakfast. Their easy friendship appeared restored, but he'd rather cement that before their next mission.

The women wouldn't be happy that a plan had already been decided. And they'd been in this manor for too long with nothing but the garden for fresh air. He grinned. There was a way to give them a day of enjoyment in hopes of softening news of the plan. He was a fool if he thought he could get away with placating the women, but they'd have a day of pleasure regardless.

"Hello, ladies." Finn gave AJ a peck on the cheek and gave Maire, Mary, and Stella a pleasant smile. "The days are certainly getting warmer. The scent of the flowers alone is enough to calm a soul."

"And we could certainly use that." Stella winked at him, and a tension he hadn't realized was pressing on him released.

"And what brings you our way, dear brother?" Several flowers lay in Maire's lap, and she selected one to weave into a small crown she was making.

"I believe there was a promise made for an outing through Hyde Park. And I thought Stella might like lunch at Rules."

Mary clapped her hands. "That's a marvelous idea, though I doubt I can talk Hensley into joining us."

"Nonsense. He has several messages to return, so he can't go to the park, but he can meet us at the restaurant."

"Wonderful." Mary sprang up, taking time to stash her needlework in a small basket. "We should probably send a messenger to reserve a table."

"It's already taken care of." Finn waited as the other women rose, and he followed them into the house and stopped at the staircase. "I'll meet you down here in one hour. Will that be enough time?" He knew AJ, Maire, and Stella could be down in fifteen minutes if they had to, but Mary would stick to protocol when going out, which meant everyone would require their best day dress.

AJ pulled him in and gave him a kiss. "You're up to something."

"You know me too well." And with that, he turned for the study. He had to tell Hensley and Ethan the plan he put together and hoped it wasn't too late to procure a table at Rules.

Stella stared at her reflection in the dressing table mirror as Sarah added finishing touches to her hair. She'd stayed the night at Hensley's after Eleanor insisted she would be alright. Now that all their secrets were out, Eleanor would want a portion of her solitude back, or as much as she could achieve with the men in the house. There was no doubt she was helping the staff care for them.

She tugged at a tendril that framed her face. It seemed wrong to be going out and having tea and pleasant conversation while Beckworth suffered. The ship wouldn't have deep, dark, cavernous dungeons, but there would be torture, assuming he ever gained consciousness after a two-by-four to the head. She closed her eyes, holding back the tears that threatened, when Sarah nudged her elbow.

"I thought you'd want to wear this." Sarah held the box with her opal necklace.

"I thought I'd wait until Beckworth returns." She stared at the opal and remembered how his cornflower-blue eyes had heated when he saw it laying between her breasts.

"Isn't this a way to let him know he's never far from your thoughts?" Sarah's gaze was encouraging.

"I hadn't thought of it that way." She nodded and waited for the expected warmth as the opal touched her skin. Sarah was right, it felt like it belonged. She squeezed the girl's hand and stood. "Then I think we're complete."

"The bracelet?" Sarah asked.

"I won't hide it anymore, but I think I'll keep that for evening attire."

Sarah bobbed her head. "That's appropriate." She stored the box with the bracelet in a drawer and pulled out a thin wrap. "The late afternoon can be chilly."

The wrap was an emerald silk that complemented her mint-green day dress. Two new dresses had arrived the day after returning from Ipswich. This was the first time she'd been willing to wear one. She didn't know what Finn was planning. His efforts to keep them happy weren't any different than his behavior in Baywood, but he was up to something. She could smell it.

They had everything they needed to plan Beckworth's extraction and had agreed the job had to be done soon before Gemini got spooked and moved him. The men had been huddling in Hensley's study all morning, and AJ grumbled that they were planning something without them. It bothered her at first, but she decided it was best for the men to work out all the logistical details. There was always time to change a plan before it was put into motion.

Stella met everyone in the foyer with Mary being the last to arrive. They were piled into the carriage with the men accompanying them on horseback. They drove through the park before the carriage stopped, and the men dismounted so the women could stroll through a section of flower gardens. As was the way with Mary, they paused occasionally for her to introduce them to acquaintances.

It was a beautiful spring day, and though the conversation kept her entertained, Stella constantly reached for her opal, rubbing it as a thought of Beckworth came to her. At times, she could hear his voice—sometimes in irritation or in soft tones as he confided in her. She refused to think about how similar this would all be once she was back in Baywood and all she had were memories. Instead, she focused on this moment and what it would take to ensure he was safely back with them.

Hensley waited for them at the restaurant with Barrington. He was in deep conversation with two gentlemen, who quickly departed after giving the group a quick nod. A private room had been arranged, and it held a single table long enough to seat twenty, though only eight table settings had been arranged.

"Where's Jamie and the other men?" Stella asked.

"Jamie wanted to check on the ship and make sure it was well supplied in case we have need of the *Daphne*." Finn pulled a chair out for AJ.

Barrington, who was in butler attire, gave her a small smile as he assisted her to her seat. She didn't know him well enough to read anything into it. But she suspected Hensley had told him of their plan, and if that was the case, she assumed Barrington was in agreement.

"Where's Thomas been?" Maire asked.

"He moved the men to the earl's London house." Ethan leaned back to allow the footman to ladle soup into his bowl. "Our group is growing large, and we thought it best Gemini didn't know how many men we we're gathering."

The group settled into pleasant conversation about the walk through the park with Hensley and Mary sharing stories about the different individuals they'd met. Once the plates were removed and the whiskey came out, Hensley got down to business.

"I know it won't settle well with some of you..." Hensley's gaze shifted to AJ, and Stella held back a smile when AJ scowled. "Ethan and Finn happened to be in my study, and the conversation naturally turned to Beckworth. We have a preliminary idea of how to extract him, and I invited Barrington to join us so he can keep the crews updated. We want them involved, but this particular mission will fall to me. I got him involved with Gemini, and I'll see him clear. The crews have risked enough to find him. Now, it's our turn to see him back with us."

"We'll actually use Beckworth's own playbook for the operation," Finn started. He moved various pieces of dishes and glassware around the table as he began to explain.

"Diversions?" Stella asked.

Ethan nodded. "But rather than one, we'll use two. We'll need to be careful because we don't want to draw attention from the local constables."

"That's where the crew will be handy." Barrington sipped his whiskey. "We can have additional diversions ready if needed to slow any watchmen that might try for the dock. Most of them leave the ships to fend for themselves so they can focus on the pubs. Fortunately, the *Phoenix* is moored far enough from the pubs to be of any concern, but we'll have friends watching out for us."

Finn moved the whiskey bottle to the center of the table. "This is the *Phoenix*. The extraction team will be Fitz, Jamie, and Ethan, who will arrive by dinghy." He slid a water glass to one side of the bottle. "Since we don't know what condition Beckworth is in, we'll need at least two men to help get him off the ship and one to run point." Finn slid an empty wineglass to the other side of the bottle. "Lando will lead the first diversion team with Thomas and someone from his surveillance team. They'll set a fire on the starboard side that rests along the dock. They'll take out whoever they run across." He slid a bowl of salt near the water glass. "I'll run the second diversion with AJ and another of Thomas's surveillance team. We'll approach from the aft with a second dinghy."

"Where will I be?" Maire asked.

"You'll be with Eleanor at Beckworth's manor preparing for Beckworth," Ethan answered. "We'll need your skills along with Bart's for whatever might be needed."

"I'll have a coach waiting with a few of the crew should any of Gemini's men follow." Barrington gave Stella a glance, as did AJ and Maire. Everyone had a role except for her.

"It sounds like a tight plan." She gave the men a glance, then focused on Finn, who'd been tasked with laying out the plan. "You left my name out."

"I have an idea where you'll be best suited, but I'm interested in hearing your thoughts." Finn gave her his signature grin, and she returned a sly smile.

"That's easy enough. I need to go with the extraction team. I know the ship, and if we enter by the gunports, I can navigate us to the holding cells where we were kept. There are stairs on each side of the passageway that can take us to the top deck."

Finn's smile never faltered. "We agree."

She blinked. Her shoulders dropped, and for the first time in days, the tension she'd held in check melted away. They'd learned their lesson and trusted her. It was enough. "How do we get off the ship?"

"AJ will be shooting arrows, so most of the crew will most likely stay out of sight except for those trying to save the ship. That should leave you a clear path to the gangplank."

"When do we do this?" AJ asked. She fidgeted like a thoroughbred at the starting gate, waiting for the sound of the starting pistol.

"I hope you all had a good meal." Hensley waved for Finn to slide him the whiskey bottle now that it was no longer needed as a prop. "Mary will provide small snacks this evening, and then you'll want to rest up. You leave at midnight."

16

After the meeting, the carriage took a last stroll through Hyde Park before returning to Hensley's manor. Sebastian waited for the group in the foyer, sitting on a bench, his head in a book. Once everyone had entered and the butler closed the door behind them, he stood. Maire hurried to him to see if he was alright.

AJ leaned into Finn. "This doesn't bode well."

"Maybe he feels left out." Finn put an arm around her as they stood back to see what bothered Sebastian enough to leave the library.

It was rare to find Sebastian anywhere but there as perusing the books was his favorite pastime except for his occasional visits to the garden. No matter how often Mary explained they had a gardener, he enjoyed tinkering with the plants, and everyone agreed he could use the fresh air.

Stella stepped next to AJ and grabbed her hand. Her brow lifted in curiosity rather than concern.

"Oh, I'm fine." Sebastian held the book to his chest. "Beckworth will be back with us this evening?"

"Yes. We just finalized the plan." Maire turned him toward

the library, but he stayed her hand and faced the group. "I'd like to wait with Bart and Eleanor. Would it be possible for someone to take me to the manor?"

Maire shook her head. "It's safer if you stay here."

"Maire's right." Hensley pushed through everyone. "Gemini must be expecting we'll do something soon. We can't be too careful, and this manor is quite secure."

Sebastian shook his head, and his chin lifted a fraction. Maire glanced at AJ, but she didn't see what she could do. Normally, the monk was accommodating, but when he made a decision on something, it was difficult to sway him.

"Is there a reason you want to be with them?" AJ asked. It seemed an obvious question and might make negotiating with him easier.

"Bart will be there to assist with any physical malady Beckworth might have. I'd like to be there for his spiritual healing."

Someone snorted, but it wasn't Stella, which surprised AJ. But her friend obviously knew Beckworth more than her. It was something AJ would probably stew on for days.

Maire wrung her hands, then glanced to Ethan, who could only shrug. When she turned back, AJ could see she was struggling for the right words. "I'm not sure Beckworth would be open to spiritual healing."

Sebastian smiled, humor dancing in his intelligent eyes, which were enough for AJ to know Maire wasn't going to win this one. "Everyone requires spiritual healing, even if they aren't aware of it. You would be surprised at the conversations the two of us have had on our journey." He patted Maire's arm. "Where will you be this evening?"

Maire hesitated, and her heavy sigh was loud enough for everyone to hear. "I'll be with Bart and Eleanor."

"Excellent. Then we can go together."

Hensley was already whispering something to Barrington,

who was nodding. Plans were being altered to strengthen the defenses at Beckworth's manor.

"Alright, Sebastian," Hensley said. "You can leave with Maire this evening. We'll have extra precautions in place."

"Most excellent." Sebastian beamed. "In that case, I think I'll retire to my room. Many things to record in my journal, and I'll need to rest." He turned for the stairs, with Maire and Ethan following.

Finn waited until the trio had reached the second floor and turned down the hall before speaking. "Do you want me to see if Jamie has extra men?"

"That won't be necessary," Barrington responded. "Hensley will send a couple of men, and we'll have the crew increase their watch."

"What could Gemini be planning?" Stella asked. "It's been over a week since she took Beckworth, and her men are already watching this manor."

"Only for the next few hours," Hensley answered. "They'll be removed before we leave tonight."

"Well, that's good news, but not where I was going. Why hasn't she made a move to negotiate for the other chronicles or the Heart Stone? She seems to have another game plan, yet she doesn't seem to be in any hurry. And what's up with Belato? He seems to enjoy staying in the background. Who's really running the show?"

The men chuckled, but it was Hensley who took her arm. "All excellent questions. Perhaps we can discuss that over a game of chess."

While Hensley led her away, Barrington kept his eye on the two as they disappeared down the hall. "I'll return this evening with the coach to take Maire and Sebastian to the manor, then meet you in the designated spot." He shook Finn's hand and nodded at AJ before leaving.

AJ took Finn's arm and led him up the stairs to their room. "There never seems to be a dull moment with this group."

Finn chuckled. "Sometimes, it's amazing that we can all agree on anything."

When they reached their room, AJ opened the drapes to let the afternoon sun shed its light. She turned to let Finn help with her dress. Once it fell to the ground, she stepped out of it and placed it on a chair for Willa to have cleaned before helping Finn with his clothes.

"At the meeting earlier, why did you ask Stella what part she wanted to play rather than giving her an assignment like the rest of us?"

He shrugged out of his jacket and waited for her to pull the shirt over his head. "She's new to the team, and while she's been actively participating in events since her arrival in this time period, I haven't seen her in action. I was curious where she believed her skills to be of best use. I'm not sure we've seen all she has to offer, but for this task, I agreed with her assessment."

"A test?"

"Not really. We would have come to an agreement, but I was curious what her thoughts were. She wanted to have her opinions heard. This was her opportunity."

She unbuttoned his breeches. "You're a good friend to her, but I also think you're trying to make amends."

He slid off the breeches, then pulled the chemise over her head. "Do you think it worked?"

"Absolutely. I won't say Stella didn't see it for what it was, but that would have made it more meaningful. She knows you're trying."

She kissed him and wrapped her arms around his neck as he lifted her into his arms. He placed her on the bed and removed the rest of their clothing. When he lay next to her, he pulled her into him, his legs entwining with hers.

"How deep are Stella's feelings for Beckworth?"

That was a good question. She'd mended her own cracked bridge with Stella, yet the two had avoided any discussion about Beckworth. And that alone had been enough for AJ to know the answer to the unspoken question.

"Enough that I don't know what decision she'll make when it's time to go home." Tears pricked her eyes, and she didn't know if they came from the possibility of having to say goodbye to her friend or knowing the heartache Stella would have to survive after going home.

"It's something you're familiar with." He kissed her temple. "The choice was easy for me, but we don't know if Beckworth's feelings are as strong."

"Don't we, though?" She moved away and lifted onto her elbow to stare down at him, brushing errant locks from his eyes. "How many would have given themselves up to save her? I suppose it was the chivalrous thing to do."

"I think most would have attempted other options for a better outcome. After seeing how hard he struggled in our time to stay alive and find a way home, the man values his life as much as the next. He gave up quickly, not wanting to take any chance on Stella's life. So, yes, I guess we do know." He ran his hand over her cheek. "I would have done the same in his situation. Without hesitation."

Her tears fell, and he wiped them away before he kissed her. It was slow and thorough, and she fell back as he rolled her over, the kiss growing heated and urgent. She ran her hands over his shoulders and down his sides as her sorrow for Stella was slowly pushed away. This was their time, and nothing came between that.

They had a mission. It would be dangerous, and she'd learned to never take these moments for granted.

When the kiss ended, she stared into his loving gaze. "Take me to the moon, husband."

"Will you never get tired of saying that word?"

"Not until my dying days, and not even then."

He moved his knee to part her legs and gave her a deep kiss, his hands roaming south to her breast, and farther still. She remembered seeing the bright light of stars as he fulfilled her command.

17

A door creaked.

Beckworth opened an eye. The other one was still glued shut from caked blood. He licked his dry lips, which were cracked and tender. It had been a while since his last drink of water, and that had been barely a couple of mouthfuls. He wasn't sure how long he'd been in this room. There wasn't a window, and what little food he got didn't arrive on a regular schedule. It seemed to happen when someone remembered, which wasn't often.

It had been like that since Gemini stopped visiting him. He wasn't sure which was worse. The little to no regard of his survival, or dealing with her unwanted advances.

The only thing that kept him sane was his last image of Stella. Her tear-streaked face reflected painful emotions while also radiating a deep desire to kick his ass. He smiled, ignoring the sting it brought to his lips.

Then flashes emerged of her in a firelit room, naked with her arms flung wide. The memory of their passionate nights turned into others—her bouts of irritation when he did something she didn't like, stomping her foot at having to ride the horse on her own, the thrill in her expression when she closed her eyes and savored her latest attempt at the perfect cup of campfire coffee, or the way she ticked off a list to make a point. His smile widened.

Ice-cold water splashed over him, jarring him out of his reverie. The water chilled him, and he sputtered at the unexpected deluge.

"Well, that wiped the smile off your face." A man of average height, average looks, and average intelligence pranced over to stare at him. "Do tell, were you thinking of my sister?"

He prowled around Beckworth, which was easy enough to do. His legs were bound to a wooden chair by iron manacles, and his arms were raised above him locked in cuffs that hung from a rafter. If memory served, he wasn't too far from where Stella and Sebastian had been held. This hold was smaller but just as much of a cage.

When he'd walked up the gangway to the *Phoenix*, the first hit across his back had been a surprise. He still felt the ache and had been lucky Gaines hadn't put his full weight behind it, or it would have broken his spine. As it was, he was barely able to walk and had been dragged onto the ship. Or so he assumed since he barely remembered falling and curling into a fetal position, arms over his head as he waited for the next blow. Gaines hadn't disappointed, but Gemini's call to stop made him sidestep, and though the blow had hit him, it glanced off the side of his head. It bled profusely, and all these days later, he still had a headache.

He'd woken in a bed with his arms and legs bound with chains. At least he'd had some mobility, but he couldn't move his legs more than a few inches before a tremendous spasm racked his body followed by a period of blacking out.

Gemini had been furious and prohibited Gaines and André —her brother—from visiting her cabin. She'd stayed with him on their journey to London, sleeping next to him, curled up as if they were lovers. Each morning she would kiss him and tell him what a wonderful night they'd shared. Someone was losing bits of their sanity, and though it was quite possibly him, she wasn't far behind.

He was fed and watered regularly, like a good pet. The only conversations he remembered involved the stones. But he wasn't able to keep up, his wounds too fresh. Then she brought in documents, and he was fairly certain he wasn't of full mind by that point. He kept mumbling as images came and went. Though his memory was fuzzy, he didn't remember signing anything. The only confirmation of that had been her rising anger. Then she'd left, and he was moved to the hold.

That's when the beatings started. And while they had nothing on Dugan's techniques, the previous injury to his back brought bouts of extreme agony. How he was still alive was a mystery.

His chin was lifted, and the man who had his sister's eyes and nose but little else stared at him. "Do you know where the Heart Stone is?"

Interesting. All this time and they were finally getting around to this. Not once had Gemini mentioned the other chronicles or the scribe.

"I can offer your freedom in exchange for it. It belongs to France."

"Why don't you ask Murphy?"

André strode around the room, and Beckworth prepared for a strike each time the man walked behind him. "My sister doesn't believe the Heart Stone is as valuable as our uncle preached. It's her opinion that with the druid's book and the smaller stones, one can travel to the future as well as back to a point in time where my uncle knew where everything was buried."

"That doesn't sound smart."

André laughed. "I agree. With enough friends in Napoleon's army, we can simply storm the monastery and find what we need. But I fear my sister has given up on being able to retrieve the Heart Stone." He stopped in front of Beckworth. "She told me a story of your brother. Now, don't scowl. We were quite sorry to hear of his death at your hands. But we believe he was on to something in using the blood of a time traveler." André lifted Beckworth's chin again. "And you've traveled to the future, haven't you?"

"It didn't work." That was the last thing he needed. To be carved up like Murphy had been.

"Reginald didn't have the right incantation nor the ability to run more tests before his untimely death. As you've learned, my uncle had great patience, which he instilled in both of us. Even with Antoinette, his letters promised she would see the glory of France again."

"Is there a reason you keep speaking of your uncle in the past?"

André snickered. "Didn't she tell you?" He bent close to Beckworth's ear. "Didn't she whisper it to you during your long passionate evenings?" He stepped back. His face was a mask of contempt. "Our dear uncle was on the brink of discovering a perfected incantation. But he got drunk, as he did every night, and stumbled down the stairs. The fool broke his neck."

Now, the pieces began to fit together. His own mind was still befuddled from an intense headache, but the story was easy enough to follow. The elder Belato had been the one to develop the incantation that allowed Gaines to travel to the future and find the right time and place to return. It hadn't been perfect, from what Stella had said, but close enough. With his death, they required a new scribe. And since they couldn't find Maire, they'd kidnapped Sebastian.

André pulled out a pocket watch. "I think I'll get more

answers from you after another session with Gaines. For now, I have to get back."

The door burst open. "Get back to what, dear brother?"

Gemini stood in the doorway, dressed in a fine evening gown that showed off her classical beauty. She was back to playing the role of Lady Prescott. But instead of the curious beauty of a lady, her face was contorted in rage. "Is this where you've been when I thought you'd slunk off to a pub? Who told you to move him?" She strode to Beckworth and lifted his chin.

What was it with this family? Did they know the pain that rippled through him each time they jostled his head?

Her touch was gentle as her thumb grazed his swollen eye and cracked lips. She glanced around and stepped away, returning with a cup of water. "Drink this slowly, my love. That's it. No. That's all for now." She turned on her brother. "We agreed that I would handle Teddy."

"Your patience until now has been formidable, but the enemy is gathering forces. It's only a matter of time before they find us. We need to speed this up."

"Nonsense. They've been searching the coastline for the ship. It won't take long before they decide to try for the monastery. No one will think to look for us here, and I've set the next stage of our plan in motion." She glanced at Beckworth, who'd tilted his head so he could watch them out of his good eye.

"I'm sorry, darling. I wish we had time to move you back to our cabin, but I'm already late for Lady Thompson's dinner party. Then I have a late-night meeting. But as soon as it's over, I'll be back, and we'll get you tucked into bed." She snapped her fingers. "Now, André, come. You've wasted enough of my time."

She stormed out. André trailed behind her but not before Beckworth caught the man's glare at her retreat as his hands opened and closed into fists. How much longer before the tension between these two snapped? The question was whether that would be a benefit or a quick way to get him killed. If the ship was hidden along the Thames, it could take weeks before someone stumbled across it—if at all.

Stella kept her eye on the ship as it drew closer. The river was calm, and reflections from nearby lights cast undefinable shapes on the water. The only sound was the slight creak of an oar as it quietly churned the water.

Ethan leaned over and whispered, "Are you ready?"

She nodded. Her heart raced like a revved-up Ferrari, her nerves prickling along her arms and spine, but Beckworth was near. She could feel it. The pistol, resting in the holster Finn had given her, hung heavy against her leg, and she ran a hand over it. No one had believed she could fire a flintlock, but AJ had confirmed she spent time at the firing range a few times a year. The men smiled and shook their heads when she'd demonstrated loading the pistol and a rifle.

The dinghy stopped when a sailor walked by the railing before disappearing.

"A guard?" Ethan asked.

"I don't think so. Probably just checking lines or leaving for the pubs." Fitz waited another minute before nodding to the sailor who rowed the boat, and they continued on until they were below the gunport closest to the bow.

She glanced up and gulped. "It didn't occur to me until now how far up it was. It didn't seem that high from the dock."

Fitz stood, the boat barely moving under his quiet steps. He lifted a grappling hook while everyone moved back to give him room. Jamie held her still so she wouldn't mistakenly jostle the boat. With a couple of swings, he released the rope, and the hook caught on the first try.

"Do you practice that?" she whispered.

Fitz simply grinned before he grabbed a pile of rope and shimmied up the line.

She turned to Ethan and Jamie. "I can't do that."

Jamie smiled. "Don't worry, lass. We have you covered."

She repeatedly ran her hands over her pants as she peered up at Fitz, who was already climbing through the hole. He fussed with something before a rope ladder dropped from the gunport. She smiled. That she could do.

"Okay, lass." Jamie pushed her toward the ladder. "Up you go."

She didn't waste any time as she put a foot on the bottom rung, tested her weight and the feel of the rope, then began to climb. It wasn't as easy as it looked, but after the first couple of steps, she got a feel for the loose rungs. She'd barely reached the gunport before Fitz grabbed her and pulled her through the gap. Ethan crawled through next, followed by Jamie, who dropped the rope ladder first then the grappling hook, which landed with a dull thud in the boat.

Within seconds the boat turned, and the lone sailor rowed away.

Their only escape would be down the gangplank and into the waiting coach. She didn't have long to think about it when Ethan tapped her shoulder.

"Which way?"

She turned around to glance at the room filled with cannons and barrels of gunpowder. A dim light shone in from the ports. This was the same place she'd exited before. She closed her eyes, recalling the path.

"This way." She took off, moving quickly with Ethan, Jamie, and Fitz behind her.

She stopped before the last turn that would take them to the cargo hold where she'd been held. The passageway was brighter than she'd anticipated.

Ethan tapped her shoulder and pointed for her to get behind him. He peeked around the corner and then pulled back.

"Two men in the corridor. Standing guard from the looks of it."

Jamie considered for a moment, then turned to Fitz. "Our first diversion should be coming soon."

Fitz didn't respond, he simply hunched his shoulders and, with his head down, stumbled around the corner, his shoulder knocking into the wall. He sang an old sailing ditty, his voice telling them how far down the hall he was progressing.

"Hey, no one's allowed down here."

The singing continued.

"Who are you?"

"He's drunk. Just let him pass."

A bang echoed through the ship, and it rocked violently to the side.

The singing abruptly halted. A scuffle followed—then two thuds.

"Let's go." Jamie immediately ran around the corner, Ethan following.

Stella shrugged to no one in particular since the men had all rounded the corner, which surprised her at their assumption that Fitz was the obvious victor. She peeked around the corner. Two men were on the ground, the other three hovered, waiting for her. She scurried down the hall, smiling at being with the winning team. Then she sobered—they were far from success.

She stepped over the fallen men and pointed to the room on her left. "We were held in there."

Fitz was tying the men's hands behind their backs. He had a bundle of rags that she assumed would be stuffed into their mouths to keep them from calling out. "They were standing in front of this one." He jerked his thumb to the one across the way.

Ethan opened the door and looked in before throwing it wide.

She was right behind him, peering around his shoulder, then let out a small squeal as she raced across the room.

Beckworth's legs were chained to the chair, but his arms were raised above his head and manacled to chains hanging from the ceiling.

"It's about bloody, time." Beckworth's words were rough, and she cringed at the swollen eye and cracked lips.

It didn't matter. The first thing she did was kiss him. At first quick, but then it lingered, and she felt his heat rise. Then she released him and ran a gentle hand over his face. "I'm sorry it took so long to find you."

"Are you able to walk?" Jamie asked. He checked the manacles. "These are locked."

"We should be able to get those opened," Fitz said.

"Not well, my back aches something wicked, and my head isn't much better. But I'll do whatever I need to get out of here."

"I'll check the path to the upper deck." Ethan ran off.

Stella ran to the door in time to see him turn left at the end of the hallway. When she spun around, the men were attempting to open the locks. They were taking too long.

She took a last peek out the door, and when the men were still struggling with the locks, she sighed. "Oh, for god's sake, let me."

She knelt by Beckworth's legs and pulled a hairpin from her hair. "Watch the door."

"I've got it, lass." Fitz leaned against the wall, peering out every few seconds.

"That's not the one I gave you."

She glanced up at Beckworth. "I'm not wearing it. The last thing I want to do is lose it breaking you out of here." She finessed the pin until she felt the lock give. Once she pulled the lock off and released the manacle, she moved to the next one.

"Where'd you learn to do that?" Jamie asked, and she heard the admiration in his voice.

She grinned as she worked on the second one. "Let's just say I didn't have a stellar reputation in my youth. I tend to be nosy."

"Teddy!" Gemini's shout froze everyone.

They looked up. The word had drifted in from an upper hatch she hadn't noticed.

"If you think I'm going to let anyone take my husband, you roaches are sadly mistaken."

18

Stella stared at Beckworth and frowned. "What is she talking about?"

"It's not what it sounds like, just get me out of these chains." Beckworth tugged at the manacles on his wrist and then glanced at Fitz.

"We're still clear," Fitz said from the doorway. "But not for long."

"It sounds like you have a wife." Stella's chest ached at the thought. And Gemini? What was she up to?

Beckworth huffed and grimaced as he moved a foot around, then tried the other one. Jamie managed to unlock one of his wrist chains. His arm seemed painful as he slowly lowered it, but when he tried to shake it to get the blood circulating, he groaned. "Now, is not the time. I'll explain everything once we get someplace safe."

"I want to hear it now."

Jamie and Fitz looked at each other. Stella ignored them.

"The faster you explain, the faster we'll be on our way to the waiting coach." Her tone was hard, and Beckworth squirmed.

"She falsified my signature, hoping it was enough to pass the magistrate's inspection. It won't be."

"Uh-huh. Was the marriage consummated?"

Beckworth paled. Jamie hid a smile, and Fitz snickered from the door.

"Of course, not. You know I hate that woman."

"It's quite possible for a body to react on its own with the right stimuli, regardless if you want it to."

"My god, woman. Can we not discuss this here and now? I need to get off this bloody ship."

Jamie was having difficulties holding in his laughter. "He's right, Stella. I know we have a second diversion, but it's best if we don't risk it."

Stella released the lock and removed the last manacle. "I just wanted to make sure we were taking this risk for a reason. You know, in case he was just in denial and preferred to stay."

"Teddy, my love." Gemini's voice was sickly sweet. "You promised to make love to me in the middle of your beautiful gardens under the moonlight. Our passion knows no bounds."

She had enough of that bitch. Since she couldn't do anything about her for the moment, she took it out on the one person she could. She stood, her anger boiling at the off chance something happened between them, even if Beckworth wasn't willing. It wasn't fair, she knew it, but she couldn't stop herself. She slapped him, then turned for the door, shaking her hand that hurt like hell. She'd put more into it than she planned and was shocked by her own behavior. All the fear that had been pent-up since watching him fall under Gaines's two-by-four had blindly surged through her.

She reached for her pistol and drew it out as she took Fitz's place at the door. Their escape would be the most dangerous. With Gemini back onboard, it was likely Gaines wasn't far away.

Ethan raced toward them from the far end of the hall. "We need to go back to the other stairwell."

Stella waited for him, her pistol aimed at whoever might have followed him. She glanced over her shoulder to see Beckworth being half-dragged by Fitz and Jamie. He was deathly pale, his face screwed up into a pain-filled mask. He would probably pass out before they made it to the coach.

She didn't want to shoot anyone. But as Ethan directed her to follow the men, Beckworth's wrecked body slumped between them, she knew without a doubt that she'd put a ball through that woman if she didn't stay out of her way.

Beckworth winced at the pulsing pain in his cheek. It wouldn't surprise him if she'd left a mark. He was lucky she hadn't used a fist, or Jamie might be carrying him out over his shoulder. His back throbbed in agony, and his headache had returned. The slap hadn't helped, and he refused to think about his tender ribs.

Stella barely glanced at him, and when she did, it was only for a second. He didn't think it had anything to do with Gemini's claims. She knew him better than that. Her anger was a reaction to her fear, and most likely the ghastly figure he made. He wanted to walk out on his own, but his muscles were weak, and he doubted he'd be able to crawl, even if he had all night.

He focused on the kiss she'd given him when she'd first stormed into the room. It was the best thing he'd tasted in days. And even with Gemini's claim, everything would work itself out, assuming they got off the ship. He was surprised Stella had been included in the rescue, but she was familiar with the ship, and he doubted anyone could have stopped her if they'd tried.

When they reached the next passageway, Gemini yelled for him again.

"I'm coming, darling. It won't be much longer."

"That's why I'm still single," Fitz said. "Wives can be demanding." He somehow managed to keep a straight face. "You know I had a bit of a taste of your missus, back when she was Lady Prescott. And I have to say, she was rather demanding in bed as well. You'll need your stamina for that."

And with a wink and a chortle, he leaned Beckworth against Jamie. "I'll go first and clear out a path." He raced toward the stairs and disappeared. A few seconds later, he popped his head out of the stairwell and called back, "Still clear for now."

Beckworth felt the vibration of the laughter Jamie was managing to hold in. Stella's lips twitched, though her face was filled with mixed emotions—humor, uncertainty, and rage.

He cried out in pain when they reached the stairs, and she was there. Her arm wrapped around his middle, and her lavender scent enveloped him.

"Put your arm around my shoulder." She clung to him, and for a moment, he wasn't sure who was helping who. "Jamie and I will try to do most of the work, but this is going to hurt, and there's nothing we can do about it. You just need to hold on a bit longer."

The climb to the top deck was slow and awkward in the close quarters. Jamie led, and Beckworth hung at an angle between him and Stella. He almost bit his tongue when the ship rocked from a second explosion. Though the sound was muffled, this blast was much closer.

Fitz waited until they reached the top of the stairs before peering out the door. A cool draft floated down—the smell of freedom laced with the heavy scent of gunpowder. He'd been right. The explosion had been close. Enough to scare the sailors and Gemini's men away and provide them the cover of smoke.

Then the door was thrown open, and the wan light from the moon revealed Jamie's determined expression. He held a pistol in his free hand, and when Beckworth glanced down at Stella, who still bore his weight, he noted the primed pistol in hers as well.

"I hear men coming," Ethan said from behind Stella. "They'll be at the stairs soon."

Fitz must have heard him because they were suddenly moving. Yells from men reached him before he exited the staircase. Most were commands to save the sails from the fire. If Gemini was still out there, her voice was drowned out by the others. Thank heavens for small miracles.

Jamie moved across the deck quickly, and Stella kept up so he wasn't pulled apart between them. He must have screamed at some point because she shouted above the other voices. "I know it hurts. I'm so sorry. It won't be much longer."

The pain in her voice made him bear the agony as they came to an abrupt halt. Fitz had engaged a mercenary, their blades clashing. Jamie fired a shot, then slid the pistol into a holster before pulling out a second one. The first shot must have counted because they moved a couple of steps.

Fitz swung his blade with power and precision, driving the opponent back. The mercenary was so focused on defending himself, he wasn't watching his footing, and he fell across a pile of rope. Fitz sliced an opening in the man's chest. It was far from a killing blow, but it would sting for some time. Fitz picked up the man's sword and threw it overboard.

Beckworth's eyes widened when he shifted his gaze to the six men blocking their path to the gangway.

"Don't worry." Stella's raised voice was filled with confidence, though she kept glancing at Jamie. "We don't have much farther."

The words were barely out of her mouth when an arrow pierced the chest of one of the men closest to them. He dropped to his knees as a second one burrowed into a man on the far side of the group. Lando burst out of the darkness, taking down another mercenary in the time it took to blink. Then Finn, Thomas, and two others he recognized were on them. Gemini's men didn't have a chance.

Ethan pushed them forward. "We're clear back here. The fire has them preoccupied, but I haven't seen Gemini."

"She most likely went downstairs, thinking we hadn't gotten Beckworth out of his chains," Jamie said. "She'll be coming up the same stairs we did. Watch your back."

They picked their way over the fallen men and reached the gangway. He must have fallen in and out of consciousness for the remaining rescue because he only remembered bits and pieces—Stella's calming voice, Finn lifting his head to get a look at the damage, AJ's questions of concern, Barrington's deep frown, a coach, and then stairs. Too many blasted stairs.

Then he was laid on a soft, sweet-smelling bed. His body relaxed a fraction as his clothes were removed. A warm cloth wiped gently at his face, dabbing softly at his swollen eye.

He opened his good one. Stella was there. Her eyes glistened, and her brow wrinkled with concern. She ran the towel over his forehead and cheeks again.

"It's okay. You're safe now. I'm so sorry."

He wished he had the strength to lift his hand and wipe away her tears. She had nothing to be sorry about. She had come. That was all that mattered.

Then arms took her away, and Maire was there, holding a cup.

"Drink this. You need water." He drank the liquid and then coughed, almost spitting it out.

"That's not water." His voice sounded rougher than before.

"I didn't say it was, just that you needed some. Though this does have water in it."

Then her face disappeared to be replaced by one of a grizzled old man. Bart.

"Bite onto this." He shoved a smooth, round stick in his mouth. "This is going to hurt."

19

Beckworth opened an eye. His other must have still been swollen, but when he raised his hand to check, he found a bandage covering it. He glanced to his left to find a head of auburn hair. Stella was seated next to his bed, holding onto his arm as she slept.

He glanced around the room. It appeared to be the guest suite at Lord Templeton's manor, a good friend of his who was rarely in London. Beckworth was free to use it whenever he was in town, as long as it was unoccupied. A fire burned in the hearth and cast a glow over the sleeping form of a young man in a chair. Lincoln. He remembered seeing Bart and Maire. Barrington must be in town and had the manor opened for them. He vaguely remembered seeing him in a blur of images during the rescue.

He didn't see Maire but assumed she would have left with Ethan for the evening. The drapes were pulled so he couldn't discern the time of day, and though he didn't think he'd been out long, it had to be close to dawn.

He ran a hand over Stella's hair, his fingers rubbing a lock. The leaf hairpin, along with several other pins, held her hair in place, though several strands had leaked out. She'd been through quite the ordeal, and he was eager to hear about the rescue, and so much more.

She stirred and lifted her head. Huge green eyes stared at him, then a hint of a smile.

"You're awake."

It was a simple statement, her voice rough from sleep, but to him, it meant only one thing—you're back, and you're safe. She rose to a sitting position and cried out, her hand reaching for her neck.

"I must have fallen asleep." She rubbed it as she bent her head back and forth then glanced around the room before her gaze fell back on him. "How do you feel? Do you want some water?"

For the moment, he was content to watch her as her brows came together to form a crease over her nose. Her lips contorted from a smile to a frown then to a smirk.

"I'm real. In case you think you're hallucinating. The hit to your head could have been a lot worse from what Bart said, but it was still a good enough wallop that you've probably been living with a mild concussion. That would explain the headaches."

Her eyes darted to the side, then roamed around the room again. He waited, anticipating bad news. She heaved a sigh and took his hand.

"Your back took more damage, but we're not sure to what extent. Bart felt a misalignment in your spine. He made some adjustments that I doubt you remember. You passed out pretty quickly when he started. You seem to have reflexes in your toes, which is a good sign, but Bart needed you awake to finish his exam."

She stopped talking but kept a grip on his hand. Then she tilted her head. "I heard you speak last night, so I assume Bart didn't do anything to block your vocal cords. Though from what Finn and AJ tell me about Maire's concoctions, they might have burnt a hole in your throat."

He smiled. "I just wanted to look at you. Make sure you were real."

She rolled her eyes. "Of course, I'm real. I told you that earlier. Are you thirsty yet?"

He nodded, then took stock of his physical condition while she stood and stretched her back after her awkward sleeping position. His fingers and arms were sore but seemed to function properly, though they felt as heavy as lead weights. He shifted and winced; his back hurt, but not nearly as much as it had. Whether that was from Bart's ministrations or whatever drugs and herbs he and Maire used on him, it was too early to tell. He tried to lift a leg but stopped when the pain increased. The fact they moved at all had to be a good sign. With any luck, all he required was time to strengthen them.

She returned from the dresser where a pitcher of water, a basin, and several jars, vials, and pouches sat. "Let's see if you can sit up without any pain." She set down the glass of water and helped pull him to a sitting position but stopped the minute he groaned.

"It's alright, keep going." His breath came out in a rush, and he squinted through a twitch of pain.

She stuffed pillows behind his back before letting him relax against them. "Does that cause too much pressure on your back?"

"No."

"You're not lying to me, are you?"

He grunted. "There was pain when I moved, but it's calming down now, so I assume it's not the new position."

"Alright. Here, let's see if you can drink this without making a mess." She draped a linen towel under his chin.

He managed to get several swallows without spilling anything before she took it away. She wiped his chin where a few drops clung.

"Let that settle before you drink more."

"How long?"

She considered the question. "Since you were taken?" She winced when she said the words. When he nodded, she said, "A little over a week."

It had seemed longer.

"You've only been asleep for a few hours. Maire went back to Hensley's with Ethan, Finn, and AJ. Sebastian is still here. He sat with you while Bart was working on you. He was quite worried." She fussed with the glasses and jars on the bedside table. "Lincoln has been like a watchdog. Eleanor is probably in the kitchen. She never seems to sleep, so I expect she'll be here soon. Hopefully, Barrington is getting much-needed rest."

"How many people are here?"

"That's everyone. Other than Thomas and his men, who are staying at the earl's London house. They'll be by later today. I think they're monitoring both manors to make sure Gemini doesn't send men. There were a few watching Hensley's manor, probably since the first time we escaped Gemini, but he had them removed before we began grouping for the rescue."

She gave him more water, and when his stomach growled, their eyes met. They laughed.

"I suppose that's a good sign." She began to stand when he pulled her back down.

"Just sit with me a while."

She ran a hand over his face, then the tears dropped. Just a few, like leftover raindrops after a storm.

"It wasn't your fault." When she shook her head, he squeezed her hand. "We were vastly outnumbered. It would have been a miracle if someone hadn't found you on the roof."

"They didn't."

When his gaze widened, she continued. "I was off the roof, running for our meeting spot, when someone grabbed me. I was watching the streets and alleys, but he seemed to jump up from out of nowhere. Then a second one grabbed my arms." Another sigh escaped along with a few more tears. "If I'd had a dagger, I could have stabbed the first guy before the second one had a chance."

"No recriminations. It all worked out."

She wiped her eyes, and then her nose. "Not as we planned."

"It doesn't always go as planned."

"That's what AJ and Finn said."

He snorted. "They would know. How are Morton and Lewelyn?"

"They're fine. They'd been at the meeting place, then came looking for us."

A knock startled them, and Lincoln jumped up, almost tripping over his long legs and the blanket that had covered his lap.

The door opened, and Eleanor stuck her head in. When she saw Beckworth, she smiled and pushed through with a tray in her hands, which Lincoln immediately took.

"I thought Stella could use some coffee, and I made a broth in case you were awake." She stormed to the bed and looked him over. "You're pale. Nothing some sun and fresh air won't cure. How's your back?"

"It still hurts but not as badly as it had."

"Bart will up be up soon to do an exam. Can you feel your toes?"

He wiggled them. "I think they're moving."

She looked at Stella, who set down her cup, and they each stood at a corner of the bed as they pulled up the blankets until his feet felt the cool air of the room.

"Wiggle them," Eleanor demanded.

He did as she commanded and watched the women's eyes since the blankets hid his feet from view. Both women nodded and smiled, and he leaned back, air rushing out. He thought his back was alright, but their pleased responses gave him more encouragement than any words could.

"It's definitely a good sign, but we'll let Bart have the final say." Eleanor brought over the broth. "Just a few spoonfuls, then I'll keep the rest warm by the fire."

"It's nice of you to let me use my skills for something, old woman." Bart pushed past her. "Why don't you women find something to do?" He took a long look at Stella. "You." He pointed at her. "Go get some sleep. You're no good to him or yourself."

When Stella's expression turned stubborn, Bart refused to be overruled. "I'm going to do an exam. Lincoln will help. Then he'll get a draught that will knock him out. You might as well get some sleep so you're not so bullheaded."

Stella glared at him, but glanced at Eleanor and then at Beckworth. "Alright. But just a nap." She put the pot of coffee by the fire and then leaned over him.

"My room is just across the hall."

"You already have a room here?"

"I've been staying here the last few days. Get some rest, and we'll catch up." She brushed his hair from his forehead and bent to give him a kiss. It was gentle but lingered for several seconds. It was as sweet as he remembered.

"I expect good news." She gave Bart a stern look, but he just waved her off.

"Everyone expects miracles."

Beckworth watched her until the door closed before resting his head against the pillows.

Bart glanced at Eleanor. "You, too." They stared at each other.

"I've already slept, but I'll give you time to do your exam while I check on breakfast." She gave Beckworth's arm a squeeze. "I'll return soon."

"Enough pampering. Let's see how much damage we're working with." Bart smiled down at him, and it wasn't one of his pleasant ones.

Stella rolled over and stared at the fire. It burned low but provided enough heat for the cooler spring mornings. For as much as she hadn't wanted to leave Beckworth's side, she'd collapsed on the bed as soon as she'd entered the room. Someone woke her when they placed a log on the dying fire not long after she crashed, and when she managed to open an eye, she was surprised it was Eleanor. Did that woman ever sleep?

She'd wanted to ask her how Beckworth was doing, but her limbs were dead weight, and she couldn't keep her eyes open. It had been the final release of the stress that had plagued her since Ipswich. She pushed herself up and noticed that someone had covered her with a blanket. That, too, must have been Eleanor.

The floor was warm under her feet, and she pushed the drapes aside as the midday sun blinded her for several seconds. She glanced down at the front of the manor as she pulled off her shirt, leaving her in a chemise and pants.

Barrington jogged down the steps and got into a carriage. She didn't recognize the driver. He could be going to Hensley's or Chester's. For all she knew, he was going to a tailor to have new clothes made for Beckworth. Then her heart sank. Or to a lawyer to determine Beckworth's marital status.

What was the reason for Gemini's subterfuge? For his

money, or to bring her a step closer to the scribes and the Heart Stone? There were a dozen possibilities, yet something nagged. It was elusive, and she'd remember it faster if she didn't push for an answer.

She was unbuttoning her pants when a knock was quickly followed by the door opening. A head popped around the door.

"Are you ready for visitors?" Eleanor pushed the door wider and brought in a tray. "I was just checking on Beckworth and thought I'd better make sure you were alright."

"How is he?"

"He's sleeping again, but Bart feels more optimistic this morning." She fussed with preparing a plate, adding small portions from a few bowls, then poured coffee into a large mug typically used for ale. "He has feeling in both feet and all his toes. Bart suspects the hit to his back misaligned his spine, and he adjusted it. Now, Beckworth needs time to heal. In order to do that, he must take a few steps in his room several times a day to gain his strength back."

"Staying in bed will work for a short time, but that won't last for long."

"That is a concern. Bart won't want him doing too much too fast. It could do more harm than good." Eleanor hung the coffee pot by the hearth. "Come sit and eat something."

Stella had changed out of her pants, opting for a simple dark-pink day dress that matched her personal taste and was a color Beckworth liked. She plopped down at the small table where two place settings had been set. "You're eating, too?"

"I do need the occasional meal."

Stella laughed. "Even when we stayed with you, you rarely seemed to eat."

The silence expanded as they ate, neither seeming to mind. Stella got up to refill her mug. "I should go downstairs and get a new pot."

"Lincoln took one to Beckworth's room. You'll want to check on him. He should wake in an hour or so."

Stella bit her lip. "I imagine some of his friends will be by to check on him."

Eleanor chewed a piece of bacon and eyed her to the point she wanted to squirm. "He doesn't blame you."

She rubbed her hands together, glancing around for her stack of paper, and realized she'd used it all. "I know. That's what he told me."

"You don't believe him."

She shrugged and stacked the dirty dishes. "It's hard to see him lying in bed knowing he's like that because he traded himself for me."

"Do you think Barrington and Chester feel the same way?"

The question surprised her, though it had been a concern when she'd first reached out to Chester. "They don't seem to."

When she began wiping a plate with a napkin, Eleanor took Stella's hand. "For all his eccentricities, he's not that complicated of a man."

She snorted. "Most aren't."

Eleanor chuckled. "See, you know the truth. He's loyal, can be stubborn, but he's always been forgiving." She squeezed Stella's hand tighter. "And I'm not saying there's anything to forgive. He's been at these games far longer than you. From what I hear, you were greatly outnumbered. It could have easily been Beckworth or one of Hensley's men who were caught." Her smile turned wily. "I heard you bit one of them."

That made her smile. "Nasty tasting, but it was worth it."

"Don't shy away from him now when he needs you the most."

"What do you mean?"

"Bart and I can tell him what he should or shouldn't do to

heal. As you said, he won't be happy stuck in bed and will do what he wants—with one exception. He'll listen to you."

She wasn't convinced of that, but Eleanor had known Beckworth for years. And she wasn't the type to lie. That wasn't something Stella appreciated about her and Bart. They said what they thought without caring if the person was ready to hear it. She was the same way, except she tended to add a shiny spin to the truth. Something she'd learned as a broker that had become second nature. Why couldn't that be applied to getting Beckworth healthy?

The question was how. He might be the simple man that Eleanor claimed him to be, but he would require stimuli to keep him from going crazy. She tapped her fingers on the table.

"I need more coffee. Then a coach. I have some shopping to do."

After Eleanor had left with the tray, Stella called for her lady's maid to help with her hair. Once she was presentable for being in public, she stopped to check on Beckworth. Bart and Lincoln were in his room playing chess. Beckworth was sleeping, and she tiptoed to the bed and sat in the chair that had been pulled up next to it.

She pushed a few locks of hair away from his forehead and felt his smooth skin. It was cool, just as it should be.

"He should be waking soon," Bart said, his eyes never leaving the board.

"That's what Eleanor said. You think all he needs is rest and exercise?"

"For the most part. Some fresh air when he can manage the stairs. He'll have some pain for a while. I'm making up medications for him, but you'll need to see that he takes them. That includes the sleeping draughts and the herbal concoctions Maire left."

"I need to do some shopping. Is Barrington back yet?"

"Not yet. Lincoln could take you, but he's not familiar with the shops."

"I know how to get to the mercantile and apothecary." Lincoln moved a bishop. "Check."

Bart growled. "I knew I shouldn't have taught you this game."

"Did you bring the chessboard or is that from downstairs?" Stella asked.

"It's my own. I don't like leaving without it. Why?"

"I think it would be helpful for Beckworth to have one nearby. I think Sebastian plays. And I'm going to check the books in the library and see if there are any he might be interested in."

Bart moved a rook. "That's a good idea."

A moment later, Lincoln said, "Checkmate."

Bart slapped the arm of the chair. "That wasn't a legal move."

"More legal than the last two moves you made." Lincoln chuckled and stood. "The coach is still here. Barrington went in another one. I'd be happy to drive you if you think the two stores I know of will have what you need."

"I think that would be perfect." She glanced at Beckworth, then at Bart. "Did you want to go with us? Or is there anything we can get for you while we're out?" She had taken a few coins from the pile she'd grabbed from Gemini's coin box. That nagging thought hit her again. It was so close, yet whatever she was trying to remember remained out of reach.

"Lincoln knows what I like. Surprise me."

She stood and touched Beckworth's hand. "We won't be long."

20

AJ stepped out of the coach and glanced up at the manor Beckworth sometimes leased while he was in London. She remembered the first time they'd stayed there. After all this time, she would have thought he'd have bought his own manor by now, but if he had this one to use whenever he needed it, she could understand not spending the money.

She hadn't seen much of him when he'd been assisted from the ship. Memories of Finn being dragged out of the dingy cell he'd been kept in gave her the shivers. Beckworth had only been held a week versus Finn's three months in captivity, but she'd cringed when she heard about the beating he'd taken with a two-by-four.

Maire thought he would be alright, but she had mentioned Bart's concern about whether his back injury would impact his ability to walk. If that became an issue, she couldn't imagine how he would take the news, and Stella would blame herself.

Finn took her elbow and led her up the steps. "I'm sure he'll be fine with rest. Jamie said he was able to bear some weight, he'd just been trussed up too long."

She nodded but didn't say anything as Ethan knocked on the door.

When the door opened, Barrington stood ramrod straight, and though he wore pants, shirt, and a leather vest rather than butler livery, he bowed. "Welcome."

"Playing butler?" Finn asked.

The group entered, and Barrington shut the door.

"I just came down from seeing to Beckworth and happened to be on my way to the kitchen."

"Is Stella here?" AJ glanced behind him and up the stairs. She didn't hear women's voices. Not even Eleanor's.

"I'm told Lincoln took the women shopping earlier today. They should be back soon."

"I forgot to thank you for your help last night." Finn held out his hand, and if Barrington found it surprising, he held his stoic expression and gripped it in return. "Is it alright if we go up?"

"He's awake, but a bit grumpy."

"Worse than Bart?" AJ smiled.

Barrington's lips twitched. "No one is grumpier than Bart."

"Truer words," Ethan mumbled.

"The hall to your left. Second door on the right." He turned and disappeared through a sitting room.

The group climbed the stairs and knocked lightly on the door. When there wasn't a response, Finn was preparing to knock again when Bart opened the door.

"Well, it's about time." Bart hobbled away as Finn led the group in. "I need to make up some more medications, but if I leave him alone too long, I don't trust he won't wander about the manor. He needs time on his feet, but short intervals, and he shouldn't traverse the stairs on his own."

"Enough, you old coot. I should know what I'm capable of." Beckworth's surly tone almost made AJ turn around to wait for

Stella in the sitting room, but Ethan and Maire blocked her escape, so she gave Beckworth a smile. Barrington wasn't wrong about his mental state, but she questioned who was the grumpier of the two.

Finn shook his hand. "You look pretty chipper. Better than I imagined when last I saw you."

Beckworth rubbed the back of his neck then scratched his head. "Better than what could have been the outcome if I'd been hit a few inches lower. Double the luck I missed most of the swing to my head."

AJ grimaced. "It had to have been painful all the same." She glanced at the bedside table and the myriad jars and vials. "And must still ache badly."

"What I wouldn't give for something out of Edith's medicine cabinet." Beckworth leaned back on the pillows, a twinge accompanying the change of position. AJ was surprised he mentioned one of the two sisters that cared for him when he was in Baywood. "The old woman had rows of little orange bottles. From what I gathered on the labels, a good portion of them were pain pills."

"I would think they'd pack more of a punch." Ethan waved Maire to a seat on the other side of the bed and dragged another one over. Instead, she reviewed the various items on the table.

"I'm not sure that's necessarily true," Maire said. "After researching the more modern medicines, I think I'd trust Bart's remedies."

"Leave the prescribing to Bart," Beckworth mumbled. "He gave me one of your tonics. I don't think I'll ever forget the nasty stuff."

The others nodded. They'd all spent time under Maire's loving care. AJ was fairly certain Maire made some of her herbal remedies taste worse than they needed to.

Maire grinned as she took her seat, unperturbed by the group's comments, which, to AJ, only proved her suspicions.

Finn moved two chairs to the bedside for himself and AJ. "Once again, it seems we have a lot to share with you." He relaxed into the chair and rested a leg over his knee. "We'd be happy to go first before you tell us your story. We want to hear the events leading up to the decision to board the *Phoenix* in Saint-Malo."

Beckworth chuckled, knowing full well that AJ wanted to confirm Stella's part in the decision, but that could wait. "Were you able to get the other two chronicles?"

Finn nodded and shared their travel across France, how they found and retrieved the chronicle, their short stop in Rouen to learn of Belato, and ending with Belato's men boarding their ship once they left LaHavre.

Ethan ran through the events of arriving in Southampton, where they heard about a fire on a ship and assumed it might have been Beckworth's doing, at which Beckworth gave a short nod, not willing to interrupt Ethan's recap. He continued with their stop at the earl's, then their surprise at how easy it had been to retrieve the second chronicle only to face an ambush outside Stokenchurch. He ended with their jump back to Baywood.

"Let me get this straight." Beckworth pushed himself up, then cried out when a back spasm made him freeze up. Maire was up in an instant, mixing herbs into a glass of water. She added a bit of white powder. Before handing it to him, she rubbed his back, slapping away his hand when he tried to wave her off.

"Don't be difficult." She appeared to be manipulating his spine, which made him grimace, but after a minute, his face relaxed. She handed him the glass. "Drink it all."

He obeyed, squinting as he took his first sip. He waited, then swallowed the rest down. "That wasn't half bad." Then he squinted again. "What was that white powder?"

"It's for pain, but you should be sleeping like a baby in an hour. So let's get on with it." She returned to her seat.

Beckworth squirmed until he found a comfortable spot then turned to Maire. "You were able to modify the incantation in order for you to return to the correct location and date?"

"I wouldn't have without the second chronicle. But without testing it one or two more times, I can't guarantee how reliable it will be."

"Intriguing." Beckworth leaned forward, a light sheen on his forehead. "Was it a slight change in the incantation you used when you all first arrived in Hereford? I believe you updated the one Gaines left for you. Or did you start over with his?"

Maire considered his question. "A little of both, I suppose, with the help of my notes from the druid's grimoire. Celtic words aren't typically that precise, but if you transpose today's calendar with the one the druids used, the date is more accurate."

"And you did it all with one of the smaller stones." Beckworth digested it, and AJ would have asked what he was thinking, but Finn spoke first, dragging them to a new topic.

"So, what happened in Saint-Malo?"

Beckworth leaned back and wiped his brow. He wouldn't have thought one could become tired lying around in bed. The ache in his back that had begun as a dull pain when the group first arrived had increased. The slightest of movements stabbed like a knife, but the unexpected spasms were the worst. The only light on the horizon was that his headaches had decreased, which Bart attributed to one of the herbal mixtures Maire had provided. They were the worst tasting, and if they hadn't proved to be helpful, he would have poured them into the bedpan when Bart wasn't looking.

The other positive note was his ability to get out of bed and take a few steps before he tired, though it didn't come without pain. Bart insisted time was all he required before he'd be back to his old self. But would it be soon enough? Gemini and her crazed brother were out there, and he wasn't happy being sidelined for what was still to come.

"Could I have some water? And perhaps a nip of whiskey." Beckworth's plea was met with sympathy from the men.

The women glanced at each other, most likely questioning the wisdom of mixing whiskey with Bart's white powder. But Murphy handed him the water and then walked to a sideboard where a couple of decanters sat. He poured three glasses of whiskey and raised one toward AJ, who shook her head, as did Maire.

After drinking a portion down, Beckworth wiped his mouth, then his brow, and settled back to tell his tale.

"I didn't think it wise to board the *Phoenix,* but we couldn't leave without Sebastian. I could have gone alone, but it would have taken longer to find him, and it might have all been for nothing. Although we couldn't be sure of Stella's information on when the ship was to set sail, we didn't have a choice. Either way, she was determined to return for Sebastian, and unless Lando physically restrained her, we had to let her go. It was quite the sight to watch her scamper back up a stack of crates to enter through a gunport. I had to admire her ingenuity if not her determination." He shared their short trip across the Channel, how he'd evaded notice during the journey, and their eventual escape.

"What I couldn't understand was why we weren't chased by Gemini's men, since I'd assumed they wanted Sebastian. She had men watching Waverly, and one unfortunate man saw me leave through the woods on my way back to Eleanor's. He surprised Stella when she was out walking, and I had no choice. I couldn't let him lead others to Eleanor's."

He stopped to take a drink and assess his guests' thoughts. They all nodded, agreeing with his actions, and he inwardly sighed. Stella and Sebastian had said he wasn't to blame, and that had been enough for him, but it was still gratifying to know the others would have made the same decision. It bothered him that he cared what these four thought, and he wasn't sure when that had happened.

He'd always been concerned about what his mother thought of him and his choice of work, and she'd never given him any reason to doubt her love and acceptance. Then he'd wasted years trying to gain the same approval from his father. A man, he discovered too late, who had no capacity for either emotion. The only positive thing he'd gained from his unscrupulous time with the man was his title. For that he was grateful. And if anyone were to ask the old widow he'd purchased Waverly from, she was happy to be rid of it.

"The trip to London was uneventful, and while we waited for word from Ipswich and your teams, we enjoyed Hensley and Mary's hospitality while participating in a handful of social engagements." He smiled at AJ. "You should have seen Stella dressed for a ball." Then he laughed out loud, which ended in a short spasm, and he pointed to his whiskey glass, which Murphy refilled.

"Has Mary shared the story of her dinner party the first day we arrived?"

They shook their heads.

"I'd say have Stella tell you, but I think Mary would provide a better tale. As I'd always thought, Stella and Elizabeth got along famously. But the best part was how easily Stella responded to Agatha's barbs."

AJ groaned. "How I would have loved to have been there for that. Did they stay long? I imagine that could have been a trying time."

He cocked his head as he considered the weekend, and he couldn't help another smile. "One would have thought so. Mary took everyone out to lunch, and when they returned, the women appeared to be getting along. It makes sense, though. Stella is as bold as Elizabeth, as you know, and I think that's what keeps Agatha in check." He gave AJ an apologetic grin before adding, "She tends to go after the weaker ones."

AJ frowned, but after a moment, she nodded. "I think we can all agree I wasn't at my best when we visited Waverly for the first time."

Beckworth held up his glass of whiskey. "I believe that was true for all of us."

"What made you try for Ipswich without waiting for the rest of us?" Murphy asked.

"It wasn't an easy decision. Hensley sent men to investigate and discovered Belato's ship was in port. It appeared Gemini was amassing a small army. When the days went by with no word from anyone, we feared you'd either run into trouble or were having difficulties finding the chronicles. We thought a small team would be best."

"It makes sense," Hughes said. "With a handful of people, it's harder to distinguish their intent, assuming they're discovered in the first place."

"The plan was to investigate and, if we thought it possible, grab the chronicle. But we learned that the blacksmith had been found and tortured. We didn't know he was dead until I was inside. At that point, we were committed."

"I still don't understand why you let Stella go with you to Ipswich." AJ's expression was defiant. She expected a definitive reason.

He didn't have one to give her, so he shrugged. "Hensley and I thought it best she remain behind, but she insisted, and quite frankly, she's an excellent shot with a firearm."

"Putting aside why you taught her how to fire a flintlock in the first place, why didn't you just tell her no?" AJ's voice rose as she made her case, her tone growing harsher.

"Have you met her?" Beckworth's tone was equally sharp.

The others glanced at each other and then grinned at understanding Beckworth's dilemma.

"I think we all know it would have been a difficult discussion." Murphy played the diplomat.

AJ glared at Beckworth, and he scowled right back. She was obviously upset as if he could simply say the right word and everything that happened would be erased. He'd been equally irritated by Stella's incessant need to be included, but he wouldn't have changed a minute of it. And that was the difference.

He sat back, lowering his gaze to the book Stella had left for him before he woke that morning. It was *Travels into Several Remote Nations of the World. In Four Parts.* It was written by Jonathan Swift. He had a later version of it in his library titled *Gulliver's Travels.* It had been an interesting selection.

"As far as the flintlock, I taught her how to load it early on, while we were still making our way to Southampton. She'd felt defenseless and wanted to feel safe if we were parted." He gave AJ a pointed stare. "Most likely the same feeling you had the first time you hefted that dagger of yours." He absently rubbed his shoulder where she'd stabbed him twice before. She had the good grace to lower her gaze.

"As far as Ipswich, we made the decision together, as we have ever since leaving Saint-Malo." He opened the cover and touched the swan Stella had left inside. He smiled. "To be honest, Sebastian wasn't any easier to keep out of trouble. He's as stubborn as the lot of you. The thing is, it's done. I can't change what happened, even if I wanted to."

He looked up, catching AJ's gaze.

It had softened, and she swallowed before nodding. She reached out her hand which he squeezed before letting go. "We're good. I thought the two of you would be like oil and water together. It's taken some time for me to realize your similarities. If I hadn't been so worried for her, I would have seen it before now."

"That's one too many heads butting together for me," Hughes said. His tone was light.

"And something I think we're all familiar with, considering our team." Maire gave Beckworth a pointed look, which only made him grin.

"I just couldn't understand what made her ride to the East End on her own." AJ pulled at her lip, though she gave Beckworth a quick glance.

Before he could ask what she was talking about, Murphy interrupted. "Can you tell us about your time on the *Phoenix*?"

"Not much to tell." Beckworth didn't want to think about Gemini or her cloying behavior. "The first couple of days are a haze. The pain was incredible, and she fed me laudanum."

"It's a wonder you remember anything with that vile stuff." Maire's response was reasonable, considering her predilection for herbal remedies.

"When she lessened the frequency, I still wasn't very coherent, but I picked up enough to know she and her brother aren't as close as one might expect. Whatever her faults, Gemini is the brains of the group. I think her brother was damaged being raised by his uncle." He turned to Murphy. "From what you discovered in Rouen, it sounds like the Belatos have never been good with planning."

"It's been enough to keep the duke and Dugan in play," Hughes pointed out.

Beckworth partially agreed with the statement. "I think the older Belato's original idea of stealing the stones and *The Book of Stones* was sound from his point of view. But I believe Gemini has been the key all along. And for all his brute strength, Dugan played a large part in manipulating Reginald. The duke might have only been given the tidbits, but he can be formidable in his strategy. His madness was his downfall. And apparently, the same could be said of the Belatos. I don't know who raised Gemini, but she learned at an early age how to get what she wanted and how to plan for the long game."

"Did she provide any clue as to what that game might be?" Murphy asked.

Beckworth rubbed his head as he tried to remember. "Between the whiskey and the potion Maire gave me, Bart's white powder seems to be working. Let me think on it."

Maire stood and motioned for the others to get up. "Some sleep should clear his brain."

Beckworth grabbed AJ's hand when she bent to kiss his cheek. "Whatever you do, don't send Stella home until I've had a chance to say goodbye."

He wasn't sure what passed in her gaze, but she shook her head. "I don't think my opinion matters in this case. She has no intention of leaving until the business with Gemini is over. She tends to hold grudges." She gave his cheek another kiss.

Once the door closed behind him, he picked up the swan and closed his eyes.

21

Stella talked Eleanor into going shopping. It served several purposes. First, she didn't think Eleanor had been out of the manor since arriving in London, with the exception of going to Hensley's manor, and second, Eleanor knew London better than she or Lincoln, even if it had been years since she'd been back.

Their first stop was the mercantile where she bought two bundles of paper. When they came out of the store with a few other things Eleanor had purchased, Lincoln took their packages and stored them in the coach. He'd struck up a conversation with two other drivers, so they left him to his new friends as they walked the street. They stopped at the apothecary to pick up a few items Lincoln thought Bart was running out of.

The kid was sharp, and from what Eleanor said, was learning from Bart to one day work in the field of medicine. Bart still had enough clout with the College of Surgeons to have Lincoln listed as an apprentice.

The two women chatted about trivial things until something in a shop window caught Stella's eye.

"Let's go in here." She tugged Eleanor with her.

"What did you see?"

"Something I'm sure no one will be happy about."

Eleanor seemed intrigued as Stella glanced about, finding a small display case at the back of the shop with items similar to the one that had captured her attention in the front window.

Eleanor's brow lifted. "Beckworth probably has several daggers with him."

She nodded. "So does AJ, but I want my own. One that fits me." The case had several, most of them too large, but two smaller ones looked interesting.

The shopkeeper finished with another customer and wandered over. He was a big man with a hefty stomach and surprisingly dainty hands. His spectacles perched at the end of his nose as he glanced down at the display.

"We have a fine collection of knives. Is this a gift for your husband? Perhaps your father?"

"It's for me."

"Aah. For personal defense, no?"

"That's right." Most of them were too large, but she tapped the glass at the six-inch blade with an etched silver handle.

The men frowned but took it out. "The size is about right, but I think you'll find the handle a bit heavy."

He handed the hilt toward her.

It was heavy. She didn't know the first thing about knives but had seen AJ train with hers. She waved it in short arcs, and her wrist felt the weight. After five minutes of training, she wouldn't be able to hold it.

"You're right. Definitely too heavy."

She tried a couple of others but wasn't satisfied. The shopkeeper seemed to sense she was ready to move on when he placed a finger by his nose as if he was thinking.

"I have a few items that just came in. If you don't mind waiting a few minutes, I think there was something that might be what you're looking for."

Eleanor had lost interest and wandered the shop. So, Stella nodded. It wouldn't hurt to wait a few minutes rather than find another store. She didn't want to go home empty-handed.

The shopkeeper returned five minutes later with a tray holding three daggers. "These are a bit more expensive than the others, but I think are better suited for you."

They were definitely more what she had in mind, and her eye immediately went to the bone-handled dagger with a double-edged blade. She pointed to it, and he smiled.

"Exactly the one I was thinking of when I remembered them." He handed it to her.

The handle seemed molded for her hand. When she waved it around, it felt light. It felt perfect. Another customer strode by. He was tall and impeccably dressed, with iron-gray hair, pinched lips, and a disagreeable expression.

"What a beautiful piece. It would look wonderful in my collection." He peered down at her. "Not really something a proper lady should require. I know the streets seem more dangerous these days, but if you're nervous about such things, your husband shouldn't allow you out without proper protection."

The shopkeeper appeared to want to help her, but he glanced nervously at the man. She didn't know who the man was, but he might be a frequent buyer, and she didn't want to ruin the shopkeeper's business. She had to remember what era she was in.

"I'm quite comfortable walking these streets. I was just looking for something easier to handle while in public rather than this." She pulled out her pistol, and the man stepped back. "It only takes me a few minutes to reload, but the weight is cumbersome." She noticed Eleanor behind the man, holding her hand in front of her mouth, her eyes lit with humor.

The gentleman was clearly taken aback. It might have been

her American accent or her manners. Either way, he mumbled something and moved on.

The shopkeeper smiled, and without saying a word, handed her another one to try. She tried all three but tapped the bone-handled one. "I think this one will do. Does it come with a sheath?" She hoped she said that right but remembered Beckworth calling it that.

"Of course." He pulled out two. "If you plan on keeping it in your pocket, I would suggest this one."

She nodded. "I agree."

Eleanor stepped up and looked over her shoulder. "I think that's a fine piece. Do you know how to use it?"

"No. But it will give Beckworth something to do while he's recuperating."

"He's going to love it."

Stella and Eleanor returned from their shopping trip, missing AJ and Maire by fifteen minutes, but they'd left a dinner invitation and suggested they come early. Before going to her room, she stopped to check on Beckworth with Eleanor only steps behind her.

If she'd hoped to speak with him, she was too late. He was fast asleep. Eleanor cleaned up the room and fetched a fresh pitcher of water while Stella sat next to him. She studied his relaxed features and even breathing. At least the pain didn't follow him into his dreams.

She opened the drapes to let the sunshine brighten the room. He might be bedridden for the moment, but that didn't mean he had to lie around in darkness all day. They had found Bart and Sebastian playing chess in the library when they returned from shopping. Bart had been able to get Beckworth up for a few steps before his visitors arrived. If he should wake and want to attempt more steps, at least he could look out at the garden.

Unsure whether he would wake before she left for dinner, she set her purchases aside and called for her lady's maid. She took a long soak in a bath and had her hair washed. Mary would expect everyone to dress for dinner, so she chose the periwinkle dress Beckworth had made for her on their first day in London. It was the only evening dress she'd brought from Hensley's, having left the rest in her room at his manor. She should have the rest of her things brought over but wasn't sure how AJ would take it.

She snorted. If that was all she had to worry about.

Once she was dressed, she stared at the opal necklace in the mirror as she rubbed it between her fingers, comforted by its warmth. The memory of Beckworth removing it from her neck the first time they made love brought heat to her cheeks. With the loss of the third chronicle and Gemini still out there, there was much to do before returning home. Even with the updated incantation to return to the past, there was still a difference between the time spent here versus her own timeline. When Maire and Ethan had jumped to escape the ambush outside Stokenchurch, they'd only been gone three or four days according to Adam, compared to the weeks they'd been in this period.

So, there was nothing to worry about at home. Adam and Madelyn were monitoring her house and business, while Alexis, her backup broker, handled her clients. She'd made a decision to stop her intimate relations with Beckworth once they left for Ipswich.

Now that the mission was behind them, it could still be weeks before she went home. Could she really look at him every day and not want to do more than smile across the table from him at meals? She'd have to reconsider her previous decision about their relationship, assuming Beckworth was of like mind.

She grabbed her wrap and glanced at her new dagger, carefully stored in its sheath. It would stay here in her room until she learned some basics. The thought of taking it with her was tempting, but since all she could do was point and stick, which might be sufficient defense, it was just as likely the blade could end up stuck in her. That was enough incentive to leave it behind.

Before meeting Eleanor in the foyer, she decided to check in on Beckworth. She'd barely opened the door to her room when she heard the male laughter coming from his. The question of whether he was still sleeping had been answered.

When the first polite knock went unanswered, which wasn't a surprise considering the volume of voices from the other side of the door, she pounded.

"Come in." The voice was distorted over the laughing and could have come from anyone.

She peeked inside and choked on the smoke before taking a step. Four men lounged in chairs on either side of Beckworth. Jamie and Fitz on one side, the latter puffing on a pipe. Chester, on the other side of the bed, also puffed on a pipe, while next to him, Barrington smoked a cigar.

Beckworth was grinning, his eyes glassy from drink or medication, and mostly likely both. "Stella," he shouted over the laughing. The others turned, and they all called her name, somewhat in unison. An empty bottle of whiskey sat on the bedside table, a second one half gone.

She clucked her tongue, then considered the situation. This was the first time they'd been together since the rescue. A life-and-death situation for all of them after days of worry of ever finding him. She wasn't their mother. They were grown men, and she couldn't help but grin at Beckworth's silly expression.

He'd endured enough on her behalf; she wouldn't spoil this. But the smoke was another issue.

"Hello, boys." She strode in and went straight for the window she'd opened only a few hours earlier. It was closed, and the drapes were drawn. She pushed them aside and reopened the window a few inches to give the smoke an outlet.

The men groaned, which only made her chuckle.

"The dark suited us." It was the first time she'd seen Beckworth pout. He must have been an adorable kid with big ears and knock knees.

She reconsidered the drapes, then pulled them together, leaving enough of an opening to help dissipate some of the smoke. "That might be, but Bart will be up to check on you, and he's an old man who shouldn't be working in a smoke-filled room." There were several clean glasses on the dresser, and she took the empty ones from the men. "Did you want another round?"

They stared at her, and she gave them a polite smile, but inside she was laughing her ass off. It was apparent they couldn't decide if she was up to something or was expecting them to make their apologies and leave. She picked up the half-empty bottle and poured six glasses.

She passed them around, picked up her own, and held it high. It took a moment before they glanced at each other and then lifted theirs. "To a successful mission and Beckworth back home with the help of good friends." She downed hers, winced at the sharp kick and burn, then set the glass down. The men followed, still a bit confused.

"Leave the window how I left it until it gets too cold. It's still dark enough in here, but make sure you let your eyes get accustomed to the light when you step into the hall. We don't need you breaking your necks on the stairs. We still have enemies to vanquish."

She stepped next to Beckworth. He still wore a silly grin, but his gaze seemed warmer than when she'd first entered. "You're lucky Eleanor is coming to dinner with me."

"You're leaving?" he asked.

"For a few hours. Mary invited us to dinner, and I haven't spent much time with AJ and Maire." She tugged his blanket up, then gave the room another glance. "Have you all eaten?" They shook their heads. "I'll have food sent up before I leave. Something that will soak up that alcohol before everyone stumbles back home or to their ship."

She bent down and kissed Beckworth on his cheek. "Don't overdo it." Before she left, she gave the group one of her best realtor smiles. "Have a good night, boys."

Though still a bit shell-shocked, they all wore their own boyish grins as she waltzed out the door.

Once downstairs, she found Eleanor coming down the hall toward her. "Do you know what's going on in Beckworth's room?"

Eleanor nodded. "I had just opened the door to check on them when you made your toast then heard you mention food. I've asked one of the housemaids to inform the kitchen." She grinned. "They're probably still talking about the redheaded siren who encouraged them to stay rather than leave.

"That's my motto: always leave them guessing."

The two laughed as they left the manor for the waiting coach.

22

Stella returned from Hensley's manor several hours later. It was good to be with everyone as they spent two hours before dinner playing games in the sitting room. Beckworth was never far from her thoughts, but the conversation and laughter were enough to keep her mind from dwelling on him and his recovery.

No one spoke of Gemini or the mission. Hensley told stories of the first time he'd met Finn and the difficulties of taming the wild Irish sailor. It was all in jest, and Finn had a few of his own stories of dealing with a stodgy old Englishman.

Mary spoke of several parties she wanted the group to attend with her and Hensley, and a dinner party to be held at their manor with a handful of close friends. AJ paled, but after a glance at Stella, seemed to retrieve a bit of her backbone. Stella wasn't sure AJ would ever get over her anxiety around the mere mention of Agatha's name. Maybe Mary could include backyard games like dagger tosses and archery. After seeing AJ's skill at those events, Agatha might learn to hold her acerbic tongue.

On their way back to Beckworth's manor, Stella began formulating a plan with Eleanor. When they arrived, she stalked toward the library while Eleanor went up to check on Beckworth. She would ensure the room was clear of others so Stella could have private time with him, even if all he did was sleep.

She was surprised to find Barrington, Bart, and Lincoln together. Barrington was reading, and Bart and Lincoln played chess. They glanced up, took note of her, then went back to what they were doing. She pulled a chair over so she sat between them, which gained more interest from the men.

"I hate to bother you, but I need a moment of your time to discuss my plans for Beckworth." Now she had their immediate attention. Barrington put his book down, and the other two turned toward her, their gazes filled with suspicion. "Take it easy, gentlemen, I just wanted to discuss Beckworth's recovery."

Once she began laying out her ideas, however, she had their rapt interest, and after thirty minutes of discussion and minor adjustments, they all agreed. When she exited the library, Bart was still chortling when he went back to his game.

Her lady's maid was waiting for her and helped her out of her dress and into a nightgown. Stella ran a hand through her hair after all the hairpins had been removed. The opal necklace snuggled against her chest. The maid wanted to remove it, but she wanted to wear it for her visit with Beckworth. It was silly, but it felt right.

She waited after the maid had left, staring into the fire, chiding herself for being nervous. It was just Beckworth. But it was nighttime, and that alone added a layer of intimacy to the setting. She glanced down at her nightgown. Maybe she should put on a day dress, but instead she pulled out the moss-green robe that Beckworth found enticing.

The man was injured. He wasn't at death's door, but the last thing she wanted was to encourage thoughts of sex. He was a man. Of course, his thoughts would travel there. But they'd stopped their evenings together, and too much had happened since Ipswich.

Stop your woolgathering and just go over and talk to the man.

When she couldn't think of a rebuttal to her thoughts, she stood and marched to his door. She paused, her ear pushed against it. All was quiet. She took a breath, then tapped.

"Come in."

Beckworth was sitting up, the lamp next to his bed was brightly lit, and a book was in his lap. He closed it when she stepped inside and hovered by the door.

"I was hoping you'd come see me before going to bed."

"I had to get out of that dress."

"It suited you." His smile was cheeky.

She returned it. "It wasn't the same without you parading around like a peacock next to me."

He chuckled and set the book on the bedside table. "Come tell me about dinner."

She sat next to the bed and shared details of the evening, and within minutes, their old banter returned. He asked questions and laughed at Hensley's and Mary's stories. His color had returned, and he only grimaced when he laughed too hard or moved the wrong way.

"How's your back?"

He shrugged. "Much better but it still twinges, and it hurts when I walk."

She considered that. "Did Bart have any opinion on that?"

"Bart has an opinion on everything, but all he said was give it time."

"With a back injury, he's not wrong. But he thinks your spine is okay?"

He nodded. "Just muscles and bruised bone."

She had some thoughts about that but would check with Bart and Eleanor before suggesting massage therapy. "Have you been up for a few steps this evening?"

"Not since before the men arrived."

She smirked. "And how drunk were they when they left?"

"The food was a good idea. They only stumbled on every other step."

She laughed. "I hope you had a good time."

"They think you're a fierce angel."

She snorted. "They don't know me very well."

"I think they know you better than you think." His eyes warmed, and her cheeks heated. He took her hand and turned it over, running a finger across her palm. "You took a great risk riding to the East End."

She'd wondered if he'd heard about her going to Chester. It was just a matter of time. "A risk worth taking."

"I owe you my life. Based on where they found the ship, it could have been weeks before Hensley's men stumbled across it."

"I owed getting you out of a spot you wouldn't have been in if it wasn't for me."

He didn't say anything but opened her palm farther as he traced a line. "You have a long lifeline. It's strong and bold, just like you." When she tried to close her hand, he forced it open. "There are tiny crosshatches all along it. Some say they're challenges you'll face, others refer to them as unexpected events. I like to think of them as adventures. We all take risks. I admit I've taken more than most, and I don't have to tell you the stones are a combination of all those things. I've learned they also bring great rewards, but not in how most think of it. I don't mean riches, power, or great knowledge, though all those could be achieved. It's taken me a long time to understand there are rewards much more valuable than those trivial items."

"And are you willing to share your wisdom?"

He lifted his gaze to hers. "The rewards are deep and lasting friendships. Friends who'll risk everything for you. Those that fall never to rise, those who are injured, those captured, and those that risk all to save them. We're a true team, and you've proven yourself to be as worthy as the rest of them. There's never anyone to blame for anything that happens with the stones. You need to put your guilt behind you. Isn't that what you preach to me?"

She lowered her gaze and blinked rapidly. "I'm finding it much easier to give advice than to be on the receiving end."

His laugh was loud and warm. "Don't we all."

She hesitated, not sure how to broach the subject, but the elephant in the room needed to be faced, and the sooner, the better. She pulled her hand back, and though she wanted to look at him, she dropped her gaze to fuss with the bedcover. "What happened with Gemini?"

He sighed and fidgeted as if trying to find a more comfortable position. "My memory isn't clear on the first couple of days. Most likely from what she gave me for the pain. I slept a great deal, and when I did wake, most things were fuzzy, as if I'd been out all night at a pub." He glanced at her, then away. "Bart thinks it was a combination of the concussion and the pain from my back." He shrugged. "All I know is that whenever she came to see me, I could only keep up with parts of the conversation. I don't know if she realized how unstable I was at the time. When she laid the parchment on my chest and handed me a quill, I was aware enough to know not to sign anything. I certainly wasn't able to read it."

He turned away from her, staring at some point in the distance, and she took his hand. "I assume she kept trying."

"From what I can remember, she brought the parchment with her each time she visited. At the time, I was just grateful Gaines didn't come with her. She must have known that wouldn't have been points in her favor. And before you ask, yes, she did try to tempt me with her body, wearing almost nothing at all at times. But the more she begged, the more disgusting I found her."

He squeezed her hand. "Do you know what kept me sane? And I don't mean just during her attempts to have me sign her document, but afterward when she decided a forgery would be just as good and left me to Gaines and Belato."

He waited for her to respond, but she shook her head, unable to speak. His smile was more a grimace, which was either a statement of his recollection or a painful twinge from his back.

"A redheaded temptress."

She blinked back a tear and wanted to say she was sorry again, but what would be the point? He'd heard it enough times already and, being the man he was, would only lecture her again. And this wasn't about her. This was his story and the events that he continued to contend with.

He knew his attempt to cheer her up had fallen flat, but it didn't deter him. "At the time, I thought she was using the men to get me to change my mind. But apparently, she'd already decided on the forgery. She didn't care what the men did to me as long as they kept me alive. She was smart enough to know I might have provisions in place to protect my finances."

"You don't seem concerned, merely irritated, so I assume she was correct?"

He nodded. "I'm the only one who can access my accounts, with the exception of Barrington and Dame Ellingsworth. Even a notice of marriage wouldn't give her, or any wife, access to my finances. I'm not sure why she didn't know that, or perhaps it was just the first step in her plan to take over Waverly. That seems to be a revolving desire, and it makes me wonder if she'd planned on seducing Reginald before his demise. That would explain why she was so angry about his death."

Something nagged at Stella, that sliver of memory that

refused to come into focus. She ignored it, staying with Beckworth. "What can you do about it?"

"Barrington has already delivered notices to my barrister and the banks. Since there was no official notice of the banns, as far as I know, nor was a license obtained, the parchment doesn't mean much."

"Another reason for keeping you alive."

"Most likely."

"I'm sorry she put you through that. I shouldn't have nagged you about it."

He snorted. "As if that would have stopped Fitz or Jamie. And as I've told you several times, I have thicker skin than that. I was only concerned for your feelings."

She wasn't sure what to say to that, but her heart clenched. He squeezed her hand before releasing it, and she missed the physical contact. "You should see the moon. It's not quite full yet, but bright enough to lighten the garden."

"A spectacular sight when the flowers are in bloom."

"Do you feel up for a stroll to the window? You can lean on me."

He hesitated, then pushed back the covers and grunted.

"Wait for me." She stood and went to the other side of the bed to pull the covers back so he wouldn't tangle his legs in them. His nightshirt hung to just above his knees, and she looked around for a robe but didn't see one. She'd seen him naked, and while this seemed too intimate, considering she'd broken off relations, she focused on the task before them.

"Now, slowly turn and take your time. Grab my arm for support."

She managed to help him rise, and before he took a step, he leaned on her to catch his breath. They shuffled their way across the room to the window. He improved with each step, but when they reached the window, she made him lean against her, though she doubted he minded with his arm wrapped around her, his hand resting on her hip. She ignored the heat running through her at his touch.

"It's beautiful." He closed his eyes and breathed deeply. Then he smiled. "The jasmine is blooming. It's unfortunate it's too early for the lilacs."

"You'll be walking through the garden before you know it."

They stood and admired the scene until she felt him twitch, though he didn't complain.

"Come back to bed."

He moved faster on his way back, and though he grimaced as she helped swing his legs back in bed and repositioned him on his pillows, he never said a word.

"Thank you." His eyelids drooped.

"Get some sleep. You have a big day tomorrow." She stood and pulled his covers over him.

"Oh?"

She smiled and then kissed him. She'd aimed for his cheek, but at the last moment, his lips looked too good to resist. He responded instantly, and the moment lasted longer than she'd planned. But she wasn't complaining. His lips tasted good, and it had been far too long since the last kiss.

She pulled away and ran a hand down his cheek before stepping back. When she got to the door, she turned to him and gave him a wicked smile.

"Prepare yourself, Beckworth. We start training tomorrow."

And she closed the door against his surprised expression.

23

The next morning, Stella ate breakfast with Barrington, Bart, Lincoln, and Eleanor as they reviewed their plan for the next few days. She'd dressed in her pants and shirt, ready for her first training session.

"His back is healthy as far as I'm concerned," Bart said between bites of egg. "It's his muscles that are sore, probably a few nerves. He's rested enough and needs time on his legs. He'll most likely tire easy the first couple of days, but he'll have his stamina back soon enough."

"Your dagger training will be a good start." Barrington spread jam over his roll. "He'll need sparring time to fully recover if he plans on going on any missions."

"I can do a bit of that," Lincoln offered. "But soon enough he'll need someone more experienced."

"That's easy." Stella pushed her eggs around, nibbling on bacon. "Finn and Ethan would enjoy the diversion. They must be going stir-crazy with all this waiting."

"The *Phoenix* left port the day after we took Beckworth," Barrington said. "Chester has a crew checking docks, and Hensley added a couple of men to help. No one believes they left

London. It makes more sense they found a quiet mooring. We haven't been able to locate Gemini, but we believe her to be staying with friends she met as Lady Prescott. The crews will continue to keep a watchful eye."

"What do you think she's up to? She just goes about her business, and what? There's nothing we can do about it?"

Eleanor sipped her coffee and pushed her plate away. "That's the problem. She's made herself so well-known with the aristocrats, she'll be missed if she disappears."

Stella groaned. "And because she's posing as a noble, there will be an investigation." She wiped her hands on a napkin and then balled it in her fist. "What about her kidnapping Beckworth?"

"There's no proof other than our own." Barrington drained his coffee. "With her Prescott persona, no one will believe she's Gemini. Hensley is searching for other options, but that will take time." He stood. "I have errands this morning. I'll see you this afternoon."

Five minutes later, the group disbanded, and Stella ran up the stairs. She was eager to check on Beckworth. It was more a mixture of nervous excitement and anxiety with how Beckworth would respond to her plan. The fact everyone else was on board, didn't mean he'd cooperate.

Once in her room, she tightened the leather thong she used to tie her hair back, then added a few hairpins for the shorter strands so they'd stay out of her face. She picked up her leaf hairpin and rolled it around in her fingers, smiling at the memory of when he'd given it to her. Then she placed it with her opal necklace and picked up the dagger, still in its sheath. Barrington had given her a belt that would fit the sheath, and she put it on and faced the mirror.

She snickered at the sight. If only her clients could see her now. All she needed was a holster for her pistol, and she'd be ready for the Western frontier. God forbid.

She marched across the hall and knocked.

"Yes. Yes. Come in."

Her brow rose at his testy response, and she almost rethought her plan. But she barged in, matching his grumpiness against her determination.

He stood, wearing a different shirt than the night before. No pants. And what a sight he made, even though his back was to her as he fussed with something she couldn't see.

"Well, bring them over. I'll need to sit to put them on."

This time when her brow lifted, she quirked a smile. "I'm not used to putting pants back on a man."

He swirled around, grimaced, and tilted to one side, a hand reaching for the bedside table. His eyes were bright, and he recovered a smile. "I thought you were my valet."

"With all the wardrobe closets and a dressing room, you only have one pair of pants?"

"I wanted a specific pair."

"Of course, you did." She began to close the door when the harried-looking valet arrived.

He was out of breath and held a pair of neatly pressed breeches across his arm.

"I'll take those." And before the man knew it, she had them in her hands. "He won't need you until after lunch. Take some time for yourself before Mr. Crankypants starts shouting orders again."

The man peered around her, and Beckworth must have nodded before he bowed and hustled away.

"I think you've scared him more than I ever could."

She shut the door and placed the pants over a chair. "You won't be needing these until later." She searched the wardrobe closets, then glanced around. "Where are your clothes?"

"In the dressing room, and what are you looking for?"

"Something for you to work out in." She'd raised her voice so he could hear her from the other room.

"Work out?"

She walked back out with a pair of pants she'd seen him wear when they'd been on the run. "These will do. Now sit down, and I'll get them started for you."

"What's all this?"

"Today, you are not the viscount, you are Beckworth, my personal trainer." When she was in reach of him, he glanced down.

"What's that on your hip?"

She looked down. "That's my dagger."

"Who gave you a dagger?"

"No one. I purchased it yesterday when Eleanor and I went shopping."

He sat, but she didn't think it had anything to do with putting his pants on. "And she let you?"

"She helped me pick it out. I think she was leaning toward the silver-handled one, but it was too heavy."

He stared at her. "What do you mean by a personal trainer?"

She gave him a saucy smile. "It's not what you're thinking." She winked at him. "I don't think either of us needs training in that area."

His eyes widened at her sexual reference. The fact he was speechless and a bit off-kilter pleased her. At least he wasn't grumpy anymore.

She held onto the pants while planting a fist on her hip. "Here's the thing. I know self-defense moves. As a woman alone meeting potential home buyers, I want the ability to defend myself. But when the man grabbed me in Ipswich, all that training went out the window. I hadn't been as prepared as I thought I was."

"There were two men."

"But I almost got away from the first one. What matters is that I wasn't prepared. And I've realized that not only do I have to remember my self-defense training in those situations, but a dagger would have come in handy. I prefer a pistol, but it doesn't make sense in a hand-to-hand situation."

When he started to speak, she held up a finger. He closed his mouth and smiled. "A dagger, properly used, makes more sense. And I'm quite aware that I don't know the first thing about handling anything other than a paring knife. I need training, you have the expertise, and it just so happens you need something to ease you back into fighting shape."

He studied her as he considered her suggestion. "I'm not sure I can handle stairs yet."

"That wasn't what I had in mind."

"Oh?"

She glanced around the room. "Lincoln will be up soon to help move the furniture around. There's more than enough room in here to teach me the basics. Or am I wrong?"

He grinned. "Then you better get those pants on me before he shows up. You wouldn't want rumors to spread."

"Oh, I think that ship sailed." She knelt and gathered the pants and gently put one leg in, then the other, pulling them up to his knees. Then she stood and held out her hand. He took it, stood, and with his back slightly bent toward her, managed to pull them the rest of the way up with a slight grunt.

"I must say, I do prefer removing them." She gave him another wink, and he grinned.

A knock at the door was met with "come in" from them both. Lincoln strode in, looked at the two of them standing together, then surveyed the room.

"Let's make some room near the window. The fresh air will keep you cool once you work up a sweat. It should be a warm day." Lincoln strode to the desk and began tugging on it when a footman appeared and took the other end. After the room had been rearranged to give them a twelve-by-twelve workspace, Lincoln followed the footman to the door. Before leaving, he turned and smiled at Beckworth. "Barrington and I will be back this afternoon for our turn."

He was out the door before Beckworth could ask what he meant. When he turned toward Stella, she'd already pulled out her dagger.

Before he could raise a question, she asked her own. "Where do we begin?"

Beckworth stared at the auburn-haired beauty. Back in her pants and shirts, she'd attempted to tame her hair with a leather thong and hairpins. The unruly locks were already finding ways to spring out about her head. And now she stood with a dagger pointing at him. The woman never ceased to surprise him.

"The first thing would be to put the dagger away." He took a tentative step, then another. The majority of the pain was gone. He was still sore, but nothing he couldn't manage, and though his muscles were weak, he was pleased with how quickly he seemed to be recovering.

The problem was the sudden spasms that could take him to his knees. He could handle it if he could anticipate when they would strike, but there wasn't any pattern to them that he could discern. The frequency seemed to be growing farther apart, but not enough for him to be trustworthy on a mission.

Perhaps the plan to focus on her training was key. If nothing else, it would give them time together, and that pleased him.

"I don't understand." She still gripped the dagger and appeared eager to stab something with it.

"I'd prefer to review what self-defense moves you already know. Some might be adapted to work with the dagger. It would be better to train with familiar movements."

She considered his suggestion, and he waited for her to come to the same conclusion. It gave him time to draw closer, his steps slow and tentative.

By the time he reached her, she'd slid the dagger back into its sheath.

"I know about ten moves."

"Show me."

She shook out her arms and went through each one, explaining their intent as she did them. The first two were stilted, but she became more fluid as she worked through them. When she completed the last one, she turned toward him.

"Do them again, but slowly this time. I want to make sure I'm catching each movement."

He expected her to complain, but she complied without hesitation. The first time through, he'd watched the woman work through the various techniques, the second time he focused on the motion of each move. Several didn't require a dagger. Daily repetition would be sufficient so the moves came naturally. They would need Lincoln to assist with the physical training until he had full mobility.

There were a handful of positions where a dagger would provide a distinct advantage, and he could work with her to learn the intricate movements on her own until she mastered them. Then she would be ready to use them in a sparring match. Baby steps first, as she liked to say.

"Let's use Lincoln to work with you on the positions that won't require a dagger. I'll monitor and suggest changes. I'd like to go over the second one you showed me. I think you called it a hammer strike. That's the easiest one to add a dagger, but I have a few modifications that will be good to practice."

She was an eager student and took instruction well.

They'd been working for an hour when he moved to demonstrate a different technique and, without warning, a spasm hit him, and he dropped to a knee. She was beside him in a heartbeat, her arm going around his waist. He grimaced as a sharp pain made him cry out.

"Do you want to sit or lie down?" Her voice was calm but insistent.

"Just give me a moment." He leaned into her, and the simple act of their bodies connecting shifted his thoughts away from the pain, refocusing them on the curves he remembered so well. He took a deep breath and stood with her assistance. "The pain is gone. Let me walk you through the steps one more time, then you can practice on your own."

When she reached for the dagger, he stopped her hand. He glanced around and pointed toward the desk. "Use that quill."

"A quill?"

"I'd prefer you become proficient with the correct movements before we add an extremely sharp instrument."

"I suppose that makes sense."

Once they went through the steps three times together, he watched her perform them three times on her own.

"Perfect. Practice that a few times today. An hour or two apart until it becomes second nature."

"That's all?"

"For today. With each lesson, we'll start with a demonstration of all you've learned, then we'll add a new movement. We'll do that each day, ending with a sparring session with Lincoln on the moves that don't require a dagger. Eventually, we'll mix up various scenarios with those that require a dagger and those that don't."

She sighed. She'd wanted to use her dagger, but he had a solution for that.

"Come help me back to the bed."

"I'm sorry. I wasn't thinking."

"I'm alright, but I can tell when I've had enough."

"You're pale. I should have seen that." She sat with him on the bed. There was a light sheen on her skin, and her floral scent washed over him, his mind conjuring up scenes from their evenings together. She absently ran her hand over the dagger's sheath.

"I'd love to see it."

"What? Oh, yes." She pulled the dagger out and handed it to him, hilt first.

He took it from her and felt its weight and tested its balance. "A decent knife. The shopkeeper appears to know his merchandise." He ran a finger along the bone handle. "This will work well. I'll get you a whetstone. You need to learn how to keep it sharp." He handed it back to her.

"How's your back? And be honest."

He'd always found it difficult to discuss his weaknesses with anyone, but somehow Stella made him want to share everything. Without a second thought, he told her about the spasms and general soreness.

"Would you be willing to let me guide you through some exercises combined with a massage that might speed up your recovery?"

"A massage? I remember something like that from your century." He couldn't help a grin, knowing it had something to do with her hands moving over his back.

Her gaze twinkled. "Think of it as a reward after your time with Barrington and Lincoln."

He frowned.

"Don't worry. I doubt the sessions will be long until you heal more. Their first task is to keep you moving around, using your muscles until you're ready for light sparring." She leaned close, her lips moving in, but instead of a kiss, they touched his ear. "Think of it as an incentive. I've changed my mind about our abstinence. Assuming you're interested."

He pulled back to gauge her honesty. It was clear by the sparks in her emerald gaze that she was serious. "Well, luv, it wasn't my idea to stop in the first place."

24

Stella threw herself face-first across the bed, her heavy panting buried within the bedcovers. The last six days of training were meant to be taxing on Beckworth as he built back his endurance. He was an evil man, who, with each passing day, seemed more determined to make her suffer.

Her arms were numb, her legs had the strength of a gelatin mold, and her heart pounded as if it were trying to burst from her chest. She wasn't sure how she'd made it up the stairs. Beckworth gained strength with each training session, where she could pass for a limp mop.

The door opened, but she didn't have the energy to turn her head. If the house was being raided by Gemini's men, she was a goner. Her only request was not to be stabbed with her own dagger.

"I thought you could use a hot bath." Eleanor strode across the room and closed the drapes.

Additional footsteps crossed the room, and the sound of the hipbath being brought in made her coo. If only her body would obey her command to rise. The simple act of rolling over seemed beyond her for the moment.

"I need AJ. I think she lied to me." Her words were muffled by a pillow.

"About what?" Eleanor opened drawers, and the sounds of ruffled fabric made Stella groan.

The thought of leaving the room, or god forbid, the manor, made her curl into a fetal position.

"Aren't I supposed to be getting stronger?"

Eleanor's laugh was like a stab through her heart. The whole lot of them had ganged up on her. Somehow, they'd missed the point where it was all about Beckworth's training and had turned her own plans against her.

"For such a smart woman, sometimes you get—what did AJ call it—tunnel vision?"

That made her roll over, and she caught the scent of lavender and chamomile. The steam rising from the bath made her drool. Eleanor shooed the maids away and shut the door.

"What are you talking about?"

Eleanor motioned for her to sit up, and she obeyed. The bath became her focal point. "Take off your clothes. I think you can manage the shirt and pants on your own."

She untied the shirt strings and pulled it over her head, wincing at the ache in her muscles.

"When you started your training sessions with Beckworth, they were barely an hour long. He couldn't do much for fear of a spasm. Between the continued training, the back therapy you and Maire devised, and the increased intensity of your sparring, your session today was almost three hours."

That jerked her head up. "Three hours? Are you sure?"

"You started right after breakfast. I've asked the cook to delay lunch by an hour so you could get a good soak, have your hair washed, and take a short nap."

She pulled off her pants and undergarments and made a

beeline for the tub. "No wonder I feel like someone deboned me."

The water was hot, but it didn't deter her from stepping in. She cringed at the heat until her body accepted it as she slowly lowered herself in. The scent was enough to soothe her muscles.

"I'll bring up some coffee. Relax for a spell, and then we'll get that hair washed."

Stella leaned back, wishing she could stretch out her legs, but soon her eyes closed, and she didn't care. She considered the last training session. Where had the three hours gone? No wonder she was whipped. She smiled. She'd held her own against Beckworth and Lincoln. They weren't as tough on her as a real bad guy would be, but she'd gotten out of both of their holds and managed to touch them in the sensitive areas of their stomachs and backs with the tip of her dagger.

She considered that a success, but it wasn't the highlight of her training. Beckworth moved with the grace she'd seen before his capture in Ipswich. He still protected his right side where he'd been repeatedly punched by Gaines and Belato. The spasms still came but not nearly as frequently, and he seemed capable of compensating for them while working through the pain.

They'd danced around each other with a promise of an evening together. There had been short kisses, and plenty of innuendos when no one was listening. She relished the increasing tension growing between them.

Eleanor returned with coffee and food.

"I thought we were having lunch downstairs." She straightened and lifted her chin as Eleanor poured water over her head and massaged soap into her hair.

"There's been a change of plans. Hensley wants us to join him this afternoon."

"Is Gemini active again?"

"The message simply asked us to join them with an expectation to stay for dinner."

"It's a planning session. He must have learned something important."

"Possibly. Beckworth has given us an hour to be ready, so I'm afraid you won't get a nap."

"That's alright. The bath helped, as long as my legs work."

An hour later, Stella managed the stairs without her knees buckling. In fact, after several cups of coffee and a few bites of food, she felt like a new woman.

Beckworth waited at the bottom of the stairs. He was once again the Viscount of Waverly, though he hadn't overdone it with the clothing. His tan breeches and dark-brown coat complimented his ash-blond hair. His cornflower-blue eyes were emphasized by the blue-striped waistcoat.

She ran a hand over her emerald-green dress. It wasn't as fancy as her periwinkle gown, but it was still within the expected parameters for dinner attire. His gaze fell on her opal necklace.

He took her hand when she reached the last step, and he pulled her into his arms. His gaze heated as it met hers. Then he was kissing her. Not a quick peck, nor a light movement over her lips. It was deep and passionate and made her knees weak.

When he pulled back, it took a second to catch her breath. "What was that for?"

"I didn't think I needed a reason. But if you require one, let's just say that one look at you in all that finery, and knowing you could stab me in the heart with the dagger you've hidden in your pocket makes me tingle all over."

She laughed and pulled him in for another kiss.

This time when the kiss ended, he took several steps back. She understood. One more minute and she'd strip off her dress and leave it in a heap at the bottom of the stairs.

He held out his arm. "Eleanor and the rest of the crew are already outside."

"Then let's not keep them waiting."

Barrington and Lincoln were in the box, opting to drive the coach on their own.

Bart was inside with Eleanor, and Stella took a seat next to her, while Beckworth sat next to Bart. Although the day was warm, a blanket covered Bart's legs. The old man moved with surprising ease, if not a bit slowly, but got chilled easily. Maire created an herbal remedy that Lincoln made him drink each evening, and though he complained about it, he drank every drop.

"Do you think Hensley discovered something?" Stella asked.

Beckworth shook his head. "I have a feeling he was waiting for Jamie's return."

"Where did he go? I didn't realize the *Daphne* had left."

"Finn and Ethan were becoming irritable with the waiting, so Hensley sent them to Southampton on another matter."

She lifted a brow. "AJ didn't mention it when she stopped by with Maire yesterday." She looked out the window and shook her head. "They were checking our progress to report back to Hensley."

Bart snickered. "For a smart woman, your observation skills appear lacking these days." He winked at her.

"Keep it up, old man, and I'll slip something into Maire's herbal tonic."

He cackled. "Make it the same thing you're slipping into Beckworth's food. He's made a surprisingly speedy recovery."

At that, three heads turned to their respective windows to survey the scenery as Bart continued to chuckle. She smiled as she watched the streets of London pass by. She hoped Hensley wouldn't destroy their good humor.

25

When they arrived at Hensley's, Mary waited for them at the bottom of the steps.

"It's been days since I've seen you all." When Beckworth stepped down first, she almost squealed. "Oh, Teddy, I was so worried about you."

Stella, not standing on ceremony, or willing to wait for a footman to help them down, and with no idea when Mary might release Beckworth, climbed down on her own. Then she turned and helped Eleanor out, who seemed as eager to exit the carriage.

She glanced around for Barrington and found him and Lincoln in hushed conversation with Hensley. It must have been important for them to ignore the coach. She elbowed Eleanor, and they assisted Bart down before Beckworth could extract himself from Mary's motherly embrace. His cheeks were pink when he glanced at Stella before Mary tugged at him to escort her into the manor.

Eleanor took Bart's other side as the three of them approached the steps. She leaned across Bart to advise Stella.

"In all the time I've known that man, even as a boy, I don't remember seeing him blush."

Stella stared at him as he bent his head to listen to Mary. "I think the last couple of weeks have given him a great deal to think about."

Eleanor smiled. "Oh, I think it's been a lot longer than a couple of weeks."

She caught the grin and tried to ignore the suggestion that she might have something to do with the small changes in Beckworth. Then she frowned. They hadn't restarted their intimate relationship yet. She wanted to make sure he was healthy. There had been kisses and small touches but nothing else. Soon, the moment would come, and with it, the concern of how to say goodbye when it was time to go home. Somehow, she'd convinced herself that spending more time with him wouldn't change the difficulty of that day.

One day at a time. Keep it simple. She'd had short love affairs before. This wouldn't be any different. But when they reached the front door and he bent down to kiss Mary's cheek, something in her chest cracked—just a little.

Beckworth released Mary once they were inside and took Stella's arm. He shouldn't have left the women to fend for themselves. "Sorry about the coach."

She gazed up at him, a wicked smile on her luscious lips. "I thought you might have forgotten all about us."

"It can be a difficult choice when surrounded by so many beautiful women."

She laughed. "Okay. You win. It only makes sense you'd be devoted to Mary."

Voices drifted into the hallway as Mary led them to the solarium. Everyone was there—AJ and Murphy, Maire and Hughes, Jamie, Lando, Fitz, and Thomas. Bart had dropped into a corner chair next to Sebastian, who immediately passed him a book he must have been reading.

Barrington entered and nodded to Beckworth; Hensley followed him in with Lincoln. They had probably been discussing the crew, and if that was the case, he'd know soon enough.

He directed Stella to a seat that faced the windows so she could see the garden. Mary had once again set up a long table that would accommodate the entire team, and the numerous windows shed the bright light of a sunny spring day. Hensley must have decided it was time to begin their planning sessions.

"It's good to see you up and about." Jamie sat to his right and gripped his shoulder. "Fitz thought we should come by for a sparring match."

Beckworth laughed. It was good to be back among them. "If you think it will be an easy afternoon, you might rethink your plans."

"That's alright, mate." Fitz bumped his chair, a plate of meat pies in his hand. "We'll bring Lando to even the odds."

Lando grunted from the other side of Jamie, and Murphy grinned from across the table. "I'd watch it, gentlemen. I hear we have a new dagger wielder in the group."

"That's right." Stella gave them a demure smile. "It won't just be AJ running around with a sharp, stabby thing." They all laughed, though the men glanced at him.

Beckworth nodded. "I'm afraid it's true. But I won't be held responsible. You can blame Eleanor for encouraging her."

Eleanor had taken a seat in the corner with Bart and Sebastian and pretended not to hear him.

"Thank you all for coming on short notice." Hensley pushed his papers, quill, and inkpot to the side then picked at the broken wax seal of a note. "Now that all members of the team have returned from their various missions and Beckworth has been safely recovered, it's time to get back to the mission of Gemini."

"You mean to getting rid of her once and for all." Fitz licked his fingers before biting into another meat pie.

"That is the goal." Hensley gave Fitz a disapproving glance, which, as usual, didn't faze the spunky sailor. "The question is how."

"I can think of a few ways," Stella mumbled, and though Hensley lifted a brow at the few snickers, he ignored her comment.

"Barrington has been working with Chester, who, as you know, was instrumental in locating the *Phoenix*, and now they've found Gemini."

"Finally," Hughes muttered.

"Agreed." Hensley dropped the note card and sat back. "Barrington, why don't you tell us what the crew has discovered."

Beckworth eyed his friend, curious why he'd never said a word about what he'd been up to with Chester. When he gave him a questioning look, Barrington glanced toward Lincoln and Eleanor, but it was Bart who smiled at him. They'd left him out on purpose. Stella, however, appeared as curious as the rest of the team as to what Barrington had to tell them. So, she hadn't been told, either. He sighed. They hadn't told him because they wanted him focused on healing. They'd used Stella's plan of assisting in his recovery to hide their own activities.

He would have preferred being kept in the loop, but Barrington was right about keeping him in the dark. He had legal issues with Gemini at the moment, and it was best he stayed away from whatever they were cooking up. For now.

Barrington cleared his throat and gave the room a quick scan, making eye contact with everyone to ensure they were paying attention as well as to let them know this was his area of expertise. "We've found Gemini hiding in plain sight. She's staying at the London home of Lord and Lady Wright, using her alias of Lady Penelope Prescott. The Wrights appear to have left London two weeks ago from what we could gather, so Gemini is either renting the manor or simply took it over with guile." He shook his head. "We've been watching her for three days. She never leaves on her own. There are at least two men with her at all times. They are well dressed and appear to be her bodyguards."

"One of them will be Gaines." Beckworth stared out the window to a bed of daffodils, a yellow flash of color against the green foliage of holly. He was sorry Stella never got to see the gardens at Waverly. "The other one is most likely her brother, André Belato."

AJ perked up. "That's likely. It's a shame we weren't able to get to either of them when we boarded the *Phoenix*."

"It makes sense she'd keep them close," Murphy said. "And we have no evidence that says she's anyone other than who she says she is."

"Where's the older Belato?" Hughes had stood to pace, but he stopped next to the window that Beckworth still gazed through. "I don't think he was on the ship. Is he even in England?"

Beckworth scratched his head and then tugged at a sleeve. "He's dead."

The group all began talking at once. He'd dropped a critical piece of information, but truthfully, he'd only just remembered it.

Hensley pounded on the table. "Enough." When they all quieted, he turned to Beckworth. "Is there a reason you're just now telling us?"

Stella's hand rested on his leg where no one could see, and

while it gave him a jolt, he understood it was her way of saying she was there for him.

"It didn't come to me until you mentioned him. All I can say is that I simply didn't remember until he was mentioned. André told me the night you rescued me. I wasn't quite myself at the time. I was in pain, and it wasn't the first time he'd visited to taunt me." He scratched his head, lost in the memories of that day and his fear he might never be found. "My headaches had been increasing in strength, and my mind wandered while he blathered on. He mentioned that his uncle had been on the brink of cracking an incantation that would improve its accuracy when the drunken fool fell down the stairs and broke his neck."

"I don't want to be uncharitable," Sebastian said from the back of the room, "but it's not a surprising ending for him."

"They do say karma's a bitch." Stella leaned over the table at the same time AJ did, and they touched their coffee cups together in a toast. Then she turned to Beckworth. "While we're on the subject, did you get any indication of who's in charge now? Gemini or her brother?"

He gave the jasmine a last look before turning to her, though he didn't have to give her question much thought. She looked fetching today in forest green. It was a simple dress, yet she made it elegant. She fingered the opal that hung from her neck. It had become a habit when she was thinking, and it pleased him that she rarely took it off. "There's no question that Gemini is in charge, though I don't think André is happy about it. I sensed tension between them."

"That begs another question that's been bothering me since our meeting with Lavigne in Rouen." Murphy rubbed at a spot on the table, his nail scratching at the linen tablecloth. "From what Lavigne said, Belato was destitute, renting rooms above a distillery. If that information was correct, where are they getting their funds? The *Phoenix* might be stolen, and the original crew dumped overboard, but how do they pay the current crew? Gemini, Gaines, and perhaps a handful of others might wait for whatever glory they think they'll find with the stones, but mercenaries don't work on promises."

The group fell silent as they considered the point. From everything they knew until now, or all that Beckworth was aware, they had to assume there was a money man. The tables filled with trinkets he'd found at the warehouse in Ipswich might pay a few days of wages, but not much else. And he hadn't been able to glean much information from Gemini while onboard the ship. Not with how little he remembered of their conversations.

"Wherever they're getting their money, we're still back to having no legal recourse to take Gemini down," Hughes said. "At least not without running afoul of the local magistrate. Perhaps we could convince someone that Gemini is working for France."

The team discussed it for several minutes, and while they did, Beckworth kept his eye on Stella, who'd grown quiet. Something was brewing in that head of hers, and suddenly, she straightened and slammed her fist on the table.

"Al Capone."

"Who?" Hensley asked.

"Where have I heard that name before?" Murphy glanced at Hughes. "Was it someone we might have met during our time travels?"

"He was a gangster from the 1920s." AJ appeared confused. "He ran a gang and was most notably known as an infamous bootlegger, what you would call a smuggler, of alcohol during prohibition." When blank faces stared at her, she tried again. "For a short period of time in our country's history, distilling, supplying, or even drinking alcohol was against the law. Capone was a violent criminal and evaded justice for a long time, though I'm not sure what he has to do with our current situation."

"I was thinking more about how they finally locked him away." Stella shifted in her seat until she perched on the edge of the chair as if she'd take flight like one of her swans. "It wasn't for the murders, prostitution, or the bootlegging. He let his henchman do the dirty work." She had everyone's attention. "The Feds, a short name for the US government, went after him for tax evasion. That's what finally put him behind bars."

"While an interesting tale, I'm not understanding where you're going with this." Hensley laid down his quill, intrigued by her story.

Stella shrugged, but he wasn't the only one who seemed to notice the slight change in her posture. Murphy and Hughes were both studying her, trying to anticipate where she was leading them. The rest of the group was still getting to know Stella, but after she'd gone to Chester, who ended up being the one to find him, she had earned their respect. If she was working out a plan, it was most likely worth considering.

She glanced around the room, then smiled in a demure manner he wouldn't have trusted for a second. Her story was meant to lure them in, and she was doing a damn fine job of it. "I need to frame this the right way. You said Gemini was using the Penelope Prescott name again, right?" Several heads bobbed. "Is that the only alias she's used?"

When no one spoke, Hensley answered the question. "It's the only one we're aware of. It's possible she has used others. It would be difficult to use a different name here in London since she's attending parties where anyone might attend."

"That makes sense, but it would be easy to use other names outside London, perhaps a location where she holes up for a while. I think we all agree the Belatos have been trying to steal the stones for years."

"Where are you going with this?" Murphy asked.

"There's a real Penelope Prescott," Beckworth answered.

"The Prescott home is in the far north, and from what Gemini told me several weeks ago, assuming it was the truth, the real Lady Prescott is spending her days along the coast."

"Exactly." His words seemed to have added steam to Stella's story. "She took their name, and I believe their wealth as well. Or at least, as much of it as she could get away with." She glanced around the room, settling on Hensley. "I assume that's illegal in England. I mean, she had no problem becoming someone else's wife with a bit of forgery." She scowled at Beckworth.

He sighed, deciding it best to ignore the statement. And while everyone else hid their grins, Bart chuckled from the back of the room, which forced a snicker from Fitz.

Hensley cleared his throat. "I understand your point of using another method to bring her to justice. And yes, it would be illegal if we had some form of proof, but Prescott is a common name."

Stella gave him a wily smile. "Would a file with dozens of business transactions and real estate sales that have the Prescott name on them be sufficient evidence? I can't be entirely sure, but I think there were other names on the documents I found."

The group began to fidget, their interest more than piqued, but it was Hensley who seemed the most dumbfounded. "Why haven't you mentioned this before now?"

She shrugged, not at all sheepish about holding back valuable information. "To be honest, it's nagged at me for the last couple of days. I didn't put it all together until just now. I discovered the documents by accident when I'd first been kidnapped. Gemini locked me in a room with stacks of trunks, which is where I ran across them. At the time, I was thinking about survival and a way to escape, not how to take her down. And after the escape and running for our lives, well, we've been kind of busy since then."

Beckworth was so stimulated by her keen mind, if they had the time, and they weren't in someone else's manor—although he wasn't sure that would matter—he'd toss her over his shoulder and carry her upstairs to demonstrate how much it affected him. When she caught his heated gaze, a lovely blush colored her cheeks.

She swallowed. "Some of you are aware of my tendency to snoop. And honestly, how can someone lock a person away for days in a room with dozens of trunks, tell them to ignore them, and then expect them not to look." She smiled, and everyone nodded. They all would have done the same thing. "Anyway, I found a file with dozens of papers at the bottom of one of her trunks. They were buried under evening gowns, purses, and other accessories."

"That sounds like something we can work with," Murphy said, turning to Hensley. "If we can locate where that trunk is, and identify it as Gemini's, can we get Lord Langdon to assist? He's already aware of the Heart Stone and its importance."

Hensley nodded. "I think he'd be willing to get the magistrate and the local watchmen involved. But they would have to find the documents on their own with definitive evidence they belong to Gemini." He tapped his chin. "We would need confirmation of where the files are currently located and someone to review them to ensure they're enough to convict her. In the meantime, I have a man in Liverpool who could find the real Lady Prescott and garner a written testimony of her identity and possibly any financial misdeeds. It would provide enough cause for a search."

"We tried this before with Reginald, and the police bungled it." Beckworth had been so irritated, he'd been ready to beat someone senseless.

"You can be assured I won't allow that to happen a second time." Hensley seemed as angry as him at the memory.

Beckworth nodded. "Barrington, how well guarded is the manor where Gemini is staying? Is it possible to get in if she and her bodyguards aren't at home?"

Barrington considered the question. "We don't have anyone inside. Other than what appears to be the normal staff, we haven't seen anyone else enter or leave except Gemini and the two men."

He turned to the group. "We need to get into that manor."

26

After dinner at Hensley's, Beckworth begged for an early departure rather than meeting the men for cigars and libations. Mary agreed, concerned about him overdoing activities while still recovering, but the only thing he had in mind was getting Stella home. And resting wasn't on his list for the evening.

At some point between their meeting to discuss Gemini and drinks before dinner, Stella noticed his singular attention. It was apparent she understood his intent, and whether it was purposeful guile on her part or sheer unwitting obstruction by AJ and Maire, she kept a polite distance from him. She sat across from him at dinner, and while Jamie and Fitz kept the group entertained with their latest sailing capers, he couldn't keep his eyes off her every time she fondled the opal. No one seemed to notice, and she flagrantly avoided his gaze. The more she avoided him, the more he wanted her.

He'd just gotten everyone in the coach and was ready to step in when Barrington pulled him away for a quick discussion with Hensley.

"Sorry to disturb the rest of your evening, Beckworth." Hensley held a note in his hand that appeared to be the one with the broken wax seal he'd been fondling during their meeting.

Beckworth inwardly sighed. Fate was working against him this evening. "Well, get it out. I'm sure I'm not going to like it."

Hensley gave Barrington a glance before handing Beckworth the message. "It's from Dame Ellingsworth. She left a party early yesterday evening after a heated argument with someone claiming to be the Viscountess of Waverly."

He groaned. "That didn't take her long."

"She recognized the woman from your holiday hunting party last year and is demanding an explanation."

"And why did she send the message to you?"

"She wasn't aware you were still in London and was apparently unwilling to wait for a return message from Waverly."

Beckworth sighed again, this time audibly. "I didn't think Gemini would have the nerve to start announcing it without me present. I thought I had time to resolve this quickly and quietly."

"She's baiting you." Barrington gave him a pointed look. "You can't let her run the game."

"He's quite right," Hensley said.

"Then the quicker we get into the Wrights' manor and find the evidence we need, the faster this nightmare will go away." He glanced at the coach and caught Stella watching them. Now that she was willing to return to their intimate evenings, and he was physically up to the challenge, he couldn't catch a break.

"How would you like me to respond to Elizabeth?" Hensley asked.

He read the note, then tapped it against his leg as he considered his limited options. "Elizabeth is a wily one when it comes to intrigue among the aristocrats. I'll need to speak with her right away. Can you send her an immediate reply?"

Hensley nodded. "What do you have in mind?"

"I need to pay her a visit this evening, but I'll need an hour to get everyone home. Tell her I'll enter through the servant's entrance. I don't need nosy neighbors spotting me at her front door."

Hensley and Barrington smiled, but it was Hensley who said, "This might be the very thing we need to keep Gemini busy while we sneak into the castle."

The men shook hands and Hensley returned to the manor to reply to Elizabeth. Barrington climbed to the box where Lincoln waited while Beckworth joined the group in the coach.

Once they left the manor, Stella asked, "What was that all about?"

He shook his head and stared out the window. "The fox is trying to outwit the wolf."

When they reached the manor, Eleanor retired to her room while Bart and Lincoln meandered toward the library for an evening drink and a game of chess. Stella remained in the foyer, staring at him and Barrington.

"Out with it." She had her hands planted on her hips in a pose he'd once considered annoying and now found endearing. "You know I'll find out sooner or later."

He handed her the note. She read it quickly as he watched her face. Her brows had lifted at being given the message, full of curiosity. It only took an instant for them to lower and that stubborn tilt of her chin to appear.

"This is outrageous. Can she do this? I mean, can I go around claiming I'm somebody I'm not?"

Barrington grimaced. "She's taking a risk. I doubt she expected to be outed so quickly, and not by someone of Dame Ellingsworth's stature."

"But it's enough to get tongues wagging." Beckworth studied Stella, gauging her anger. Was it directed solely at Gemini or at him as well?

Her expression changed, and though her brows still knitted

together, she appeared to be thinking rather than raging. Maybe she was doing both. He glanced at Barrington, who had also been watching her, and when he turned his gaze to Beckworth, he shrugged, as curious as he was.

He didn't think she was aware that she'd begun to fold the note into a swan, and he suppressed a grin.

When she finally spoke, her conclusion fit with theirs. "You need to speak with Elizabeth. There has to be a way we can use this to our advantage."

"We agree. I plan on going over there now, but I want to change into servant's attire first."

She nodded and glanced at Barrington. "You'll follow him?"

"Naturally."

"Good." She took Beckworth's arm. "I'll walk up with you. I need to get out of these shoes."

Beckworth returned to the manor two hours later and handed the reins of his horse to Barrington. "Take the morning off. I only ask that you get my message to Chester."

"I'll take it myself. I'd like to spend some time in the East End."

"Say hello to everyone for me. And make sure you thank them again for their help."

"You know it's not required."

"I know. I'd like to have it said just the same."

Barrington nodded and led the horse away.

Beckworth glanced up at the manor. Would she still be awake? It wasn't that late, but it had been a long day. The manor was quiet, the lights dim as he made his way up the stairs. He hated the thought of Gemini spreading rumors around town.

But once he explained the events of his capture and rescue to Elizabeth, as well as the discovery of the Prescott documents, he was reminded of how crafty the old woman was.

Stella had been right about Elizabeth finding an advantage. She'd already developed a plan, but after what he'd shared about his capture, they worked together to modify it to solve two problems—make Gemini out to be a schemer and provide a distraction for the team to gain access to the manor.

He smiled as he walked down the second-floor hall to his room but stopped to stare at Stella's door. Would she be in a congenial mood after reading the message about Gemini calling herself the Viscountess of Waverly? He decided to change out of the servant's attire while he mulled it over.

When he opened the door, he was surprised at how dark it was in the room. He expected his valet to leave a lamp on after laying out his evening attire, but the only light came from the hearth where a fire steadily burned.

He shut the door and was almost to the bed when a movement in the shadows made him stop. A quick glance at the windows confirmed the drapes were shut. Either an intruder had shut them after entering, or they walked up the main staircase. Perhaps they came from the servant's stairs. He slowly reached for his dagger—then stopped.

She stepped into the firelight like an ethereal wood nymph. Her long robe was lightly tied at the waist, and though he only saw her outline, he knew what lay beneath the silk fabric.

His cock stirred with excitement. She had waited for him.

Her steps were measured, and it wasn't until she stood mere inches in front of him that he could make out her features, though slivers of shadows still lurked. She didn't say a word as she ran her hands up his chest and pushed the jacket from his shoulders. It only slipped partway down his arms as she untied his shirt then ran a hand up to his neck to pull his face to hers.

Her kiss was light, and her tongue played at his lips before he answered her call and met her tongue with his own. The kiss deepened, and he wanted to touch her, but his arms were tangled in the jacket.

She untied her robe but kept it on as she pressed against him. The feel of her curves sent fireworks through him. She knew what game she played. And she proved it when her hand slipped from his neck and traced light fingers down his chest, and past his stomach until she cupped him.

"I wasn't sure how long you'd be gone." She whispered the words against his lips, then kissed the skin below his chin before running her tongue over the base of his neck. It was impossible for her not to feel the throbbing under her hand.

"I was hoping you'd wait." He wasn't sure how he got the words out. It was a miracle he still stood.

Her hands were suddenly at his waist, unbuttoning his trousers. "I gave your valet and my lady's maid the evening and morning off."

He groaned when her hand danced over his manhood before pushing the pants down just low enough for him not to be able to walk anywhere.

"I seem to be at your mercy." And he loved every moment of it.

The edges of her robe fell away, exposing a portion of her breasts, stomach, and the soft hair below. Her fingers traced up his sides until her arms were around his neck and she pressed herself against him.

He moaned. "If you don't release my hands, luv, I can't be responsible for what happens next."

Her chuckle was low and sultry, which did nothing to relieve the situation. But she relented, her movements slow as she circled him, pulling off his jacket and releasing his arms. He wanted to turn around and finish what she started but was curious to see what she'd do next.

She stepped back as he sat to remove his boots. When he stood and began to remove his shirt, she stopped him. With her robe still open, she stepped close and gave him another languid kiss, running a hand up his chest, her fingernails leaving a soft trail. She lifted his arms and pulled the shirt off.

He couldn't remember anyone undressing him in such a manner, and it was all he could do not to toss her on the bed. She pushed him onto it instead, and when she straddled him, he thought he might lose his mind as the silk fabric rubbed against his legs and chest.

Her hair fell around her face as she leaned over him, her breasts brushing against his chest. She placed a soft kiss on his lips and then on the tip of his ear before she whispered, "Show me what you've got."

In one swift move, he stripped the robe from her shoulders and down her arms as he twisted, rolling her over until she was under him. "I'll do my best not to disappoint."

Stella woke to strong arms holding her and the scent of coffee filling the room. A low fire burned in the hearth, and she struggled with staying like this for several more hours or sneaking out of bed for a cup of brew. While she considered her options, Beckworth stirred.

She stretched as she turned to face him, finding him wide awake and amused.

"I'd wondered how long it would take for the scent of coffee to wake you." He kissed her, and for a moment, she forgot everything else.

"How long was it?"

"At least five minutes, perhaps a minute or two longer." He pulled her to him, nuzzling her neck.

"That long?" She pulled back to study the lines of his face and gave him a sly smile. "To be honest, I couldn't decide whether to sneak out of bed to grab a cup or stay nestled in your arms."

He frowned. "I have a feeling the coffee won out."

She snorted and ran a finger down his chest. "I would have come back to bed. After last night, I needed something to re-energize me."

He grabbed her traveling hand and kissed it. "Let me see if I have the power to bring life back into those tired limbs."

Thirty minutes later, he squeezed her ass and left the bed. "Don't move. I'll be right back."

"Honestly, I don't know how you have the strength to walk."

"A man on a mission for his woman has the strength of ten warriors." He strode naked to the hearth, where he removed the pot of coffee and placed it on the table, filling two mugs. It hadn't taken him long to decide mugs required fewer refills, considering how much she drank.

He handed the mugs to her before climbing back into bed. She had fluffed the pillows so they could lean against them and savor the morning.

"I gave your valet and my lady's maid the morning off. How did you get coffee sent up?"

"My valet, Jeffries, was sent over by the gentlemen's club I belong to. He'd been sitting in the hall for two hours before I poked my head out."

"You knew he'd be there?"

"Of course. I've known him for a few years now, and he's as stubborn as Barrington."

"Two hours just sitting there?"

"I wouldn't worry about him. It's peaceful in the hallway, and

I noticed the book he shoved behind him before he stood to take my breakfast order."

"Well, that makes me feel better. Does that mean our breakfast is getting cold?"

"It's warming near the hearth."

She relaxed against him. "Then all is right with the world."

"At least for this morning."

"You never mentioned what Elizabeth had to say when you visited her last night."

"If memory serves, I wasn't given time to mention it."

She elbowed him in the side. "I don't remember you complaining."

"No complaints. Just stating facts." He put an arm around her shoulders and tugged her close. "You were correct about Elizabeth. She'd already come up with a scheme before I arrived. Thankfully, things aren't as bad as I feared, meaning Gemini didn't stand at the top of the stairs and shout out her stolen title."

"She wouldn't have to. From what I've seen, or experienced, all it requires is telling one person, and within an hour, dozens know."

"And Elizabeth believes that was Gemini's intent all along. Gossip has more power and spreads faster than the banns advising of a marriage, which of course, in this case, were never printed."

"Does she think the rumor will be believed?"

"It would have for many if Elizabeth hadn't called her out on the lie in front of several influential women. Most of the aristocrats know me as a bachelor who, as I've told you before, had never attended a social engagement with a woman by my side. However, many of them remember me flaunting a particularly gorgeous redhead at several social events this season. Needless to say, they were confused when a blonde, who only a few were familiar with, claimed to be my wife."

"What did she hope to achieve?"

"With Gemini, your guess is as good as any other. But I suspect she had no idea Elizabeth would be there. Why she hadn't noticed her, I can't say. She should have remembered her from my hunting party, but she spent most of her time flirting with the men."

"Thank heavens Elizabeth was there. I wish I'd been there to witness it."

He scratched his chin where his morning whiskers gave him a roguish appearance. "Fortunately, Elizabeth has friends in many places. She sent a message to a friend who throws a masquerade ball every season. We're in luck that the event is in two days."

"And that helps us how?"

"Lady Prescott, or the viscountess, I'm not sure how the invitation will be addressed, but I presume the latter, will be receiving hers later this morning."

"The use of a title will make Gemini believe she'd made traction with the aristocrats. But how does that help us?" She shook her head and took a long swallow of coffee. "Never mind. I wasn't thinking. We expect her to attend, leaving the manor free for us to get in."

"Elizabeth also requested additional invitations be sent to Hensley's manor as well."

"We'll have spies to keep an eye on her."

"That's the idea."

"Now we just need a plan on how to get in."

"I've decided to leave that to Chester."

"Why?"

"Because he's the best budge in the business."

"Budge?"

He laughed. "A burglar. Specifically, one who breaks into homes."

She nodded and stored away the term. "Who else will you send in with him?"

"It's not my decision. And before you raise those hackles, there's no point in arguing. It's common practice for the person running the game to make the call, and Chester won't have it any other way."

In an attempt she was positive was either meant to stop her from whining or prevent her from listing out the reasons why she should be part of the crew, he took her mug and set it aside.

Then he rocked her world one more time.

27

Beckworth welcomed his guests, which included all the regulars, including the men from the *Daphne* and Sebastian, and directed them to the dining room where Bart and Lincoln had already found their seats. He would have preferred the library or the solarium where he could look at the garden, but this wasn't Waverly, and he was only borrowing the manor.

Templeton retained a small yearly staff to maintain the manor. Additional staff were brought in when someone was in residence. He could have asked the housekeeper to set up a table in the solarium as Mary had done, but it wasn't worth the staff's effort for the short time it was required. Against his wishes, but unable to deter her, Eleanor assisted the housekeeper with arranging the meal and the dining room.

He made a short announcement about the news Elizabeth had shared the night before and the upcoming masquerade ball that might provide them the diversion they needed to get Gemini out of the manor. Then Eleanor called the footmen to bring in a light buffet, and he circulated among his guests, encouraging the group to mingle as they ate. This gave Chester, who had met most of them and worked closely with some, time to socialize and finalize his team.

Beckworth had given him his recommendations, and while Chester would take his advice to heart, it didn't mean he would. No doubt Barrington had also chimed in, and while his advice would be similar to his own, it wasn't a guarantee.

Breaking into the manor where Gemini stayed and remaining unnoticed wouldn't be easy and required specific skills. Beckworth would have preferred to be part of the selected crew, but considering the awkward position Gemini had put him in with her forged marriage documents, he couldn't be found at the manor if something went wrong.

Once the majority of the group had finished eating, they began to find seats around the table. Hensley, as Beckworth requested, sat at the head of the table. He'd brought his own stationary, quill, and inkpot, and had been writing messages while the team conversed. Chester, an equal to Hensley in this mission, dropped into the seat at the opposite end of the table.

Beckworth waited for the footmen to clear the empty plates and refill glasses. The buffet remained specifically for Fitz, who had a bottomless stomach, but he'd requested dessert to be included so Fitz didn't eat alone.

When it was obvious the side conversations weren't going to end, he tapped the table several times then cleared his throat before raising his voice to be heard. "Let's settle down and get started."

It was as if he hadn't said a word. He understood Hensley's frustration at keeping orderly meetings and noticed the man smirking at him. He opened his mouth to try again when a shrill whistle carried through the room.

It had an immediate impact. He turned to Stella.

Her smile was innocent. "Sorry. It just seemed faster."

He grinned and noticed the others give her a tolerant nod as they quieted. At least they'd all become familiar with her particular style.

"I appreciate everyone coming today." Beckworth had purposely chosen a seat in the middle of the group. He might be the host, but he wasn't the lead in the mission. "While we've had success meeting brawn with brawn in dealing with the duke and Reginald in the past, we don't have the isolation of the monastery to deal with Gemini. We have eyes on her here in London, but we don't know where the rest of her mercenaries are. In addition, we're in the city. Neither the magistrate nor the watchmen will take kindly to a personal raid on a citizen who hasn't appeared to have broken any English law. But circumstances have changed.

"We have recently discovered how Gemini is most likely financing her game to steal the chronicles, the stones, and eventually the Heart Stone. The task before us isn't to take the evidence, but to ensure we know where it's located." He nodded toward Hensley.

Hensley set down his fork and wiped his mouth. "I've been in contact with Lord Langdon. He's as eager as the rest of us to put this business with the stones to rest. As most of you know, his daughter-in-law was an unwitting victim of Reginald. He's discussed the issue with John Fielding—"

"The Bow Street Runners?" Chester interrupted.

"They know nothing of our business arrangement, nor will they. I told Langdon of the sworn statement we should soon receive from the real Lady Prescott. They're very interested in knowing what the evidence of her missing fortune might entail. They, of course, have no idea how we aim to obtain that information, but trust I will be prudent in the matter." He scanned the group, and seeing that everyone was following along, continued. "After discussing the matter with Beckworth, we agreed our best option is to use one of the crews to infiltrate the manor where Gemini is staying and search for the papers. With any luck, we'll find it in the manor."

"And if it's not there?" Jamie asked. He would already know the answer, and most likely asked the question to make sure everyone else knew the problem if what they sought wasn't at the manor.

"Then it's most likely on the *Phoenix*," Beckworth answered. With a nod from Hensley, he took over the meeting. "Most of you have worked with Chester and his crew in the past, specifically to save my sorry backside." That earned several nods and chuckles. "This type of infiltration is a specialty of Chester's, and he'll be in charge of this mission. To make sure you understand, this is his operation for two reasons—to keep Hensley's hands clean and because Gemini and her team, even after my rescue from the *Phoenix*, won't know his crew. What this means is that it's his decision how to run the mission and who will be included in the team."

He studied the faces around the table, waiting for nods of acceptance. He anticipated pushback from Murphy and Hughes, but they seemed to look at him differently now. It was Stella's doing, though he wasn't sure if it had been something she'd said, or the fact he'd sacrificed himself for her in Ipswich. Either way, he told himself it didn't matter—but deep down—it did.

It was one more thing he owed Stella. He glanced her way. She folded one of her swans as if he were planning a hunting party and not a dangerous invasion of a private home. He shook his head. Was there nothing that fazed that woman? And as much as he tried to ignore it—it meant a great deal that she trusted him.

Chester cleared his throat, and Beckworth rejoined the conversation.

"Sorry. The room is yours."

Chester removed a pipe from his pocket and barely glanced

at the people gathered around the table. He scratched his head and leaned back, rubbing the bowl of the pipe. The shiny, worn spot on the surface of the clay showed how often he performed the ritual. After a moment of silence, he gave the group a more thoughtful appraisal, seeming to take a final measure of the team he had to choose from.

"I'll be using four from my own crew as lookouts." There was grumbling from the group. "They're excellent with last-minute diversions and have the ability to disappear faster than anyone at this table, including Beckworth or myself."

Chester gave him a toothy grin, and Beckworth understood he wasn't going to like the team he'd selected.

"This job requires a small group. No more than three. I think we can all agree on the importance of a successful mission, so I'll be going myself. I'm still the best budge man in London and, if necessary, can assist with a diversion."

Eyes turned to Beckworth, who nodded. "That's why he's in charge of the job."

"In addition, we'll need someone to review the documents if we find them. For that, I'll ask Jamie to join us. You'll need to pass for a footman, someone who usually goes unnoticed. And finally, I'll need Stella."

The room erupted, and through it all, Stella quietly made her swans with a slight smile. Had the two of them planned it from the beginning? It wouldn't surprise him. They'd gotten close during his absence. He didn't like it, but he couldn't argue after telling everyone it was Chester's decision.

This time, rather than yelling over the group, he used Stella's technique and gave a sharp, loud whistle. It took a couple of minutes before the group calmed again.

"Give the man a chance to explain his decision." Beckworth was interested in hearing it as well.

Chester took his time packing tobacco into the pipe. Then

with a nod of approval from Beckworth, lit the bowl. Soft tendrils of smoke lifted into the air and filled the room with the scent of cloves. After a couple of puffs, he gave the room a stern look.

"I selected Stella for several reasons. I've had time to get to know her and see her determination to complete a goal. She's cool under pressure, and I have it on good authority that she can pick locks, and while I can as well, it never hurts to have a second person with that skill. She also has a contentious history with Gemini." Chester gave him another grin.

Stella had many reasons to want to see Gemini put away, but he bet Chester's smile had more to do with Gemini's illegal marriage to him, and Stella's irritation with it. He scowled in return.

"If for some reason, Gemini unexpectedly returns early, and my outside crew can't stop her, I have no doubt Stella's presence, while annoying to Gemini, wouldn't be a complete surprise considering the current situation Beckworth finds himself in."

Beckworth was beginning to question why he considered Chester such a valuable friend. Everyone seemed to be getting good sport out of his predicament with Gemini as they looked from him to Stella before resting their gazes on Chester.

Everyone nodded in agreement, though several were still disappointed. He expected them to continue to needle Chester in hopes of a change of heart. But Chester took two more puffs, smothered the embers, and tucked the pipe in his jacket as he stood.

"I need to prepare my team." He eyed Jamie and Stella. "I'll meet the two of you at a pub down the street from the crew's meeting place on the evening of the ball. Eight sharp. Beckworth will provide the location." He pointed at Stella. "You need to be in a dress, but one you can climb in."

With those words, AJ mumbled something under her breath.

Everyone in the room knew how well she could climb. But he'd seen the manor, and access to the second floor wouldn't be that difficult, even for someone inexperienced. Besides, he'd seen her scamper up the side of a ship and duck into a gunport. Her main problem would be keeping her skirts raised so she didn't trip on them.

Stella nodded and waved goodbye as Chester walked out the door.

AJ stood and stared at her. "I don't even know who you are anymore. Haven't we had several discussions about your recklessness?"

Stella chortled. "It's a risk for anyone at this table, and I dare anyone to challenge my ability to perform the task." She glanced at Beckworth, and AJ followed her gaze.

He shrugged. "As much as it pains me, I can't argue Chester's decision of either Stella or Jamie. I think several men here could replace Jamie, but Stella is the right choice. She also knows where to search. With any luck, they'll find the third chronicle as well. But that doesn't mean the rest of you don't have a role to play. We have a masquerade ball that a few of you will be attending."

Maire sighed. "The last one we attended didn't go exactly as planned."

"Fortunately, we don't have to steal anything or create diversions. The team simply needs to observe and send a message if Gemini leaves earlier than planned." He gave Maire a wink. "At least this time you won't have to go disguised as a scullery maid."

She brightened. "This sounds more promising."

"I believe Murphy, AJ, Hughes, and Maire make the perfect couples to attend the event. Invitations should be arriving at Hensley's before the day is out if they haven't already arrived." He nodded to the back of the room where Eleanor stood. "Eleanor will help with your costumes, hair, and makeup. I doubt Gemini has given up on her search for the scribe or the Heart Stone, so it will be imperative that everyone is properly masked." He waited for Murphy or Hughes to argue, but they again nodded their acceptance.

He was beginning to think this was too easy. "And finally, we'll need Fitz and Lando to play coachmen. The two of you will also be our teams' contacts to deliver messages should Gemini depart early. Even dressed as a coachman, it won't be out of protocol for you to be seen in the kitchen. That will be the easiest location for any of the four to get a message to you. If that should happen, one of you must race to Gemini's manor and inform Chester's lookouts. The other will get our team out and back to Hensley's without incident. I'm going to ask Lincoln to go as well and remain in the coach. He'll assist with providing cover should any of you be detected. Any questions?"

While not everyone got the part they might have hoped for, they all had a role to play.

"And where will you be in all of this?" Murphy asked.

He attempted a smile but didn't quite pull it off. "Right here with Barrington, wearing a path in the carpet."

Hensley chuckled. "Not as easy as one thinks waiting for others to run an operation. I think we have a good plan. Once we confirm the evidence, I'll contact Langdon, and then we'll all have to wait for others to take Gemini."

Grumbles sounded from around the room, and Beckworth understood. It would be a letdown to have someone else finish the job they had all in some way suffered through.

He stood and gathered two bottles of whiskey from the sideboard and nodded to the footman to bring glasses. "Until then, let's toast to a successful mission."

28

"Sorry for my outburst in the meeting." AJ stepped next to Stella, who looked out the solarium windows at the garden.

Stella put an arm around her waist. "I know you worry for me." She snorted. "I worry about myself, but not from Gemini or the dangers of sneaking into her manor."

AJ didn't say anything for a moment. "It's Beckworth, isn't it?"

She stepped away. "Let's go to the garden." She led the way and waited for AJ to catch up. From what Eleanor told her, the garden didn't compare to Waverly, and she missed her own. The truth was, she didn't want Beckworth overhearing anything, not sure where the conversation might lead.

A large elm tree offered shade from the afternoon sun. Though spring had barely arrived, the weather had warmed the last few days. She dragged a wrought iron chair out from the table and patted the one next to her before sitting and leaning her elbows on the table.

AJ's brows gathered in a frown. "You know your silence tells me everything I need to know."

"I wanted to get away from the house and wandering ears."

She ran a finger over the design on the tabletop. If she'd only thought to bring paper to fold swans.

"How serious is it?"

She shrugged. "More than I expected." When the silence dragged on, she blew out a breath and sat straighter, turning to look at AJ. "I'm not planning on staying. I know what I have back home, and while I've adapted here better than I thought, I don't think I could survive here."

"Well, this is a topic I know something about." Her frown disappeared, but she didn't fool Stella. AJ did understand and had made her own difficult decision to return home. Finn loved her enough to follow.

Stella didn't know Beckworth's feelings. He never spoke of them any more than she mentioned hers. But she suspected he still didn't feel worthy of love, and she had no more words to give him to help him see the truth. It was now up to him and whether he had the fortitude to face it.

Finn left behind his ship and his way of life for AJ. Beckworth had spent his life digging himself out of poverty, left the crews, and came to terms with a father who was incapable of giving Beckworth the approval he'd sought. And he earned the hard-won acknowledgment that he didn't need his father's acceptance. Nor did he want it. AJ didn't understand that part of Beckworth. Not like Stella did.

Even if he wanted to return with her as Finn had followed AJ, what would he do in the future? He'd have to start all over. He wasn't someone who could sit in a dull office cube with the monotony of an eight-to-five job. Outside of this era, he had no marketable skills. Finn had the inn, his horses, and a new interest in making furniture. That wouldn't suit Beckworth.

"I know I don't fit in this world any more than he would fit in mine." Stella gazed at the lilacs with their tiny buds. His favorite. "But I can't deny what there is between us, and I made the choice to let it go as far as it has. And this is as much as I care to discuss the topic. You know me. This isn't the first time I've had an intense relationship and probably won't be my last." She reached for AJ's hand. "So let me enjoy it while I'm here."

"For heaven's sake, please say yes and stop your moping around."

They turned to see Maire strolling toward them. "It's been Stella this and Stella that ever since she disappeared from the inn." Her smile was wide, and she squeezed Stella's arm as she dropped into the other chair next to her.

"It hasn't been that bad." But AJ's expression and tone weren't convincing.

"Well, now you know that all is well." Stella gave her one of those Stella-knows-best stares.

AJ laughed "I get it. And while you're climbing up to a second-story balcony, I'll be drinking champagne and hobnobbing with the aristocrats."

"The sacrifices some of us face," Maire said and pointed to AJ. "Eleanor is looking for you. She had an idea for your costume. Mine has already been decided. She's not doing much in the way of fancy dresses. Most of the work will be with the masks and our makeup."

"I'll make sure to stop on my way out."

Happy the conversation had turned away from her, Stella focused her attention on Maire. "So, where have you been hiding these past days? It wouldn't be pigeon-holed with Sebastian over some dusty chronicle."

Maire's smile was ethereal, as it always got when talk turned to *The Book of Stones*. "We've been working on the fourth chronicle, the one AJ retrieved in Bréval. As we suspected, it mostly speaks of the torc. At first, we didn't think we'd get much out of it. The druids seemed to ramble at the end. I wish Emory was here to give his opinion. Sebastian was quite interested in hearing about Emory and his studies on Celtic lore. He was fascinated the topic was of such interest in the future.

"But as we've reread several passages, we think we can modify the incantations for the Heart Stone and the individual stones. I think what most of the scribes and druids have had difficulty with is transport to the future rather than the past."

Stella leaned back in her chair as Maire rambled on, part of her listening to her friend's insatiable curiosity about the past, part of her thinking about the mission she'd be undertaking. A slight shiver of excitement and anticipation flowed through her, sparking nerves and making her antsy. And the job was still two days away. She'd be as tightly strung as a string on a violin if she didn't get some release. Her first thought went to Beckworth. Would anyone mind if she locked him in a room for two days? She giggled, and as AJ and Maire stared at her, she realized she'd stopped paying attention.

"Sorry, I didn't mean to interrupt. You were saying something about the incantations working better for going to the past?" As she said the words, something nagged at her, as they had with Gemini's hidden documents. When Maire spoke, the thought vanished.

"I can't imagine where your mind might have wandered." Maire grinned before giving her a pointed look. "Yes, that is what I'm saying. Sebastian agrees, but we don't know why that would be since the druid's sole purpose for their initial ritual was focused on predicting the future."

"It's not like their first attempt went the way they'd expected." AJ had leaned into the table, completely absorbed by the discussion. "I wonder if anything would have happened at all without the lightning and the eclipse."

Maire shrugged. "I think whatever they'd hoped to achieve would have failed. Emory believes it's what he calls the trifecta or the perfect storm of events."

"You said you can modify the incantations further?" AJ asked.

Maire nodded. "For travel to the past. As far as we can tell, other than the incantation that allows a smaller stone to search for the Heart Stone, which is how Ethan and Finn traveled through the future and how we return to the inn each time, the torc is required to provide enough power to move through the future. But without a traveler knowing where to go, it could be dangerous. For example, if I'm in London and want to go to a future London, the torc could probably get me there. But if I wanted to go to a city that exists now, but for some reason doesn't exist in the future, let's say because of war or an invasion, we don't know if the torc simply won't work, or if it would send the traveler someplace else."

"I'm not sure that's something I'd be willing to try," Stella said.

They all shook their heads.

AJ slapped her hand on the table. "That would confirm why Reginald and the druid could never get the smaller stones to work in their attempt to travel to the future."

Maire nodded. "According to what the druid wrote in the grimoire, he had some success traveling to the future with the Heart Stone. But I don't believe the jump would have taken him very far, probably no more than a few years."

"Do you know what might be in the third chronicle that Gemini has?" AJ asked.

"From what Sebastian can remember, he believes it discusses the connection between the Heart Stone and the torc. Since the second chronicle spoke about the smaller stones, it makes sense. I only hope Gemini has hidden the chronicle with the documents Stella will be searching for."

"Do you know what we need?" Stella asked.

Maire eyed her suspiciously. "I'm almost scared to ask."

AJ snickered, but Stella ignored her, though she couldn't help but smile. AJ knew exactly what kind of trouble she could conjure up.

"This sitting around and waiting for the big event is nerve-racking. What we need is a ladies' day in London. We should invite Mary and Elizabeth to join us. The weather has been fantastic. We could take a ride through Hyde Park, do some shopping, and have tea somewhere. Anything to get our minds off the ball. Maybe we can find both of you new dresses for the party."

"Do you think Eleanor would go?" AJ asked.

"Hmm." Stella considered it. "If her plan for the ball is focused on masks and makeup, maybe she'd like to help select dresses. If they need tucking in here or there, that wouldn't take her very long."

"I thought another day of combing over the chronicles would be enough to keep my mind occupied, but I like your idea. I have a few things I'd like to pick up."

"But the men can't come with, and they'll fuss about us being out on our own," AJ said.

Stella patted her hand. "Don't worry. I have a feeling that will work itself out."

After the meeting, Beckworth walked Hensley and Sebastian to their coach. Hensley had dispatches to send, and Sebastian was eager to return to his study of the fourth chronicle, mumbling something about Maire spending more time with it than he had.

After watching the coach drive off, he was still smiling as he made his way back through the manor. He found the men in the study, the room already filled with cigar smoke and the telltale scent of earthy tobacco from Fitz's pipe.

When he'd first seen Fitz with his pipe, he'd thought the man had spent too long at sea, but now he found the pipe fit the man. For all the sailor's bravado and his love of brawling, he was more of a thinker than most gave him credit. The man was younger than him, and he had no doubt the first mate, who had no desire to captain a ship, would one day settle down as a fisherman in some Irish port with a lass and several babes, his evenings spent in a rocking chair, smoking that same pipe.

"So, how's the back?" Murphy asked.

Beckworth strode to the sideboard and poured a whiskey. "As good as new from what I can tell. The sparring sessions haven't bothered it."

The men gave each other a look that made his back itch. There was no telling what they'd been discussing while he'd been seeing the coach off.

"We're all feeling on edge waiting for the mission." Jamie had taken the chair behind the desk and propped his boots on its corner, his glass resting on his stomach.

"And too much time in port," Lando agreed as he leaned against a bookcase.

"Do you ever sit?" Beckworth asked. "You're like a vulture waiting to pick bones off a carcass."

Lando sneered. "You are many things, little man, but funny isn't one of them."

The men laughed, and he ignored Lando's nickname for him, though he wished the man would find a different one.

"We need time away from London." Fitz gazed up to the ceiling, wheels turning in his head. "Or a good brawl."

"I almost miss the days of Reginald and the duke." Hughes had sprawled on the sofa next to Murphy, and as much as his statement brought back bad memories, he had a point.

"We never had to sit around waiting for so long," Jamie concurred and lifted his glass in solidarity.

"I almost miss running from Gemini's men." Beckworth didn't want to share how much he missed those days but not because it kept him occupied. Those had been the days when it had been just him and Stella.

"All the more reason to consider Finn's plan." Jamie dropped his legs and sat up, pointing to Beckworth. "And we'll know for sure how well you've healed."

He eyed the group suspiciously. "What exactly do you have in mind? You need to be in one piece for the ball."

"And we need to be refreshed, not stodgy from sitting around like old men playing card games in the sitting room." Murphy sat up, his elbows resting on his knees, his glass of whiskey slowly rotating in his hands. "Hensley has connections with a hunting lodge outside Richmond. I sent a message a couple of days ago. It's an hour's ride out of the city with plenty of forest." He gave Beckworth a grin. "No better way to test your back than a day in the saddle."

Beckworth considered it. Murphy wasn't wrong, and he felt healthy enough. If his back bothered him, he could always go back to the lodge, as humiliating as it would be. "What of the women?"

"Eleanor's working on costumes. We can make sure Stella goes with her to Hensley's where they'll be safe." Hughes's eyes sparked with excitement, which was rare for the stoic man.

He felt his own blood surging with a need to get out of the city. A long evening with Stella and a day on a hunt, followed by another evening with her. He couldn't think of a more pleasant way to live. The more he thought about it, the more he liked the plan.

"I'll bring Bart and Lincoln along with Stella. Those two

need a change of scenery, and they'll enjoy spending time with Sebastian."

The next hour was spent planning their hunt, and for the first time since being dragged onto the *Phoenix* in Ipswich, Beckworth felt like the Viscount of Waverly. He only hoped Stella wouldn't mind being stuck at Hensley's for the day.

29

Beckworth knocked on the door, and when Stella snapped, "Come in," he reconsidered entering. It wasn't that he hadn't been around her when she was waspish—it was usually from something he said or did. Since they were currently on better terms, intimate ones to be exact, he couldn't think of anything he'd done or said that would make him the cause of her current mood.

That left one thing. The job. On her first mission with the team, he'd been the one to be saved, so he had no idea if this was her normal mood as the time of the event grew near. Either way, he wasn't going to let her go without wishing her luck. He squared his shoulders and forced a neutral expression as he entered.

"It's just me. I thought I'd check on you before you left to meet Chester." She was dressed in her moss-colored robe, which was tied at her waist, but she gripped the material closed at her neck as she stared into the wardrobe closet.

She didn't respond.

"Is there something in there I should defend you from?"

"Yes. A dozen dresses that are all wrong."

He stepped behind her and laid his hands on her shoulders, gently massaging them. "If I had my way, you'd have dozens more, but I'm sure we can find something within this limited number."

She leaned against him, her floral scent filling his senses. He closed his eyes, his arms moving around her waist. She seemed to melt into him, and without thinking, his hand moved under the edge of the robe, his fingers finding the soft curve of her breast. When she arched under his touch, his senses exploded. The world shrunk to only one thing—this woman in his arms.

She turned around and took his hand, kissing it and placing it on her waist before she wrapped her arms around him. "We have a couple of hours."

Her tone was soft and sultry. It dissolved his ability to consider his actions. He was in the moment, but he would simply hold her until she gave the signal to proceed. She leaned back and stared up at him.

"Are you game?"

He chuckled. "With you, always."

She pushed him backward until his legs hit the edge of the bed. Her fingers were nimble as they unbuttoned his breeches and then tugged his pants down to below his knees.

Her grin was anything but sweet. "Sit and relax. Stella's in a mood."

She certainly was. He'd never seen her like this and wasn't sure what to expect. Her gaze locked with his and was filled with heated passion. She bent down and kissed him. It wasn't soft or languid. She devoured him, and he barely registered her pulling her robe aside to climb onto his lap. She covered him, and he grabbed her waist as she moved around to find just the right spot.

If she was in a mood, it was becoming one of his favorites, and he was at her mercy.

An hour later, it might have been longer, they sprawled across the bed. Her body was tangled in her robe. At some point, he couldn't remember when, she'd pulled his shirt over his head but wasn't sure where she'd tossed it. His pants were still around his ankles, and he was surprised the maid hadn't interrupted them. Or maybe she had. He'd been in a land far, far away that only included Stella.

He turned his head to find her staring at the ceiling, a soft smile on her face. This woman continued to surprise him. "Is Stella still in a mood?"

Her throaty laugh stirred him, but he didn't think they had time for another round.

"It's much improved."

"Is there anything else you need of me?"

She considered it. "Yes. Find me a dress that would be presentable enough should I come face to face with that bitch, yet still be able to climb to the balcony."

"That I can do."

She rolled over until her head rested on his chest. Her hand strayed lower. "On second thought, I'm still a bit nervous. I think we still have time."

"You, Stella Caldway, are incorrigible." But he didn't give her time to respond, planting his lips on hers and finding just enough energy to make her forget the mission.

Stella stared up at the back of the manor from her position in the garden. Chester and Jamie were on either side of her as they squatted behind a hedge. She grinned. If only Beckworth could see her next to a bush. At least she had something to dive into should the job not go as expected.

Earlier that day, Beckworth had left for an appointment. With nothing to do during her long wait for the evening and no one to talk to other than Bart and Lincoln, she went with Eleanor to prepare AJ and Maire for the ball.

It helped. They'd found two dresses while out shopping the day before that were perfect with the masks Eleanor had made.

Mary prepared an afternoon lunch in the garden. Eleanor worked on taking in the seams and hems on the dresses while Mary entertained them with her stories. AJ and Maire grew excited about the party while she fought to calm her overabundant nerves.

She didn't want to back out of her role. It was the waiting she hated, and she'd overeaten to compensate. She cut off the coffee by mid-afternoon. It would be more than embarrassing if Chester and Jamie had to wait while she peed in a bush.

If Beckworth hadn't come along at just the right time, she would have climbed the walls with her pent-up energy. She smiled at the memory. Now her thighs burned from squatting for so long. She glanced around and then sat, thankful the grass where they waited wasn't damp. She'd need every muscle in her legs to cooperate for the climb.

Jamie had picked her up at seven-thirty, and they'd arrived at the meeting place right on time. Chester introduced them to the crew that would be their lookouts and diversions. Most were mere children. They were thin with ragged clothes, but their eyes showed wisdom far beyond their years. She'd imagined Beckworth at that age. They'd never have a childhood. They were too busy finding ways to feed their families.

Beckworth had warned her about this, and with his blessing, she'd brought biscuits with her. She pulled them out of her pocket, and after getting Chester's nod of approval, handed them out. They'd grabbed several, and after receiving final instructions, disappeared into the shadows.

Chester had circled around the manor next door before entering the garden from an alley. While they waited for Gemini to leave, Chester reviewed the plan again.

"I'll go up first." Chester scanned the yard then pointed. "See that trellis?" When they nodded, he continued. "I'll test it to see if it's strong enough to climb, but I worry about your skirts tangling in the vines. It will probably be best to climb the edges of the stone."

Stella shook her head. "Don't worry about that. I tested several dresses." She pulled her wrap around her against the cooling air. "I can tuck my skirts up so they'll be out of the way. Not very ladylike but better to climb. I'll tie the wrap around my head and waist."

When Chester looked at Jamie, he nodded. "I'll climb the stone wall once Stella reaches the balcony. I don't want to stress the trellis. She'll need it for the climb down."

She tilted her head and smiled at Chester. "You're not having second thoughts on your selection, are you?"

He shook his head. "No. I knew you'd find a way to adapt."

Fifteen minutes later, a light bird call came from behind them.

"That's the signal. Let's go." Chester stood, glanced around then raced to the patio.

Stella didn't waste time as she jumped up to follow, Jamie on her heels. When they reached the back of the house, Chester took a moment to study the climb, then he tugged on the trellis. The vines had sprouted most of their leaves, but there were still several open areas for footholds. He climbed the trellis partway before grabbing the bottom edge of the balcony and pulling himself up to use the fancy edging for foot and handholds.

While she watched him climb, she stuck the hem of her skirts inside the waistband of her petticoat, then pulled the wrap over her head, tying its tails around her waist. Jamie nudged her, and she grabbed the trellis. Her fear of heights suddenly gripped her, and she wished there wasn't a hard stone patio to land on if she fell. She second-guessed her original thrill of being selected for this mission and considered why climbing up the side of the *Phoenix* on a rope ladder hadn't caused such anxiety. Falling into the water should have concerned her. It shouldn't have surprised her the difference was Beckworth. She would have done anything to rescue him.

When she was nudged a second time, she thought about Beckworth and his confidence in her. She put a foot on one of the trellis's crossbeams and hauled herself up. She remembered AJ's words of advisement from lunch. Don't look down, and don't look up until you think you've reached the top. Focus on each foot and hand placement. Test before putting her full weight on each beam. She added an element to the process by counting each step. She had no idea how many steps were required; the point was to maintain focus.

Before she knew it, Chester was patting her head. She took another step up, then he held her arm as she stretched her leg for the railing. Once her foot found it, she was pulled over. She glanced down and scowled at how quickly Jamie followed her up.

Once they all stood on the balcony, Chester tested the doors. He fussed with the latch before one of the doors opened. He peered inside, then disappeared. Stella followed with Jamie staying behind her.

It was close to a full moon, and after he closed the door, Jamie pulled the drapes back far enough to give them some light.

"This is the master suite," Chester whispered.

"Then there should be a dressing room," Stella whispered back.

"Over here." Jamie disappeared and a moment later a light

glow leaked from the doorway. Stella raced over and followed him in while Chester remained at the entrance.

Several trunks were stacked along the walls. A few dresses hung on one side, but otherwise, the dressing room was bare.

"She must have had the owner's belongings moved." Stella went to the first trunk, opened it, and rifled through it. "These are Gemini's things, but the files aren't in this one."

Chester entered and picked up one end of the trunk she'd just searched. "Help me take this down so she can search the bottom one. Then we'll move to the next."

They continued the pattern of searching the top and bottom trunks as they moved around the room. They had finished the trunks along one side of the room and against the back wall when a sound froze them in place.

The candlelight disappeared, leaving them in darkness. The outer door opened, and light footsteps crossed the room before an audible intake of breath.

Stella pushed past Chester to peer out. It was a maid, and she was staring at the opened drapes. Beyond them, the door stood partially open. It must have slipped the latch.

30

The two couples stepped from the coach, and AJ glanced down the street where other coaches lined up. Finn took her hand and led her up the stairs, but before entering, she took a last look over her shoulder as Fitz clucked his tongue and the carriage moved off.

The men had made a last-minute change. Lando rode a horse rather than joining Fitz in the box. If Chester's crew had to be notified, a horse could move swiftly through the streets and go places a coach couldn't.

She caught a glimpse of Lando as he rode by the manor in the opposite direction of the coaches. He gave the barest hint of a nod as he passed by Fitz. Once Gemini arrived, he would tie his horse someplace close and wait in the kitchen for word.

Finn squeezed her hand. "Don't worry. Everything will work out." He bent to kiss her cheek. "I'm glad it's me escorting you to a ball this time."

She was, too. The last time she'd attended a ball, Ethan had escorted her while Finn searched for the druid's book. A plan that had been doomed from the start and ended with him getting caught and her leaving him behind in the hopes of saving the rest of the team. It had worked, but Finn spent months tortured and starving, certain he'd never see her again.

This evening wasn't going to end up the same way. All they had to do was wait for Gemini and keep an eye on her.

They arrived early, hoping to miss the others' notice. It was the one time Gemini might have spotted them. They didn't believe she knew what any of them looked like, except for Gaines, who'd briefly met Finn at the meeting in Basingstoke. Eleanor made his mask larger so it covered his forehead and half of his face. He looked like the phantom of the opera. It didn't help that his breeches, boots, waistcoat, and jacket were all black.

Ethan and Maire stepped next to them once they reached the far side of the foyer. "We'll make a pass through the first floor, but I doubt she arrived this early."

Finn nodded. "We'll get something to drink and find a corner to watch the entrance."

For more than an hour, Finn and AJ stood behind a tall fern, partially hidden from view but not enough to appear suspicious. They looked like young lovers, his hand resting on her waist and hers on his arm, their heads bent low.

AJ's nerves got the better of her. "Maybe we should take a walk around the ballroom. She might have come in a different entrance."

He shook his head. "This is the only one she'd enter through if she wants to be seen."

"I suppose it would look odd for you to bring a chair over?"

He pulled her closer. "I'm sorry. You should have known to wear comfortable shoes."

She kept her head lowered, and her whispered tone came out harsher than she expected. "I didn't think we'd be standing in the same spot for so long."

Finn snapped his fingers at a footman with a tray who

wandered close by. He exchanged their flutes with fresher champagne. "Stay here, and I'll find Ethan. Maybe she arrived before us."

She watched him walk away. He didn't think Gemini was here. It was more likely he wanted to give her space. It wasn't his fault her feet hurt. She hadn't made the wisest choice in shoes, but they did look smashing with her dress. Good god. She'd been in this timeline too long if she was thinking like an aristocrat. Then she grinned. She'd make it up to him tonight.

She sipped her drink and glanced at the entrance—and froze.

Somehow it was the tall man behind the blonde woman that first caught her eye. He was dressed in black like Finn, but her gaze locked on the cruel twist of his lips. His eyes were the dark color of his simple mask. She'd never forget that face from the cabin at Basingstoke—mask or no mask.

She turned her focus to the woman and the second man behind her. Though they were better hidden behind their masks, it was easy to note the similar feminine lines along their chins and cheeks. Their eye color was light, but she couldn't discern if they were blue or green. They had to be related.

The woman moved with grace through the crowd, and the guests appeared to naturally make room for her. She was stunning.

She hated this next part. Finn should know better. She didn't mingle. Rather than stick to one spot, and afraid she might say something and have her American accent draw too much interest, she moved slowly from one group to another.

Each time the woman stopped to speak to someone, the other women's eyes widened beneath their masks. Was she introducing herself as the Viscountess of Waverly? She felt for Beckworth. Between the duke, Reginald, Dugan, and now

Gemini, he never seemed to catch a break. If she could just get close enough to hear the conversation.

She pulled her fan out and worked her way around the crowd, inching closer to her target.

Once they left Finn and AJ in the foyer, Ethan led Maire through the ballroom. Though they'd arrived early, there were already quite a few people milling about, and the musicians played simple melodies, preparing for when the dancing would begin.

Ethan grabbed two flutes of champagne from a tray, and they made a complete circle around the room, confirming they didn't see anyone that could be Gemini. Two women had caught Maire's eye as they strolled by, but the men with them weren't either of her bodyguards. One man was too portly, the other too old.

Although Gemini could introduce any man accompanying her as a brother or uncle, she expected to see Gaines. She hadn't gotten as good a look as Ethan had but knew he was Finn's height and had dark hair and a muscular frame. It would reduce a large portion of the crowd.

After they'd come full circle, Ethan steered her to the dining room, where a light buffet had been set up. The room was too busy, and neither of them thought Gemini would waste her time eating when there was a ballroom full of people to share the news of her fake marriage.

She almost felt sorry for Beckworth. He'd changed a great deal from the viscount she remembered, and though she'd mostly forgiven him for those eighteen months as his prisoner, albeit in the finest of surroundings, she still couldn't completely forgive him. If Gemini's pursuit of him didn't hurt Stella as much as it did, she'd have a good laugh at it all. It was a failed plan from the start, and Gemini couldn't be thinking straight if she thought it would be easy to steal a dime from Beckworth. If she'd known his history as a London street urchin working with the crews, she would have rethought her strategy.

Since no banns had been printed and no special license obtained, Beckworth should be able to ignore whatever Gemini was up to, though with enough gossip, the matter might end up with the magistrate. Beckworth couldn't tell them about the kidnapping. It was too much of a risk to expose the stones and the crews. The forged document should be enough to clear him.

Her deeper concern revolved around the planned raid by the Bow Street Runners. What if they discovered the chronicle? They hadn't been able to confirm if Gemini had the rest of the smaller stones, but she had at least one of them that Gaines used to kidnap Stella.

"Are you listening to me?" Ethan asked.

She looked up, completely unaware he'd been talking. If she were one of the women who normally attended these balls, she would have batted her eyes and given him a vapid stare. But she wasn't one of these women, and she would never play with Ethan's emotions.

"I was lost in thought. I'm so sorry." She gave him the most endearing smile she could, then leaned into him, her chin raised.

He knew what she wanted and didn't hesitate to meet her lips for a quick kiss. "You can make it up to me this evening."

She stared into his stormy gray eyes. He was everything to her. She'd always feared she'd end up married off to an Irish farmer and live in the same town and the same house until she grew old and died. She'd wanted to be a Traveller when she was young. It seemed a fascinating life, moving from one town to another, studying herbs.

It was the influence of the Travellers that had driven her to leave with her cousin for London rather than wait for Finn. She wanted an adventure that wasn't shadowed by her brother. Little did she know her first trip away from home would drop her into Beckworth's world. Then she'd caught a whiff of the stones and their alleged magical powers.

When AJ arrived, and ultimately with Finn's return, her whole world turned upside down again. Then Ethan Hughes walked into her life. He was loyal, kind, and brave. He wasn't a farmer and never would be. He lived a life of adventure, and he'd been smitten with her the moment he saw her. A woman could tell these things.

What he didn't seem to be aware of after all this time together, in this century or the future, was how much he meant to her. She couldn't imagine a day without him and had learned it the hard way when she'd been foolish enough to get kidnapped a second time. Six months apart. Never again. Yet something held him back from moving their relationship forward, and she believed she knew why.

It was her. Ethan seemed agreeable to live in any century, as long as he was with her. But she'd been unable to make a decision on whether to remain in this century or in the future with AJ and her brother. She didn't see why they couldn't commit to a future together regardless of which century they were in.

He was staring at her. She'd been caught wool-gathering again only minutes from the last time.

She laughed. It was one of her deeper laughs, and it forced a grin from Ethan. "I can't believe I did it again. You must think me a horrible companion. It seems impossible to stay focused."

He hugged her to him. "Perhaps a dance will put aside whatever thoughts are floating around that lovely head of yours."

"You're too good to me, you know. Most men wouldn't tolerate my behavior."

"Then it's a good thing I'm not most men."

"I'd say." She winked at him. His eyes warmed, and she cursed the fact they were on a job. She had to stay focused on their search for Gemini.

Before either could say another word, Finn stepped up and tapped Ethan on the shoulder. "Have you taken the opportunity to dance?"

Ethan shook his head. "We were discussing it."

The three of them walked toward a quiet corner, keeping their voices low.

"I could use your assistance on a matter if you don't mind stepping away from your wife for a moment." Finn played his role should anyone overhear.

"I think that can be arranged." Ethan turned to Maire. "I'll see about getting you another drink before I return. You don't mind mingling, do you, darling?"

"Not at all."

The two men walked away, most likely to see if Lando was in the kitchen. Finn's words had jolted her when he called her Ethan's wife. It had given her warm tingles, but she shook it off, and when a footman strolled by carrying a tray of appetizers, she took something that looked like a mini pie. It was filled with tasty minced meat, and she devoured it.

She wandered around the ballroom, making two circles before moving toward the sitting room where she spotted a group of ladies. Even with the mask, she remembered one of the women and her distinctive laugh from the last time she visited London.

When she approached, one of the younger women dabbed at her eyes. They were red-rimmed, and her face had become blotchy. Something had certainly created an outburst.

"Now, now, it's still early. Is it possible your young man will step up to make his intentions clear?" an older matron asked.

The younger woman blew her nose. "He had planned to, but when Lord Minken asked for my hand, he became undecided. When I asked why, he said he wanted what was best for me and that he couldn't provide what Lord Minken could. I told him it didn't matter, but I don't think he's listening to me."

The other women stared at each other, knowing it was most likely too late for this young woman in love. And all because her young man wouldn't stand up for her. He preferred to be heroic, but would that comfort him in six months when it was too late?

She stepped back, preferring to watch a couple of older gentlemen play chess. A perfect spot to analyze the new thought that sprang to mind when hearing the women's discussion. It came to her when it was mentioned the young man thought the lord could provide a more stable future for her.

That was the exact reason Ethan held back. She was sure of it.

His ability to support her wouldn't be an issue in the future. He owned a security company, and though it had suffered while he'd been away, he would be able to rebuild it. But what did he have in this time period? He'd given up his position with the earl. And though the earl would welcome them back, he didn't have much time left before the estate would transition to someone else. Ethan couldn't inherit. If he stayed as part of the new lord's guard, he'd report to Thomas. He could work for Hensley, but he'd be gone often, and most likely without her. Either way, it would be a difficult life.

Would he let her go thinking she could make a better match?

"There you are." Ethan took her arm and led her back to where the main crowd gathered. "Lando wasn't in the kitchen, so he must still be waiting for Gemini. I hope this wasn't one event she decided to ignore." When she didn't respond, he tried again. "Maire. Is your head still in the clouds?"

She didn't respond, though his voice jarred her from her musings.

"Come with me." She grabbed his hand and pulled him toward the hallway. When a footman passed, she stopped him, drained the last of her champagne, and set the empty flute on it.

He didn't stop her as she led him deeper into the manor, but he hesitated when she entered the music room. It was empty, and no fire burned, which made it the perfect spot.

She closed the door behind them and twirled to face him. "Why have you never asked me to marry you?"

31

Ethan's eyes darted around the room before landing on Maire. "What?"

"You heard me. Why haven't you ever proposed? Was that never your intention?"

No words came to mind. What the hell had brought this on? Not once in their entire time together had she given any sign that this was something important to her. He wasn't prepared for this conversation and fell back on the only question running through his head.

"Don't you think this might be an inappropriate time to discuss this?"

"AJ and Finn can watch for Gemini. We have time." She walked across the room and sat on the piano bench. Her hands were folded across her lap in a demure manner that wasn't fooling him.

He strolled along the edges of the room, needing time to consider the best way out of this. It was a discussion long overdue, but he couldn't understand why now of all times. This was something that should be done in the privacy of a drawing room, or on a picnic, maybe during a ride through Hyde Park. It shouldn't be done in the middle of a mission when other lives were at risk. That was the answer.

"We have people depending on us to keep eyes on Gemini."

"You said Gemini wasn't here yet. Even if she showed up before Finn returned to AJ, she'll stay at least an hour before leaving. She'll want time to press whatever advantage she believes she has by posing as the Viscountess of Waverly. We have a few minutes."

It was apparent she wasn't going to budge until he complied. Her stubborn Irish temperament. He had planned out his entire approach for when the time was right. Now that the moment had been thrust upon him, he couldn't remember a word of his practiced speech. Everything seemed jumbled now, including why he had waited.

She was still sitting, staring at a spot on the wall, or maybe at the harp across the room. He pulled a chair over so it faced her with only inches separating them.

He placed a hand on her knee, and the foot she'd been lightly tapping stopped. "Can you tell me what brought this on?"

He didn't think she'd answer when a minute ticked by and then another, but he used the time to pull his thoughts together. There was an explanation for his hesitation, but her focus shifted before he could finish his thoughts.

She smiled and held his hand. "I suppose it's silly now that I think about it from your perspective. I was thinking about my life and the choices I've made. They seemed like mistakes in the beginning, but then I met AJ—and you. Then I was caught up in the mystery and adventure of the stones, even though it's been difficult at times."

Her gaze dropped, and her expression dimmed like the sun setting before its time. She'd been thinking of her time in Reginald's prison cell.

"And that's what made you ask the question?"

She lifted her head and gave a shrug. "Not in itself." She blushed a lovely shade of pink that was rare to see. "While I was waiting for you to find Lando, I stood next to a group of women. One of the younger ones was distraught. A lord asked for her hand in marriage, but she loves another. But the other man won't interfere because he believes the lord is a better match for her."

"Ah. I see." His feelings for her, and his delay in discussing their future weren't quite the same. Not at all. But one thing was. He was making the decision for her, rather than giving her the truth and letting her determine her path.

She'd pulled her hand away while she'd shared her thoughts, and he reached for it, not letting go when she tried to tug it back.

"Listen. You asked why I haven't proposed. What my intentions are. Give me a moment to tell you." He waited until she relaxed and leaned toward him, her sea-green gaze locked on his.

"Tell me."

"I've loved you from the moment I saw you. It made no sense, but I knew it just the same. But you were focused on the stones and getting AJ home, and I wasn't sure how to approach you. Then a miracle happened."

Her smile brought the sun. "I'd like to think it was fate."

His heart clenched at her admission. She'd felt it, too. He shook his head. "When we forced you to go to the future, I'd thought I'd lost you. But you adapted so well. Curious about everything. Yet, I knew *The Book* and the stones called to you." He wasn't sure if he could get the next words out. To know the truth of her feelings and whether they had a future together.

"Now we're probably running out of time, and my brother will come looking for us. So tell me." She was still smiling. The patient saint except when she wasn't.

"I didn't want you to make a decision about where your future lay because of a commitment to me."

"You don't think we'd be possible in this time period."

"I think it would be difficult, not impossible."

She nodded. "I can see that. But you can't determine a decision about us based on where we live." She gave him an impish grin. "Or which time period. We're not waiting to live our lives, Ethan. We're living them now—the two of us—regardless of where we are." She took both of his hands, her expression blissful. "Marry me, Ethan. While the earl still lives. When this is done, take me to Hereford. Let the earl wed us."

His chest hurt until the air rushed out of him. He pulled her to him and kissed her. And then she was pushing him away. "What?"

"Was that a yes?"

"You've watched too many movies."

She snorted. "Perhaps. But to be honest, I was getting tired of waiting. I was considering asking Finn to talk to you."

"I think he already tried."

She stood. "Let's go. We need to check in with AJ and Finn." She pulled him toward the door, but he stopped her. When she turned to look at him, she had a puzzled expression.

"Yes."

She tilted her head as if she forgot her question. Then she grinned as she threw her arms around him. "We'll celebrate tonight." Then she was tugging him toward the door again.

He gave the room one last look. Of all the places for a proposal, this would have been the last place he'd have considered. Women always had to be different. A silly grin was stamped on his face as he followed Maire down the hall.

When Finn left Ethan and Maire, he got a twinge along the back of his neck. Lando hadn't been in the kitchen, but all that meant was that Gemini hadn't arrived yet. He should have asked Ethan to check again. They might have just missed him. He had one of those hunches. The one he got in the middle of a mission when something was wrong.

He returned to the foyer, but AJ wasn't where he'd left her. In fact, she wasn't anywhere in sight. He scanned the room but didn't see anyone fitting Gemini's description. AJ must have seen someone that might have been her and followed her.

He reversed his steps and entered the ballroom, remaining near the door as he scanned the crowd. The number of guests had grown since the few minutes he'd left, and he wouldn't find AJ without entering the fray. It took time to work his way through the throng of people deep in conversation, laughing at someone's fanciful tale, or those watching the dance floor.

He was halfway around the room, a small bead of sweat working its way down his temple, but he didn't see her anywhere. AJ wasn't the timid woman she used to be at these affairs, and that could get her in trouble, even at a ball. The last thing they needed were tongues wagging about the American woman wandering through the ball unescorted.

Then he stopped when he spotted her. He didn't have a good feeling about this. Her focus was pinned on someone, and when he followed her line of sight, he understood. There was no question in his mind that Gemini had arrived. The woman was the right stature, blonde hair curled loosely about her head, and while her simple gold mask glittered, it did nothing to hide the face behind it. She was a beauty, as the men who'd met her had described.

What truly confirmed it was the man at her side. Gaines.

There was no question about it. He wasn't as tall as Dugan or as broad of shoulder, but he wasn't a man to be taken lightly. Rather than walk arm and arm with Gemini, he walked a pace behind. The sign of a bodyguard.

Gemini stopped and spoke with several women, and when he glanced back at AJ, she was creeping closer. What the hell was she thinking? He pushed his way through the crowd, apologizing as he went. He had to get to her before she got too close. If Gemini saw any of them it would be enough to spook her into moving her location, and all of this would be for naught.

AJ was approaching two couples in deep discussion. Gemini had finished her conversation and was turning toward her. Before Gemini took a step, Gaines bent to whisper in her ear, giving him the chance to grab AJ's elbow, twirling her away onto the dance floor just as Gemini lifted her head.

Finn turned his back to them, moving AJ farther into the dancers. He bent his head. "What were you thinking?"

He wasn't following the correct dance steps, but no one seemed to notice, and when he spun AJ around, Gemini had moved on to another group of people. Gaines's attention was focused on a different point in the room.

"I wanted to hear what she was telling people."

He moved her to a point just off the dance floor, staying within the crowd but close enough to watch Gaines and the top of Gemini's blonde curls.

"That wasn't the plan." His voice was tinged with anger.

"I'm sorry. You know I don't mingle well, and I thought I could stay hidden behind people. The ballroom has filled up quickly."

He put an arm around her. "You worry me with your recklessness at times."

"That seems to be a behavior we have in common."

He couldn't stop the grin. She was right, but it didn't change his concern that something wasn't right. "We should tell Ethan and Maire. Though I expected them to be somewhere in here."

"Maybe they decided to check the other rooms since you didn't know Gemini had arrived. Or did Lando tell you she was here?"

"Lando wasn't in the kitchen. He probably showed up minutes after Ethan and I left."

Loud voices came from the direction Gemini had been heading. They were women's voices, and one sounded familiar.

"What's happening? I can't see over everyone's head."

He steered her closer to the commotion rather than away from it.

Some guests were moving away from the heated words, but others were drawn to them, and Finn kept them in the flow moving toward what was now outright yelling. AJ clutched his jacket.

"I know that voice. It's Lady Agatha."

Of course. "Elizabeth said she wasn't attending the ball."

"Agatha must have decided to come anyway."

Gaines turned around, and blonde curls bobbed behind him. They were headed for the foyer.

"It looks like they might be leaving." Finn pushed his way through the people to follow them.

"Maybe they're just going to another room." Her tone didn't sound convincing.

They both knew the outburst would taint the ball if one of the women didn't leave. When they passed where the commotion had started, he caught sight of Agatha. She held a mask attached to a stick that she waved about in her agitation as she spoke with several others who nodded in unison. When they reached the door leading to the foyer, he caught sight of Gaines directing Gemini in that direction.

"Damn it. They're leaving." He turned them left, stopping to peer into the less crowded rooms of the sitting room and the dining room. "Where did Ethan and Maire disappear to?"

"Maybe we missed them in the ballroom. If they were on the other side of the room, they might not have heard the argument over the music."

It was possible, but it didn't matter. They needed to get to the kitchen. He turned down another hallway to see Ethan and Maire rushing toward them.

"What's wrong?" Ethan asked before Finn had a chance to ask where they'd been.

"Gemini's leaving."

"Already? She must have just gotten here." Maire looked chagrined as she glanced up at Ethan.

For the first time, Finn noticed a strange expression on Ethan's face. But Ethan had already turned toward the back of the manor, yelling over his shoulder. "We need to find Lando."

The four of them scurried through the hallways, down the stairs, and into the kitchen. Lando stepped away from the group of drivers drinking coffee and sharing tales.

"What's wrong? I just got here."

"And they're already leaving." Finn explained the disagreement Gemini had with Lady Agatha.

"That's not good. Get to your coach. I'll head for the manor."

Finn watched Lando rush off. There wasn't anything more for them to do other than return to Hensley's. He led the group back up the stairs, rushing them down the hallway and through the foyer. They waited by the steps for several minutes before their coach came into view. There was still a thin line of carriages arriving late. It would have slowed Gemini's departure as well, which should give Chester's team more time, but it was going to be close.

When Fitz brought the coach to a stop, he leaned down. "I

saw them. They have five minutes on us. But the crew is already on their way to the manor."

Finn helped AJ and Maire into the coach then nodded for Ethan to enter.

"To Hensley's?" Fitz asked.

He was going to say yes but changed his mind. "Take us to Beckworth's."

32

Stella stared at the maid and reached into her pocket, her fingers grazing coins Beckworth had given her. Before she'd left that evening, he'd given her pointers about the mission. He suspected Gemini was a hostile guest and paid the critical staff like the butler and housekeeper well to keep them compliant during her stay.

But did she pay the maids? Most likely not, leaving that to the owners of the manor. She took a step toward the room when Chester pulled her back. He shook his head, but she laid her hand on his arm and nodded. He glanced at Jamie, who shrugged.

They could either take a chance the maid could be persuaded to leave for an hour and forget she'd seen her or hope she didn't blather to the housekeeper about the open door. She didn't like the odds, so she pulled away from Chester who sighed but let her go.

She waited until she'd taken enough steps to block the maid from the door to the hallway then whispered, "Excuse me."

The girl spun around and let out a light screech.

"Shush. I won't hurt you, but you need to stay quiet."

"Who are you?" The maid stepped closer, lifting the lamp in her hand to get a better view of her. She probably came up to add wood to the dying embers in preparation for Gemini's return. She was young, and though her eyes were wide, she didn't appear scared.

"This is a bit awkward, and to be honest, I feel a bit foolish." She kept her voice low and fidgeted with the edges of her sleeves. "The lady of the manor took something from me, and she won't return it. It's rather precious, something my father had given me. I know it's not ladylike, but I climbed the trellis, hoping to find it."

"The true lady of the manor would never steal anything." The maid straightened her shoulders. The kid had sass written all over her face that didn't mesh with the demure maid who'd first faced her.

She could work with this. "I'm sorry. I think the woman I'm talking about might be visiting the true lady of the manor. Perhaps family?"

The girl's eyes rounded with understanding. She spit on the carpet.

That was unexpected.

"She has no relationship with my lady, and she's not much of a friend. She's shifty and mean."

"That sounds like her." Her hand went to her throat as if it was something she always did. "It was an opal necklace. Perhaps you wouldn't mind if I looked for what she took? Assuming she didn't wear it to the ball."

The maid tilted her head. "You waited until she left and then sneaked in. How do I know you're not a thief?"

She sighed. Maybe it would have been better to take the chance the girl wouldn't have mentioned the open door to anyone. "I'm not sure how I can prove to you I'm only here for my necklace. Lady Prescott will never admit she stole it."

"And now she'll think I took it."

Damn. She hadn't thought of that. This girl should be working for Beckworth. Then she acted as if a thought just occurred to her. "There must be any number of people in this house who have access to this room." She jangled her pocket, then reached in and took out two coins. They were crown pieces and should be an enticing offer. "Perhaps this would be enough for the risk you take."

She held out the coins, and the maid stepped closer. When she kept her palm open, the woman took one, felt its weight, then snapped the other one up.

The maid's grin was sly. "You have thirty minutes. The housekeeper will be up to ensure the room is prepared, so I'll be waiting close by." She glanced around the room. "And don't make a mess." She slipped past Stella, shutting the door quietly behind her.

She raced to the dressing room. "You heard?"

Chester nodded. "That was a close one."

"Yeah. I wasn't sure she'd take the bait."

"No one in service turns down two crowns for simply walking out a door." Chester waved to Jamie, who relit the candle. "Let's get that next trunk down. We need to pick up the pace."

Stella found the documents two trunks later. She pulled them out and spread the pages across the top of another trunk, then backed away for Jamie to review them.

She moved to the door, leaving Chester with Jamie to replace the trunk once the documents were put back. If they had more time, they could look for the chronicle, but it would be a risk after running into the maid. She was a few steps from the door when the light from the candle reflected off something metal. Curious, she pushed garments out of the way and smiled.

"Well, hello sweetheart. Remember me?" It was the small

chest she'd found under the bed of her not-so-glorious accommodations when she was a guest of Gemini's. The one with all the coins. Jamie was still reviewing documents, turning pages faster than before.

She pulled a hairpin from her updo and picked the lock. It clicked open as Chester stepped next to her.

"What are you doing?"

"Just checking to see how much money Gemini has left in here."

Chester shook his head until the lid opened. "What's this?"

"A bit of a long story. I don't know if this is all her money or just what she keeps close. She's probably stealing items and selling them for coins. This is just as full as it was weeks ago." She dug in and took a handful.

"We only came to verify the documents." He said all the right words, but he was tempted.

She stuck the coins in her pocket. "Does it look like I took any?"

He shook his head, and she took another handful, stuffing them in her other pocket.

"I got the impression Beckworth was taking care of you."

"He is. This isn't for him or me." She moved the coins around so they didn't look disturbed, then shut the lid and reattached the lock.

"Then what's it for?"

"For you and those starving children you have working for you."

"What are you two doing? Help me with this trunk." Jamie closed the lid, the documents back inside. She had no doubt he put them back where she'd found them.

Chester helped move the trunk back, then Jamie extinguished the light, and they rushed toward the balcony door. Stella shut the drapes and was closing the door when yelling came from below. When the sound came again, she recognized the sound of an angry woman.

She pushed Chester toward the railing. "Gemini's back. Hurry." She tucked her skirts back into her petticoat, the weight of the coin making it trickier. Jamie picked her up and set her on the railing.

"Take it slow. One step at a time. It will take her a while to come upstairs, and she won't think of looking for anyone."

She nodded and grabbed onto the trellis, searching for a beam to step on. Chester was already on the ground, and Jamie was incredibly patient as she worked her way down. It had been easier going up, but AJ's words came back to her. One foot at a time, search for the beam, test her weight, then search for the next step. She used the mantra until hands grabbed her waist and pulled her to the ground.

Chester glanced around as Jamie dropped next to them. She wanted to race for the shadows of the yard, but Chester took his time, his focus on the alley, the manor, and all points between. They reached their exit point through a back gate where two urchins waited. They hurried behind the kids until they were a block from the manor.

They stopped, and she leaned against a wall. Her heart beat like a drum solo in her chest. When Chester and Jamie looked at her, she grinned.

"That was exhilarating."

33

Stella peered out of the carriage to follow Beckworth's path as he strode to a coach parked farther down the alley. Finn and Ethan disembarked, and the three of them continued on, meeting two men who stood in the shadows—Hensley and Lord Langdon. If it wasn't for the safety of his daughter-in-law, who would eventually become the first Keeper of Stones, and Gemini's possible connection to France, she doubted Langdon would take such a personal interest.

She wouldn't be sitting in the coach, watching the men speak in hushed voices, if Hensley hadn't agreed with Jamie's assessment that the documents Gemini kept hidden were questionable, and at the least, deserved further investigation. And while Hensley still waited for word from the real Lady Penelope Prescott, Langdon was satisfied with the evidence at hand.

The raid was set for seven o'clock to ensure the occupants didn't leave for a party or other appointment. They'd kept eyes on the place all day just to ensure Gemini, Gaines, and André were present.

The evening before, after she'd returned from the job with Chester, and Finn and AJ had seen for themselves that she was alive and unharmed, Beckworth had a lavender-scented hip bath waiting for her. He'd prepared it himself and described in grand detail the difficulties the extra effort required, punctuating it with an occasional wink and well-placed kiss. He washed her hair, seeming to revel in gently pouring the warm water over her head. When he ran a soapy towel over her body, she almost pulled him into the water with her.

His mock complaining stopped once he'd towel-dried her entire body. After a long session under the covers, she told him about the job and confessed about the coins she'd taken from Gemini's chest. She expected him to be mad or deliver some admonishment about risking the team. But all he did was laugh and assure her that Chester would see the money put to good use.

It had felt good to sleep in his arms. He woke first, as usual, to ensure there would be a coffee service for when she woke. What luxury.

"What do you see?" AJ nudged her elbow. "Either start talking or move aside so I can look."

She blinked away the erotic thoughts that had been forming and glanced out the carriage window. Barrington had stopped the coach next to a building, and AJ and Eleanor's windows had a spectacular view of a brick wall.

"There's nothing to see." Maire stuck her head out the window and looked in both directions. "There's only the men standing in a circle."

"Why do we have to stay in the carriage if the men got out?" Stella asked.

Maire and AJ glanced at each other, and then all three turned to Eleanor.

"I don't know why you're looking at me. They're your men." She glanced to her right, as if forgetting there was nothing but a wall there. Then she ducked her head and peered across the coach and out Maire's window. "Besides, I have no desire to stand around in the chilled air. I only came along as moral support. If you want to go see what's happening, I'm not averse to gossip."

They laughed, then admonished each other for making too much noise as Stella peeked out the window to see if the men heard. No one turned their head toward them. When the giggles settled down, Maire opened the door and stepped down, turning to assist Stella, and then AJ.

Barrington was still in the box holding the reins, and he glanced down, gave them a frown, then returned to watching the street.

The women, bolstered by his indifference, strolled arm-in-arm together as if enjoying a day at Hyde Park.

They slowed as they reached the men and formed their own huddle. One by one, they tiptoed to the end of the building and peered around the corner. Then they'd scurry back, and the three would formulate their thoughts on what was happening.

"These men appear to be more skilled than the constables who tried to capture Reginald." AJ scratched her nose then pulled her wrap tighter as she bounced on her toes.

"That's because Langdon is using John Fielding's elite force." Maire's eyes were wide as they darted from one point to another, taking it all in, waiting for something to happen. "From what I heard Beckworth tell Ethan, the crews keep a fair distance from them, but they're just as corrupt as the rest. Still, we should expect better results."

Somewhere along the way, Stella stopped listening. Everything could be over tonight. Her adventure coming to a quick end. If that were the case, AJ would be eager to leave for home. It could be as early as tomorrow.

And she wasn't ready.

From the future's perspective, she'd been gone less than a

week. She deserved a vacation. Some time to decompress before going home. It was putting off the inevitable, and would only make it harder, but she wasn't prepared—not even close.

"They're going in."

She wasn't sure who said it. Maybe Ethan, maybe Hensley. All she was aware of was Beckworth's arm around her as the men joined the women. They stepped out of the shadows of the alley and into the street, waiting to see who came out.

It was quiet for an unbearably long time. Since they were a block away, they wouldn't hear much unless someone fired a weapon.

"They sent in eight men. A second team circled the house in case someone runs." Beckworth shared his commentary though no one had asked.

"Didn't they have someone in the back before they went in?" Ethan asked.

"No. And that was their mistake the last time." Beckworth squeezed her, but she wasn't sure if he did it out of comfort or as a reflexive motion that revealed his frustration.

"Do you think someone warned her?" Finn asked.

"How could they? Unless she's paying someone." AJ's comment had the men giving each other worried glances.

Maire's words about the Runners being corrupt came to mind, but she decided not to share that tidbit. The men would already be aware of it.

"Surely, they would have considered that. Langdon knew how slippery Gemini has been." Ethan's tone wasn't convincing.

It was wartime, and everyone was feeling the pinch. No one would be above a bribe if they were trying to feed their families and keep a roof over their heads. It was a hard time for anyone who wasn't part of the wealthy class.

Thirty minutes later, men left the manor, and as they entered the street, one man with his hands tied in front of him was being led to an enclosed wagon.

"It's André." Beckworth sighed, and Stella felt the muscles in his arms harden with tension when no one else exited.

"They don't have her. Was she not at home?" Finn asked though Stella didn't think he was expecting an answer.

Hensley spoke in hushed tones with Lord Langdon as the two rushed toward other men who'd gathered near the wagon.

Ten minutes later, which seemed too quick from Stella's perspective, Hensley returned. He stopped for only a moment. "Let's go back to the manor and discuss this." Then he strode off toward the coach the men had arrived in.

Beckworth saw the women back into their carriage then mounted his horse to follow them. They made a quick stop at Beckworth's manor so Eleanor could get out, claiming she'd had enough for one evening.

Stella was tempted to do the same thing, but Beckworth needed her. Because one thing was for certain. Gemini had slipped the net.

Beckworth stared into the hearth, the flames dancing as the logs fed the fire. The only thing that kept him from punching something was Stella's steady caress on his arm, and her lavender scent tickling his nose. They gathered in Hensley's library, and even the women were drinking whiskey.

"Other than the staff who work for the Wrights, André Belato was the only other one on the premise." Hensley leaned back in a chair with his legs propped up by a footstool. "He was passed out drunk in one of the guest rooms. It took them several minutes to get him to his feet."

"What will happen to him?" Murphy asked.

"Will they use him in a prisoner exchange?" Hughes's question was a worthy one, and Beckworth held his breath for Hensley's response.

"No. Napoleon doesn't do exchanges. Belato will be held at Newgate until they can transfer him to Portchester Castle, where he'll remain until the end of the war."

"That should remove him as a threat." Maire waved at Murphy to refill her glass. "He might start out thinking revenge, but after years as a prisoner, it won't seem worth it, especially seeing what it did to his uncle." She seemed different this evening, more lighthearted than he'd seen her in some time. And if he didn't know better, Hughes also seemed less morose. They were holding hands. What happened at the ball?

Beckworth cleared his throat. "I agree with Maire. André doesn't have what it takes to do anything on his own, and after years in a cell, he'll have nothing when he goes back to France. Gemini is financing her operation from stolen property. Did they recover the documents?"

Hensley grunted. "It will take them a few days to sort through it all before they can give me an inventory. As difficult as it might be, I suggest we take the next few days to relax and consider our next move while we wait for Langdon's news."

"We need to find where Gemini went." Murphy stood and walked to a map of England that was framed on a wall. He studied it for some time. "Is it possible she's headed back to France? This would be an opportune time to go to the monastery."

Beckworth hated the thought of crossing the Channel, and when he glanced down at Stella, her expression was mixed. Her face had paled, and her hand went to her stomach, which probably lurched at the thought of another ship. But that stubborn tilt to her chin and the determined set of her features told him she wasn't ready to give up the fight.

He'd already considered that Gemini might flee to France. "It's fortunate the crew found the *Phoenix's* new mooring. We've kept it under surveillance with a few of the street crew." He nodded to Hensley. "I can have someone go down this evening and see if the ship had any arrivals other than drunken sailors."

"Then let's call it a night. It's a waste to make guesses until we have more information." Hensley stood, and the rest followed his lead. "Until then, Mary would love to have everyone to dinner. Let's say tomorrow night. Include Bart, Eleanor, and that young lad Lincoln. Come a couple of hours early. I'm in the mood for chess."

Beckworth tied his horse to the carriage so he could ride with Stella on the short drive to the manor. Neither spoke, but she leaned into him, and he simply held her. She'd been quiet since the raid, and he couldn't measure her mood. It was rare for her to be so quiet, and when she was, it was typically because she was upset. Everyone was frustrated with Gemini slipping through their grasp, but for Stella, he didn't think it was as simple as that. Perhaps she was simply tired.

Once back at the manor, he stood next to Barrington and watched her walk up the stairs, her lady's maid following behind her.

"The study?" Barrington asked.

He nodded and led the way. Once there, he placed two glasses on the desk and filled them with whiskey. "Any word on Gemini?"

Barrington's grim face was enough of an answer, and the shake of his head confirmed it. "We'll keep the normal watch, but she's gone to ground someplace other than the ship." He took a long drink of whiskey and leaned back. He played with a silver ring he'd begun wearing since he'd arrived in London.

Beckworth didn't think he'd ever see it again and wondered

what made him take it out now. But that wasn't a topic for him to raise.

"Eleanor and Bart are becoming antsy. They want to go home."

"It was just a matter of time." They wouldn't be the only ones going home soon. He rubbed his chest and pushed the thought aside. "I'm surprised they've stayed this long. Do we have men to take them? I don't want them unguarded."

Barrington nodded. "I'd like to go with them."

It wasn't a surprise. For most of his life, Barrington had lived in London, but Waverly was his home now. Chester would be available if they needed the crew again. "Hensley has asked us to dinner tomorrow. With any luck, he'll have news from Langdon on what items were recovered from the manor. You can leave the following morning."

After they finished their drinks, Beckworth trudged up the stairs. He wanted to spend the evening with Stella, but she hadn't said anything before going to her room. Instead of stopping to check on her, he went to his room to change.

When he opened the door, he smiled. Two lamps spread a golden light through the room, and a new log had been placed on the fire. And though he couldn't see her, the lump in the middle of his bed didn't require explanation, and a pleasant warmth snaked through him.

He tossed his clothes aside. When he slid in, she rolled over and ran a hand across his stomach.

"I'm too exhausted for anything more than you holding me."

He kissed her forehead. "Whatever you want, sweetheart." She nestled against him, and all his worries about Gemini melted away. What didn't go away was what he'd do once they put Gemini behind bars and it was time for Stella to go home.

34

Dame Ellington's London house was located near Kensington Palace, and the richly appointed manor was the grandest Stella had seen. According to AJ, her country home was more impressive.

The day after the questionable raid on Gemini, Beckworth had given the staff the day off, and they made good use of it. Eleanor, after a severe scolding from Beckworth to not bother, made their meals and performed minor cleaning. She muttered that if she didn't do it, the men would starve. Stella had laughed because it was more the truth in this century than her own.

With the house staff gone, Eleanor cleaning, and Bart and Lincoln holed up in the library, no one questioned where she and Beckworth were. They might have known and simply not cared. Either way, she took every advantage of spending a day with him. After a light breakfast and a full pot of coffee, they lounged in bed—talking, napping, and having glorious sex that she was certain made her cheeks a rosy pink. They barely had time to dress for a late afternoon at Hensley's. At dinner, when Mary suggested a garden lunch with Elizabeth the following day, Stella was more excited than AJ and Maire. But she had developed a different relationship with the dowager.

It was a beautiful, mildly warm spring day, and after a tour of Elizabeth's house, the group settled in the garden under a maple tree. They were served a three-course lunch, and as they ate, it didn't take long for the conversation to turn to Gemini.

"I still don't understand why she went to such lengths of forging a marriage license." AJ took a bite of her poached fish and chased it with a sip of wine. "She must have known she couldn't get away with it, especially with Beckworth alive."

"She's been quietly announcing her new title at a number of social engagements." Dame Ellington barely ate her food, but the footman kept her gin glass full. "If they hear it enough, they will eventually believe it to be true, and it could tarnish Teddy's reputation. And that I won't tolerate, which was why I called her out on the lie at Lady Jane's party."

"Apparently Lady Agatha was of the same mind at the masquerade ball," AJ said.

"It was a good thing we were able to get out of the manor before she caught us." Stella wasn't sure it was the best thing, but it sounded better than admitting she would have preferred waiting for Gemini in the bedroom so she could give her a solid punch or two. It didn't seem like too much to ask.

"Do you think she got away with the Prescott documents?" Elizabeth asked.

"We haven't heard from Lord Langdon." AJ picked at a spiced apple tart. "There was only a short window where no one watched the back of the manor. Finn thought there would have been enough time for her and Gaines to sneak out, but not with anything more than maybe a single trunk, assuming they had a coach waiting."

"Well, I don't believe any of it will pass muster with a magistrate. Of course, Teddy has other legal recourse, especially if they can prove the document was forged."

The topic made Stella sick to her stomach, and she pushed her plate away. It shouldn't mean anything to her since she'd be going home, but she wanted Beckworth to be happy, even if it was without her.

"Well, perhaps I can speak of a happier marriage proposal." Maire sipped her wine, her gaze pinning each of the other women as she peered over the rim of her glass. A slight smile seemed ready to burst.

AJ jumped up. "Ethan asked you to marry him?"

"Not exactly."

AJ slumped back into her chair. "Well, that was a quick letdown. Who are you talking about?"

Stella barked out a laugh. Something to finally brighten her mood. "You asked him."

When Maire's smile broadened, Elizabeth chortled. "Good for you."

"Oh my." Mary looked like she could use a fan. "Is that true?"

"He needed a bit of a push. I know he was waiting for the perfect time, but honestly, when would that be? Although, we do want to keep it quiet until after this business with Gemini. And he wants to speak with Finn, but I just couldn't hold it in any longer."

"When did this happen?" AJ stopped picking at the tart and shoved the whole small morsel in her mouth.

"At the masquerade ball."

The tart was almost spat out, but AJ was able to mumble her response. "While we were supposed to be watching for Gemini?"

Maire shrugged. Not a single sign of remorse reflected on her face. "I was bored. And, I don't know, it felt like it needed to be addressed."

"Where will you hold the wedding? When will it be?" Mary became more animated. "There's planning to be done."

Maire laughed. "We didn't get that far. Though I have some ideas."

"You know, Elizabeth has the most amazing blooms in her garden. There are several that would be perfect with a garden wedding."

Stella listened as Elizabeth and Mary shared stories of their weddings. Then everyone but Stella and Elizabeth wandered the garden in search of the best wedding flowers.

Elizabeth had her drink refreshed while Stella tapped her glass and smiled at the footman, who filled her wineglass.

"I gather you didn't take Gemini's marriage claim well."

That was a touchy area. It had been a stab in the heart, but that information wasn't anything she wanted to share. Not even with AJ.

"Why would you say that?" She attempted to sidestep the topic.

Elizabeth gazed off to where the women stood around a collection of colorful blooms. "I've known Teddy for a long time. I never thought I'd see the day he would find love." When she didn't respond, Elizabeth trained her gaze on her. Stella squirmed under the steady perusal. "He doesn't have to say anything for me to see what's in his heart. He's changed over these last couple of years and has taken his role of viscount seriously. After the trouble with Reginald, he's become a welcomed landowner in Corsham. But I've seen a greater change in him since he met you."

"He's a good man." Her heart was stuck in her throat, and she didn't think she could say anything else. Nothing safe. Nothing that would change their situation.

"I can see you don't want to discuss it, and I won't push. But you should know one thing. That man would follow you anywhere."

Beckworth stood in front of Newgate prison. Murphy and Hughes stood next to him, Murphy's watchful eyes scanning the city streets. Hughes spoke in a low but stern tone with the captain of the guard as the man read a parchment Hughes handed him.

They'd already talked their way through two previous guards who, even with a signed document from England's war office, weren't eager to allow the three men inside. It wasn't surprising they'd want someone with more authority to allow them entrance. The document granted access to the section where war criminals were held pending transfer to a prisoner of war facility.

Lord Langdon had been delayed in reviewing the inventory confiscated from the raid but had received Hensley's request for access to André. Langdon had agreed, but Beckworth surmised it was more likely his interrogators weren't having success retrieving any worthwhile information. Hensley's group of spies might have better luck.

It would be a miracle if they got anything valuable regarding Gemini, and for all of André's bluster, Beckworth doubted the man cared a trinket about Napoleon, the English, or the war. While the Belatos might have been a name known during the Terror, they were never interested in reform. They saw an opportunity to finance their crumbling inheritance by stealing artifacts from the churches.

If it wasn't for their involvement in resurrecting the secret of the stones, which began this whole nightmare, he would never have met Stella. And for that, he was grateful to the Belatos. And wasn't that thought sheer madness?

He glanced at the tall walls of the prison. This was their last chance for a clue to where Gemini went. Chester had spoken with two other crews, but there wasn't a sign of her anywhere, and with the *Phoenix* still in port, if she fled to the monastery, she'd found other transport. The assumption was that Gaines was still with her, in addition to an indeterminate amount of mercenaries. He turned to Murphy, who still had his gaze locked on their surroundings, watching for any sign of trouble, before glancing at Hughes, who appeared to have made some progress.

"You'll need to be checked for weapons, and then Sergeant Matthews will see you in." The captain handed the parchment back to Hughes. "You have one hour."

"Understood. We appreciate your cooperation."

"You won't get anything out of that bloke if you had a week, but it's not my time you're wasting." The captain waved at the guard to open the gate and let the men pass.

Hughes said nothing more to the captain as the three were led down the path to the main doors of the prison. Once inside the dingy foyer, they were searched for weapons, taken through several locked doors, and then down old-stone stairs to a lower level.

The place stank of unemptied buckets of excrement, blood, and sickness. The cells were small considering the spacing of the doors, and Beckworth shuddered at the living conditions. He'd seen worse, but not by much.

When Matthews stopped in front of a door at the end of a hallway, the three huddled next to the man. Murphy glanced at Hughes, who nodded. Before they'd arrived at the prison, they had discussed several options for meeting with André. They wanted to go in together, but the guards, especially where

French prisoners were being held, weren't exact in following orders.

To be certain that Matthews or someone with a key to the cell remained close by, it was decided that two of them would go into the cell while one remained with the guard. Hughes, being closely associated with the Earl of Hereford and was once his Sergeant of Arms, made the most sense to ensure their timely exit.

Beckworth entered first, with Murphy right behind him. He'd prepared himself for a possible attack from André, but the man was curled up on a small pad in the corner. He didn't turn around, most likely expecting someone to clean out his bucket.

"André. We need a few words." Beckworth kept as much distance as the ten-by-ten cell would allow, not knowing whether the man would leap up.

André rolled over and peered up at him, his face a swollen mess, the skin already bruising. He scowled before rolling back into his partial fetal position. "Go away." He'd been beaten. Besides the blows to his face, he'd taken several powerful punches to the ribs and kidneys, if he had to guess.

"We don't want much of your time. Can you tell us what happened the night you were taken?"

When the man didn't speak, he tried a different approach.

"We're searching for Gemini."

At that, the man sputtered out a laugh, then coughed. It wouldn't surprise him if a bit of blood had been spat out.

"I don't think you have much loyalty to your sister." Beckworth's voice was soft, with a touch of understanding. "She never gave you credit for your intelligence or the knowledge you carry from your uncle."

André shifted.

"You're in this particular part of the prison simply because you're French and they suspect you're a spy for Napoleon."

André released a sharp laugh then clutched his stomach, confirming the severe beating he'd been given. He didn't have any sympathy for the man, but he did have a bargaining chip. He knew the man wasn't a spy. Despite his words regarding the man's intelligence, he didn't think André had the instinct for it. He hadn't committed any particular crime other than his role in Beckworth's torture, and he didn't have anything to do with Gemini's ill-gotten financing. But he was a danger where the stones were concerned if anyone listened to his fanciful tales.

But did he deserve the continued beatings? Imprisonment for the next several years then released penniless would be punishment enough for his crimes.

"If you provide us with the information we seek, we can assure the right men you aren't a French spy. You simply came to visit your sister, looking for a way out of the war, and got caught up in something not of your making. You'll be held until the war is over. Maybe you'll be lucky enough for a prisoner exchange. Either way, we can have you moved to a different cell and have the beatings stopped while you wait for a wagon to Portchester Castle."

He waited and glanced at Murphy, who shrugged. He didn't have anything more to offer.

"You're lucky to have someone to speak on your behalf. Your sister didn't waste time getting out of the manor."

André spat on the floor. "That bitch is no sister to me. She's lost sight of the greater prize. The comforts of being a lady—" he snickered, "—have driven her away from our goals. Years of planning and waiting, and now gone in a blink of an eye."

Beckworth glanced at Murphy, who stepped closer. They were both interested in hearing more.

"Wasn't your game to steal the stones and *The Book of Stones*?" Murphy asked.

"And the torc. We let Reginald play his games with the

grimoire and his trials for traveling with a smaller stone. No one thought it would work, but it didn't hurt to see if we might be wrong." His laugh was short and menacing. "We weren't. Gemini and Gaines were irritated that you killed him, but our uncle knew Reginald was too weak to fit our needs. We had to stop using puppets and do what no one else could achieve."

It was interesting information. Not overly helpful for their current situation, except for his use of the name Gemini rather than his sister's true name. But did he see her as a sister? It must have been years since he'd seen her. Of if he did, the visits were likely short.

He stepped closer and squatted, keeping distance between him and André, though the man's poor condition was enough to keep him on his pad. "You weren't able to get the financing you required to build a private army, but Gemini found a way."

"When she was young, she worked as a maid in some low nobleman's house. More as a slave since she wasn't paid, and being French with no family, she didn't have much of a choice. But she's smart. She learned English and lost her accent over time. Her first money came from the same man who bought her from our uncle. The stupid fool kept money in the house, and after several years when she was of age, he had an unfortunate accident that killed him. His stash of money was enough to set our plans in motion."

"And since then, she's been the one funding the operation, snuggling up with Dugan to control her marks, and leaving her to believe she's the one in charge."

"It would have been different if our uncle had been able to stay sober long enough."

Beckworth doubted that, but it no longer mattered. "So what happened that night in the manor? How did you get left behind?"

"She was paying someone in the guards. I don't know who,

and he wasn't very important, but he saw the orders that were sent down from the top. She received a message about thirty minutes before the doors were busted open. It might have been longer. I was drunk. Just like my uncle. Just like my father. I thought it was an invitation to another party. She never said a word to me."

The poor bastard. Gemini was probably looking for a way to get rid of him. "Do you know where she went?"

"No." He pinned his gaze on Beckworth. "And believe me, if I knew, you'd be the only one I told. I will give you one fair warning. She's turned her attention away from the stones for now. Her entire focus is on you."

That shook Beckworth. How had he become so intricately woven into this business with the stones? The duke, Reginald, and now Gemini. He stood.

"I'll keep my word to find you better accommodations and have the beatings stopped."

André's chuckle was eerie. "It's more than my own sister has done for me."

35

Two days later, Hensley asked everyone to attend a meeting. Beckworth and Stella arrived quickly to find Murphy, AJ, Hughes, and Maire already in the study. Everyone but Hensley appeared anxious, which suggested Hensley had waited for everyone to be present before sharing his information.

Hensley got right to the point. "I received a message from Langdon this morning. It was rushed, as he was going into another set of long meetings with the war council. He reviewed the list of inventory taken during the raid. The manor was thoroughly searched, and the only relevant items of interest, as we know, were located in a dressing room.

"After reviewing the number of trunks from Langdon's inventory and the number Jamie and Stella provided, Gemini took one of the trunks with her. Fortunately, it wasn't the one that held the files of the property transactions. There were multiple noblemen named in the documents, all of whom are deceased. The timing of the transactions in relation to the time of their death is suspect. We also received word from the real Lady Penelope Prescott, who was left destitute at a seaside cottage. There's more to investigate, but Langdon believes they have enough to hold Gemini for questioning as the rest of her game is unraveled."

"What of the third chronicle?" Maire asked.

"There was nothing in the report that spoke of anything resembling a book. Just the financial documents."

"Which means Gemini most likely has it with her," Murphy said.

Beckworth didn't like this. Stella squeezed his hand, somehow sensing his growing tension. "Whether we believe André's story or not, she would be a fool not to keep the chronicle close. It's a bargaining chip if nothing else."

"You don't believe she's given up on the stones?" Hughes asked.

"I think it's always been her plan, and she hasn't shifted from it. She's simply redirected her focus to restore her finances." He didn't have to spell it out for them. They all knew he was her target.

Hensley redirected the conversation as the silence became uncomfortable. "The question is, now that she's wanted by the local magistrate, I can't see her taking the chance on staying in London." He glanced around, seeming to want confirmation.

It was Hughes who gave it to him. "Based on what we've seen to date, unless she knows she has the upper hand she disappears. But we'd be the fools to think she's given up the game."

"We need the third chronicle." Maire would never rest until the entire book was put together. Beckworth couldn't blame her. No one liked an unsolved puzzle.

"Has Sebastian received messages from the monastery?" Murphy asked.

Before Hensley could respond, the study door burst open, and the men jumped up to face the intruder. It was a footman, standing next to a road-weary man. Or so Beckworth guessed based on the dust covering his clothes. He recognized the man.

It was one of his guards from Waverly. His heart skipped a beat, and his stomach lurched.

"Sorry, sir, he said it was urgent. Life and death." The footman backed away at Hensley's wave.

"What is it Henderson?" Beckworth stepped in front of the other men.

Henderson turned and seemed relieved when he saw him. Barrington must have directed him to Hensley, knowing the spymaster was always in residence while in London.

"It's Gemini. She's taken Waverly."

Beckworth left the study and stopped in the foyer. A sole trunk, the one brought down from his room, was all that sat on the polished floor. The front door opened, and Henderson rushed in. The man still looked haggard but refused to rest before leaving.

"Did you already take Stella's trunk out?"

"No, sir. I was just coming to have a footman help me with yours."

As if on cue, a footman came in from the sitting room and went to the trunk when Henderson waved toward it.

"I'll see it's ready in fifteen minutes. Find something to eat after you load my trunk." Beckworth took the stairs two at a time, and a sharp pain in his back reminded him that while he had full movement, the occasional twinges might be with him for some time.

He gave a short rap on Stella's door before entering. She was still in her robe, standing in front of the wardrobe closet, staring at all her dresses. Sarah was busy arranging stacks of undergarments, wraps, and cloaks. The large trunk he had sent up an hour ago sat empty.

"Why aren't you ready yet?"

Speechless for one of the rare moments of her life, she turned and looked down at a pair of pants and a shirt she'd been holding. "I'm not sure what to wear." She turned to her wardrobe. "Or what to take. I'm not even sure where we're going."

His previous anger evaporated, and he took her gently by the arm with one hand while taking the clothes from her with the other. He handed the pants and shirt to Sarah.

"Pack everything except a simple day dress for traveling. Put one pair of pants, shirt, and her boots in the duffel. Pack her jewelry, including her opal necklace at the bottom of her trunk.

"No." Stella shook her head, clutching at the necklace around her neck. "I'll wear the opal."

He pushed her toward the bed. "Sit here while Sarah packs. Now, look at me."

She did, and though her eyes watered, her expression was a mixture of anger, fear, and defiance. At least it was something he'd seen before. "I heard the *Phoenix* left port. Where do you think it went?"

She'd been thinking about Gemini, but he didn't think the ship was what worried her. "It's hard to say, but if Gemini is at Waverly, then best guess is Bristol. Perhaps Southampton." He pushed a loose strand of hair away from her face. "It's nothing to worry about now. We need to focus on today. The footmen are waiting to load your trunk into the coach..."

Her gaze flashed with irritation. "That will take too long."

That was the Stella he was used to seeing. The spark of their first days together.

"That's right. But we need more information before we can determine our strategy. Lando and Fitz have gone ahead to see what's waiting for us. They'll check on Bart and Eleanor first, and most likely move who they can to Bart's. It's a safer distance from Waverly, and that's where we'll go. At most, we'll lose half a day if we change horses en route.

"I've also asked Thomas..." He put a finger to her lips before she interrupted, his grin impossible to stop. "Yes, Thomas is still in town with a handful of men. They've been visiting friends and family and enjoying some well-deserved rest. Which means they're ready to do something more physical than lifting pints."

"They'll be our escort." She nodded, seeming to accept the plan. Then her head shot up. "What of Sebastian?"

"He'll travel with Hensley and will be heavily guarded. Now, help Sarah decide which dress you want to travel in and everything else gets packed. Weapons in the duffel, but keep your dagger on you."

"Are we only taking one coach?"

"Yes, the women will travel in the carriage, and the men will ride as guards. Hensley will remain in London for a couple more days to close the house. He's sending Jamie with a message for the local magistrate in Bristol. He'll be our best option for dealing with Gemini. Jamie will sail with the next tide."

"I'm sorry." Her voice was low, and her eyes filled with sadness.

"About what." He wiped away a small tear that slipped down her cheek.

"That everyone keeps trying to take away your home."

He kissed her, and it lingered. It was all he could do not to take her in his arms and just hold her for a while. But Sarah was in the room, and the others would be waiting.

He stood, his gaze still locked with hers. With everything happening around them, her first thought was of him and his home. She was quite aware of how much he loved Waverly. He'd wanted her to see it, but not like this.

He made one promise to himself as he gave her a last glance

before leaving the room. She would walk through the splendor of Waverly gardens at least once before she went home.

Stella stuck her head out the window of the carriage as it slowed, eager to get a glimpse of Bart's home. After hearing AJ and Maire's description of the place, she had visions of one of the abandoned cabins Beckworth always seemed to find during their escape from Gemini.

All she saw was a decrepit gate as the coach pulled to a stop.

"It's me, you wretched old goat. And I've brought friends." Beckworth yelled at the top of his lungs. She wasn't sure how far Waverly was, but they could probably hear him.

Several minutes passed before a man slid out of the bushes. Fitz.

He was grinning. "What took you so long? We thought you'd be in time for lunch."

She breathed out a sigh of relief in unison with AJ and Maire. Fitz pulled the gate open, and the coach drove through it. She glanced behind and caught a glimpse of him closing it behind the troop of men. It was a miracle the weathered slats hadn't broken into pieces from sheer orneriness, just like the homeowner. Then her head swiveled to the front until the coach turned a bend, and the house came into view.

It could use some repairs and a fresh coat of paint, but she'd seen so much worse during her time here. Eleanor's house was slightly larger and had better curb appeal. Good grief. She was two hundred years from her future and still a realtor at heart.

"The inside is cozier than it looks." AJ leaned her head against the back of the coach with her eyes closed. She'd been to Bart's several times before, and it probably felt like home. "Though it's too rustic for my taste."

Maire snorted. "I'd say rustic for anyone other than Bart."

Stella stretched her arms as far as they could go with the low ceiling, then twisted one way and then another. If she saw another coach anytime soon, she'd walk. She laughed, and the women stared at her. "I was thinking how much better the ride would have been on a horse."

AJ snorted several times in a row, and they were all laughing as they were helped from the coach. The men had the good grace to not ask.

Lando and Bart were lounging on the front porch in wooden chairs while Lincoln sat on the top step, leaning against the railing. All they needed was a bottle of beer, or at least a glass of lemonade. The front door swung open, and Eleanor stepped out to stand next to Lincoln, her hands on her hips as she noted the entourage.

"I knew you'd want to make an entrance. Fortunately, I made enough stew to feed the lot of you. Wash the road dust from you while I set the table."

Stella followed the women toward the porch but turned to search for Beckworth. He was helping Fitz unhitch the horses from the carriage. The rest of the men lumbered toward the barn, their horses looking as weary as them.

Inside, Maire had poured steaming water into a basin and was adding cold water to make it more tolerable. While Maire and AJ took turns cleaning their arms and faces, Stella helped Elizabeth with setting the table.

The women ate at the table with some of the men while others sat on the porch. After lunch, Fitz took Thomas and his men to the barn to show them the area that had been cleaned out for them. The night would be clear enough to build a fire in the yard where some preferred to lay a bedroll.

The remainder of the afternoon was for rest. They'd get down to business before dinner. Stella glanced around the cabin, searching for a place to be out of the way when Beckworth grabbed her hand and, with a blanket under one arm, led her out of the cabin. She didn't argue as he led her down a trail and into the trees. When he turned down a narrow path, she checked her pocket to make sure her dagger was still with her. The last time she'd been in the woods, Gemini's man had surprised her. Even though Beckworth was with her, she wasn't going to stand by helplessly.

When she saw the stream and a short grassy area, she smiled. She took a corner and helped him spread the blanket, then dropped down next to him.

"And will we sleep under the stars tonight?" she joked.

"If the nights weren't still so chilly, I'd say yes. But this might be the only time we'll have to ourselves once we hear what's happening at Waverly. Things will move pretty quickly at that point."

"Then let's not waste it."

His kiss started lightly, and she responded in kind, but soon neither of them could seem to control the passion. The only feeling sweeter than the soft spring air cooling her skin was his hands as they caressed her, heating every inch of flesh he touched. She lost track of time and didn't care. The pull of home called to her. It moved closer and became stronger every day, so she took what joy she could and pushed everything else aside.

Afterward, as the sun moved closer to the horizon, she lay on her stomach, propped on her elbows as she picked at the grass. He lay next to her, shoulder to shoulder, hip to hip—all bare skin—the sun keeping them warm.

"I suppose you're going to sacrifice yourself again." She didn't want to break the solace of the afternoon, but it slipped out, and she prepared for his temper, or worse, his denial that would be a lie.

"Why would you say that?" His question surprised her, as did his tone, which was lazy and curious.

"Because you need to save Waverly. You worry about your people."

He turned on his side, facing her, and slid a tendril of hair behind her ear. "How did you come to know me so well so quickly?"

She snorted and gave him a side glance. "You're an open book for anyone willing to look closely."

His eyes flickered upward as if to search for the bird twilling from a high perch. "And I suppose there's no way to stop you from charging in after me."

She grinned. It appeared he knew her equally well. Though to be honest, he had several opportunities to witness her brash foolishness. But still, it was nice to know he paid attention. "I can't wait for someone else to save your sorry ass."

His arm reached out as fast as a snake, pulling her to him as his lips crushed hers. He pressed his body against hers, and she couldn't help but notice how much he felt like home.

"Won't we be late?" Her tongue seemed too thick for her mouth, but she managed to spit the words out.

"They'll wait."

"That will be a bit embarrassing. It's not like they don't know where we are or what we're doing."

"I don't mind. I like to see pink in your cheeks."

She beat her fist playfully against his chest before she grabbed him around his neck and pulled him down for more.

36

Stella stood next to Beckworth and stared down at the two hand-drawn maps. A second table had been pushed against the main table to allow more seating, but the chairs had been moved aside so the larger group could gather to view the maps.

No one had noticed them slip into the cabin thirty minutes earlier when they'd returned from the stream. The group was in full conversation mode. A few argued over some point or other as they discussed the maps, but most spoke of other things as they snacked on the cheese, fruit, and something that looked suspiciously like corn fritters as they drank ale and waited for the meeting to begin.

Beckworth waited until the voices quieted and faces turned to him. Though Fitz and Lando had been the ones running surveillance, Waverly was Beckworth's, and no one knew it better than him.

"Let's start at the beginning with what we know." Beckworth took the time to meet each person's gaze. Stella didn't know if he was sizing each person up or mentally organizing them into their specialties. It was most likely a bit of both if she'd learned anything about his strategizing.

"Henderson—" he nodded to the man directly across from him, "—is one of my guards and was able to escape Waverly with a note from Barrington, who's in the manor, either acting as butler or under guard. But we'll come back to that. Do you want to share what you know?"

Henderson cleared his throat. "Four days ago, Barrington received word of a raid on a neighboring farm by outlaws. The message claimed they were under siege by a dozen men. Barrington sent half the garrison—that's fifteen men—to assist." He scowled. "It was a ruse, which Barrington thought it might be, but we couldn't take the chance it was real. The rest of us were spread in a perimeter around the property. The men hadn't been gone for more than an hour when Waverly was attacked. I was on the line at the rear of the property, but there were just too many of them and not enough of us. I ran for the stables and found Barrington already there. He had a horse saddled, and I happened to be the first one to reach him. He handed me a note, and I took off through the back of the property, barely evading the perimeter guards. Two men followed me before I made it to the road to Corsham. Let's just say they didn't make it back to Waverly."

"Were you able to get a count?" Finn asked.

"No, but I'd say double the men we had. So at least thirty, maybe a few more."

"They probably lost one or two in the raid," Ethan said. "But Waverly probably lost a few as well. If not all of them."

Beckworth nodded to Fitz, who finished the fritter-looking thing he was eating and took a long swallow of ale.

"I don't think so." Fitz wiped his mouth and stared at the map he likely drew. "While Lando went to investigate the town and check Eleanor's house, I went to Waverly. I've been there on a couple of occasions, so I know the layout fairly well. They've set their own perimeter around the entire property, and then a second one closer in." He made a circle around the manor that reached the main road, then made a second circle halfway between the house and the outer circle. "I counted twelve on the outer perimeter. The second perimeter is about a hundred yards from the manor, but there's not much cover, so they're easily spotted. That's another eight men."

He pointed to a building across a small meadow from the main house. "This is the garrison. They have four men stationed there, two at each door, and work a fairly routine rotation around the building."

"Which means there are men being held in there." Finn closed his eyes as if picturing it. "If I remember correctly, there are windows along both sides of the buildings, on both the first and second floors."

"Yes," Beckworth said. "Both floors have two rooms that can accommodate ten men comfortably. There's another larger room on the ground floor that's used for meals and social time. There are four smaller private rooms on the second floor for the four team leaders as well as a storage room for food. There's an armory that we have to assume has been emptied. But there's a hidden door on the second floor with another armory, assuming it hasn't been discovered. The men know they're outnumbered, so they'll stay put and wait for word. But chances are, if we can free them, they'll be armed."

Finn chuckled. "Always a trick up your sleeve."

Beckworth smiled. "I've been surprised too many times."

"What can you tell us of the manor itself?" Thomas asked.

"I couldn't get all the way to the manor, so I have no idea how many might be inside." Fitz tapped another building on the map. "I made it as far as the stables. There are twenty horses inside, and another thirty in outside pens."

"Fifteen of those would be from Beckworth's guards," Thomas said.

"And another six from my private collection." Beckworth scratched his chin. "Are the outer perimeter men on horseback?"

"Some are, but those that are on foot have horses tied close by. The inner perimeter guards are all on foot." Fitz tapped the manor house. "There are four men outside the manor, working their own rotation."

"That still leaves almost a dozen unaccounted for." Thomas glanced around the table. "We have to assume they're inside the manor."

"They don't have enough men to hold the manor." Finn pointed to the various spots Fitz had reviewed with them. "They have two perimeters and men in the correct locations for the number they have, but the outer perimeter is a lot of ground to cover with only twelve men. Based on the count of horses, unless they're keeping more someplace else, that doesn't leave enough men to cover more than a single shift."

"Are there men in town?" Stella asked. "Or maybe at Eleanor's?" She didn't like the way the numbers were adding up. They had to be sure of the number of men they were facing.

"Eleanor's home was empty both times I stopped there." Lando was the only one not standing at the table. He seemed to prefer the window, keeping an eye on the road. "It's possible one or two men might have ridden by doing their own surveillance. If there had been more than that, the ground would have been obviously disturbed.

"I checked the pub and both inns. There are a handful of men that have been there for four days, which fits when Gemini came for Waverly." He smiled at Beckworth. "It would appear, little man, that the town has some respect for you. The man at the mercantile has been more than helpful in providing details."

Beckworth scowled at Lando, and Stella held back a smile. Lando's nickname rankled him, but while it might have started out as a way to irritate him, it was more than that to Lando. The big man respected Beckworth if only he could see it. Or maybe he did.

He softened his expression and nodded at Lando. "The mercantile is the hub of the town. Tobias is a natural gossip and always has eyes out for strangers."

"And it's a good thing. The news is heartening. The men Barrington sent to the other farm found a small group of men harassing the farmer, who they now suspect were Gemini's men. Beckworth's guards put the men to their final rest. When they arrived back at Waverly—at that time they didn't know about Gemini—they discovered the manor has been overrun. They went to Corsham and are hiding with family and friends, waiting for word."

"That evens the odds." Thomas hit his fist on the table and grinned. "We're an equal match now to seize Waverly."

"But not without bloodshed," Ethan added.

"And that's unacceptable. We need to be smart about this." Beckworth tapped the table, considering ramifications as various ideas crossed his mind. He picked up his mug of ale. "Let's give this some thought. I want to minimize the loss on our side. There are innocents in the manor that Gemini and Gaines wouldn't think twice about killing if they thought it would aid their cause."

"What are you thinking?" Finn gave him his signature grin, but his emerald gaze was hard as it met Beckworth's.

Stella responded instead. "He's planning on sacrificing himself for the cause."

The group broke up to give what they'd heard some time to settle as they considered options. Some found chairs in the house while others congregated on the porch. The ale continued to flow, and Stella helped Eleanor prepare dinner for the masses while Maire and AJ ensured the men had enough drink to keep their inspiration flowing.

Bart sat near the hearth, grumbling about this or that while he played chess with Lincoln. When the young man left to care for the horses, Doc limped to the back room, mumbling something about checking his inventory. Stella shivered at his comment. There would no doubt be casualties no matter how well they planned. She wanted to keep an eye on Beckworth to gauge his mood, but he'd been one of the men to go outside.

Once dinner was cooking, Eleanor suggested the women should take a break and enforced it by kicking Stella, AJ, and Maire out of the kitchen. "Go find your men and make sure they're resting. Their minds will be fresher."

Stella didn't hesitate to search for Beckworth, who wasn't on the porch anymore. She didn't see him anywhere outside. AJ sat with Finn against a large elm tree, while Maire and Ethan remained inside. There was a small group of men under a tree on the far side of the yard, but he wasn't there. Then her gaze fell on the barn. Lincoln must still be in there since he hadn't returned to the house. Maybe he'd seen Beckworth.

The strong odor of horse, hay, and manure hit her when she walked through the door. She grinned at how comforting the scent had become during her time in this century. Lincoln was to her left, brushing a horse. When he turned to find her there, he nodded toward the other side of the barn. She returned the nod with her smile still in place as she ventured deeper into the building. Horses had been tied up in the aisle for feeding since there weren't enough stalls to hold them, and she slid quietly around them.

On the back end of the barn, one of the stalls opened up to an outside corral. A horse was tied to a post, and Beckworth was checking its hooves. She leaned against the stall door and watched him work. He'd fussed with all four hooves and had brushed one side of the horse before he noticed her.

His smile was warm, and his gaze swept her from top to bottom. It didn't make her blush, but it did heat her blood. "Did they send you to check on me?"

She gave him a half-shrug. "Eleanor wanted to make sure everyone was resting."

"I'm too worked up to rest."

"I think she was more concerned with a mental rest rather than physical."

"She's spent too much time with Bart."

"Maybe she's just a wise woman. There's something to be said for giving one's subconscious the time to work through the amount of data we just covered."

"Apparently, she's not the only wise woman in the group."

She'd been slowly walking toward him as they spoke while he continued to brush the horse. When she reached him, she ran her hands up his back until they reached his shoulders, which she began to massage. She worked on a particularly rough knot until he yelped, dropping the brush.

She giggled when he turned and lifted her off her feet, planting a kiss on her lips that made her forget where she was. When he set her back down, he whispered in her hair, "You're a distraction."

"Yes. But it's too late."

"What do you mean?"

"You're not out here considering strategies and weighing options. You've already decided."

"Is that the only reason you came looking for me? To distract me into something less daring?"

She sighed and hugged him, her cheek resting against his chest. "I might have thought so in the beginning, but I know better. It's not your way."

He pulled back. "It will be alright. It's a good plan. You'll see."

It wasn't like she had a choice. "Well, put the horse away, and let's go tell them. There's no reason to make them struggle with the perfect plan when you already have one."

She waited until the horse was returned to its stall then tugged him back through the barn. When they walked into the sunshine of the yard, Stella shouted out. "Come on, everyone. Let's get this done. Beckworth has a plan." She stifled a grin at their grumbles. At least she wasn't the only one thinking it.

"Gemini has only one purpose for being here—to lay claim to Waverly. But it won't do her any good without my signature in addition to my personal contact with the banks and magistrate to make our so-called marriage real. The plan is to give her half of what she wants—me."

He waited for the mumbling to stop. "Trust me, if I could convince her that one of you blokes would be just as good, I'd do it in a heartbeat."

This time the laughter tickled her. She rarely saw any of these men smile, let alone give up deep belly laughs.

"I'll make an entrance riding down the drive as if coming direct from London. Walking through the doors of my home will only be the trigger." He pointed to the outer perimeter line. "We need twelve of our stealthiest to take out all twelve men at the same time."

He stopped and monitored faces. They were intrigued, and he continued. "The barracks are in between the two perimeters. We need four men who can take out the guards within minutes of the outer perimeter falling. At the same time, they can release the men inside. Those men know Waverly almost as well as I do. We'll use them as part of the strike force once we flush the chickens from the roost."

"This looks efficient, but who are we flushing from the manor?" Ethan asked.

Finn answered. "We don't know how many are in the house. We need them to come out rather than take the fight inside."

Ethan nodded. "Nothing worse than fighting in close quarters."

"What about the inner perimeter?" Thomas had been staring at the map during the discussion, his bushy brows drawn together. "I'd wait until we got the men from inside the manor pushed out, then surround all the exits and close the net."

"I agree." Beckworth wasn't exactly smiling, but he was pleased. He gave the men a start then stepped back and let them do what they did best.

Stella had only heard about their various missions secondhand and after they were long over. It was a sobering experience to be in the middle of it as it played out. AJ had told her on numerous occasions that the team preferred to work with those they knew. This was a bonded group that could anticipate what another team member would do before it happened. The whole experience made her tingle.

Finn scratched his chin. "Lando can go to Corsham and round up your other guards. Henderson can help with that." He glanced up, scanning the table for Beckworth's man, who nodded when Finn met his gaze.

"How do you plan on getting those in the house outside?" Lando turned from the window and leaned against the frame. His biceps strained the seams of his shirt, and he held a smirk as he waited for Beckworth to answer.

Beckworth grinned. "I'm hoping to add a surprise or two for

that. We need to wait for Fitz and Jamie and whatever crew he's bringing before I can answer that."

The group looked around for Fitz and seemed perplexed when they couldn't find him.

"I sent him to Bristol after our earlier meeting." Beckworth stared at the map, putting his words in order. "We need more men. I don't want to be evenly matched. I want to overpower if we can. That's the only way to reduce casualties among our own as well as those held in the house."

"When do you expect Fitz to return?" Thomas asked.

"No more than a day or two, unless Jamie was delayed at sea."

"I hate the waiting." Ethan placed an arm around Maire, who leaned into him. "We should start drills."

Finn nodded. "For everyone. We need to be sharp. Do we know where everyone will be assigned?"

"I thought we'd wait for Fitz and Jamie before deciding that as well. There's one other thing everyone needs to be aware of." Beckworth placed a mug just outside the outer perimeter. "There's an old outbuilding that sits here. It's a stable structure though not livable. However, there's a room that was used for food storage that has a trap door that goes down to a small cellar. That cellar has a secret door that connects to a tunnel that goes to Waverly."

Finn laughed. "I remember now. That's how you escaped during Reginald's masquerade ball."

Beckworth nodded. "It leads to various places in the manor including my bedroom, which I have no doubt Gemini has taken for her own. It also gives us access to a door at the back of the manor."

"What are you going to be doing inside, little man, when you walk through those doors?" Lando asked.

"I'll keep Gemini and Gaines occupied, giving the team

coming through the tunnel free access to the manor while bartering for the life of my staff."

Stella had stopped listening. She'd heard about the secret tunnel they'd used to sneak into Waverly. It was where Finn had been caught, but Beckworth had gotten away, something she thought he still blamed himself for.

One way or another, she was going to be part of the team that used the tunnel. Because one thing was certain. She wasn't going to let Beckworth suffer at the hands of Gemini and Gaines again.

37

The following day was spent running drills and making optional plans, each dependent on how many men Jamie brought with him from the *Daphne*. Stella joined AJ and Lando for the first part of the drills to work on her dagger skills. When AJ moved on to target practice with her bow, Stella switched to firearms. Ethan and Thomas welcomed her to the group of men who were running through blade work and taught her tricks to load the pistol and rifle faster. Then they set up targets for her. If they questioned her abilities before, their respect for her skills was evident in their broad smiles when she quickly eliminated the targets.

Afterward, she returned to the cabin to help Eleanor with dinner preparations. She'd only seen Beckworth a couple of times when he was running sword drills and then standing with others over a table filled with maps. He seemed to be in his element, so she left him with the men.

Jamie and Fitz arrived just before dinner with a dozen sailors from the ship. They were quickly brought up to speed on the main plan and various options for deploying the team.

"Sounds like an excellent plan, but on Beckworth's request,

we brought something that should add a touch of excitement to the party." Jamie nodded to Fitz, who placed a small keg and a roll of what looked like twine on the table.

Ethan whistled. "Gunpowder?"

The group glanced around, then they all smiled and nodded.

Fitz tapped the top of the keg. "It will definitely be an explosive evening."

The team left Bart's late the following afternoon, leaving Bart and Eleanor behind. Lincoln wanted to go with the group, but Beckworth convinced him he needed to provide protection in case someone came around if things went wrong.

Stella had eaten little that day, her stomach already threatening trouble from her nervous energy. Eleanor seemed to understand her dilemma and kept her busy with work. But it was Beckworth who took five minutes before their departure to calm her with sweet kisses behind the barn in between walking her through her part of the mission. It had been like old times, and his magic worked to temporarily settle her nerves.

Then the team mounted up and rode to a hunting cabin Beckworth said was rarely used. It was on his neighbor's property just north of Waverly and two miles from the road that led to Corsham. When they arrived, they found sixteen of Beckworth's men waiting for them. Henderson had ridden to town earlier that day to gather the men, and Beckworth spoke with each of them, shaking their hands and patting their shoulders.

The group gathered, and they reviewed the plan they'd finalized the evening before. They quickly determined how the team would be divided. The first group was twelve of Beckworth's men who would replace Gemini's men on the outer perimeter. Once the fireworks started, they would move in to close the net.

Thomas and Henderson along with the other three from Beckworth's team would take out the guards at the barracks and release the rest of Beckworth's men. This was one of the questionable areas since they didn't know how many men had survived the initial attack and would be in shape to fight.

Ethan, Lando, Jamie, and AJ, along with six sailors, would wait until the outer perimeter was theirs, then head for the stable to set up the first diversion. Finn, Fitz, Stella, and Maire would take the other six sailors and go through the tunnel to the manor. From there, they would split up with Fitz arranging an additional diversion.

The team broke into their assigned groups, but Stella followed Beckworth to his horse.

"I suppose I don't have to tell you to be safe and don't take chances." She put her arms around him and hugged him tightly.

He kissed her—hard and quick—which was enough to make her stagger a bit when he pulled her arms away. "I should tell you the same, but I won't waste my breath."

"Because you know I won't take chances, or because you know I'd just lie?"

He chuckled. "We are a pair, you and I." He kissed the tip of her nose and mounted. And with a swift kick, his horse carried him away into the dusky evening.

Beckworth took his time once he reached the road, keeping the horse to a walk until he nudged it to a canter when he turned down the tree-lined road to Waverly. The team would have begun moving into position as soon as he left. The first part would be the most difficult as his guards worked their way around Waverly for their assault on the outer-perimeter defenses. They were skilled men and knew the terrain well, but even so, it only required one of Gemini's men to be out of position for someone to sound an alarm. He trusted the other teams would be able to adjust if that occurred.

No one stopped him, nor did he see anyone until he reached the manor. One of the guards yelled for a stable boy. The boy was hesitant at first, but when he glanced up and saw Beckworth, a flash of relief lit the boy's gaze before it disappeared.

He nodded at the boy and ruffled his hair as he handed him the reins. "Make sure he gets a good rub down and fresh hay."

"Yes, master." The boy's simple words told him all he needed to know. The staff was playing the same roles as they did whenever he took on the full viscount persona. But underneath the facade, they were his personal crew and would be his eyes and ears for the rest of Waverly.

He turned and strode to the front door and almost smiled at Gemini's man, who tried to run in front of him. When he reached the door, Beckworth let the man open it, then knocked him out of the way as he entered his home. Two guards stood in the foyer. Where were the others?

A footman entered from a side door, looking mildly surprised.

"Where's Barrington?"

"In his room, sir." The footman glanced at the guards. "He's only allowed out with supervision."

"I see." He tilted his head, listening for voices or something that would tell him where everyone was.

"They're in the dining room, sir."

He nodded and strode down the hall. The guard who followed him into the house seemed perplexed whether to continue after him or return to his station. The man decided to trail behind. He ignored him and pushed the doors to the dining room open without preamble and before the guard could move past him.

Gemini and Gaines were in the middle of dinner, and they both jumped when he stormed in. Two of his footmen were stationed to serve, and another two of Gemini's men stood on each side of the room.

"Dare I ask what possessed you to enter my home without my knowledge or permission?" He frowned and let the full force of his pent-up rage surge.

Gemini almost choked on her food before dabbing her lips with a napkin. "Teddy, I wasn't expecting you without a message first."

"I've told you not to call me that."

She ignored his reprimand. "Why would I inform you of my arrival since you didn't provide the same courtesy?"

"You mean your invasion?"

She clucked. "Nothing more than a wife coming home to her husband. How did I know those men weren't the invaders?"

"For the last and final time, you're not my wife, and you damn well know it."

She cut a piece of fish, took a bite, and closed her eyes. "The cook is truly amazing." She eyed him. "Sit down, Teddy. You there—" she pointed at one of the footmen, "—gather another place setting for your lord."

A crash made them jump and face his direction. Remnants of a vase and scattered flowers lay on the floor. What was once a lovely table dressing had been destroyed, and he was sorry for the mess the staff would have to clean.

Beckworth stared at Gemini, his full anger pushing to be released. "You will not address my staff in such a manner."

She studied him, her brows raised, then shrugged. "As you wish."

A maid rushed in to clean the mess.

"Sorry, Elsa."

"No worries, sir." She glanced at Gemini, then back at him.

He bent down and gave her a smile, whispering, "I'm doing my best to get rid of her." Her lips twitched, and he stepped back, dropping into the chair at the opposite end of the table. He leaned back and propped his boots on the table. "Douglas, get me a glass of whiskey."

The footmen gave a slight nod and poured a generous amount before delivering it.

He took a long swallow and leaned his head back. "Why are you really here? Hoping to find more chronicles, or perhaps, the stones? Or have you given up?"

She frowned and stabbed at a piece of fish. "I've sent dozens of men everywhere trying to keep up with the lot of you. It was tiring and boring. And honestly, I didn't see a reason to find them on my own. Well, with a few exceptions. The men that followed your little ragtag group were meant to ensure you uncovered the chronicles. Gathering everything up for me with a nice bow."

He knocked back the rest of the whiskey. "And then what? We're supposed to just hand everything over to you?"

"Of course. And since you walked into my web, you won't be leaving again until you have someone bring me the other chronicles." She pushed her plate away, snapping her fingers at a footman, who rushed over to take the plate. "I might also mention, I have a group of men in London who are right now sneaking into Hensley's manor to take the scribe."

He kept his expression bored, though it was difficult. At first, he thought she meant Maire, but she was here, prepared to break into his bedroom. Did she know Maire had left London, or was she talking about Sebastian? Hensley's manor was well guarded, but would it be sufficient? Worse case, if they were to grab the monk, they would bring him here, which could become sticky, depending on tonight's outcome.

"What, no response?" Gemini asked.

"You seemed to have left London rather quickly. I hope there weren't any difficulties."

Her face reddened, and Gaines pushed his chair back, but with a motion from Gemini, he didn't rise. "What do you know of that?"

Beckworth smiled. "André sends his regards."

And with that, Gaines flew across the room.

Stella watched her footing as Finn led them down the dark, earthy tunnel. Thick timber posts and beams had been strategically placed to prevent cave-ins, but she'd be happy never to do this again. Every third person held a lamp, but they barely kept the shadows at bay.

Maire kept pushing her on. She didn't mean to slow down; it was more a reactive decision her brain made. It seemed like they'd been walking for hours when her logical mind told her it had only been twenty minutes.

She thought she'd weep with joy when Finn stopped at a door. They had to be at the manor. He held a finger to his lips and handed her the lantern. The door didn't have a handle, and he ran his hand along its edges and then along the stones that had been used as a doorframe. The top corner stone slid back an inch, and the door cracked open.

Finn pried at the edges until it swung wide. The tunnel continued, but this time, it was stairs rather than dirt inside what appeared to be part of a stone basement. There was a small landing area at the foot of the stairs, and they all gathered in the tight space until the last man closed the door.

"From what Beckworth told me," Finn said, "the stairs go up a floor before branching out to two exits on the main floor. We'll continue up another set of stairs that will take us to Beckworth's bedroom. From there, another set of stairs will lead down again, this time leading to a hidden room on the first floor. There's a single door that leads outside to the back of the manor. We'll divide up when we reach the path to the bedroom."

Everyone nodded, and they began their climb. It didn't take long to reach the second floor, where most of the men had to duck their heads with the low ceiling. They squatted at a junction.

"This is where we split up." Finn nodded to Fitz. "You have everything you need?"

He nodded and tapped the burlap bag filled with gunpowder hanging from his belt. "We wait five minutes after the first diversion to make sure the inner perimeter teams move in. Then we'll exit out the back, surprise the guards patrolling the manor, and with any luck, any stragglers from the perimeter."

"Good luck, gentlemen."

Stella watched the men go, each of them patting Finn's shoulder on their way past. AJ mentioned once that Jamie had added new crew members after becoming captain, but many of the men that worked under Finn still remained. It appeared those were the sailors Jamie had brought with him.

Once they were gone, only three remained—Finn, Maire, and herself.

Finn gave them his signature grin. "Here's to hoping Beckworth is in place and keeping everyone occupied."

AJ trotted behind Ethan, with Jamie and Lando behind her, followed by the sailors from the *Daphne*. The men who would be taking out the perimeter guards brought up the rear, and one by one they left the group as they came to the approximate location of their target.

Their mission was to take out Gemini's men as soon as they found them, and then take a position in a slightly different spot in case Gaines sent someone out to check on them. Then they just had to wait for the fireworks.

She grinned. They hadn't used explosives before. The closest they'd come to that was their first battle against the duke at the monastery, when she'd convinced Jamie, who'd been first mate at the time, to use the *Daphne's* cannons as a diversion. There weren't fireworks then, just cannonballs breaking through rocks and trees as they landed.

They had put distance between them and the barracks as another group, led by Thomas and Henderson, broke off with their small strike team in their attempt to release Beckworth's guards. Ethan never hesitated after giving Thomas a hand signal, and only looked back once to see another man sneak away for the perimeter.

Ethan came to an abrupt stop and held up his hand, turning to face the left. A dim light reflected through a small door in the stables. The six sailors formed a tight circle around them as they waited. They were the only team that had a specific time to set off the first diversion. Then everything else would fall into place.

All was quiet, except for one of Beckworth's men sneaking through the trees ten yards in front of them. He stopped, glancing around before freezing as he peered to his right and another five yards ahead. He moved with a stealth anyone would be proud of, and then grabbed a man AJ hadn't seen.

It was over in an instant as Gemini's man slid to the ground.

The man turned and waved Ethan and the group through. They stayed low as they came up to the back of the barn. Once they'd grouped up again, Ethan crept to the back door and found it partially open. First, his head disappeared, and then the rest of him. Jamie tapped AJ, who slid her bow and quiver to her back and sprinted through the door.

One lantern provided the only light, keeping most of the interior in shadows. Ethan was speaking with two stable boys, who listened intently with an occasional nod. Jamie and Lando stopped behind her. The sailors would remain outside. Their task would be to join with those rescued from the barracks to take out the inner perimeter men and those that fled from the manor.

Ethan waved the group over. "These two lads will get the horses out of the stalls and keep them in the aisle until we're ready."

The lads' eyes were as wide as their grins. AJ smothered a chuckle. They were equally fearful and excited. *Welcome to the club, boys.*

"AJ, check the front door and make sure it's free to open when the blast goes off. Jamie, get your surprise set up."

AJ slid between the horses that were already out of their stalls. She slowly opened the door to check the area when a man pulled it from her and stepped inside, pushing her back.

A bulky man entered, and the scent of stale alcohol smothered her.

"Well, what do we have here?"

38

Beckworth was ready for Gaines and stood just as the man barreled into him. They crashed against the wall with the force of the hit. They rolled on the ground until Beckworth ended on top. He punched Gaines in the ribs and then in the face, but Gaines turned his head, catching the brunt of the hit on his chin. Blood spurted from his mouth, most likely from biting his tongue.

Gaines managed to tangle his legs with Beckworth's, forcing him over. Beckworth held on tight and leaned hard to the right to put them into a roll. They crashed into the side table and decanters of alcohol rattled then tipped, dousing both men.

Someone was screaming. He didn't know who it was, nor did he care. His complete focus was to beat on Gaines until the man couldn't move. A phrase he'd heard when he was in Baywood came to mind—paybacks were hell.

He took a hit in his kidneys that made his eyes water and created a spasm in his back. But he didn't stop. He pounded on Gaines—the ribs, his face, stomach, then back to the ribs.

He felt the fight going out of the man. Something smashed over his head. Once. Then again.

Everything went dark.

Stella had squatted next to Finn, waiting for his decision on when to proceed.

"What are we waiting for, brother?" Maire's tone was filled with anxiety and eagerness.

Stella wasn't fooled, and it was doubtful Finn would be. She always got like this when something involved *The Book*. She wondered if Maire had some sixth sense when part of it was near. Or perhaps a psychic link. She snorted, then held back her grin when Finn gave her one of his scary looks that worked on others but never fazed her.

"We're waiting, dear sister, to give Beckworth a little more time to gather everyone on the first floor. We'll wait another five minutes."

Maire slipped from her squat until her backside hit the floor and placed her hands in her lap.

She was irritated, and Finn grinned. Stella would have loved to have seen these two when they were younger. They had a strong bond and were completely loyal to each other, but they had bold personalities that didn't always see eye to eye. She leaned her head against the wall and let her mind drift to Beckworth. Gemini wouldn't kill him. She might have allowed the torture, but she needed him. She scowled. It was more than that. It was true she wanted his money, but as much as she didn't want to admit it, the bitch had feelings for Beckworth. And the more he fought against her, the more she was drawn to him.

Finn nudged her and snapped her out of her self-made hell. "You're going first."

That surprised her and she pushed herself up. "I'm ready."

"The passage goes in about fifteen feet, then stops at a door.

There isn't room for all of us, and there's limited head space. The door enters directly into the bedroom. We'll have to go single file, and the person in front goes in first.

"This would have been a great time to let Maire take the lead," Stella mumbled as she duckwalked toward the door. Halfway there she glanced over her shoulder. "You know it's not smart to open the door with the lantern lit up like Christmas. It's not very stealthy."

She turned back to the path, smiling at Finn's annoyed stare, but he didn't stop her. He stayed back and blocked most of the light with his body. The passageway became darker, and with every step, she kept a hand in front of her, expecting the door at any moment. And there it was.

"Press on the top right corner." Finn's voice filtered from behind her.

She put her ear to the door but didn't hear anything other than the steady thrumming of her heart. That was helpful. She didn't really need a reminder of her anxiety. Taking a deep breath, she pressed the corner.

Nothing happened.

She pressed again, giving it a harder push. Click. The door slid a few inches without a sound. She pushed it wider and cursed. A low light was in the room, and it was bright enough to show the figure of a man hovering a foot away—waiting for her.

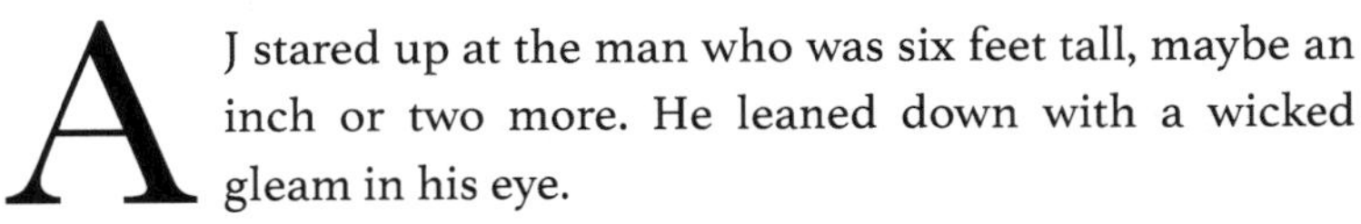

AJ stared up at the man who was six feet tall, maybe an inch or two more. He leaned down with a wicked gleam in his eye.

She took a step back.

He blinked then gave her a longer perusal, his gaze falling on her bow and quiver. "What's this? A bit late to be out hunting."

She raised her voice to make sure the others heard her. "It depends on what you're hunting?"

His lip lifted in a leer, and he licked his thick lips.

She did her best to stand firm and not cringe as her hand slid into her pocket. Her fingers wrapped around the dagger.

"And what might you be huntin'?" He took a step closer.

She took another step back and gave him her sweetest smile. "I've heard vermin has invaded Waverly."

It took him a moment to register her words and understand them for what they meant. She was pulling the dagger out of her pocket as he lifted a hand to slap her. Before she could take a step back, the man's eyes bugged out, and he arched before dropping to the ground in front of her.

Lando stood behind the fallen man, his dagger slick with blood. He glanced down at the one in her hand. "Apologies. We don't have much time to waste."

She slipped the dagger back into her pocket. "I could have taken him." She pushed the bow and quiver farther up her shoulder. "I just wanted him all the way in the barn so I didn't have to drag him."

He grinned. "Once again, sorry for not anticipating your stealth."

"Fine. My idea would have taken longer." She glanced out the door. "Did you see anyone while you were out there?"

"No." He lifted his arm and signaled the others. "Jamie is ready."

"That was fast."

"There's not much involved."

Ethan stepped in from the front of the building, followed by two sailors. "Let's go." He slipped back out the door.

AJ followed with Lando behind her. They closed the door behind them. The sailors stood at the entrance and would pull the doors open once the gunpowder blew. The three huddled together just to the side of the barn.

"Remember to stay as close as you can, and don't stop." Ethan glanced at the side of the barn. "The horses should stay together long enough to get us to the manor." When they nodded, Ethan called out. "Jamie, we're ready."

A light flashed, and she turned to watch the tiny fire work its way up the cord.

Jamie raced for them. "Cover your heads."

They knelt and did as he said. The blast was loud, and she wished she'd thought to cover her ears instead.

After that, everything moved quickly. Someone pulled her up as the barn doors swung open and terrified horses raced out of the building. Then she was running for the manor, heading for the door to the kitchen or as close as they could get.

All she heard was the screaming of the horses as they trampled anything in their path on their way to safety.

Stella stared up at the dark figure. With the light shining from behind, all she could discern was that he had to be a man.

"It's about time." The voice was a harsh whisper, like a teacher reprimanding an errant school child late from recess.

She snorted before releasing a relieved sigh. "Barrington."

She stepped into the room, stretching her back. Finn and Maire followed behind her, and Barrington reached out to shake Finn's hand.

"Is Beckworth alright?" she asked.

"He won't be for long from what I've been told." He strode across the room. "Gemini had two trunks with her when she arrived. I believe they're in the dressing room."

"How many men does Gemini have in the house?"

"A dozen from what the footmen tell me."

Finn glanced in the dressing room. "Do you need help?"

Maire shook her head. "No. We have it."

Finn leaned against the wall across from the dressing room. "Why are footmen keeping you apprised?"

"Gemini had me locked in my room. They might know I'm missing by now."

"Where are they?"

"In the library."

"How is it they don't know where you are?"

Barrington snorted. "When we heard Beckworth had returned, we knew he wouldn't be alone. We've been waiting to make our move. And Gemini can't be bothered with how the servants move around the manor."

Maire laughed behind them. "They aren't aware of the secret passages. The one we came through wasn't the only one in this house." There was rustling and then a surprised, "Oh."

The men turned toward the dressing room. Maire held up the chronicle. "Bingo." Her grin was wide.

Behind Maire, toward the back of the dressing room, Stella had been scanning Beckworth's wide array of clothes before she knelt in front of the second trunk. Had Gemini taken the first trunks available to her in the rush to leave, or did she take these for a particular reason?

She opened the lid, happy that Maire had found the chronicle. But it was worth taking a quick peek at this one. She carefully reviewed each item as she took them out and placed them next to her. This trunk was familiar. It was the one she'd taken the purse from, the one that was now in her trunk with the last of her stolen coins in it. There were several other purses inside, and she was placing the fourth one in the stack when she paused and went back to the third one.

It seemed heavier than it should be for its size and the silk material it was made from. It was puffy, and it wasn't until she pressed down on it that she felt rough edges. Curious, she opened it. The inside was stuffed with scarves. She pulled out one, and another, and another until she found a lace pouch. More money?

"What are you doing, Stella?" Finn moved into the dressing room. "Maire found the chronicle."

She didn't respond as she opened the pouch and poured out the contents. Three small stones fell into her palm. She didn't require more light to know what they were. She stared up into Finn's awestruck gaze.

He fell to his knees and held out his hand, and she dropped the stones into his palm, one by one. "I'll be damned. How did she get her hands on them?"

She couldn't answer and didn't think he expected her to. Sebastian might be able to piece it together, but Gemini was the only one who could tell them.

"Maire," he called. But she was already standing beside him, Barrington behind her. "You need to take these and the chronicle and get out of here. Go back through the tunnels and wait at the outbuilding until I have someone come for you. Do you understand?"

He was still looking at the stones. Stella thought Maire would argue, but after a minute, she took the stones from Finn's palm and stuffed them back in the pouch. She stuck them in the pockets of her skirts and backed up.

"Let me call two of the footmen to go with her." Barrington looked at Finn. "You can trust these men. They were hand selected by Beckworth."

Finn considered the butler and then nodded. "Be quick."

Barrington rushed to the bedroom door with Maire following.

An explosion ripped through the night.

Barrington raced back to the dressing room. "Was that your doing?"

Finn nodded. "There will be another one in five minutes somewhere along the back of the manor."

Barrington nodded then disappeared.

"Help me put this stuff back." Stella began tossing things back into the trunk. Finn passed her dresses and small jewelry boxes. Once everything was in, she stamped them down, and Finn closed the lid while she latched it.

"We need to find Gemini, right? Make sure Beckworth is okay."

He nodded. "Barrington and I can do that. You should follow Maire."

She shook her head. "I'm not leaving without him."

He studied her for a moment, perhaps assessing her commitment, but then he nodded before standing and leaving the room. She leaned on the trunk to help her stand and noticed a small trunk sticking out from underneath a great coat. She brushed the fabric aside.

"Like Finn said. I'll be damned."

She stuck her head out of the room just as Maire ducked into the secret passage with two footmen behind her. "Barrington. Can I speak with you?" She held up a finger to Finn. "It will only take a moment."

A few minutes later, the two of them rushed out of the room and met Finn at the door to the hallway. While Finn checked the hall for Gemini's men, Stella glanced at Barrington and smiled. When he winked back, at least part of Gemini's damage wouldn't be in vain.

Beckworth woke to a blinding headache. Not again. He kept his eyes closed, mostly to take stock of what else hurt, but also to determine if he was alone. He wasn't. The scratch of a quill on paper was unmistakable.

His legs and wrists were tied to a chair with rope. It wasn't a dining room chair. It felt more like one of the chairs in his study, or perhaps the library. He was bruised in a few spots, but other than his head, he felt fine. And even that pain was beginning to subside.

His first thought was how much time had elapsed. He assumed Gemini's first perimeter had been taken, but had they set the diversions? Since no one appeared panicked, he had to assume no. It was possible their attempt to take out the first perimeter hadn't been successful, and the team had to regroup. Only one way to find out.

He opened an eye and then the other before blinking a few times to clear his vision.

"Ah, you're awake, darling." Gemini's voice was soothing. "I imagine you might have a headache, and I am sorry for that, but I couldn't have you killing Gaines."

"What did you hit me with?"

"A silver tray. It required a few attempts until you finally stilled."

He scanned the room—the library—but Gaines wasn't anywhere in sight. Not dead, but he had to be feeling the effects of the fight. More so than he did.

Gemini sat at a writing desk, a stack of messages on one side, and she finished another before sanding it, folding it, and applying a wax seal. She added it to the stack.

He wasn't going to ask what she was doing. With any luck, it soon wouldn't matter, and he didn't want to feed into her delusions.

"I don't know why you have me tied up. Gaines attacked me."

"I don't want either of you hurt, but you left me no choice."

"Like on the ship where you left me to André and Gaines's gentle care?"

She grimaced. "I do apologize for that. As I've told you before, Gaines can be a bit aggressive in his treatment of prisoners. I'm still working on refining his techniques. From what I can tell, André never had a proper upbringing. Not his fault, really, but I'm afraid he was too far gone for me to help him."

"So, that's why you left him when you and Gaines scurried out the back door like rats on a sinking ship."

Her face pinched with anger. "I take it you had a hand in that, and I'm afraid Gaines will expect something in return. Though I've also taken offense. I had to leave many precious things behind."

"Like the documents of your misdeeds with forged property transactions. Do you think you can do the same here?"

She shrugged, but her face was still tinged with frustration. "It will be a bit more tricky, but you know how long it takes for news to travel. And it won't be the first time I've had to change my plans." She moved the stack of messages aside and stood, picking up several other documents. She moved to the front of the desk, her skirts brushing his knee as she passed him.

She laid the documents along the edge of the desk, then moved the inkpot and quill near the first parchment. "The only thing you need to do this evening is sign these documents. Then I'll help you to bed and ensure you get a good night's sleep. By morning your headache will be gone, and yes, I can clearly see by your squinting eyes that your head hurts. In a couple of days, I'll be gone."

"We've been through this before. I won't sign anything."

Her smile was serene. "Of course, you will. You might not care for your own life, but you care for your staff. You've made that clear enough. It was Gaines, actually, who suggested using those you hold dear as part of our negotiations. It's a shame that little trollop you passed off as AJ Murphy isn't close at hand."

Thank heavens they hadn't found her. Was she even close to the manor, or still stuck behind the perimeter? "I believe it was Gaines who passed her off as AJ Murphy."

"Semantics at this point. I was thinking maybe one of the maids might be a good place to start, but I've decided to begin with your butler." Her lip curled. "He's a most disagreeable man."

Was Barrington still locked in his room? If the staff knew something was up, they would do whatever they could to free him.

"Why don't you simply marry Gaines and get on with your life?"

"Why do that when I can have a lovely estate, or at least the money from it, as well as a devoted lover on the side?"

"Or perhaps a lover to console a widow?" Gaines entered the room, holding his side where Beckworth had landed several good blows. He glared at him, then scowled at Gemini. "The butler's gone."

"What do you mean gone?" There wasn't immediate panic in her gaze, but the news startled her. "Damn it. One of the servants must have let him out. Search the house. If he'd gotten outside, one of the guards would have seen him."

Beckworth chuckled. "I suppose you were in too much of a hurry to think this all through."

"The guards are already searching for him." Gaines stepped closer. "There's nowhere for him to run. But while we wait for him, why don't we see if we can't get a signature or two without him." He stopped in front of Beckworth and pulled out a dagger. With one quick swipe, blood appeared on Beckworth's sleeve before he felt the sting of the blade.

Gaines turned to Gemini. “Let’s see if losing a few inches of flesh doesn’t change his mind.”

An explosion shook the windows.

Gemini and Gaines ducked and looked around. Boots raced down the hall, and a man stuck his head inside.

“It came from the stables.” The man’s gaze was wild, but there was a spark that read payback. He would be dangerous.

“Well, don’t stand there. Find out what’s happening,” Gaines barked.

Gemini stood in front of Beckworth. She grabbed his hair and pulled his head back, increasing the ache until darkness edged his vision. “What did you do?”

39

Finn, Barrington, and Stella ran down the hall until they came to the stairs. Finn threw out an arm to stop them. Stella cursed. Gemini's men were supposed to have left the manor.

"There's a guard." Finn looked behind them.

"Just one?" Stella asked.

Finn leaned against the wall. He was thinking up something, but Stella had an easy answer.

"Let me lure him upstairs," she suggested. "He won't shoot me, but he'll come after me."

When Finn didn't seem convinced, Barrington added, "We can hide in this first guest room. If she can lure him inside, we'll be waiting."

That seemed logical enough, and Finn nodded. "Don't do anything fancy."

She simply rolled her eyes and walked toward the stairs. Before she became visible to the guard, she hunched her shoulders and tiptoed as if she didn't want to be noticed. When the guard didn't notice her, she sighed. They always noticed the person in the movies. She didn't know why they bothered hiding. It appeared Gemini hadn't brought her A team. The only thing she could think of other than yelling at him was to fake a trip, and she stumbled into the banister.

When the guard glanced up, he did a double take as Stella gave him a wide-eyed stare then turned and ran. Boots on the stairs followed her, and she saw the backside of Finn running into the room. She glanced over her shoulder to see the man reach the top of the stairs.

She turned back, ready to go through the door when she spotted AJ running toward her, bow held in front of her, an arrow nocked, and the string tight under tension.

"Drop." AJ's call was a light echo through the hall, and Stella hit the deck, her jaw scraping the wood floor.

The arrow whizzed by, and something hit her at the same time she heard a thud.

"What the..." Finn had stepped outside, Barrington behind him.

The butler chuckled. "That's going to be quite the story around the hearth." He hurried around Finn and grabbed the man's legs.

The second explosion made them all duck. Stella laughed. "Like we weren't expecting it."

"That should clear the last of them out." Finn walked to Stella, and she waited for some smart comment from him, but he seemed to change his mind.

Stella pushed at the man, who had landed across her legs. Finn grabbed the man's shoulders and lifted lift him off her. Her gaze froze on the broken end of the arrow stuck in his chest. The arrow had broken when the man hit the ground. She glanced up at AJ. "Nice shot."

"I'm so sorry. I didn't know Finn was here. All I saw was you running from him." She took Stella's elbow as she pulled herself up.

Stella hugged her, trying to stifle a laugh that was half hysterical and half relief. "We did have a plan, but this works, too."

Once the dead man was dropped into the room, Finn hugged AJ. "What are you doing here?"

She shrugged. "Using the horses for cover worked better than expected. Thomas and Henderson ended up with a larger group of men than we planned. Gemini's men are surrounded. They haven't given up, but Ethan said it was just a matter of time. Jamie and Lando came in with me. We're searching for any of her men that stayed inside."

Barrington gave the group a quick study. "Now that there's four of us, why don't we break up? You both know the manor well enough. Go back toward the master suite and take the servant's stairs down to the first floor. Stella and I will work our way toward the west wing. We'll meet you in the dining room, which isn't far from the library."

Finn nodded and touched AJ's arm before running off. She followed but glanced back to wave at Stella, who waved back.

Stella watched her friend leave to chase after bad guys. She had so much respect for AJ at that moment. What a different woman she turned into since the stones came into her life. And with Finn at her side, she couldn't be happier for them. As long as they both got their backsides back home safe and sound.

Barrington nudged her. They needed to move. She didn't know how she knew, but they were running out of time.

She stayed close to Barrington, who slowed as they passed by rooms and came to a complete stop when they had to cross a hallway. They'd reached the end of the hall where a door led to the servant's stairs. He pushed her inside.

"Wait here. I'll be right back."

He was gone before she could ask where he was going. It had

barely been a couple of minutes when he returned. He held a sword in his hand, and that made her feel better.

"Shall we go?" she asked.

"Stay close." He raced down the stairs, passed the landing for the first floor, and continued down another flight to what had to be the kitchen. Delectable scents tickled her nose and made her stomach growl. They were clearing food off the platters and plates. The meal must have just ended. Had Beckworth dined with them? She would have loved to hear that dinner conversation.

He peeked through the door as she caught up. She'd slowed on the stairs, not wanting to miss a step and break her neck. He took a step backward, almost stepping on her toes, and grabbed her arm to turn her around when a burly man came through the door.

This guy wasn't part of the staff. It wouldn't matter what he wore, he'd never fit in as someone who worked in service. It was probably the beady eyes.

In a flash, Barrington brought up his sword and cleaved the man's middle. He dropped like a rock, his blood pooling on the floor.

That was unexpected.

She swallowed, then ignored the dead man as she had others in the past and sidestepped him in a rush to keep up with Barrington, who was already racing away. The use of his sword was just as quick and deadly when they ran into a second man.

He barreled his way past without pause or remorse. Waverly might belong to Beckworth, but this was his home, too. Would she be any less fierce? Maybe it was the juxtaposition of seeing the estate's butler as a warrior. But she'd witnessed his continued loyalty to Beckworth time and again, so maybe it wasn't as odd as it seemed.

She reached into her pocket, felt the weight of her flintlock, then pulled out her dagger. Gemini had better keep Beckworth alive. When a woman screamed, Barrington ran faster.

Beckworth's arms and legs were going numb, and he pushed against the restraints even though they would be impossible to break. But if he could stretch the ropes, his circulation would return. The only thing worse than being tied down was listening to Gemini drone on and on about her inability to stop Gaines once he got an idea in his head. Just sign the documents, and they'd leave—for now.

She didn't seem to understand his resolve to not give up something he'd fought so hard for. But Gaines was right about one thing—he wouldn't allow his staff to suffer. Not if he could prevent it. The second diversion should happen soon. Gemini was already irritated. How would she fare with another disruption?

The house shook with another explosion. Right on time.

Gemini spun toward the door and then back to him. "I'll ask one more time. What have you done?"

"You don't seriously believe I came alone, do you?"

Her face paled. "Gaines? Get in here." She paced, her eyes jumping back and forth between the door and him. "How many? Who's out there?"

He remained silent, waiting to see where this would go.

The strike came so fast he never saw it coming. It stung. Her fear had been replaced by rage.

"Gaines!" She screeched it.

"I'm here." Gaines rushed in. He was under more control than Beckworth would have preferred. "The guards have gone to investigate."

Beckworth smiled. Exactly according to plan.

"We need to speed this up." Gemini paced. "We can't leave until he's signed those papers. Is the coach prepared?"

"Yes, but we might need to take horses instead."

"Let me go."

He recognized the woman's voice. It was Libby. He closed his eyes. He didn't want to see anyone hurt, but Libby was a fighter. She might help delay whatever Gaines had in mind.

A man entered, dragging Libby with him. She fought him all the way, her irritated gaze shooting to him for an instant before she refocused on her struggle. Then Gaines punched her, and she dropped like a broken marionette.

"Leave her alone." Beckworth growled the words as he struggled harder against the ropes.

Gaines pointed to a chair. "Tie her up over there."

"What do you hope to gain with this?" He understood the game, but he had to play for time. Gaines assumed he'd be willing to do anything to prevent Libby from getting hurt. They were right. But how far was Gemini willing to go? Would the fact Gaines selected a woman to hurt have any effect on her?

They were about to find out. Unless he found a way to delay the inevitable.

"I'll sign." He hated to say the words, but he just needed a little more time. Someone must have let Barrington out by now.

Gemini stared at him. "Untie him."

"No." Gaines took her arms and shook her until she refocused on him. "Can't you see he's playing you? He's given in rather fast, even for someone who worries for his staff." He glanced toward the door. "We have time. Let's see this through. We've come too far."

She nodded as he spoke, and a new resolve seemed to overtake her. And Beckworth knew he'd lost his moment. Whatever Gaines was to her, she trusted his instincts. She pushed his hands away.

"You're right. Wake her up."

Gaines gave Beckworth a wicked grin. "Let's see if you're truly ready to sign." He threw a cup of water on Libby then lightly slapped her face. "Wake up, little girl. Let's see how much your master cares about you."

When nothing happened, he went to the sideboard and grabbed a bottle of whiskey, pouring a cup full. He tossed it in her face, and this time she sputtered and moaned as she pried an eye open.

She screamed.

It was ear-piercing, and he slapped her again. This time harder. When he lifted his hand to do it again, Gemini grabbed his arm.

"Let her calm down. Her screams won't get her anywhere."

"No. But this isn't about her." Gaines glared at Beckworth. "He's already worried about her. And we're running out of time." He pulled out his dagger. "I say we carve a little bit. We'll know when he's truly ready to sign."

Gemini looked from Libby to him, and there was a flicker of concern before she shielded her emotions. How deep had she buried her humanity?

Libby glanced at him, but she'd hid her fear behind her anger. *Good girl, Libby. Hold on a bit longer.*

Gaines glared at Beckworth and stalked toward her. "Time to have some fun, little girl."

Beckworth wasn't going to play the game, so he turned his attention to Libby. He didn't smile with encouragement or show sympathy. He kept his expression blank, and she followed his lead, lifting her chin a fraction. She was bracing herself, not willing to give in. She was a Londoner. She was crew. She was family.

Gemini searched Beckworth's face, and he could only guess what she was looking for, but whatever it was, she didn't find it.

She gave a nod to Gaines then turned away, fiddled with the documents, then nudged the inkpot an inch to the right.

"Hold her still," Gaines said to the man standing behind Libby, and he complied, gripping her shoulders.

She flinched as the man dug his fingers deep. Gaines stuck the blade into the soft flesh just above her right breast, and she released another ear-piercing scream.

"Stop."

The single word was said with such force, Gaines stepped back as everyone turned their heads to the door.

Murphy stood in the doorway. AJ was a step behind him with her bow raised, an arrow already nocked. But she had a poor angle and knew it. Did Gaines?

Quicker than Beckworth thought possible, Gemini held a dagger to his neck. Stalemate.

Gemini smiled at Murphy. "I don't think you understand the situation."

"That's Murphy." Gaines all but growled it, and Gemini smiled.

"Well, it's about time we met." She straightened but kept the knife at Beckworth's throat. "I'm sorry we didn't have a chance to do so sooner. And who's the little girl with the bow?"

"I'm AJ Murphy. I think you've been looking for me." AJ didn't let the bow slip an inch.

Gemini held her smile, but Beckworth guessed it was taking every ounce of her patience. Suddenly, the arrow pointed at them became more real.

AJ took a step to her left, and now she had an excellent shot. Her arrow was pointed directly at Gemini.

A shout echoed through the hallway. "Invaders. We need help."

The next minute was almost impossible to follow.

The man behind Libby moved, and without hesitation, AJ

turned and let the arrow fly. It caught the man in the chest, and he fell back.

Murphy went after Gaines, but he had already turned for Beckworth, the dagger still stained with Libby's blood aimed at his heart.

Beckworth struggled to tip the chair over, but it was too heavy to move.

"No!" Gemini's scream echoed through the room. She moved toward Gaines, and Beckworth wasn't sure if she intended to protect him or stop him. Either way, Murphy dove for his legs as an arrow hit Gaines in the shoulder, forcing him off balance.

Gemini wasn't able to step out of the way soon enough, and the dagger struck her below her chest. She teetered and glanced down, gripping the knife as her legs buckled. Gaines caught her as he fell.

"Oh, god. No. No." Gaines words, laced with fear, were screamed.

Blood seeped through her hands, her gaze sliding to Beckworth.

Finn had rolled into the desk, and he was shaking his head. AJ had run to his side and was helping him up. Neither of them caught Gaines brushing Gemini's hair aside before he pulled out the dagger. She grunted as he placed her hands over the wound.

He stood and faced Beckworth, the dagger in his hands, the blade now dripping with blood from two different women.

He came at Beckworth, the dagger raised to strike.

Beckworth refused to flinch or close his eyes. He'd always promised himself to face death head-on.

The crack from a flintlock startled him.

He shrank back as Gaines kept coming. Then a circle of crimson marred Gaines's shirt, and it spread as if it were a bud blossoming to full bloom. His gaze was wide and focused on Beckworth. He dropped, never knowing who shot him.

Beckworth lifted his gaze after Gaines fell at his feet. He couldn't help but smile.

Stella, a self-satisfied expression on her face, gripped a pistol, the smoke still curling around it as the acrid smell filled the air.

40

Beckworth tossed the ropes aside as Finn cut through them. He glanced at Stella, who had taken a few steps into the library and was staring down at the tableau of Gaines and Gemini. She needed a few minutes to come to terms with what she'd done. She'd saved his life, but had taken one in return.

Death was never to be taken lightly, even after battle. He'd once told AJ that once you took a life, the world was never quite the same. Her first one must be worth the price. He could talk to Stella about it, but she would seek AJ for solace. That was best.

He went to Libby first, where Barrington was untying her. Her bodice was bloodstained, and he pulled down the edges to find the cut. Barrington handed him a linen, and he pressed it against her wound.

"Hold this until they bring Greta."

"Enough with the both of you. It's a cut. I've dealt with much worse." Libby stood, swayed a bit, then gave Beckworth a sorrowful glance. "I suppose a glass or two of whiskey wouldn't hurt."

Beckworth smiled. The girl would be fine if she was already bargaining with him. "Of course. Barrington will see to it."

Then Beckworth went to Stella and grasped her shoulders. Her focus had shifted from the scene on the floor to Libby. "Are you alright? I thought you might need some time."

She tore her gaze away from Libby. "Of course. I'm not the one who got stabbed."

"No. But..." He wasn't sure what to say. How to make it better.

She grasped his wrists but didn't try to dislodge his grip. Somehow her touch calmed him, even when he wasn't the one that needed it. "I'm alright. It was a life-or-death situation. There was no question what I had to do. No one else would have gotten to him in time." She gave him a slight smile. "Although I wouldn't be averse to what Libby's having."

He grinned. "Of course." He led her to the sofa where Libby sat.

Barrington handed a glass to Libby then poured another for Stella. The two women looked at each other, seemed to size the other up, then clinked their glasses together with weary smiles.

"I want the both of you to stay put for now." When they both nodded, he rushed to where Finn and AJ knelt to one side of Gemini. She lay on the floor with a pillow elevating her head. Finn pressed another pillow to her chest in an attempt to staunch the bleeding.

AJ gripped her hand. "Hold on a bit longer. We've called for a doctor."

It would take too long to bring a doctor from Corsham, and Bart was farther away. Barrington had already called for Greta, one of the kitchen staff who was also a midwife. But there was too much blood on the floor.

Finn stepped aside as he knelt next to her and looked at AJ. She knew what the outcome would be. He glanced down at Gemini, who'd been watching them.

"This wasn't exactly the ending I had planned, darling." She managed a weak smile.

"You always demanded to do things your own way." He wasn't sure what else to say. For everything she'd done and all the pain she'd caused, he wouldn't berate a dying woman. This time, he'd play her game.

"It could have been wonderful, you know."

"You always dreamed big."

She gripped his hand. For a second, it was full of strength, but then it went limp. Her expression was peaceful as she gazed at something beyond his shoulder. For all she'd endured in her life, for all the wrong she'd done, he still wished a better afterlife for her.

Finn gripped his shoulder. "We've called for the magistrate. We have prisoners."

Beckworth nodded and stood, then held out a hand to AJ, which she took as she rose. Neither had anything to say.

He returned to Stella, who was placing a bandage over Libby's wound. Apparently, she wasn't going to wait for Greta.

"I've asked for a guest room to be prepared for you."

Stella glanced up at him, and he shook his head. "Not for you. Your trunk will be taken to my room once the maids change the linens and have it cleared of Gemini's things." He took Libby's hand. "The room is for you. Two days of bed rest and no arguments. You can have visitors, but I want you to take time to recover. I'll talk with you in the morning. Now, Barrington will help you upstairs."

"That's not necessary, my lord." Her tone was demure, and he clucked his tongue.

"You're among friends here, so stop with the 'my lord' stuff. You're a tough old bird for as young as you are, and you have my gratitude. But more about that tomorrow." He glanced up at Barrington, who nodded.

"Come, child. Let's get you settled." Barrington helped her up.

"Child? Now who's playing games." She picked up her empty glass, but Barrington took it from her. "You can have a nightcap once you're in bed."

Two maids rushed in. "We'll take her up, sir. We've been worried about her."

Once Libby was gone from the room, Barrington called for footmen and more maids.

Beckworth sat next to Stella. "I didn't mean to come to you last." He gripped her hand and brought it to his lips.

"I'm sorry about Gemini. I wish I'd gotten here sooner."

"It all happened so fast. Gaines was filled with rage. I'm not sure it could have ended any other way. Gemini wouldn't have survived prison, though it might have been possible to have her sent to the colonies. She only knew one way to live. Her youth wasn't much different than mine."

"It was a great deal different. You made friends, even being poor, and you considered others. She only had one goal in life that was driven by her uncle's greed. And she never cared who she hurt in the process. She wanted to change the future to her advantage. That road leads to damnation, or so my mother would have said."

AJ, who'd been speaking with Murphy and Maire, came over and sat on the other side of Stella.

"Are you okay?" When Stella nodded, AJ shook her head. "You're as deadly as Maire with flintlocks. I'm sorry, that didn't come out right."

"No. You're right." Stella nudged her with a shoulder. "The timing might have been a bit off." The two laughed, but Beckworth caught the tension in it.

"I heard you were just as deadly this evening." Beckworth leaned back, bringing Stella with him, which gave him a clearer view of AJ.

She shrugged. "It wasn't any easier than the first time, but they chose their side. They weren't good people, and while it's not my place to judge, I can't let those I love be hurt by men like that."

Murphy, Hughes, and Maire joined them and dropped into nearby chairs.

"I can't believe this is over." Maire had a glazed look, and he didn't think it was from the danger of the evening—at least not all of it. She glanced around the group. "Is it over? I mean truly over?"

Murphy nodded. "The older Belato is dead. André is in prison and will most likely remain there until the war is over. Even if he's sent home before then, he didn't seem interested in his uncle's game. He was as much a victim as Gemini had been. At least as children. Maybe if she'd stayed in France, the two of them might have walked away from it all."

Beckworth changed the subject, not wanting to give Gemini any more due. "Barrington is arranging rooms for everyone and is having the coach brought in, so you'll have your trunks soon."

"Aye, and I've sent a messenger to Hensley. We'll stay until he arrives, and then we'll go home."

Quiet descended, and Beckworth found it difficult to breathe. He knew this day had been coming. He stood. "I need to see to the estate and check on my men and the staff. Please, make yourself at home." He winked at Maire. "If you need assistance, Maire knows where everything is."

When she stuck her tongue out at him, he chuckled. Stella squeezed his hand and made to get up. "Stay put until the rooms and trunks are ready."

He left the group, all at once feeling like an outsider. The one that wouldn't be leaving. He was already home.

Stella stretched and rolled over. Beckworth had left early, wanting to check on everyone and see to his guards. Neither of them had slept much, finding comfort in holding each other until, at some point, she'd fallen into a deep sleep.

He hadn't left too quickly, since he'd taken the time to have a pot of coffee brought up, assuming her nose wasn't playing tricks on her. She rose from the bed, waited for her equilibrium to catch up, then stumbled to retrieve the pot from the hearth.

After she poured a mug, she stepped out to the balcony to marvel at the garden. It was massive, with an elaborate pond in the center. Several seating areas, some with smaller water features, were tucked away, providing private settings in an otherwise very public garden.

She selected one of Beckworth's favorite day dresses then went downstairs. She skipped breakfast, the weight of the previous evening still fresh, and meandered through the rooms, stopping to check out each one. She picked up bobbles here and there as she imagined him spending a quiet evening at home.

Did he spend it in the library or in his study? Maybe he lounged in his bedroom wearing nothing but a robe. It was something she would never witness.

She passed through the solarium and drank in the scents of a small indoor garden before venturing outside. Unsure of where to start, she turned to the right and took a path that flowed through the flower beds like a river. She found a small grassy path next to a flowering hedge and followed it. At a small break in the bushes, a hand snaked out and grabbed her arm, pulling her through.

She considered screaming, but her brain was running through the possibilities of who'd snatched her. It had to be one of Gemini's men, but she didn't see how. Then she was brought up against a hard frame, and his scent washed over her.

It reminded her of the cliffs in Oregon where the fir trees grew right to the edge with the ocean fifty feet below. On winter days, when she was feeling low, she'd drive to the coast and walk through the woods until she reached the point where she could watch the waves crash to shore. Between the wicked waves and the wind ripping through the trees, the experience felt like she was riding a storm. Wild and without limitations. That was what Beckworth's scent reminded her of—a wild storm, fierce and unrelenting,

His kiss was swift and hard, but then it softened, and he pulled her to the ground.

"You're wearing one of my favorite dresses." His tone was teasing as he ran a hand up her leg. She stretched back on the grass, thankful it was dry. Under normal circumstances, she might be shy being outside with all her friends just yards away in the manor. But their time was short, and she wasn't going to waste any of it.

She worked at his pants, but with everything his hands were doing, it was difficult to concentrate on her task. He pushed her hands away, and she watched the leaves rustle in the breeze. The intricate latticework of branches revealed an azure sky beyond, and when their bodies met, her senses mixed with the scents from the garden. She forgot time and place. There was only Beckworth.

Sometime later, she wasn't sure how long, he sat up and pulled twigs from her hair.

"I don't know what it is with you and bushes." His gaze was still heated.

"You can't blame me this time, you pulled me in."

He touched her leaf hairpin, then pulled her up as they helped each other dress. She took his hand as he led her through a short maze before coming out to a path that ran along the lake. They strolled every inch of the landscaped yard, occasionally stepping into a private grotto or behind a tree to sneak kisses.

When they arrived back at the solarium, they raced through the hallways and up the stairs to his bedroom, slamming the door behind them. As the afternoon passed, and she fell asleep in his arms, she thought of Elizabeth's words that Beckworth would follow her anywhere.

Hensley, worried about the team, had quickened their departure from London and arrived at Waverly late that afternoon. Mary had put off the rest of the season parties, preferring their country estate after all the excitement of London. Beckworth gave them a room to rest and pushed dinner to an hour later than normal.

Everyone met in the sitting room a few hours later after receiving a note to dress as if it were a social gathering. Stella wore her periwinkle evening gown complete with her opal necklace and bracelet that AJ and Maire oohed over, which pleased Beckworth. He would want to see her dressed like royalty one last time. Conversation flowed easily as the tension from the last few weeks ebbed away. But they had much more to celebrate now that the issue of the stones had been put to rest.

A pop from a champagne cork being released quieted the group, and they turned to find Ethan holding the bottle with nary a drop falling. He filled a tray of glasses then let the footman pass them around as he pulled Maire to him.

"I imagine there might be a few of you aware of what I'm about to say, but we felt, now that the business with the stones is done once and for all, it was time to share our news." He glanced down at Maire while Mary squealed in the background.

Maire's smile was radiant as she scanned the group. "It's true. We're getting married."

After the cheering and toasts stopped, Fitz couldn't help himself. "I heard it was Maire that asked for Ethan's hand. From what AJ tells me, that's how it's done in the future."

"I said sometimes." AJ shook her head and swatted the first mate.

He grinned and rubbed his arm. "Close enough."

"And where will you get married? Here or back in Baywood?" Finn asked.

Ethan sipped the bubbly and glanced at Thomas. "We've decided to head to Hereford after the morrow."

Maire was glowing and couldn't seem to stop fidgeting. "The earl has the ability to marry us, and with his failing health, we wanted him to see Ethan married. It won't be forever. Sebastian..." She pointed her glass in his direction, and he lifted his in return. "Well, he'd like to see the earl one last time before he follows us back to Baywood."

AJ's grin faded. "Are you sure, Sebastian? That's a big decision."

Jamie glanced at Sebastian. "I see an end to a perfect smuggling operation coming to an end."

"Not at all." Sebastian's smile was ethereal as he glanced at Hensley. "I've already sent missives to the monastery explaining my last wishes. The operations will continue, and the monastery will remain an information hub for Hensley's work.

"I've spent a lifetime watching visitors come and go. Some —" He winked at Maire, "—with experiences more exciting than others. I'm old and have given the monastery all I can. It's time for the younger monks to use the skills I've taught them."

"That's why there's no trace of your last days at the

monastery." AJ glanced at Maire, who met her gaze, her eyes sparkling with excitement.

"I've told the monastery I was on a personal quest and wasn't sure when or if I would return."

As excited discussions broke out, Stella glanced at Beckworth. He kept his expression guarded as he spoke with Ethan and Jamie.

Everyone seemed content with the future that lay before them without the worry of the stones hanging over their shoulders. She was over the moon happy for Ethan and Maire and their decision to eventually return to the future. However, hers didn't seem as bright.

She didn't know what Beckworth was thinking as their time together grew to a close. They both continued to evade the topic. But tonight she would ask him to come with her. Tomorrow she would be going home.

After dinner, the women gathered to discuss dresses, flowers, and colors for the wedding at Hereford, although Maire continued to insist the event would be simple, with just the earl and the manor's staff. Mary, who shared the news that she and Hensley would be traveling with them, advised Maire to think bigger. The earl wouldn't have it any other way.

Stella broke away from the group in search of Beckworth. It was time to swallow her pride and ask him to come home with her. It would be a difficult question. He loved Waverly. She'd seen his pride in it, and his sorrow when he found where flowers and bushes had been trampled in the team's efforts to help him take back his home. Part of the barracks had been destroyed with the first siege, and other parts of the manor and stables had been damaged from the explosives. Nothing major, Beckworth had assured her, but enough that she understood it bothered him.

She found Barrington in the dining room, speaking with one

of the footmen. He didn't wait for her to ask. "The men were in the study, but I believe they moved to the library to wait for the women."

She nodded but decided to check the study first since it was on the way to the library. The door was ajar, and she was ready to knock until she heard Hensley speak.

"This will be an excellent assignment now that this business with the stones is over."

"Aye, it will be good to perform simple information gathering for a change." Jamie sounded excited. "Before leaving London, I heard from a close contact there might be a French spy in the King's court. It will be an easy way to get back to your work."

"Someone is always claiming there's a French spy somewhere." Beckworth's tone was bored, but she heard a bit of interest.

"The source is someone on the war council," Hensley added.

"That is serious." Beckworth's voice came closer, but Stella stayed her ground. He probably just moved closer to Hensley or perhaps was pouring a drink. "Do they suspect they're gathering details on ship deployments?"

"That's our primary concern."

Stella stepped away, finding an empty room and a corner to sit where she wouldn't be easily found. She wanted to stick her head between her knees and stop her head from spinning. A heavy weight threatened to crush her chest.

He had important work to do. Work for the Crown to help England fight Napoleon. She knew how it all ended, of course, but not the details. Would Beckworth's work with Hensley help end the war sooner than it would have otherwise? He could save lives, save families. This was work he loved. What would he do in the future?

She snorted. He had enough wealth to be a man of leisure,

but it wouldn't be long before he was bored. He was an intelligent man who needed a purpose. How could she ask him to leave all that he'd built behind? He'd be as frustrated in her time as she would be staying in his. Either way, they'd end up bitter and resentful, and she didn't want that. Not for herself and not for him.

She stared at a tapestry on the wall until the tears dried and her resolve settled. Tonight would be a special evening. Their last one.

41

Beckworth visited the men in the barracks and took stock of the necessary repairs after Gemini's raid on Waverly and the explosives he used to take it back. He left the barracks and strode to the stables, ducking through the door and welcoming the comforting scent of horses. He was settling the saddle on the horse when Barrington approached.

"Why didn't you have one of the boys do that for you?"

He picked up the bridle and fit it over the horse's head, then tossed the reins over the animal's neck. "They're busy." He checked the stirrup length and tightened the saddle. When the silence continued, he glanced at his friend, who leaned against a post, his arms folded.

"You know they leave today."

"I know."

"And yet you leave."

"I'm just running an errand. I'll be back."

Once his horse was ready, he turned it toward the door, then stopped when Barrington straightened.

"Did you ask her?"

Beckworth dropped his head. "She wouldn't be happy here."

"You don't know that."

"Oh, not at first. As much as she's adapted, there's so much more she'd have to learn. But then what? She's an independent woman who needs something to do during the day other than needlework and managing a house. She'd be confined to insipid discussions except for the rare few that would put up with her outspoken opinions. What we have would eventually crumble from frustration and confinement."

"She would say yes."

"Maybe. But it wouldn't change the eventual outcome."

Barrington stuck his hands in his pockets and looked at the horse. "Where are you going?"

He walked the horse out, Barrington at his side. "I wanted to check on Bart and Lincoln."

"Don't bother checking on Eleanor, she'll be here soon."

Beckworth nodded and glanced at the manor. He couldn't see his room from this side of the house, but he couldn't help wondering what Stella was up to.

"Will you be back in time to say goodbye?"

He gave his friend a weary smile. "Of course." He turned the horse to mount when another voice startled him.

"I was wondering if I could have a moment of your time before you left."

He turned to find the monk standing next to Barrington. "You have an exciting trip ahead of you."

Sebastian glanced at Barrington. "Yes. I'm looking forward to it. It will be quite the adventure."

"I'll leave you to it." Barrington nodded and strolled toward the manor.

"Well, Sebastian, what can I do for you?"

Stella leaned against the stone railing and watched the clouds give way to the sun as it spread its rays across the garden. The colors of the blooms grew deeper and bolder as if someone tapped the petals with a magic wand. She hadn't gotten nearly enough time to enjoy their splendor, but she'd remember this place. She wiped a tear and ran a hand down the dove-colored dress Beckworth enjoyed seeing her in. Her laugh was melancholy. He seemed to love every dress she wore.

The clothes she'd come in were long gone, except for her raincoat, and though it was tattered, it had been cleaned and was packed in a duffel AJ had brought for her. She'd also packed one set of her pants and shirt, another day dress, this one emerald green, her periwinkle evening gown along with her opal bracelet, and the purse she'd taken from Gemini's trunk with the handful of leftover stolen coins. She wore her leaf hairpin, and the opal necklace hung warmly against her chest.

Whenever her fingers grazed it, she remembered Beckworth's cornflower-blue gaze staring down at her, scorching her skin. She closed her eyes.

Their last evening had been amazing. He'd done things with her that made her blush—and she rarely blushed. They'd woken and talked about nothing for an hour as they drank coffee and watched the fire that flushed the chill from the air. Then he'd given her a sweltering kiss before he left to run his errands.

It was time.

She strode to the door and picked up the duffel. After taking one last look around the room, she walked out the door and bumped into Sebastian.

"I can't believe you're coming to Baywood." She hugged him.

"We'll be there before you know it. It will be good to see the earl again." Sebastian smiled up at her. "I was wondering if you had a moment to talk."

"Sure."

When he didn't move, she turned back to the bedroom. "Come in. The balcony has a beautiful view of the garden."

"That's perfect."

Several hours later, Stella and AJ stood next to Maire and Sebastian. They were in the woods beyond the garden. From what Stella had been told earlier, this was where AJ, Maire, and Ethan had jumped to evade Dugan's men during Reginald's masquerade ball. This was also the location where they'd landed when they came back to find Finn. While it wasn't critical they traveled home from here, they decided to use the same spot, though no one could explain why other than sentimentality.

"What did you decide to do about the torc and grimoire? Are you sure you want to come with us to the future?" AJ asked. "Sorry. Too many questions."

"Not at all, my child." Sebastian smiled up at her. "With the chronicles in the future, *The Book of Stones* will not exist in this time period. If the stones are also in the future, then neither the torc nor grimoire will be of any use."

"Unless someone finds the torc or grimoire in our timeline." When they frowned at her, Stella shrugged. "I know we won't go looking for them. I'm just saying."

Sebastian chuckled. "I have no fear of that. As far as my decision to go to the future, it's really quite simple. Should someone still be out there, not that I think there is, then those with the knowledge of *The Book* will be out of reach." He leaned in, and the women followed his lead until their four heads were bent together as if they were in a football huddle. "I'm quite curious how the cider is."

The women laughed as Stella scanned the area, but Beckworth wasn't in sight. She'd asked AJ and Finn if they could leave earlier than planned. They seemed surprised but didn't question it. She assumed Beckworth might arrive too late, believing them to leave later in the day. It was what she needed to do, yet she wanted to see his face one last time. But perhaps it was best to remember him as he was that morning.

Jamie, Fitz, and Lando walked toward them through the trees. They shook Finn's hand.

"I'm not sure if this will be the last time we'll see you." Jamie handed him a bottle of Jameson. "It never seems to stick."

Finn looked at the bottle. "You know there's Jameson in the future."

"Aye, but it can't possibly be as good as this."

Finn laughed. "You'd be right that it isn't the same."

Fitz handed him a thin scroll, his neck turning red. AJ stepped next to Finn. "What is it?"

Finn unrolled it and stared, unable to get a word out.

AJ leaned over and gasped. "Oh my god, that's beautiful."

Stella looked over Finn's shoulder. It was a pencil sketch of the *Daphne Marie*, and it was quite detailed, right down to the rigging, ratlines, and crow's nest. She smiled. She'd learned a thing or two about a thing or two. She was a little sorry she never got to sail on her, but two trips across the Channel had been enough of an experience.

"When did you have time to do this?" Finn asked. "I thought we were keeping you busy enough."

Fitz rocked back and forth and scratched his scruffy beard. "I've been working on it awhile. Thought I'd better finish it once it looked like this might be the last mission with the stones."

"I'll treasure it." Finn's voice choked up, and AJ put an arm around his waist.

"I know of a perfect place in your office."

"Aye, I was thinking the same thing."

Ethan stepped close and shook Finn's hand. "I expect we'll follow in a few months."

Maire hugged her brother and then AJ. "Remember to water the plants."

AJ laughed. "Give our best to the earl. I wish I could be at your wedding."

"We understand. It's a long ride to Hereford. I expect plans for a grand wedding once we return."

"And you'll have it. Right, Stella? Stella?"

She reached out and hugged Maire. "Of course." She wasn't sure what she'd just agreed to; her mind had wandered. Her gaze returned to the trees and the garden beyond. Still no Beckworth.

Then Barrington was there, leaning against a tree. He nodded, and she nodded in return. He was a man of little words, but she understood his meaning. She'd miss him, too.

It seemed like a lifetime ago that she'd been dragged into this time period. She'd been scared and angry. And as much as she knew she had to go back, it wasn't an easy decision. Beckworth hadn't asked her to stay, but he wouldn't have complained if she did. But they both knew their relationship, while hotter than the noonday sun, couldn't last. Neither could survive in the other's time period, and if their days together had to end, she'd rather it be with happy memories rather than indifferent misery.

Hensley and Mary joined the group and expressed their good wishes and hopes to see everyone again one day. When enough goodbyes had been shared, the three travelers walked away from the group.

"Where's your stone?" Finn asked Ethan.

Ethan chuckled. "Safe and sound in the manor."

Stella drew the duffel over her shoulder and grabbed AJ and Finn's hands. She stood where she could see the garden beyond the trees.

AJ began speaking the incantation, and Finn's hand tightened in hers. She glanced over her shoulder and saw the fog coming. All of a sudden, she questioned her decision.

Then she saw him.

He walked out from behind a tree. His gaze never left hers. He wore his periwinkle breeches and jacket, his hair tied back in a queue.

She blinked, and the opal hung heavy around her neck. He began to disappear, not in the fog but behind her blurred vision. Tears fell, but she couldn't release her connection with Finn and AJ.

He never wavered and never looked away. His cornflower-blue eyes locked with hers until the fog moved in and all she saw was a bright white light.

42

Baywood, Oregon - current day

Stella hit something hard, and she wrapped her arms around her stomach that clenched with nausea. She heard the grunts and groans from AJ and Finn, and she opened her eyes. When she saw the dock and the path that led up to the inn, and people running down it, she shut her eyes. As the footsteps grew closer, she rolled over, pulled up her legs, and fought back the tears. But they were relentless, and her body shook from the effort.

What had she done?

"Stella, honey. Are you alright?" AJ's words were tender, which only made her cry harder.

"I need some time."

After a moment, she felt AJ's hand on her shoulder. "Wouldn't you feel better at the inn?"

"No. I need to be left alone for a bit."

"Let her be," Finn said. "Let's take her duffel up and get everyone back to the inn."

Multiple voices whispered their concern.

"Is she injured?"

"Was she a prisoner all this time?"

"What happened?"

At some point, the voices disappeared, and there was nothing but the sound of the bay slapping against the pier and the gulls greeting AJ home.

She was numb. It was the twenty-first century, and Beckworth was long dead. She only now began to understand AJ and Finn's sorrow the first time they returned home. All she could do was let the tears continue to fall.

The first thing she noticed was the chill. Her body shook, but this time it wasn't from crying. She was all cried out for the moment. It was still daylight, the sun another hour or two from setting, but a cool mist had blown in, leaving her clothes damp.

She rolled over and laid flat on the hard wood of the dock. The last thing she wanted was to face her friends and answer dozens of questions. They would mean well. After she gave it some thought, AJ and Finn would have already given them a recap. It was more likely she'd be greeted with general happiness to see her, gratitude that she was safe, then they would clam up about any other topic, waiting for AJ and Finn to decide what was safe to talk about.

She could handle the few minutes required to deal with her friends. They meant well, but she wasn't fit for company. And it might be a long while before she was.

She managed to roll over and get to her hands and knees. Then, with more effort than she thought possible, made it to a standing position. She pushed everything to the back of her mind, setting her sights on one goal—getting home.

She trudged up the path, feeling the cold and welcoming it.

When she reached the top of the hill, Isaiah stood near the back steps to the deck before disappearing toward the house. A sentinel to let AJ know she was coming.

She entered the house without knocking and continued on to the kitchen. The conversation stopped when they saw her, and she tried a smile that didn't come close to fooling anyone. Madelyn was the first to run to her and hugged her tight. She patted the woman's arm and glanced around.

"Can someone drive me home?"

It took a moment as everyone glanced at each other, then Adam jumped up. "Let me grab your duffel."

He walked past her, giving Madelyn's arm a squeeze. "I'll be right back." Then he took Stella's arm and turned her toward the door. "You'll be home before you know it."

The knock at the door wasn't unexpected, but it was unwelcome. Stella was being uncharitable and remembered doing the same thing to AJ when her father had died. Now she understood how annoying she'd been, though it had eventually gotten AJ out of her slump. But she'd given her two weeks before she started leaving food at AJ's door, and it was several days after that before AJ was willing to face the world.

She'd only been home for ten days. She knew that because she'd scrounged through her home office before she found a paper calendar a client had given her. It was one of those monthly calendars with the company's business name printed along the bottom of each month and a picture of some historical site in Oregon.

She'd hung it with magnets on the refrigerator, moving Charlotte's crayon artwork to the side. Every morning, when she made instant coffee, she'd make a mark through the previous day. One more day without him. Then she'd take the horrible-tasting coffee back to bed, only drinking half of it before pulling the covers over her head.

The first day she'd been back, she found enough energy to school her emotions to call Alexis, the realtor who cared for her clients whenever she was away. Stella claimed she'd returned home with a horrible virus and would be out for some time and even went as far as telling her to keep the clients and the commissions.

She tried to ignore her old-fashioned answering machine whenever she heard someone leave a message. The first couple of days, everyone left her in peace, but then AJ left a message, concerned about a call she received from Alexis. She ignored it like she had all the others. Madelyn tried a couple of times, but those attempts ended quickly enough. She finally unplugged the machine.

Stella ignored the knocking and rolled over. She thought it was great progress that she'd made it as far as the chaise lounge in the garden. It had been difficult because it made her remember the garden at Waverly and the flower vendors at Whitechapel. And whatever progress she'd made disappeared, and the grief rewound, starting all over again.

She couldn't be sure, but it sounded like someone had unlocked the front door. If she was being robbed, they could take everything except for the items she'd placed in her floor safe. The light footsteps made her sigh. Damn her friends for being so caring.

The footsteps stopped at the slider, and Stella closed her eyes, waiting. Maybe she'd go away.

"I'm not leaving until we talk."

Damn it.

AJ moved into the garden and sat in the wicker chair. She

knew every creak that old chair made. Then the release of a cork. She'd brought wine or found a bottle out of Stella's stash.

"Is it red or white?" Stella's voice was scratchy from disuse.

"Does it matter?"

"If you want to have any form of communication, then yes."

"It's red."

Damn it.

After several minutes went by, AJ said, "We don't have to talk. Finn said to leave you alone, and that you wouldn't starve to death. But honestly, there's nothing in the refrigerator, and the only thing in the trash is a pile of old coffee pods. Cobwebs have grown over your coffee pot."

Stella snorted. "It hasn't been that long."

"Well, I beg to differ. I have a glass of wine here, but you have to roll over before I'll let you have it."

She sighed. The only way she was going to get rid of her stubborn friend was to at least appear fine. She rolled over and figured she missed the mark when AJ grimaced.

"That bad?"

AJ smirked. "Not if I was to compare you to a corpse. Then I'd say your pallor was an improvement."

She snorted and pushed herself up. Her hair was tangled, her caftan wrinkled, and when she took a whiff under her arm, she wrinkled her nose.

AJ brought her the glass of wine, and she clutched it to her as if it were her life's blood. She drank a quarter of it down before glancing around the garden. The sprinklers were on automatic timers, so everything was green and various blooms colored the beds, but it was becoming overgrown. Maybe she'd get to it next week.

"Everyone must think I'm an idiot."

"Everyone understands you suffered a dangerous ordeal and are recovering from a loss."

A loss. That certainly summed it up.

"Mom's worried. Madelyn's even worse. Adam's keeping everyone's spirits up, though he's probably the most concerned."

"And Finn?"

"Like I said. He wanted me to give you a few more days."

"At least the two of you have a better understanding of—" she glanced around, "—whatever I'm going through." She fingered her opal necklace as she took another sip of wine. It was good, but she set the glass down on the table next to the lounger.

"We're having a barbecue at the inn tomorrow. Just the family and the Jacksons. You wouldn't have to stay long. Finn can pick you up and bring you back home whenever you give the word."

"I don't know."

"Baby steps. Remember?"

She really hated when her own words were used against her. "Maybe for an hour. I can drive myself."

"Finn will pick you up at two."

"Fine."

"And I'm going to ask for one baby step today."

She sighed. "And what must I promise?"

AJ stood. "Take a shower. I can smell you from here."

43

London, England - 1805

Beckworth reined in his horse, dismounted, and threw the reins to the footman before bounding up the steps. He growled at the doorman as he passed through a throng of newcomers. He didn't want to be here. His being in London didn't imply he was available for the seasonal parties and balls. The only reason he was in the city was for a job. He ignored the fact that he needed one because he couldn't stand being home. Her scent still lingered in the most unexpected places.

He'd annoyed Hensley to the point the man gave him whatever assignment had come up next. It wasn't a particularly difficult job, but it kept him busy. If he hadn't received the threatening message to appear tonight or else, he wouldn't have bothered. But the "or else" was too open-ended and risky for his own liking.

He pushed his way into the reception hall. He'd been to several of Lord Melville's parties and knew the manor well. First a drink, then he'd search for the person who thought it had been a good idea to threaten his attendance, especially at such a grand affair.

Several guests greeted him as he worked his way through the room. Some he provided a quick hello, while others he stopped to join in small conversation. They were too important to ignore, either as dear friends or possible connections in his profession as one of Hensley's spies.

The only problem, other than staying longer than he wished, was the endless parade of young women that were presented to him. Mothers and aunts who saw the opportunity to corner one of London's infamous bachelors.

If they only knew the true background of the Viscount of Waverly, they wouldn't give a schilling to be seen with him let alone introduce him to their virgin daughters. Though a couple of them he knew were far from pure. It didn't really matter. Redhead, brunette, blonde, or raven-haired, each and every one was either insipid, manipulative, or simpleminded. None would ever compare to Stella. No one could.

An hour passed before he found his third whiskey. He was on his way to a private corner he'd discovered earlier when something tapped his shoulder. It was a long ivory fan, and he couldn't help but smile when he turned to meet Elizabeth's steely gaze.

"I was becoming concerned you would ignore me." She was regal as ever in a royal-blue gown. "I haven't had to admonish you yet for missing one of my requests. I'd hate to start now."

"Your message was quite clear there would be consequences, and I've spent too many years avoiding that potential outcome." He kissed her proffered hand.

She gave him an odd smile before taking his arm and leading him into the ballroom. They walked the room, once again stopping along the way to greet friends and enemies alike.

And through it all, she wore that same strange smile and a look that seemed to say she knew something he didn't.

When they reached the halfway point around the room, he attempted cajoling, teasing, and finally outright demanding she tell him why it was so important to meet with her. By the time they reached the point where they'd begun, he was ready to give her a thousand crowns if she'd just tell him what secret she appeared to be holding.

She turned to him and gave him one last appraising look. "I appreciate you coming this evening."

His temper flared. "That's it? You sent me a threatening invite just to walk you around the ballroom with that tiresome smile on your face. If you have something to tell me, just get it out."

"Why should I tell you something you already know?"

Then she walked away before he lost his mind and scratched her eyes out. Blasted woman.

Two hours later, he sat at a table in a crusty old pub in the East End. The servers were buxom wenches who were eager to earn an extra tip by providing more services than the pub owner allowed. They had pooled their resources to rent a small unit in the building next door to support their activities.

He had planned on meeting with Chester and the crew. Before he made it halfway there from the gentleman's club where he stayed, he discovered he didn't have the heart to see his old mate. He felt bad after everything the man and his crew had done for him in their fight against Gemini. But Chester would probably ask about Stella, and if he didn't, it would leave an even larger hole. That damn woman had insisted on meeting his friends. She had to know more about him. And he let her crawl through all parts of his life, never truly understanding what a mark she'd leave. He didn't know if it would be a week, a month, or more before he'd be ready to see Chester. All due to that vexing woman.

"Hey, luv. Buy me a drink?"

He turned to find a blonde pixie on the seat next to him. Her eyes were the color of a bright summer sky, still beautiful despite the tinge of red that said she'd worked a long day. He waved a finger at a server who quickly dropped a shot of whiskey as she passed their way. He pushed it toward the young woman.

She tossed it down in one swallow and drew closer. "How about you come out back with me? We have an open room."

The old Beckworth would consider it, but that person would never have seen how special Stella was. She wouldn't have given that Beckworth the time of day.

"Not tonight, luv." He stood, placed coins on the table for the drinks, and then tucked a crown into the young girl's hand. "Save this for a rainy day."

He let the horse pick its own pace as he rode back to the club. When he arrived, he had a message to meet a contact in the lounge. Would this night never end?

"Hello, Richmond." Beckworth dropped into a chair next to the man, who'd been sitting at a table where he could watch the entire room.

The man lifted his glass, but he shook his head. He'd swilled enough whiskey for one evening.

Richmond shrugged. "The information you provided is more than we could have hoped for. Hensley was quite pleased."

"Excellent. What's next?"

Richmond glanced away then down at his glass of whiskey.

"Come out with it. I'm tired of the special treatment as if I'm a half-wit."

"Hensley said to go home. He'll have something for you in a fortnight or two."

Beckworth growled. He suspected that would be coming, and there wasn't a damn thing he could do about it.

"I'm grateful to be of service to the Crown." He pushed away from the table, never feeling quite as uncharitable with Hensley as he did at that moment.

He bought a bottle of Jameson and dragged himself to his room. He might have provided some helpful information on behalf of the war effort, but all in all, it had been a wasted trip. And now he faced six long hours of sleep with nothing but a redheaded wraith to fill his dreams.

44

Stella applied mascara, using half the makeup she used to. She pulled on the colorful caftan that Beckworth had once seen her in when he'd been caught in this time period and adjusted the opal necklace.

It was taking every ounce of energy to get this far, and she glanced at her bed, eager to get the afternoon over with so she could hide beneath its comforting covers. This must have been how AJ felt when Finn had been missing. How had she been able to bear it, especially not knowing if he was still alive? At least she knew Beckworth was healthy. Well, maybe. He had a dangerous job, so anything was possible, but he was crafty.

The knock came and yanked her out of her musings. Everyone was worried about her. They most likely thought she'd returned with PTSD or some other trauma. She might as well give them the wounded lady they were expecting.

She swung open the door, expecting to see Finn. "What are you doing here?"

AJ pushed her way in. "That's a fine way to welcome a friend."

"I thought Finn was supposed to pick me up." She followed

AJ into the kitchen and wasn't surprised when she grabbed a bottle of wine from the rack and two glasses from the cupboard. "Oh, I get it. You were worried I'd refuse to come, and Finn wouldn't want to deal with tears, so you decided to strong-arm me."

"I don't know. You look like you're planning on going somewhere, and I assume a barbecue with friends would be the least challenging."

"I came to the realization that the longer I hide away, the more difficult it becomes." She took the glass AJ offered and savored the first swallow. "I haven't had wine since we returned until you stopped by yesterday."

"That's a record."

"Right?" They laughed, but there wasn't much joy in it—at least not for her. "This probably isn't something you want to hear, but I'm having a problem remembering his face. It seems too soon for that. The image is there, but the edges are becoming fuzzy. My memory seems to fill in the missing pieces, but some days I can't remember the shape of his nose or lips."

She swallowed a large gulp and pulled a piece of paper from a nearby stack. She hadn't made a swan since she'd returned, and halfway through she shoved it aside.

"For all that I'm having trouble remembering, do you know what I *can* remember? The feel of his fingertips trailing over my skin. His breath near my ear when he's come undone. His long, slow kiss that brands me from the inside out. His voice when his words were enough to know that he loved me. God, AJ. What have I done?"

AJ reached for her hands and held them tight.

"Did I make a mistake? Should I have stayed?"

"I don't know, Stella. It was a difficult decision for me. I don't know if I would have been able to return home if Finn hadn't decided to come with me. But he didn't have as much to give up as Beckworth. He had the *Daphne*, but he'd already been questioning how much longer he wanted to captain. Beckworth fought hard for Waverly to let it go so soon." She snorted and squeezed Stella's hand. "He doesn't have the fondest memories of his time here."

"And I just continue to bat a thousand."

"I think the saying is batting zero." When Stella rolled her eyes, she said, "I guess it doesn't really matter. Maybe time—"

"Don't you dare tell me time will make it better."

"I was going to say, time might give you a better perspective for what you want to do. Maybe when Ethan and Maire return, they can provide their perception."

Stella was tired of talking about it. AJ was trying to help. She understood that, but it wasn't what she needed. It just made the proverbial stake in her heart twist deeper. She finished the glass of wine and stood.

"Let's get this done."

Beckworth finished reviewing the meal plan for his next hunting party with Mrs. Walker. It would be the first one since the interior repairs to the manor had been completed. It would take several months to finish the damage to the barracks, stable, and surrounding landscape.

He entered his study, ready for time to be alone with a glass or two of scotch, and pulled up short to see Barrington sitting in front of his desk with a decanter of whiskey. Two glasses had been poured, but one was already half empty.

"This isn't a good time for one of your talks." Beckworth strode to his desk, untying the cravat from around his neck before the blasted thing suffocated him. He arched a brow at Barrington when his butler didn't respond or get up.

Then he noticed the wood chest sitting on his desk. He stared down at it. It was a decent size, wide and deep enough to hold ledgers, but overall was similar to dozens of others. Broad iron bands circled the box and fortified the corners. The lid was dome-shaped with no inscription. There was an iron clasp, and the lock and key sat beside the chest.

"What's this?" He picked up the glass of whiskey and drank two swallows.

"I was supposed to wait and give it to you when I felt the moment was right." Barrington took a drink, and though the glasses weren't empty, he refilled them.

"On whose request?"

There was a slight pause. "Stella's."

He froze. God, how he hadn't wanted to hear that name again. It was bad enough a day didn't go by that she wasn't in his thoughts. And his nights? He barely slept, and when he did, she was always there. It had been a mistake to bring her to Waverly. As much as he'd wanted her to see it, he would forever be condemned to see her walking the halls, laughing at the dining table, or waiting naked in his bed.

He cleared his throat. "Where did she get this?" He wanted to look inside, but he wasn't sure if it was safe. What could she have possibly left that required a locked chest?

"I think it's best if you open it first."

He swallowed hard, took a deep breath, and did as Barrington suggested.

What the hell?

It was filled with coins. Gold, silver, and copper coins of all sizes. An envelope sat on top of it, and he set it aside, digging his hand into the coins.

"This is a lot of money. Explain how Stella would have something like this."

Barrington shifted in his seat. "She found it in your dressing room when they discovered the chronicle and the rest of the stones."

He had to think for a minute. "This was Gemini's chest."

Barrington nodded. "Stella originally discovered it when she first arrived from her time. It was when she'd run across the Prescott property files. I believe she took a handful of them in case she found a way to escape."

He remembered the coins. She'd finally shown them to him when they'd arrived in Saint-Malo. She wanted to make sure he could rent a good room with a hearth and plenty of wine. He couldn't help but smile. She'd been so worried that by revealing the coins so late in their escape that he'd think she hadn't trusted him. She'd confessed onboard the ship that she'd lied about AJ's trust in him. He still remembered the blush to her cheeks when she told him.

"And she told you about the chest." He lifted it. "She couldn't have carried this."

"She asked me to hide it. She was adamant the magistrate not find it, worried the wrong people would end up with the money. It appeared she'd given a lot of thought to the matter and asked me to send money to Doc, Lincoln, as well as Chester to share with the crew. Then she wanted me to give you the rest."

"I don't need this." It rankled him she felt the need to pay him for what he'd done for her.

"It's not specifically for you."

His head popped up from staring at the coins. "What do you mean?"

"She wanted Eleanor and the staff to get a bonus or something nice and trusted you'd think of something. Her concern about the damage done to Waverly and its gardens seemed to be her primary reason for leaving the money to you. She wanted part of the money to go to the renovations. If there's anything left, she assumed you'd find suitable recipients, whether it be one donation or several."

His hurt pride diminished, and he felt horrible that he would have thought the worst of her.

Barrington stood. "I'll leave you to the letter."

He'd forgotten about that. He picked it up and noticed his name but didn't recognize the handwriting.

"She apologizes for the blotches and hopes you can read her words. She's not practiced with the quill."

His heart leaped to his throat. She'd left a letter. He wasn't sure whether to read it now or save it for when he was more fortified. When he glanced up to dismiss Barrington, the man was already gone, the door to his study closed.

He shut the chest, poured another glass, and took it to the hearth where he dropped onto the sofa. Time must have passed because the logs that had barely caught were now the deep orange of a good burn. He stared at the envelope for another long moment before he had the courage to open it.

Dear Teddy,

I hope it's alright to call you that now. I didn't want to tell everyone about the chest I took from Gemini. There would be hours of discussions and talk of ethics and morals, and well, I decided it was best that you determine what should be done with it. With the damage to your manor, perhaps consider it insurance for repairs rendered. I've already given Barrington instructions on where I'd like some of it to go. Good grief, this is beginning to sound like my last will and testament.

And writing with this damn quill is taking forever. I don't know how Sebastian does it.

Anyway, this wasn't really your fight. I suppose it wasn't mine, either. Yet, you were always there. Always trusted to do what's best.

I've already told you everything I could think of. So, I won't get all sappy. Except, I want you to remember that you're a good man. And if you ever doubt it, think of me if you can.

I love you, Teddy. I always will. My leaving was the hardest thing I've ever done. And I might spend the rest of my days questioning whether it was the right thing. But know my heart will always belong to you.

Love,

Stella "The Swan" Caldway

He wasn't sure whether to rip the letter to shreds or carry it in the pocket closest to his heart. He lifted it to his nose. The soft scent of lavender tickled his nose, and for the next hour, he did nothing more than stare into the fire, waiting for it to provide answers.

Beckworth strode from his office, Stella's letter tucked safely in his breast pocket. His face was an emotionless mask unless you counted the frustration and despair leaking from him. He peeked into rooms and down hallways and was almost to the foyer before a footman appeared. Either Barrington had given the staff the rest of the day off, or they were avoiding him on purpose. He couldn't blame them.

"Douglas," Beckworth barked.

The footman jumped and turned around. "Yes, sir?"

"I need a horse." He stormed by and took the stairs two at a time. He'd barely entered his bedroom when he called out, "Nigel, where are you?"

His valet stuck his head out of the dressing room. "Here, sir."

"I'm going for a ride." He tossed the cravat he'd already untied onto the floor.

"Very good, sir." Nigel disappeared into the dressing room,

and Beckworth had his shirt and pants off before the valet rushed out with his riding clothes.

He was impatient while he waited to be dressed. Some days, more and more, he was falling into the role of viscount. She wouldn't have liked that.

He pushed Nigel away when he tried to add a cravat and strode out the door. His horse had better be ready. He had to get away from the manor. His luck was with him, and his horse waited when he reached the stables. Without a word, he mounted and drove the horse to a gallop, flying down the drive with no destination in mind.

Two hours later, a tired rider and horse returned. He handed the reins to one of the stable boys.

"Make sure you give him a good rub down. He's had a hard run."

"Yes, sir. Not to worry."

He couldn't help but smile. It felt like his first genuine one in a long time.

When he reached his bedroom, he was about to call for Nigel but decided to change on his own. While he undressed, he remembered a conversation with Stella. She spoke of getting itchy when she spent too much time at home.

The one thing his long ride did was clear his mind on that topic. The itchy feeling he was experiencing wasn't from needing something to do, but having someone to do it with. That person had been Stella, and he couldn't imagine there being anyone else.

He dressed in pants, shirt, and jacket, then unlocked one of his secret hiding spots. He opened the linen-lined box that might hold a ring. He stared down at the stone and the piece of paper that held the updated incantation. Perhaps she wasn't out of reach after all.

The lights at the inn were in full blaze. A handful of cars were parked in the lot, and she could hear the upbeat Caribbean music from the outdoor speakers. The sun played chase behind the clouds, but even when it hid, the ocean air was warm, and her caftan ruffled from a light breeze.

Instead of taking Stella directly to the kitchen, AJ led her around the porch to the back deck where Jackson and Isaiah watched Adam at the grill.

"So, what's the master griller preparing this evening?" Stella braced herself for their comments.

Adam dropped his tongs on the sideboard and rushed to her, giving her a huge hug. "Ribs and burgers. And a couple of hot dogs for Robbie and Charlotte."

"Patrick has graduated to burgers?" she asked.

"According to him, hot dogs are only worth eating at baseball games."

"True that." She hugged Isaiah and squinted at Jackson. "How much work did you actually get done while we were gone?"

"Enough, woman. I only owe AJ and Finn an update on my schedule. When you hire me, then you can complain."

Stella laughed, honestly happy to see the cantankerous old man. "Fair enough. It's good to see you."

He smiled and stuck his unused pipe in his mouth. "Likewise."

She braced herself and entered the kitchen through the French doors. Charlotte ran to her, her arms hugging Stella's legs. "You're home!" the little girl screeched.

"You're looking really good, Stella." Madelyn pulled Charlotte away to give Stella space.

"I suppose it's better than laying on the dock in a fetal position. Sorry for my overreaction. Now I know it's impossible to understand everything AJ and Finn have been through without actually being there. And that's enough talk about the past for one night." She took the glass of wine Finn handed to her.

"That's a lovely hairpin." Helen stepped close. "It looks like an antique."

"It was a gift. I'll have to keep my eye on AJ and make sure she doesn't sneak into my house in the middle of the night to steal it." She winked at her friend.

After quick hugs, the talk turned to current events, which put her at ease. But as the evening went on, she quickly became tired. She only spoke when someone asked a question, and soon she had trouble keeping up with the discussion.

Helen was clearing the table when Finn bent down next to her and whispered, "Let me take you home."

She'd never been more grateful to someone than she was with Finn at that moment.

When she got home, she kissed Finn on the cheek for respecting her privacy, then waved before shutting and locking the door.

She dropped pieces of clothing along her path to the bedroom, where she crawled in and slept until noon. When she dragged herself out to the kitchen, she ignored the coffee pot and made herself a single cup in the pod machine that she considered instant coffee. It was passable, and she sat at the counter. But she couldn't sit idle and was soon pacing.

She never paced. So she made a path through the house, walking and thinking. Along the way, she pulled a knickknack from the back of a shelf. It didn't seem a conscious act, and she glared down at the snow globe in her hand. True to its name, the scene inside was a wintery Christmas in a small town complete with shops, a few families, and a dog—a Golden Retriever, if she had to guess. She hated it. Her mother had sent it to her as a Christmas present one of the first years Stella had moved to Baywood. She never owned a snow globe growing up and had never asked for one. But her mother sent her one—as an adult. Stella never responded, but it was her mother's way of asking her to come home. She kept it as a reminder of who she was and that she'd never go back.

Now she found herself at another crossroads. Who was Stella Caldway, and what did she want out of life? She'd never been concerned about being the third or fifth wheel. When AJ and Finn got together, she was happy for them. Still was. Soon, Ethan and Maire would be coming home, and they'd be planning another wedding. Again, she was thrilled for them. It was inevitable, and the only question that plagued them was whether to stay in this time period or their own.

It was all just fine until she'd fallen in love. It was a new feeling for her that confirmed her earlier suspicions. As much as she enjoyed time spent with other men, she'd never been in love. The breakups never came with this down to her soul, heart-crushing pain.

She tossed the globe in her hand. Is this what she'd come back for? Material objects and twenty-first-century conveniences? Were they worth the love of her life? A love like no other. A love tested through fire.

Her temper flared, and she threw the globe at the plate glass window that looked out at the garden. When the window shattered, so did Stella. She crumpled to the floor like an abandoned Raggedy Ann doll and wept. Her chest hurt to the point she could barely breathe, and she was blinded by a flow of tears that came from an endless well of grief.

It was evening when she opened her eyes, curled up in the dark and shivering from the cold ocean air. She used an end table to stand. Without a thought in her head, she stumbled down the hall to her bedroom and fell into bed. She slept for twelve hours.

When she woke, her attitude was the brightest it had been since returning. That wasn't saying much, but at least she wasn't questioning anything anymore. She went through the morning rituals she'd been skipping, including making a full pot of coffee, eating a healthy breakfast, and pulling business files together. She typed several pages of instructions, printing one set and emailing the others.

After dressing, she pulled down a hat box from the back of her closet and set it on the dresser. Inside was the purse she'd stolen from Gemini. She opened it and felt the two pouches inside. She ignored the heavy one and pulled out the other. The tiny piece of paper prevented the other item from coming out, so she stuck her fingers inside, fishing around to get a grip on the object. She pulled it out and placed it on her palm.

The small Mórdha stone wasn't a priceless gem, but it generated a warmth that promised her future.

45

AJ paced Adam's office. "This seems awfully fast."

The noise of the espresso machine nearly drowned her out. Stella waited until the last drip landed in the cup before dumping the spent beans and adding more. She started a second cup and let it run while she placed the first one on Adam's desk.

Adam was finishing up her power of attorney, which included the instructions she provided him from what she'd put together that morning.

She finished the second cup and started a third. "I don't know if you need this, you're already wearing a hole in Adam's beautiful carpet." Once AJ's cup was ready, she set it on the edge of the desk and leaned against the opposite corner. "Does it make sense?"

"No," AJ snapped. "What happened that made you come to this rash decision?"

"I wasn't talking to you. I was talking to Adam."

Adam finally glanced up and saw the espresso. "This is perfect. Thanks." He took a sip, closed his eyes for a moment, then focused on the computer screen. "Your house and personal property are simple enough. AJ will have control of everything. The transfer of ownership is predicated on the date you add at the bottom of the signed document. It takes effect one year from that date once you add your second signature."

He glanced through several papers on his desk. "I don't see the deed for your business location."

"A year doesn't seem like enough time." AJ took a sip of the espresso then set it down. "You're right about one thing, I don't need more caffeine." She pushed her hair back, blowing out a long sigh. "I get that you miss him and that you need to see him again. But all this business about power of attorney and transfer of property." She dropped into a chair. "It just seems so sudden. We didn't even talk about it."

"I must have left the deed at the office." Stella grabbed her purse. "It's only five minutes away. Do you have time if I run over and grab it?"

Adam finished the espresso and rubbed his hands together before pulling AJ's cup over. "Yeah, this will take me another thirty minutes to finish up."

"Great. We'll be back." She grabbed AJ's arm. "You want to talk, let's do it on the way."

Stella drove the few blocks to her real estate business and pulled into the parking lot. "This property will go for a nice sum. I was thinking of a trust for your children. Something to help with college."

"How will you know if we ever have children? You won't be here."

Stella got out of the car and raced to the front door. She was pulling files from a safe in her office when AJ caught up to her.

"You really do love him."

She glanced up. AJ stood in the doorway, and her heart tightened at her best friend's sad expression. "Yes." She pulled the deed from the pile of papers and stuffed it in her purse, then waved for AJ to sit next to her on the couch. "You said you would have stayed in the past with Finn if you had to."

AJ wiped her nose. "I know. And I would have."

"And we would never have gotten a chance to say goodbye. But now we do." She took AJ's hands. "You have a husband that would walk into fire for you. You have a loving mother who's got a new man in her life. And your relationship with your brother is the best it's been your entire life. And you'll have lots of friends."

"Not my best friend." She sniffled, and Stella couldn't stop her own tears.

Stella wiped her face, thankful she hadn't put on much makeup. "I'm losing mine as well." They didn't say anything for a while, then Stella said, "I know I could live my life without him. I might even find someone down the road to spend the rest of my days with. But I know in my heart and deep down in my gut that I won't find anyone that comes close to knowing me like Beckworth. He'll always be the one that got away. The one I should have risked everything for."

AJ wrapped her arms around Stella. "If I didn't have Finn, I don't think I'd understand what you're feeling. But I do. And I can't ask you to give that up. I wouldn't dream of it."

They sat and stared out the window for another five minutes, joking about the first time they'd each met Finn and Beckworth. Then they wiped their eyes. Stella gave one last look at the business she built and shut the door to the building.

When they arrived at Adam's office, he was printing documents.

"Here's the deed." Stella handed him the paperwork.

He glanced up at the women and paused when he took the deed. "Is everything alright?"

The two women smiled, and Stella answered, "Yes. We're good."

"Wait." AJ paled. "You're going to need the Heart Stone. We need to ask Finn about that."

Adam handed Stella the papers. "The Heart Stone? What are you talking about?"

"Oh my god." Stella slapped her forehead. "It must have been all that drowning in my own sorrow. I completely blanked on telling you." She pulled the pouch from her pocket and dropped the stone in her hand. "I have my own."

"Where did you get that?" AJ's tone was filled with awe, but then her brows dipped, and she gave Stella an accusatory look, her voice raised an octave. "Did you steal that?"

"No." Stella tried to look affronted, but she had to admit, she did have sticky fingers on occasion.

"Wait." Adam held up a hand. "I'm confused."

Stella ignored him. "Sebastian gave it to me the morning we jumped." She fished out the slip of paper and waved it at AJ. "And it comes with its own incantation."

"What do you mean its own?" AJ took the paper from her as if she could read Celtic.

"Stop. I'm getting dizzy. What's happening here?" Adam was standing now, his head swiveling as he glared at the two women.

Stella shrugged. "I'm assuming Sebastian came up with it."

"And you trust it?" AJ asked.

"It's Sebastian. He's a scribe, isn't he?" Stella took a quick glance at the documents and then added the dates and signatures to the multiple copies.

"Yes, but I'd feel better if Maire looked at this?" AJ gave the note another review until Stella snatched it back.

"Well, I trust him." She put the stone and incantation back in the pouch and then her pocket. "Did I sign these correctly?"

Adam's forehead was scrunched, and if Stella had to guess, steam should be coming out of his ears at any moment. He seemed a bit lost as he scanned the documents. "Yes, they look right."

He was still staring at them as Stella grabbed her purse and marched out of the office. AJ shadowed her out the door.

"Hey, wait a minute," Adam yelled from his office. "This has today's date on the year countdown."

Stella smiled. For the first time in a long time, this was a decision she didn't second-guess. Her heart, gut, and brain were in sync. This was her future.

Finn sat cross-legged on the stone floor of the foyer and chiseled the bottom of a rail, blew the dust away, and pushed it into the hole he'd made earlier that morning. He grinned. All it needed was some sanding.

"That's going to be a fine rocker." Jackson set down the two-by-four he'd just cut and leaned his elbow on it. He rubbed his jaw. "Is that going to be your first sale item, or do you have a spot picked out for it already?"

He chuckled. "You know this one is going in your living room by your bay window."

"We talked about this. You need to be making inventory."

"What I need is someone to test it out, and the best way to do that is for someone to use the first one and tell me what needs to be fixed."

"Ah, I see." He scratched his stubbled chin and stared at the ceiling. "So I get the first edition where everyone else gets the new and improved model."

Finn would have been worried about insulting Jackson if he hadn't seen the old man's lips twitch. "Some say the first edition holds the most value. Especially if the creator personalized it with a maker's mark."

"Well, those someones need to live long enough for that to be true." He cackled as he picked up the two-by-four and headed for the stairs.

"Do we need to pack more lumber upstairs?"

"Not yet. I just need this one for now."

"Hey, guys!" Isaiah's worried query trailed in from the dining room, where he was finishing the crown molding and minor detail work. "I think we have a problem."

The two men glanced at each other, but Jackson spoke first. "You better not have scratched or dented anything that needs to be refinished. I'm done with that room."

They chuckled to themselves. Isaiah was always worried about damaging work that had already been completed.

"That's not what I'm talking about. Have you seen this fog?"

Finn dropped the rail and sandpaper he'd been holding and raced toward the kitchen. The fog was leaving, and he wouldn't have questioned it except it was moving faster than he would have expected, as if an immense fan sat on top of the cliff blowing it out of the bay.

He stepped onto the back deck and glanced around. The bay couldn't be seen from where he stood. Isaiah and Jackson walked up to the railing and stood to either side of him.

"The wind's picked up." Isaiah turned his head toward the swaying trees. "Maybe it was a squall."

"That makes more sense than the other thing." Jackson seemed more hopeful than sure of himself.

"Maybe." Finn wiped his hands on the short apron he wore that was already filled with bits of sawdust, then removed it, dropping it on the kitchen counter on his way to the front door.

The knock came before he could grab the doorknob. Maybe Ethan and Maire were already returning. Worry replaced his good judgment as he opened the door before checking to see who it was.

"Hello, mate."

"Beckworth?"

"I'm sorry if this is an awkward time, but I was hoping you could help me out."

Finn pushed him back a step so he could scan the parking lot and then the path to the bay.

"It's just me. I came alone."

"You came on your own?"

Beckworth held up a stone. "I've got my own stone. Remember?"

Finn scratched his head, then stepped back into the house. "Of course. Come in. You've just caught me off-guard."

"Well, that seems to be one of the downsides of the fog."

Finn laughed, but he was still on edge, curious what this was about. Then it hit him. Of course. Stella. His grin widened as he glanced around. "Sorry, you caught me working on one of my projects." He stepped over the pieces of wood and tools and caught Beckworth eyeing them with curiosity as he followed.

Isaiah and Jackson waited by the dining room table, each with a tool in their hands. They didn't look friendly.

"Stand down, gentlemen. We have a friend, not foe." Finn opened the fridge and pulled out three beers and a pitcher of tea. "It's time for a break anyway."

He handed Beckworth a beer and an opener. "No twist off."

Beckworth grinned. "I guess I'll need training again."

Isaiah took a beer and poured Jackson an iced tea.

Finn pointed to the deck. "Let's have a seat and tell us what's up."

Beckworth waited until everyone was seated around the patio table. "I think you can already guess."

"Did you come to stay or take her back?" Finn opened his beer and took a long swallow, keeping an eye on him.

"If she wanted to stay, she would have." He ran a hand over

his head, careful of his queue, then tugged on his sleeves. "The two of us never spoke of the future. Even that last morning. I'd always assumed she would go back unless she asked to stay."

"Maybe she expected you to ask her."

Beckworth sighed. "I thought of that. But she's a modern woman. Bold and independent. The first few months would be bliss, but then what?"

He nodded. "And wouldn't that be the same problem for you?"

"Not to the same extent." He glanced around and still holding his beer, swept his hand in an arc as if to encompass the inn. "This didn't come from AJ's salary. And it didn't come from whatever it is that keeps you busy in this timeline. You brought the money with you, or it's from whatever you managed to invest during your time jumping."

Finn nodded. "You're right. I'm in a position where I don't have to work, and I suppose the same would be true of you."

Beckworth shrugged. "Only something that can keep my mind active. But could you see Stella managing a manor, sitting around planning garden parties, and learning needlework?"

He laughed. He couldn't. "She'd be good at it. Probably not the needlework, though."

"I'd say." Isaiah's eyes widened. "Sorry, didn't mean that to come out."

But the other men laughed.

"Did you come with just the clothes on your back?"

Beckworth smiled. "My bags are on the front porch. I didn't want to scare you. Do you know where she is?"

"AJ went to Stella's a couple of hours ago. She might still be with her. I'm not sure what their plans were."

"I hate to push, but I really need to see her."

Finn stood and set his beer on the table. "Let's go."

Stella did her best to stay within the speed limit. They'd only driven two blocks, and when she passed the next one, AJ would know Stella wasn't going back to her house.

"Hey, you missed a turn."

She smiled. Right on cue. "No. I didn't."

"Where are we going?"

"The inn."

"My car."

"Finn can drive you back to get it."

"Or you could..." Her voice trailed off. "You're leaving now. From the dock."

"It's where it always happens. I'm a believer in going with what works."

AJ turned to look out the window.

Stella reached out and touched her arm. "I'm sorry. But waiting will only make it worse. Just like a bandage, right?"

"Right."

Stella rolled her eyes, but her chest hurt. She was going to miss her friend, and it almost choked her.

AJ twisted in her seat until she was facing her. She pushed her hair behind her ear. "Are you going dressed like that? No bags? Or are your toiletries in your purse?"

"I have a bag in the trunk."

"Unbelievable. How long have you been planning this?"

"Since this morning."

"Good grief, Stella." She laughed.

Then Stella laughed and pushed down on the accelerator.

Murphy pulled up to a quaint cottage-styled house with colorful flowers along the front and down the path to the curb.

"This is her house?"

"Yes. It's larger inside than it appears, and her backyard is a completely enclosed garden. Not as grand as yours, but I think you'll like it."

A lilac tree bordered the neighbor's yard, and it was full of purple flowers. It was a sign he'd made the right decision. If he wasn't sure before, he was now. Yet, nerves twisted his gut. What if she'd left for other reasons? He touched his chest where her letter rested. She said she loved him. That leaving had been a difficult decision. This was how he'd find out for sure.

"She's had a difficult time since returning." Murphy turned to face him. "If it helps, I think she'll be happy to see you." He chuckled. "I can't believe I'm giving you advice on wooing my wife's best friend."

Beckworth laughed. "It's been a strange life since meeting you, Murphy."

Something chirped, and Beckworth looked around, focusing on Murphy when the sound came again. Murphy reached into his pocket and pulled out a phone. He lifted it to show Beckworth. When it chirped a third time, he looked at the screen and sighed. "I should check this."

"I can wait." While he worked his courage up all over again.

"Finn. You have to stop her." A man's voice came through loud and clear. "I'm not sure she's in her right mind."

"Slow down, Adam." Murphy shrugged as he glanced at him. "What are you talking about?"

"Stella. She was just here with AJ. She wanted me to make up a power of attorney for her business and personal assets."

Beckworth understood, and alarm bells sounded. There could only be one reason she did that, or so he believed.

"I didn't understand at first," the voice on the phone continued. "I thought she was just getting her affairs in order like I've bugged her to do. But the date, Finn. The power of attorney had a start date that would begin the clock on turning all assets over to AJ in one year."

"Get to the point, Adam." Murphy started the truck.

Something must be wrong.

"She added today's date, Finn. She has a stone. She's going back."

"Got it." Murphy closed the phone and tossed it in the bin between them. He pulled onto the road, tires screeching.

"How did she get a stone?"

"I don't know."

"Where are you going?"

"Back to the inn. She's going to the dock."

Beckworth held onto the door as Murphy made a turn, barely slowing down. Where did she get a stone from? She was the one who found the pouch, but Barrington would have noticed if she'd taken one. He thought back to the new incantation Sebastian had given him the morning Stella had left. He'd been curious why he required an updated one, but it had worked. Had the devious old monk given Stella a stone?

He hoped there would be time to find out.

Stella parked the car and opened the door as she shut off the engine. She rushed to the trunk and pulled out a single duffel.

"That's all you're taking?" AJ asked.

"My clothes won't be needed. I grabbed a few personal

items." She slammed the trunk shut and marched to the path leading to the bay.

"Wait. You're not going right this minute?" AJ glanced around. "Don't you want to say goodbye to Finn? What about Madelyn or Charlotte? My mom."

Stella paused. "I can't. I can't wait another minute. You can explain it to them." She was still walking, and AJ raced to catch up.

"An hour or two won't make a difference."

"What did you tell me before? A week here is like three months there. What if I'm already too late?"

"Six months or a year, do you really think Beckworth would find someone else? Hell, no one expected him to fall so hard for you."

"I can't take that chance. What if he's doing something dangerous?" She could barely see the path, she was already crying, imagining the worst. She stumbled on a rock and almost went down. "Damn. I wish I'd had time to buy new boots." Her laugh was melancholy. "He really liked those red boots."

AJ kept pace with her all the way to the wooden dock. Stella dropped the bag and checked her pocket. It was empty. She had the pouch at Adam's office. Had it fallen out? Then she checked the other pocket and relief flooded through her. It was in a different pocket. That had to be proof her head wasn't on straight. Maybe she should wait for the others. Open a bottle of wine, talk about good times, and then let them send her off.

She pulled out the incantation and stone and stuffed the pouch back in her pocket. She wiped her eyes, but her vision was still blurry, and she could barely see the letters. She grabbed AJ and gave her the tightest hug she could. Tears reformed when AJ's return hug almost squeezed all the air out of her.

She pushed AJ back and swung the duffel over her shoulder, wiped her eyes again, and spoke the incantation. Something wasn't right. Sebastian had told her to practice saying the words before using them with the stone. What if she said a word wrong and ended up in some other place or time?

Honking from above made her look up. AJ squinted at the top of the path. It was Isaiah waving his arms. For heaven's sake. It was nice to be loved but honestly, didn't anyone care about what she wanted?

She tried the incantation again but kept getting stuck on one particularly long word. She tested it silently, but she couldn't remember how to pronounce the last syllable. She was horrible with languages. After running the word through her head three more times, she spoke the incantation out loud once more, only slightly stumbling over the words. But the electric sensation that had come over her the last time she jumped didn't come, and she dropped into a sitting position on the dock hard enough to bruise her backside.

Now the tears came fast and furious. What was wrong with her? She used to be smart. Thought things through. Rarely made rash decisions, and when she did, way too many martinis had been involved.

"Stella."

She heard her name, and though she thought someone was yelling, she couldn't make out who it was over the rushing sound in her ears.

Someone was crying. It had to be AJ. Or maybe it was her.

Then someone grabbed her shoulders and lifted her up.

"Stella."

She struggled to get out of their arms. Foolish to believe it sounded like Beckworth. But she'd definitely gone off the deep end—full speed ahead, pedal to the medal, road runner and coyote nuts.

"Stella, darling. It's me. I'm right here."

She froze. Was she hearing things?

"It's me. I'm here. You don't have to go anywhere."

Terrified to look, but drawn like a pin to a magnet, she turned and blinked. He hugged her to him, and she pushed back, not trusting his scent that washed over her.

She squeezed his arms, patted his chest, then looked up into cornflower-blue eyes that shone with tears of his own.

"I can't believe after everything, I almost missed you. Impatient woman." He crushed her to him. Then his lips were on hers.

And she melted into him. No one else had ever kissed her like that, and she gripped him tight.

She pushed him back again. "Beckworth? Is it really you?"

"I must say, I thought for sure we'd miss you. Wouldn't that have been something?" He kissed her again. "And I thought you said it was time to call me Teddy."

46

Baywood, Oregon - Seven months later

Beckworth put an arm around Stella as they watched the sunset from the inn's back deck. They were huddled under a blanket, and he tugged it closer as he kissed her temple. "I never realized how beautiful a sunset could be."

She glanced at him. "Aren't you supposed to be looking at the sunset when you say that?"

"Hmm. I'm pretty sure I am."

She laughed. "I think you need to pinch me again. I'm having one of those I can't believe you're here moments."

"You're silly, but I understand. There are times when I wake before you and just watch you sleep, grateful that I took the leap."

"Are you two going to be out there all night?" AJ asked. "We're trying to pick the best date for Ethan and Maire's wedding."

"We'd better go in," Stella said. "You know she's not going to leave us alone until we do."

He led her in and found their seats at the extended table,

which still wasn't large enough to fit the entire group of family and friends. He looked around. "Where's the whiskey? Finn, can you grab that bottle I brought?"

Stella smiled. It was strange to hear Teddy call Finn by his first name, and Ethan, too. She glanced over to where Ethan sat with his arm around Maire. "I'm glad you were able to be with the earl." They'd arrived two weeks earlier. The earl had married them shortly after their arrival in the spring, and he died two days after Christmas.

Maire used a new incantation, similar to the one Sebastian had given Teddy that allowed the time jump to the Heart Stone to be more accurate. Instead of the three months in the past to one week in the future, only two weeks separated their arrival from the date when they jumped.

Sebastian huddled with Emory over a Celtic book AJ had found at an estate sale farther up the coast. Helen, her arm wrapped around Emory's, listened to the two as if it was the most interesting topic she'd heard.

"If you waited until spring, we could have that gazebo finished, and you could have the wedding right here," Jackson said.

"The spring can be unpredictable for an outdoor wedding." Adam pulled a sleeping Charlotte from around his neck and passed her to Madelyn. "Can you put her down? You know if I do it, she'll wake up."

Patrick moved first and took his sister. "I'll do it. Come on, Robbie, let's play that new video game."

"Ask Finn first," Madelyn said as she poured another glass of wine. "Which one of us is driving home?"

Adam swallowed a sip of whiskey that Finn passed to him. "I thought it was you."

"You know you're staying here." Finn pushed the bottle to

the middle of the table. "That's why I rushed Isaiah to finish the guest rooms."

"Thank heavens you decided no on the crown molding." Isaiah laughed when his mother, Olivia, slapped his arm.

"You still have molding to put up in my new quilt room."

"Yes, ma'am. I'll be starting that right after the first."

"I agree with Jackson." Beckworth put his arm around Stella and savored the whiskey. "The house is large enough if you have to move inside."

"What about having it at the McDowell house? Didn't I hear you say you'd put in an offer to buy it?" Madelyn asked.

"We'd have to wait for summer if we did that," Maire said. "There's so much that has to be done."

"We could put the work here on hold and focus on getting your house in shape for a wedding," Finn offered.

"The only problem with that is making sure the two of you make plans to go on your honeymoon right away or get a hotel room." Helen sat up, engaging in the conversation. "It takes forever to clear a house after a wedding. No one wants to wait for guests to leave on their wedding night." She winked at AJ, who blushed.

"I think we have enough information to make a decision." Ethan took Maire's hand. "What do you think?"

"It would be nice to have a wedding in a more personable location. Let's see what needs to be done to get both places presentable."

"I think a wedding at the McDowell house would make the house more meaningful in some way." Stella winked at Maire. "Perhaps exorcise the curse on the place. And why not have the reception here? That would get the guests out of the house to give the newlyweds more privacy."

"You should take a long trip around the country and see the sights. It's something we've been discussing." Beckworth took a handful of nuts from a bowl. "I'd be happy to oversee anything you need at your security company. You should have several customers in place by then."

"That would make me feel better," Ethan said. "You seem to have a knack for security."

Stella laughed. "Who better to secure a place than someone who worked on a crew?" She laid her head on Beckworth's shoulder and squeezed his thigh.

They made their excuses fifteen minutes later, but Stella doubted they'd fooled anyone. Even after seven months, the two of them rarely left the other's side for very long. She'd cut back on her real estate business to the point of accepting the occasional client only through referrals. Beckworth had taken on a consulting role with Ethan's fledgling business, which, at this point, only required his attention for a day or two.

The rest of their time was spent reacquainting Beckworth's knowledge of this time period. She adored every minute of it.

"Come to bed. I turned the fire on."

She turned off the bathroom light and tossed her moss-colored robe across the end of the bed. He pulled her into his arms as soon as she tugged the covers over them.

"What do you have planned for tomorrow while I'm gone with AJ and Maire?"

"Edith and Louise asked me to take them to the aquarium. There's an exhibit on old sailing ships."

"That's wonderful." She snuggled closer. "It's amazing how they've accepted you back into their lives."

"It took some convincing them about my recovery and why I disappeared for so long. I have to admit to something akin to a fondness for them."

"I'm sure it has nothing to do with Louise's cookies."

He laughed. "Of course, not. That would make me a truly shallow man."

She pinched his chin. "And that is definitely not you."

He leaned in for a slow kiss but pulled back too soon. His face became anxious when he revealed a box in his hand. A ring-sized box.

She inwardly sighed. And everything was going so well. It wasn't that she didn't want him to propose to her someday. But it was too soon. She enjoyed this getting-to-know-you period and wasn't ready to give it up.

He'd seemed to be as equally satisfied with how things were going, but maybe she'd misread him. Either way, she had to open it. Maybe it was earrings.

With trembling hands, she lifted the lid and paused. Not what she'd been expecting, but maybe they did things differently in 1805 England.

There were two rings. One feminine and one definitely masculine. But they didn't look like wedding rings or her perception of one.

Then it hit her. Each ring had a single stone in the setting. It was rough cut and looked exactly like the small Mórdha stones.

"Are these our stones?"

"Yes. Here. Try yours on." He took one of the rings and placed it on her left ring finger.

She didn't mean to pull back and stopped immediately, but he'd sensed it.

"I understand the significance of this particular finger, but it will go mostly unnoticed if it appears to be a wedding ring."

She looked at the setting. "Are these Celtic symbols?"

"Yes. Maire says they're used in protection ceremonies."

She took the other ring and placed it on his ring finger. "And why rings?"

He shrugged. "They're small, easy to wear, and can also be put on a chain if necessary. I wanted something easily transportable."

"That's an odd choice of words."

"Not really. I wanted to ask if you'd be interested in traveling back to Waverly to celebrate the new year."

She stared at him. "Time travel, you mean?"

"Of course. I've spoken with Maire and Sebastian. They believe they have the incantation for traveling back in time perfected. Or the best that can be expected without the Heart Stone or torc. It's the incantation Sebastian gave you.

"They're certain we can arrive at Waverly within a day or two of a specific date. Part of the trick was using the lunar calendar, which is what the druids would have used in their time period."

She glanced at the rings then back at him. He looked like a kid at a candy store, waiting for permission to select a single item. The others had jumped several times, and they were fine. She couldn't deny the tingle of excitement in going back. It would be nice to see everyone they'd left behind.

"So, tell me, what does one do for New Year's at Waverly?"

"A hunting party, of course. But let's talk about that in the morning."

His kiss was demanding, and she responded in kind. The excitement of going back to Waverly seemed to stoke their passion, and she giggled when he disappeared under the covers.

What an adventure awaited them.

Dear Reader,

Thank you for taking this incredible journey with *The Mórdha Stone Chronicles*. And what an adventure it has been. AJ, Finn, Stella, Beckworth, Maire, Ethan, and all the other wonderful characters from this time period and the past couldn't have come alive without you—the reader.

As a reader myself, it's always a bittersweet moment when I reach the end of a favorite series where I've grown invested in the characters. As an author, it's even more difficult considering how much time I spend with them during first drafts, revisions, and edits.

But all stories must come to an end, and this series is no different. So we say goodbye to *The Book of Stones*, the *Mórdha Grimoire*, also known as the druid's book, and the Heart Stone. However...

I don't know about you, but I simply can't quite let go of Stella & Beckworth's burgeoning love story. And you might have noticed I left a bit of an opening. So, let's keep in touch.
Kim

If you're interested in other stories written by me, you might enjoy my new series, ***Of Blood & Dreams***, an urban fantasy romance. A touch of mystery...with just a pinch of spice.

Seduction in Blood, Of Blood and Dreams - Book 1

A thief. A vamp. A walk on the wild side.

Cressa Langtry is the best cat burglar on the west coast. But she owes a large debt to the wrong kind of people. Her only way clear is to steal something for the city's notorious and ancient vampire – Devon Trelane.

Devon Trelane can't forgive the one man who cost him a seat on the Council. Luckily, a thief has fallen into his lap. A woman with the skills he requires to take down his greatest enemy.

There's only one hitch—a simple business arrangement becomes complicated when their dreams collide.

After my shameless pitch for how to stay in touch with me, keep reading for the first two chapters of *Seduction in Blood.*

Want to know when my next book will be available?

Sign up for my newsletter at www.kimallred.com.
Follow me on Amazon, Goodreads or Bookbub.
Connect with me on Facebook at kimallredwriter and on Instagram at kimallredauthor.

As an additional thank you for signing up for my newsletter, a free copy of *A Legacy of Stone* is available for download. This prequel to the *Mórdha Stone Chronicles* introduces Lily Mayfield, the last Keeper of Stones...until AJ that is.

A
LEGACY
OF
STONE
EXPANDED VERSION
KIM ALLRED
A MÓRDHA STONE CHRONICLE STORY

SEDUCTION IN BLOOD

Chapter One

I inched along, my toes curled as I pressed all my weight into the balls of my feet. The heavy fog coated the three-inch ledge with slick moisture, making it impossible to see more than a few feet ahead. With little to hold on to, the thirty-foot walk was precarious. At least I'd made a good selection on footwear when I'd splurged on that new pair of light sneakers.

The fog wrapped itself around the building like a thick blanket, almost making me forget I was crawling around the top of a four-story building. It wasn't my first walk around a ledge in the mist, not with the amount of fog we got in Santiga Bay or anywhere else along the California coast. But something hadn't felt right when I'd arrived earlier, and my nerves were on edge. Without a safety harness, it would be a long way down. I pushed the image of that landing away and refocused on the tricky part of the walk, turning the corner into the windy side.

When I poked my head around to test the wind, I could already hear the familiar voice bitching about the weather.

"Can you hurry it along? For Christ's sake, Cressa, I can

barely make you out. That is you, isn't it? I'm freezing my balls off with this bloody window open." Harlow couldn't seem to find pleasure in any situation. The one time I'd taken an ill-advised vacation with him to Los Angeles, he'd complained the entire time.

His words fell away with the wind as I focused on my handholds. The breeze was minimal with the dense fog, but it was strong enough to push my short locks from my face. I braced against the cold. Not far now.

I was five feet from the window when I planted my foot on a loose piece of cement and slipped. My breath caught as I dug my fingertips into the rough surface of a stone window casing. My heart pounded so loudly it blanketed Harlow's voice, which was more of a benefit than an additional problem. An image of my head split open on the asphalt flashed for an instant, and the muscles in my legs screamed as I pushed down on my right foot. My fingers tingled with numbness as I held on, moving my left foot around for a solid piece of ledge.

Sweat dripped from my forehead, leaking into my eyes, and I blinked away the moisture, trying to make out the dim shadow hanging out of the window. Harlow, his arms flying about, tried to grab my leg. I kicked his hand away when it almost caught me. What was he planning on doing? Dangling me from the ledge by a leg? Why I kept joining his heists, I'd never know. But he was the best mastermind in the business. When my left foot connected with a solid surface, I scurried the last few feet until Harlow's strong arm grabbed my waist and hauled me through the window.

We fell onto the carpeted floor, his body resting on top of mine.

"That is you, luv." His smug grin showed off his perfectly white teeth in the dim light. "I'd know this body anywhere."

"For fuck's sake. Aren't you supposed to be on the bottom if you're saving me?" I pushed against his chest. A wiry man, he was stronger than he looked, and he didn't seem to be in a hurry to move.

"I like my women on their backs. I thought you knew that." His smile, the only charming thing about him, only widened as he took a second to run his hand over me from my upper leg to the edge of my left breast. "But I'm willing to have a go doggie style if you want to roll over."

"Get off me." This time I used both hands to push while I tangled my legs with his, attempting to roll him over.

He tightened his grip as we rolled, so I was locked in his embrace, his hands using my breasts for leverage when he landed on his back.

He laughed. "I see what you mean. I think I could get used to this."

I was ready to punch him in the face, but the third voice that crept through the room was as good as dumping ice water on him.

"I'd suggest removing your hands from her breasts if you want to live past the next minute."

Harlow's smile vanished. "Trudy, Princess, I didn't see you there." His eyes widened as he rolled his head back in a vain attempt to catch a glimpse of his jealous lover.

"Uh-huh." Trudy stomped over, her famous steel-toed boots planted inches from his head. She held out a hand and pulled me up. "Thought I'd save you the trouble of punching him. We need those precious fingers of yours." She gave me a nod before glancing down at Harlow. "Pick yourself up. We still have a sensor blocking us from the room."

Trudy, who wore an automatic rifle strapped around her shoulder, held the weapon in a two-handed grip and whipped it around as she moved back out of the room. She was our muscle, and she stopped just outside the door, monitoring both ways for surprise visitors.

"Where's Stan?" I assumed he would be on the computer trying to get rid of that last sensor, but sometimes there was a hardwired backup rather than one controlled by a software program.

That was where Harlow came in when he wasn't fucking around. But I imagined that besides him being a prankster, he was simply bored. He was the strategist, as hard as it was to believe, but he had the mind of a genius that was unfortunately wrapped with a foul mouth of sexual innuendos. The trials of a working team.

"He's having a problem breaking the last encryption. We need Harlow." Trudy glanced back in the room. "Today would be good."

Harlow sauntered by Trudy, slapping her on the ass on his way out.

She pointed the rifle at his back and yelled, "Pow." Harlow waved his hand without turning back. "Damn, why do I love that man?"

"Brain damage?" I couldn't help but smile at her scowl.

She shook her head. "God help me." Then, she grinned. "At least the sex is hot."

I waved both my arms before covering my ears. "I don't want to hear it." I cringed. "Too late. Ah, man, now I have that image stuck in my head."

Trudy chuckled as she followed me down the hall where Harlow had disappeared. "I don't know why you didn't just come in the way we did."

"I need the practice, and it makes for a quick escape if I need one. Besides, there's another job I've been casing with the same architectural structure." I shrugged and glanced at the artwork we walked by as we made our way to the opposite side of the historic mansion. "It's a small job. The artifacts will be slow to sell, but I need to stay limber."

Trudy grunted. "They have gyms for that."

"Gyms don't have shiny baubles."

She laughed. "I can't argue with that."

We rounded a bend and took the main staircase down to the second floor. I'd been surprised when Harlow had approved my risky entrance, which had added time to the job, but with the amount of security required to get in the place, I'd go crazy waiting on Stan to bypass the alarms. I'd also been the one who found the job. The mansion was owned by some puffed-up politician who was currently out of state. I'd seen a newspaper article from a year earlier about his purchase of the Alistair diamond. The job required three months of surveillance and influencing one of the staff to confirm the diamond was on site. From there, a hack into the security company told us the type of safes on the premise and their locations.

Luckily, there was only one safe in the second-floor master suite closet. No surprise. Most safes were either in the bedroom or the study. The wealthy just weren't that creative. The actual surprise, however, was that it wasn't digital. Not that it made a difference. I had the tech knowledge to break through any digital safe. But the old-fashioned ones, especially those with sophisticated locking mechanisms, made my nipples tingle. Those were the type of safes that started my illustrious and highly illegal career. The thought almost brought tears to my eyes. I was inwardly laughing by the time we reached the bedroom.

Harlow and Stan were in front of the closet, near a floor lamp they'd turned on. Stan tapped at his computer, working on bypassing the last of the sensors. When he nodded, Harlow entered the impressive walk-in closet and pulled open the false door, revealing the floor safe.

"All right, Pandora, come open the box and let's see what horrors await." Harlow stepped back, bowing low as I ignored his reference to my street name, my focus on the safe.

The security company files were correct. It was a vintage Schwab safe, one of the best in its time, but a newer combination had been installed. Safes weren't easy to crack if you tried to figure out the combination. It was doable if you had the time to manipulate the lock. Time most burglars didn't have, not if they weren't taking the safe with them. Drilling was the next option and the one I used most frequently if I couldn't find the code another way. Fortunately, our inside person—a disgruntled house cleaner—found the last two digits of the combination. Doing my research, I'd discovered it was two numbers in the wife's birth date. I had memorized the birth dates of all the family members, including grandchildren.

If this were my heist and I was alone, I would have enjoyed practicing my skills in graphing the combination. But my expertise lay with the ability to combine my burglary skills with knowing my target. I researched their lifestyle, their habits, and how lazy they were. It was surprising how many people never changed the try-out combinations that came with the safe. After that, the most common combinations were typically birthdays or anniversaries. That's why I kept my jobs to residential thefts rather than jewelry stores or banks.

After dropping my backpack, I rolled my neck, flexed my fingers, and relaxed my muscles before crouching to get a look at the lock. I leaned close and dialed the first combination, immediately knowing it wasn't going to work.

The second and the third combinations didn't work either, so I reset the lock and considered my options. I could pull out my drill, but Harlow was pacing. The soft shuffle of his boots on the thick carpet began to irritate me. I gave Trudy a glance over my shoulder and nodded toward Harlow.

"Come on, Harlow. Let's check on Jamal." Trudy grabbed the back of his shirt and hauled him out.

"Put a foot on it, luv. Time's a tickin'," Harlow mumbled as he was dragged away.

I turned my attention back to the safe, blew out a breath, and tried again. On the sixth combination, I heard the satisfying click and the release of the door. The correct combination had been the daughter's birth month, the son's day of birth, followed by the wife's birth year. It was fortunate they had a small family. I had to give the guy credit—but if I had the Alistair diamond in my safe, I wouldn't have used any number associated with family. Not that I had much of one to begin with.

"Bloody time." Harlow must have been hovering by the door. I'd barely opened the safe.

I stepped back, letting Harlow have his moment to pull out the treasures. I might have been the one to discover the gig, but Harlow had fronted the job and pulled in his team. The money I would see from my share would make a significant dent in what I owed—and the timing couldn't be better. My name had gone on the bounty list two days ago.

Harlow stuck his head in the safe and pulled out three stacks of money that I'd guess to be around a hundred grand, two bearer bonds that would take some time to move but would provide a decent payday, and five jewelry boxes.

Harlow opened each one before tossing them to me. I shook my head at the first three. They were lovely jewels, two necklaces and a bracelet, but they would take time to fence. The fourth held the prize—the Alistair diamond. I took it out of the box and held it up to the light of my headlamp. The team gathered around to take a moment to bask in the glory of our find.

"How much did you say that was worth?" Trudy asked.

"A cool million, Princess. And our little Pandora here already has a buyer. Isn't that right, luv?"

I stuffed the diamond back in the box and tossed it to Harlow. "Just remember that when we split up the take." I ended my obvious threat with a wide smile. "We'll have the money before the week's out."

"Boss, we have a problem," Stan called from the bedroom.

"Is it the patrol?" Harlow asked as he grabbed half the stash while I snagged the rest.

Stan glanced up from his monitor, the glow from the screen making his pale face appear green. "They weren't there a second ago."

Trudy ran to the bedroom window. "I don't see anything."

I crammed the stash in my bag and pulled my backpack on.

"Where are they, Stan?" Trudy's voice, though still calm, held an edge.

He was shaking his head. "They're all around us."

Harlow slammed the monitor shut. "Get your gear. Now."

"There's no need to hurry."

Everyone froze. I did a quick survey of the room, already knowing I wouldn't find an exit, but my gut reaction to run was instinctual.

"And I would drop the weapons." The man's voice came from inside the room near the shadows.

Two more men walked in, pushing Jamal, our exit man, to the floor.

I finally turned, shutting my headlamp off and taking a small step back, hoping the darkness in the room was enough to hide my face.

"Hello, Pandora. I've had a devil of a time finding you."

SEDUCTION IN BLOOD

Chapter Two

My gut clenched at the sight of the man standing near a large armoire. I couldn't see his face in the dim light, but I recognized the voice.

I stepped out of the shadows, blinking as one of the goons turned on the bedroom lights. Now that I'd been found, there was no place to run. But how the hell had he found me? No one else would have known about this job. I glanced at Harlow. His face was as white as the proverbial ghost, which told me he wasn't our snitch. A quick scan of the others told me the same thing. If any of them had loose lips, surely one of them would have looked more comfortable under the bounty hunter's menacing stare.

"Sorrento." I kept my tone level and firm, not wanting to appear intimidated while I determined his mood.

Sorrento was an impressive man with powerful shoulders and a barrel chest that suggested a future slide to fat. But now, he was thick with muscle, easily seen beneath the leather vest he wore sans shirt. His biceps bulged to an abnormal size as he crossed his arms. His legs stood apart as if he was bracing himself on a ship, and the muscle in his thighs stretched the seams of his cargo pants. And while all that was enough to scare the shit out of most people who found themselves face-to-face with the man, it was his tattoo that made you pee your pants.

A Cobra tattoo covered the left half of his face, the snake's fangs large and impressive as they arched over the man's eyes. The ink covered a nasty scar. Only rumors surrounded how he received the old wound, each meant to add to his badass reputation. As if being the region's most successful and brutal bounty hunter wasn't enough.

He stepped forward, and the two other equally large men took a position on either side of him. They each carried a pistol in their hand and silver swords on their hips. The blades were meant for magical creatures that could only be stopped by decapitation. The guns would have silver bullets, just in case.

Harlow's crew wasn't supernatural. Neither was I. But a bullet was a bullet.

From the doorway, three more men and one of the tallest women I'd ever seen entered the room and spread out, ensuring each of them was close to one of Harlow's people. We were outnumbered, outclassed, and I was shit out of luck.

Sorrento stopped in front of Harlow and took the duffel from him. He tossed it to the woman, who opened it and looked through the stash. After opening two of the jewelry boxes, she threw one to Sorrento. He removed the diamond and held the gem up to the light. He whistled before turning to me, one eye drawn down as if he was winking at me. "Is this all you have for me, pet?"

"If you had waited a couple more days, you'd be getting a large pile of cash instead of a rock." I crossed my arms, trying to show I wasn't scared. I was actually ready to piss my pants but still hoped to talk my way out of this pickle.

"You must know this little trinket will only pay off a portion of what you owe." He tucked the diamond in his pocket then sat on the edge of a dresser, one leg swinging in a slow arc. "The thing is, I have paper for your immediate capture."

Yeah, I was going to piss myself. Damn. How did this happen? Who else knew about this job?

"We've worked out our differences before." I could come up with something if my brain would slow down and let me think.

He smiled. The predatory grin and long perusal of my body told me exactly where his thoughts were headed.

"Do you have another job for me? Something that would take the sting out of my run of bad luck." My luck had actually been pretty good up to this point, but he didn't need to know he was messing with my record.

"Interestingly enough, I have something like that in mind." He nodded to Harlow. "Take your crew, what's left of your loot, and get out."

Harlow glanced at me, then his crew.

"Don't overthink it, Harlow. Take what success you can from this." Sorrento patted Stan on his shoulder, and I thought the hacker was going to have a heart attack. "And grab Pandora's duffel. She probably has part of your take in it, and she won't be needing it."

Harlow nodded and gave me a pathetic apologetic glance as he removed the duffel from my shoulder. "Sorry, luv."

I nodded. Any assist, and he would end up dead. I couldn't blame him. But if I found out someone from his team snitched, well, that would be a different story.

Harlow glanced at the rest of his team. "Let's go."

Jamal closed up the duffel the tall woman had picked

through, swung it over his shoulder, and followed Trudy out. Gone in less than ten seconds. Harlow helped Stan, who shook like an upset chihuahua, get his monitor in his backpack. He gave me one last look before he pushed Stan through the door and was gone.

Once I was alone with Sorrento and his team, I planted hands on my hips, close to my weapons. "So, now what? A ride to your place?"

He grinned again, and that smile, along with his Cobra ink, made me squirm. "You've always been a smart girl. Except with your finances, that is."

I never caught the signal, but before I knew it, the muscle man, who'd moved behind me, grabbed my upper arms in a grip as tight as a vice. My knees buckled when he kicked my legs out but kept me upright with his own strength.

"We're going for a long drive. I hope you fed the cat." I wasn't sure what he meant. I didn't own a cat. Then, the tall woman bent her head near mine, and I didn't know whether she was going to whisper in my ear or kiss me. It was hard to tell. But all she did was take a deep breath as if she was smelling me.

"Down, Patrice." Sorrento's voice held a harsh edge, which didn't bolster my confidence.

Something stuck me in the neck—sharp and quick. I tried to move my arms, but they were still locked in a fierce grip. I struggled before my legs turned to rubber, the edges of my vision blurred, and I slipped into utter darkness.

Thank you for reading!

Pick up your copy today - available on Amazon, Kindle Unlimited, Print, Audible & I-Tunes

If you'd like another free peak into the world *Of Blood & Dreams*, grab a free copy of *Lyra, A Prequel*

ABOUT THE AUTHOR

Kim Allred grew up in Southern California but now enjoys the quiet life in an old timber town in the Pacific Northwest where she raises alpacas, llamas, and an undetermined number of free-range chickens. Just like her characters, Kim loves sharing stories while sipping a glass of wine or slurping a strong cup of brew.

Her spirit of adventure has taken her on many journeys, including a ten-day dogsledding trip in northern Alaska and sleeping under the stars on the savannas of eastern Africa.

Kim is currently creating worlds while shooing cats and dogs away from her lap, and the mighty parrot, Willow, from her keyboard. Willow can peel the keys from the board in fifteen seconds flat.

Kim's current works include her time travel romance series, **Mórdha Stone Chronicles**, and the urban fantasy romance series, **Of Blood & Dreams.**

Check out her website at www.kimallred.com.

To stay in contact with Kim, join her newsletter (https://www.kimallred.com/contact/), her Facebook group (https://www.facebook.com/groups/588539362866139), or visit her website at www.kimallred.com.

Made in the USA
Middletown, DE
10 September 2023

38286125R00248